Nolander

Nolander

Becca Mills

Recompense Press

Cover design by Marion Sipe

Interior formatting by Indie Designz, www.indiedesignz.com, with
alterations by the author

Cover photograph copyright 2007 iStockphoto.com/kevinruss

Interior glyph font is Entypo, by Daniel Bruce,
www.fontsquirrel.com/license/entypo

Nolander is a work of fiction. The names, characters, places, and incidents
in this book are products of the writer's imagination or have been used
fictitiously and are not to be construed as real. Any resemblance to real
persons, living or dead, or to actual events, locales, or organizations is
entirely coincidental.

For my family, my best work.

Prologue

THE GREAT BEAST slid through tall, dead grass. The wind had led him here. It had things to show him.

His once-paws sensed broken asphalt and the hardened earth of early April in the northlands, the damp soil still mixed with particles of ice. His crystalline coat moved as the evening breeze greeted it.

The wind was getting reacquainted with him, here. He had not visited the north during the long years of ice, when the storms scoured the surface of the glacier, and the land beneath was remade. When the ice drew back, the fresh place attracted him. He had spent many days here, of late.

The humans brought newness as well, of course, but that interested him less. It had come so quickly. Surely it was ephemeral.

I would know this beast as Ghosteater, though that was not his name. I can't say his name. No living thing in this world remembers it, though he's far from the oldest of creatures.

He gazed at gray clouds, watched as they pressed and crowded one another across the sky. There would be a full moon tonight, but its light would be dim.

He lowered his eyes to the broken place that stood before

him. In days past, the humans had used it. Now other creatures came and went—bats, owls, mice, coyote.

But tonight, something here would change, the wind whispered in his ear. No, that wasn't quite right, he thought, sifting through the wind's strange language, seeking understanding. Tonight something would change, and it would begin here.

The wind suggested it concerned him. He could not imagine how. Nevertheless, change was interesting. He settled down to wait.

Chapter 1

I KEPT MY face turned to the window, so Matt wouldn't see I was still crying. The streets of Dorf were largely dark—only a few folks around here stayed up this late, even on a Friday night. I watched the houses slide by, picking out the ones with the bluish glow of a TV on in the living room or a warm yellow light upstairs. One in five, maybe.

The silence from the driver's side was oppressive. Matt was really pissed. And probably embarrassed. I wiped quickly at my face. Everything was damp—my neck, even the top of my shirt. It was like I'd sprung a permanent leak.

Finally Matt shifted and took a deep breath, performing his patience for me.

"I just don't see," he said in a gritted-teeth voice, "what could possibly be so scary at T.G.I. Friday's."

"I know."

My voice sounded rough and choked.

"So what happened?"

I shook my head. I couldn't explain it.

I'd been having panic attacks all my life, and I'd never understood them. They tended to happen more often when I was in a crowded place, but sometimes they happened when I was sitting alone in my house. Sometimes they even woke me out of a deep sleep. There was no consistency, no predictability. It was some unknown thing that lurked just under the surface, and when it got hungry, it sank its teeth in and dragged me down.

"I don't know, Matt. I don't get it either. I'm sorry."

He didn't say anything. I guess "I'm sorry" doesn't make up for having your date start shaking and crying, clutch her chest, and then fall out of her chair and barf in the middle of a busy restaurant.

We pulled up in front of my house, and I got out of the car.

"Bye, Matt. Thanks ..."

I couldn't very well add "for a lovely evening," so the sentence just petered out.

"Bye, Beth."

I knew finality when I heard it.

He pulled away, leaving me standing on the terrace. I sighed and tried to push back the tears. Matt Kelsey had lasted longer than most. I'd been going out with him for about three months.

I'd been really excited about him at first. It wasn't all that often that someone moved to Dorf, Wisconsin. Only about three thousand people lived there, so everyone pretty much knew everyone, or at least knew about everyone. What they knew about me was that I had fits. That didn't exactly put me at the top of Dorf's datable-women list.

But Matt had just moved to town—he'd been hired as a gym teacher at the high school in Frederick, the next town to the west. So he didn't know about the list, and he didn't know about me. And he was a hottie. With a steady job and no kids, even though he was twenty-seven. Quite a combo.

But with the excitement came worry. No one I'd gone out with had been able to put up with the panic disorder. Standing there on the terrace, I felt the last tendrils of hope withdraw. Three months had been enough time to have four attacks in his presence. I guess he'd reached his limit.

I turned toward my house. The porch light should've been welcoming and cheery, but instead it seemed white and harsh.

I let myself in and saw my camera bag sitting on the entryway table. I immediately felt a little calmer. What I needed was a good photo session. Tomorrow. It would make me feel better.

For now, my bed was waiting for me. I climbed the creaky stairs and dropped my vomit-splattered clothes on the bathroom floor. I showered briefly, then got in bed, tucking Sniggles the bear under my arm. He reminded me of happier times.

Things hadn't been perfect back when Sniggles was a young bear. There'd never been enough money, and I'd always been the kid with the weird problem. But I hadn't been alone. Not like now.

Now I could hear the emptiness all around me. The quiet house was full of it. I lay in my cold sheets and listened. Emptiness sounded like the hum of the furnace and the soft brush of air. It sounded like people turning away and thinking of other things.

Chapter 2

I STAMPED MY boots on the concrete stoop. Clumps of gray slush fell off, speckled with crystals of rapidly softening ice.

"Betty! How you doing, sweetie?"

Fixing a smile on my face, I turned and waved to Suzanne Dreisbach, my next-door neighbor. Looked like she was just getting home from the store. She always shopped on Saturday afternoon. You could set your clock by Suzanne, she was so organized.

She waved back and gave me a bright smile, shifting the paper bag she was carrying from one ample hip to the other. Suzanne was a good neighbor. She'd come to my rescue with my spare key about a dozen times. I was good at locking myself out.

That said, I really hated being called "Betty."

"I'm fine, Suzanne. How're you today?"

"Can't complain, can't complain."

Actually, Suzanne could complain like a champ. Her complaining was one of my guilty pleasures: she was a big gossip and always seemed to know something new about everybody in town. But I just wasn't up for it at the moment. My toes were cold, and my nose had a big drip forming. If she got going, I'd be standing out here for half an hour.

"Good, good. Hey, sorry, gotta get my camera inside pronto—think it got damp out there in all this muck."

Suzanne nodded obligingly and said we should get coffee tomorrow after church. That was nice—sometimes my weekends got lonely. I told her I'd come find her after the service.

I hung my coat up on the porch and left my boots out there, too. Northern winters are tough on carpets. Grit, salt—once that stuff gets inside, you never really get rid of it.

I dumped my camera bag on the floor and padded through my little-used living room to the kitchen, where I turned the flame on under the kettle. Not ten minutes later, I was warmly settled in the den, feet curled under me, with a hot cup of tea and a cheese sandwich. I turned on the TV and channel-surfed a little. A very little—I couldn't afford cable, so I only got a few stations.

I think my mind drifted.

I can't really remember what I thought about. Probably it was on the gloomy side, what with the Matt thing weighing on me. No doubt I was grumpy about the weather. I might have worried about seeing my bitchy sister-in-law at church the next day. Maybe I wondered if I'd be able to cover my credit card balance that month, or if I was going to end up paying interest.

It sort of bothers me that I can't really remember what I thought about. Those were the last moments of my old life. Of the old me, actually. I can almost think of that young woman on the couch as someone else. So let me just pause for a moment and mark her there, thinking about something of no consequence, living her boring, lonely, frustrating life—a life that had perks she didn't recognize until they were gone.

❧

Dorf is in north-central Wisconsin. That part of the state is farm country, and it's sprinkled with towns like mine—little places where farmers can shop, drink, worship, and get a haircut. I'd grown up there and never left. I worked as a receptionist in a doctor's office.

Well, to be more accurate, I lived in the same house I grew up in, and the doctor I worked for was the one who'd been listening to my heart and tapping on my knees since my mother brought me home from the hospital.

If you're from a bigger city, this probably sounds too cute to be true. But that's what life is like in plenty of small places like Dorf: there are only so many people, only so many houses, only so many jobs. Spend a few decades there, and you'll be able to call the whole place up in your mind—not just the landscape and streets and buildings, but all the people, for better or worse. You'll see their connections to one another in your mind's eye. You'll know their histories, stretching back like long, knotted tails. And you'll be able to see their futures stretching ahead of them with nearly as much certainty.

When I was growing up, I hated that sense of having a rigid place in the scheme of things. That's why I was going to leave. I was going to live in the bigger world. I was going to do interesting things. I was going to be someone interesting. So I worked hard in school, got good grades, made friends with the teachers. I was class valedictorian, believe it or not. All so I could get out of Dorf.

But when I went to college, the panic disorder flared. I'd always had attacks a couple times a week, but in Madison, I started having them every day, sometimes three or four times a day. Sometimes in the middle of class. I felt like I was floating in dark water, and terrifying things were sweeping by me at random, brushing my legs. The sense of terror was constant, overwhelming—crippling. I didn't last a semester. I didn't even last two months.

After I got back to Dorf, I figured I'd get an apartment of my own, but then my mother passed. My brother and I inherited her house on Fourth Street. I wasn't quite nineteen, and Mom's death hit me pretty hard, so Ben thought I should just stay in the house.

"What am I going to do with this old place, anyway?" Ben had asked. "Try to find some stranger to rent it? You know Justine'd hate it if I took that on."

Of course Justine would hate it—she hated just about everything.

So there I was, more than four years later, holding down the old fort. I paid Ben a little rent since he owned the place, too, and had four kids and a stay-at-home wife to support.

One part of me hated living in Dorf. It was claustrophobic. Everyone was in everyone else's business, and nothing ever really changed.

Then again, Dorf had its up-sides: I could afford it. It was easy. And people here knew about my problem. If I had an attack in public, or if I went running off when I felt one coming on, people around here knew what was happening. If they didn't, there'd be someone standing next to them who could lean over and explain in a stage whisper about "poor Betty Ryder." Embarrassing, yeah, but better than waking up in an ambulance and getting the bill a few months later.

Most importantly, being here seemed to calm me a bit—I didn't have nearly as many attacks as I'd had in Madison. And being in Mom's house reminded me of her. If I couldn't have her, at least I could be in the place she'd made a home.

Nevertheless, the more time passed, the more uncomfortable I felt. The year before, it had gotten particularly bad. It's hard to describe the feeling—itchy and antsy, like someone was always watching and judging me, and I could never get any real privacy.

That was new. Sure, I'd had the panic disorder for ages, but except when I was in Madison, I'd always felt reasonably good between attacks. Of course I worried about when the next attack was going to happen. But being intensely anxious all the time? No, that wasn't me.

I figured my growing sense of my own limited future was getting to me, but there wasn't much I could do about the future. I couldn't leave Dorf. My six weeks of college had taught me that much.

What I needed was a diversion. So I'd taken up photography. It was simple chance, really: I came across an old camera at a church flea market. It was silver and black and took pictures on good old-fashioned film. I paid $10 for it and a couple lenses. I bought a few other things used—tripod, flash, that kind of stuff—and found a scanned copy of the camera's hokey 1970s instruction manual online. I printed it up on the sly at work and studied it.

Turned out I wasn't half bad at taking pictures. My subjects weren't adventurous—landscapes, animals, street scenes, shots of people I knew—but I ended up with some pictures that really appealed to me. Sometimes they seemed to capture some essence of the subject that I couldn't have described in words.

Taking those pictures made me feel better. I'm not sure why.

At any rate, after a few months, I realized I'd need to do my own developing and printing. I just couldn't afford it, otherwise. So I switched to black-and-white film and set up a darkroom in the old canning closet in the basement.

It wasn't hard. I got used versions of the small things online. I stretched a hose into the closet from the sink next to the washing machine and ran another out to the drain in the center of the basement floor. Voilà: running water. The chemicals and paper weren't expensive, so long as I limited the number of prints I made. The only pricey item was the enlarger, and I found a used one for a couple hundred bucks. It was a little beat-up, but it worked. Ben got it for me for Christmas.

So there you go. It wasn't the spiffiest darkroom out there, but it saved me a lot of money. And I enjoyed it, too. All the exacting little steps appealed to me—checking temperatures and timing things. I liked how precise and orderly it all was.

On this particular evening, I went down to the darkroom after I'd warmed up on the couch for a couple hours. I unloaded the film I'd shot that afternoon—just a single roll of pictures I'd taken up and down the street of stores, bars, and eateries that Dorf calls its downtown. I developed the film. That created negatives, which I could use to make prints. I let them dry for an hour, then went back to see what might be worth printing.

The weather had been dismal, so I didn't really expect to find many keepers—I always had better luck when I had sunlight and strong shadows to work with. But two frames caught my attention when I held them up to the light.

They were shots of J.T.'s, one of the three watering holes on Center Street. I'd gone across the street to photograph the bar and had gotten a good shot lined up, but just as I was pressing the shutter button, Jim Foley had walked out of the bar. I'd wanted a picture of just the building, with no people, so I'd waited a few seconds until Jim was clear and had taken a second shot.

I remembered this very clearly, but the negatives didn't match my memory. In the first shot, I could see Jim coming out of the bar, but I could also see a second person just entering the field of view from the right. In the second picture, the one I'd been certain showed just the bar, this unknown person was in full view, walking along the sidewalk.

It was a short, slight person—probably a man, given the flat chest. He walked with a pronounced slump. After a few seconds, I realized what I wasn't seeing—clothes. Weird. It'd be pretty remarkable to walk through downtown Dorf naked any time of the year, but in early April it was particularly bizarre. It had been no warmer than the mid-40s that afternoon. It's one thing to get arrested. It's another to get arrested and freeze off your naughty bits at the same time.

Speaking of which … I looked more closely, but the guy's leg obscured his groin.

Feeling a little embarrassed at my own prurient interest, I sat back and tried to figure out who he was.

I knew he wasn't from Dorf because the negative showed hardly any coloration on his skin. Since negatives are reverse-colored, that meant he was actually very dark. Dorf had to be one of the least diverse places in the world. Only a few African Americans lived in town, and none looked like this guy. And I didn't think any of them would go for a walk in their birthday suit, either.

Well, an unknown African American wandering around in the buff was sort of noteworthy, in the way any little thing is noteworthy when you live someplace where nothing happens.

I turned the lights back off and made prints of the J.T.'s shots. After they were dry, I brought them up to the kitchen to examine under good light. The stranger was very slender, but sinewy—I could see ropey muscles in his arms and legs. His posture was oddly stooped, as though he'd been trying to bend over and pick something up while he walked. He had a long neck with a pronounced Adam's apple and was quite small, less than five feet tall, I thought. He had a tiny nose, a prominent mouth, and a weak chin. He seemed to be bald.

Who could he be? Dorf wasn't on the tourist map. What through-traffic we got tended to be Wisconsinites traveling between Wausau and Eau Claire.

Maybe he was a hunter up here for turkey season. But no, a hunter wouldn't streak in downtown Dorf. More likely a college kid on spring break making good on a dare from his buddies. That made sense.

But the more I looked at the photo, the weirder it seemed. The back of my neck started to feel prickly. After I few more seconds, I actually broke out in a nervous sweat.

I didn't understand my own reaction. Okay, he was a stranger, and he was naked, but he'd been walking right through the downtown, not skulking in alleys and peeking in windows. If he was a nut, the police had probably already picked him up.

I felt myself flush—maybe I was anxious just because an unknown black male had shown up in town. God, was I really that much of a racist?

Then again, he had walked right through the picture I was taking, and I hadn't seen him. That was weird, right? Yep, downright spooky—it'd give anyone the creeps. I decided to stick with that explanation. Better to be kooky than a bigot, right?

The next morning, I slid into an empty seat next to my sister-in-law just as the processional was finishing. I was usually late to church, which annoyed Justine to no end. She expressed her irritation this time by pointedly not looking at me, though Ben did shoot me a quick smile from the far end of the pew.

Ben was eight years older than me. We actually didn't have the same father, but Ben still looked a lot like me—we both had Mom's pale skin, dark brown hair, and gray eyes. Ben and Justine had been married twelve years. They had four daughters, ranging from Tiffany, who was on the verge of teenhood, to Madisyn, a squirmy three-year-old.

Ben and I got together sometimes for lunch, but I was rarely invited to his home because Justine didn't like me. I came to church largely because that way I saw my brother and nieces at least once a week.

I resented having to do it, though. I wasn't much of a believer, and it rubbed me the wrong way to have to pretend otherwise just to see my own family. In contrast, Justine took her faith seriously. She must have known I was faking it. It probably made her dislike me even more.

It had been different before Mom died. When she was around, the Fourth Street house had been our gathering place. Justine hadn't liked me much better then, but she hadn't been willing to snub her mother-in-law, so the whole family got together for dinner a couple times a week. With Mom's death, things fell apart pretty quickly. Mom had been what made things work in a lot of ways.

My eyes wandered down the row toward the kids, and Justine finally glanced my way. The anemic sunlight coming through the windows showed the lines around her eyes and mouth. She looked angry. Angry and mean.

I never could see what Ben saw in her. Maybe what he'd seen was that she'd gotten pregnant with Tiffany by accident, and he'd just had to make the best of it ever since.

The nasty thought was satisfying and left only the slightest aftertaste of guilt. When it came to Justine, I'd long since given up on policing my thoughts. Just policing what I actually said was enough of an effort.

After the service, everyone trickled down to the community room for coffee. I got hugs from Ben and the girls and an oops-I-just-got-distracted-by-someone-who's-not-you from Justine.

"Aunt Beth! Guess what?"

This from little Madisyn, who was twisting around and hopping from one foot to the other. Either she was excited to tell me something, or she had to pee. Maybe both.

"What, baby?"

I reached out to tousle her hair, but she ducked away.

"I'm not a baby," she said crossly.

"'Course not. What'd you want to tell me?"

"I forgot," she said with a pout.

"Then tell me something else."

"Okay, but it's a secret," she said in a semi-whisper, looking around. Our fellow churchgoers were standing about, chatting and drinking their coffee. No one was paying attention. Madisyn took a big breath.

"Nanny Hansen's doggie has glass fur."

I really wasn't sure what to do with that.

"Really? Wow."

"Uh-huh."

Madisyn was grinning up at me excitedly. I wracked my

brain for a follow-up.

"Does he talk?"

Madisyn looked surprised.

"How'd you know?"

"Well, lots of dogs can, you know. But they only talk to the very nicest people."

"I don't think most of them can talk," Madisyn said doubtfully.

"Tell the truth, Madisyn," Justine cut in. "Dogs can't talk at all."

Her tone seemed unnecessarily severe to me. Then again, it often did.

Madisyn looked up at her mother with a strange expression. Then she looked at her feet, pushing at the floor tiles with one toe, then the other.

"The doggie says Mommy's leaving us."

Shocked, I glanced up at Ben. He just looked back at me, equally surprised. But Justine reacted with fury.

"Madisyn, shame on you! No lying! Go stand in that corner. Not a sound 'til I come get you."

Madisyn burst into tears and ran to the corner. Practically everyone in the room turned to look. Justine flushed in embarrassment. So did Tiff and Jazzy, the older girls. Lia, who was five, just looked confused and scared. Her lower lip quivered.

I got mad. Justine was overreacting, as usual. Madisyn was a really sweet kid, and she wasn't a liar. She just had a weird imagination and the impulse control of, well, a three-year-old. I took a breath to give Justine a piece of my mind, but she beat me to the punch.

"This is what comes of having your influence around," she hissed. "Stay away from us!"

"Me?" I was totally taken aback. "What could I possibly

have to do with it?"

Justine didn't respond, but she stared at me with such unmistakable hatred that I backed away a few steps. I'd always known she didn't care for me, but were her feelings that strong?

"Okay, okay, let's all calm down," my brother soothed. "That was a real humdinger, but it's just attention-getting behavior. Let's not make too much of it."

Justine got a crazy look on her face.

"Oh, 'attention-getting behavior,' is it? What, you been watching Dr. Phil in your spare time?"

This was the point where their arguments always devolved into the "why are you so jealous?" and "why do you always take her side?" stuff, only with more cussing. And a lot of screaming.

That's probably where Madisyn's comment came from, actually. I bet she'd heard Justine threaten to leave a dozen times. That's got to make a kid anxious.

Ben and Justine were looking daggers at each other. Justine was too proper to have any more of the fight here in church, but she'd certainly be dragging the family out the door ASAP to get her licks in.

There was nothing left for me here this week. Feeling sad and angry, I murmured an excuse about having coffee with Suzanne and stalked off.

☙

My hands were still shaking as I stirred a fourth sugar into my coffee. I wasn't sure why Justine's outburst had thrown me so badly. It's not like I wasn't used to her craziness. I'd been on the receiving end of it since I was a kid. I guess this time it had taken me by surprise. I'd thought we were in strained-but-cordial mode, and I got blindsided.

I looked up to see Suzanne studying me a bit too attentively as she stroked her pretty silver hair. I smiled sweetly and asked her what she'd thought of Pastor Ezra's focus on the metaphor of rebirth in that morning's sermon. Suzanne blinked at me, jolted out of the gossipy tidbit she'd probably been cooking up about how upset I looked after my fight with my sister-in-law.

Gossip about me generally dredged up my mental illness, dead mother, pathetic dating life, or failed try at college—or all four—so diverting Suzanne during her moments of creation was pretty important. It wasn't that she didn't like me—care about me, even. But for Suzanne, all things bowed before the god of gossip.

I reached for the creamer. Dorf wasn't sophisticated enough to have an actual coffee shop, but the ownership of Pete's Eats didn't mind if you sat and talked over a beverage. Unfortunately, Pete's coffee wasn't good—especially the decaf. At home I drank my coffee black. At Pete's I added enough cream and sugar to make it taste like coffee-flavored ice cream. Otherwise, it was too bitter to get down.

Suzanne and I chatted about the weather, which is where Wisconsin small talk almost always starts. From there we moved to the exploits of her son, Tommie, who was a forty-something Milwaukee lawyer and who probably hadn't wanted to be called "Tommie" in several decades. We talked a bit about my work, but since I was always careful not to spread gossip about Dr. Nielsen or my best friend, Janie, who was his accounts manager, that part of the conversation didn't last long.

Suzanne then filled me in on the latest goings-on about town. Samantha Werthauser had left her husband over his affair with Sandy Foley. Josh Smith was thinking of becoming a Catholic. Johnny Cooper, who read meters for the electric co-op, had been caught red-handed trying to steal Godfrey Dingle's best hunting dog. Its collar had gotten caught on the fence Johnny was trying to stuff it over.

"That poor dog set up a yammering you could hear a mile away," Suzanne said. "Even Godfrey could hear it, and you know how deaf he is. Came busting out his back door and nearly filled that boy's ass up with buckshot!"

Suzanne blushed a bit as she laughed. I could tell she was a little proud of herself for saying "ass."

The litany continued. Callie McCallister was trying to organize a boycott of Big Screen Video because they stocked a few NC-17 movies. At the same time, her boyfriend had moved in with her, which was pretty hypocritical. Someone had knocked down fourteen mailboxes over on Marsh Road. Tess Kreugger was in trouble with Animal Control again for putting out peanut butter for raccoons in her back yard.

"She said it was for woodpeckers," Suzanne said, "but how could woodpeckers eat six pounds of peanut butter? That gal's gonna get rabies if she's not careful."

Dorf was going to levy an assessment on downtown property owners for new sidewalks. The Lakeshore Supper Club had a rat infestation. Sara Goshen was expecting twins. It went on and on.

Some of it was old news. For instance, everyone knew the old mill at Bilford Crossing was still burning—the column of smoke off to the northwest had been visible since Saturday morning. Everyone also knew that Kingston Brown, last year's Frederick High homecoming king, was about to undergo a shotgun marriage to Carly Knavel. But some of Suzanne's items were pretty surprising—the thing about Callie living

BECCA MILLS

with some guy amazed me. Others were infuriating. Some were surely untrue.

I rolled my eyes a few times and generally laughed along with her. Suzanne was a pretty good storyteller. Just so long as none of her stories were about me.

When she finally ran out of steam, there was an awkward silence. I could tell she was disappointed I wasn't providing any new tidbits. The economy of gossip worked on a barter system, after all. But that was how I justified my bad habit of listening to gossip—I never provided any and never passed on what I'd heard. Fortunately, Suzanne enjoyed the act of giving too much to let my stingy ways put a hitch in our relationship.

But then it occurred to me that, just this once, I did have something to offer. I didn't know the person involved, so I didn't feel honor-bound to silence. And maybe I could get some info that would set my mind at ease.

"So, I saw someone new downtown yesterday when I was taking pictures. Short, balding African American guy with a slender build. You know who he is?"

Suzanne shook her head, looking intrigued.

"No, I haven't run into him yet. Where's he from, Chicago?"

Folks here always seemed to think any black person they encountered was probably "up from Chicago." It was one of those things that gave me Dorf-claustrophobia.

Then I remembered how the picture had creeped me out the night before. Maybe I wasn't any better myself.

"I don't know. I didn't actually talk to him. I just saw him walking in front of J.T.'s."

"Sure it wasn't Grange Consecki or Bob Garter?"

Bob and Grange were the only African American men who lived in Dorf.

"No, he was way shorter than them, and he was really thin. And his skin was super dark."

"Like a Hershey bar?"

"No, more like licorice."

I did not just say that. Oh my god, what was wrong with me?

"Huh. Well I'll ask around and see who he is," Suzanne said. "You know Twanda will want to hear if there's a new man in town," she said, giving me a wink.

Twanda Sullivan was the only single African American woman in town.

Great. Now Suzanne would talk to Twanda, and Twanda would think I thought she wanted to jump every black man who walked through town, no matter who he was.

Why did I bring this up? I needed a fire alarm, so I could escape in the chaos. Or maybe a fistfight. Suzanne would forget all about the mystery man if that happened.

Unfortunately, no one chose that moment to faint or moon us or do anything else the slightest bit distracting.

"Well, we'll just see," Suzanne said, looking like I'd put her on the hunt.

Thank god I hadn't included the nudity thing—that would've had her asking every person in town about him, for sure, and probably calling the cops, too.

It took another twenty minutes to get out of Pete's. I drove home feeling especially shitty for reasons I couldn't exactly put my finger on—some combination of acute racial embarrassment, Justine's outburst, and a nebulous sense of anxiety.

Since the light was better that afternoon than it had been the day before, I picked up my camera and drove out to the old cemetery behind St. Mary's. I shot a whole roll of film. It made me feel better. After that I did the week's grocery shopping. Then I went home, ate dinner, and hit the darkroom.

✒

I stood there holding a photo of a nineteenth-century grave marker. The eroded carving wasn't legible in the picture, but I'd looked at the stone many times and remembered what it said: "Daught. Died Dec. 25, 1859. Aged 2 yrs. 9 ds." It was such a strange, sad monument. It offered no name for the dead child, yet told us exactly how long she had lived and that she had passed on Christmas Day.

This time, I hadn't noticed the problem on the negative and had printed the picture, expecting nothing unusual. But holding the print, I could see that someone had again walked right by as I took the shot. He'd passed no more than a couple yards in front of me, leaving the frame just as I opened the shutter. His foot, ankle, and a little bit of calf were plainly visible, flexed like he was pushing off for his next step.

There had been no one besides me in the cemetery, certainly not that close to me.

The foot was huge and bare. Its skin was patterned with darker-colored, donut-shaped blotches. It had jagged, horny toenails.

It was a monster foot. Strike that. It was a cliché of a monster foot. If someone had asked me to imagine a monster foot, that's what it would've looked like.

It had to be some kind of joke. But how? I couldn't think of any way someone could've gotten the foot into the picture.

I looked again at the print. I could see the tendons and muscles of the lower leg flexing. It wasn't just some rubber Halloween-costume foot someone had dangled from a tree.

The darkroom's walls started pressing in on me, and my breathing sped up. I backed up to the wall and sat down on the floor. I gave the rubber band on my wrist a hard snap and started focusing on breathing more methodically. In, out, pause. In, out, pause. Slowly the room stabilized.

I groped for an explanation. There had to be one.

A double exposure.

But this had been a new roll of film. I'd opened it that afternoon. The empty box was still in my camera bag.

Still, someone could've played a trick on me. They could've stolen the film, opened the box, loaded the film in their own camera, shot an image of a fake foot in middle of the roll, taken the film out of their camera, returned the roll to the box, glued the box shut, and put it back with my film stash. Elaborate, maybe, but possible. April Fools' Day had been, what, a week ago?

But how had they gotten into my house? And who would do something like that? I didn't think anyone I knew would go to the trouble of such an elaborate prank. I didn't have the kind of friends who would enjoy making me freak out and then laughing about it with me later, and I didn't have enemies committed enough to go to so much trouble.

There was Justine.

I remembered that look she'd given me at church.

I'd never thought of her as an enemy, per se. She'd been more in the category of "family you can't stand, but they're still family." Maybe I'd been wrong, though. Ben did keep a key to the house. She could've gotten in. She didn't work during the day, so there'd have been plenty of opportunity.

But could she have set me up to double-expose a shot like this? Did she even know what a double exposure was or how to use a real camera?

Someone could've helped her.

I studied the print again. The grass the foot was stepping in was of a piece with all the rest of the grass in the picture: dead, wet, and a bit too long to look well kept. The foot was wet and had little bits of sodden grass stuck to it. How could two separate exposures have integrated so perfectly, just by chance? Plus, it just didn't look like a double exposure. The images weren't ghostly and overlapping. It looked real.

Maybe I was hallucinating. The naked guy had also apparently walked right in front of me, and I hadn't seen him. That image looked real, too, but maybe it wasn't.

Serious mental illness often emerged in your early twenties, right? And I already had one—panic disorder. Maybe that put me at risk for others.

But if I really was hallucinating, wouldn't I believe I wasn't?

I slid the photo up on the counter, out of sight, and sat there rubbing my hands on my jeans. I couldn't get rid of the clamminess. I tried to come up with another plausible explanation for the monster foot, but the more I thought about it, the more my chest tightened up.

Finally I pushed the whole issue away, and my mind settled into a fragile state of blankness. Then I could stand up, so I did. Carefully *not* thinking about the photo, I went upstairs, went to bed, and slept until morning.

❧

I woke up with a plan. It was so simple I should've thought of it the night before. I would show the weird pictures to someone else and see if they saw what I saw. If they did, then I wasn't going crazy, and it was just a matter of finding out who was messing with me, and why. And how.

Chapter 3

"WHAT *IS* THAT?" Janie said, scrunching up her nose adorably. She was holding half of her BLT in one hand and the cemetery picture in the other.

Since it was just the three of us in the office, Dr. Nielsen always closed up for an hour at lunchtime. Janie and I usually ate at our desks to save money, but every other Monday, we came to Pete's. I'd put my possibly hallucinatory photos in a folder and brought them along.

Clearly, she could see the monster foot. Some clenched-up thing inside me loosened. I quietly slid the other two photos—the ones of J.T.'s with the mystery man—back into the folder. If the foot wasn't a hallucination, surely Mr. Streaker wasn't either.

"I'm not sure. Someone must be pulling my chain, but I can't figure out how. Any ideas?"

"Dunno … this isn't from a digital camera, is it?"

"No, I took it on film, and I developed and printed it myself. No computers involved."

"Huh. Someone must've been there, and you didn't see them."

"But they would've been so close to me. How could I not

have seen them?"

"Huh." Janie turned the print this way and that. "What do you think, Jackie?"

I hadn't realized our waitress was standing behind me. Jackie, a tall, spare redhead, came around to look at the picture. She rolled her eyes.

"Gimme a break. It's some guy wearing a costume." Jackie looked me up and down, not very flatteringly. "You must've been zoning out, and he snuck up on you."

I blushed at the implication that I was spacey. Then I got embarrassed at blushing so easily, which made me blush more. Jesus, I was such a dork sometimes.

"I only knelt there for a few seconds to get the shot. I don't see how someone could've snuck up on me that fast without making noise."

"Well, if you're not paying attention, you don't hear stuff going on around you, do you?" Jackie said, arching an eyebrow as if I were denying the obvious.

Maybe I was. But my memory of the moment seemed so clear. I hadn't zoned out when I was taking those pictures. I'd felt pretty focused. Photography usually made me feel that way: sharp and observant and detail-oriented. It was one reason I liked it so much.

"Sure, that can happen, but if he snuck up on me while I was lining up the shot, where was he when I stood back up a second after I took it?"

"Behind a tree, maybe?"

"What're you gals arguing about?" Doyle Schumaker asked.

Doyle was having lunch with Billy Wozowski at the next table. Billy and Doyle were police officers. Doyle's K-9 partner, a German shepherd named Abby, was snoozing under their table.

"Someone's trying to put one over on Beth. She took this picture at St. Mary's yesterday afternoon, and it has a weird foot in it."

Janie gave him a flirty smile and tossed her hair a little as she handed him the photo.

I spent a little bit of each work day envying Janie. It's not that she'd dated some guy I wanted. I just wished in general I could be more like her, at least in some ways. She was pretty, yeah, but more than that, she just seemed comfortable in her own skin. She was never anxious, never restless. She seemed grounded, like she knew what was important to her and was sure she was going to get it eventually. For lack of a better word, she seemed satisfied. I'd never felt that way.

Maybe it came from growing up in a big farming family. I used to love hanging out at her place when we were kids. There was always a lot of noise and bustle, and plenty of arguments, but it was clearly a happy, loving group of people. Not that my mother hadn't loved me plenty, but for much of my life, it had just been the two of us. Janie's family was different. With a family like that, you'd never be lonely.

Doyle took the print from Janie and looked at it. His expression turned serious. He looked up at me searchingly.

"What time did you take this, exactly?" he asked, casting a meaningful glance across the table at Billy, then handing him the picture.

"Um … about 2:00 in the afternoon, I think. Is something wrong?"

"I might have to take this in as evidence, Betty."

I felt a little breathless.

"Really? Why?"

"About that time yesterday, there was an APB out for a seven-foot-tall bagel monster," he said, waggling his eyebrows at me.

Jackie, Janie, and Billy laughed, and I blushed all over again. Even worse, people at the tables around us started asking what was so funny. Soon the picture was being passed around Pete's Eats to a mixture of guffaws and speculations about Photoshopping.

If Justine had somehow engineered this to make me look stupid in front of the whole town, she'd sure as hell succeeded.

I went back to my meal, watching out of the corner of my eye as Jackie circulated among the tables, laughing with folks—no doubt at my expense. Someone's gaze caught mine. It was Callie McCallister, Dorf's most committed moral crusader. She was holding the photo and looking right at me, fear and revulsion plain on her face. Great. My picture was in the hands of the one person in town most likely to think I'd actually photographed a monster.

Sure enough, on her way out of Pete's ten minutes later, Callie stopped to drop the picture on our table. Her tiny hands were shaking. When she spoke, so was her voice.

"Elizabeth, you have to stop spreading this image. Glorifying hellspawn this way—it's unlawful."

"Callie, come on," I said. "It's just someone's idea of a prank. I'd like to know who, so I can smack 'em."

Callie's expression didn't change one bit. She was a little wisp of a thing, but when she'd made up her mind, she didn't back down. The whole town knew it from experience. Janie rolled her eyes.

A man reached down to our table and picked up the folder containing the other two photos, the ones of the mystery man in front of J.T.'s. I looked up at him in surprise. He was standing right beside Callie, but I hadn't noticed him. Maybe this was the new live-in boyfriend Suzanne had told me about.

He was looking at my pictures without permission, so I didn't hesitate to give him the once-over. He was a white guy of average height with brown hair and eyes and bland, even features. He was wearing jeans and a blue sweatshirt. Thoroughly uninteresting. And really rude.

"Excuse me, you didn't ask to see those," I said, reaching for the folder.

He ignored me except to turn slightly, so that the folder would be out of my reach. Just as I took a breath to object, Janie cut in.

"So," she said, drawing out the word in a way that made me cringe, "you're the one who's living with Our Lady of Christian Virtue, here? Living together outside the bonds of matrimony? Are you sure that's *proper?*"

Oh god. This was the part of Janie I didn't admire so much: she had the subtlety of a sledgehammer.

The man ignored Janie, but Callie sucked in a scandalized breath and turned tomato-red. That heavy, quiet feeling instantly surrounded us, the one that means every person within earshot is holding very still and listening. Two short-order cooks and a busboy stuck their heads out of the kitchen to watch. Jackie paused with her water pitcher cocked over someone's glass. Pete himself stood up from behind the counter, hands full of the straws and napkins he'd been stocking.

"He's not ... I mean, we're not ... he's just a houseguest!"

"Oh, right, he's a *houseguest*," Janie echoed in a knowing tone, added a wink and air-quotes for good measure. "Got it, got it."

"He is! I'd never ... you know."

"No, no, *of course* you wouldn't," Janie said in a soothing tone, which she immediately undercut by snorting loudly.

"Oh," she said, "excuse me." And snorted again.

The man slid the photos back into the folder and reached over to put it back on table. A thick, red scar ran across the back of his wrist. I hadn't noticed it earlier. Yuck. No wonder he wore long sleeves.

Callie stood there another few seconds, stammering out protests. Then the man put his arm around her thin shoulders and guided her out of the restaurant. I could hear her talking as they walked down the sidewalk. I couldn't understand what she was saying, but I could tell from her voice that she was crying.

After another few seconds, conversation and the sounds of eating picked back up. Janie leaned over to me with a grin.

"Whatcha say we tee-pee her house tonight?"

Doyle said "I heard that!" in mock outrage.

"Did you get a load of that guy with her?" Janie said. "Blandy McBlandsville, if you ask me."

"Yeah, I've forgotten him already," Doyle said.

A few people around us laughed.

It was bad. I mean, of course I couldn't let Callie go around claiming I was consorting with demons, or something. Dorf was a fairly religious town, and if people heard that kind of accusation enough, some of them might start believing it. But Janie's way of defending me had been over the top. I had profited from it—before Callie came to our table, I'd been the laughing stock, and now the laughing stock was her. But I felt like a shit.

Janie got busy chatting up Doyle and didn't notice how quiet I'd gotten.

We finished up and headed back to the office. Once there, I set about returning the calls on the answering machine, but I didn't give the task much attention. My mind alternated between feeling guilty over Callie and thinking about the photo.

It was good to know I hadn't hallucinated the foot—for Christ's sake, practically half the town had seen the thing.

But there still wasn't a good explanation for how someone'd managed to create the effect. That was a problem: having been humiliated, Callie would probably be out for blood. She'd be spreading all kinds of crazy ideas about me.

I needed a logical explanation for the photo, and I needed it soon.

❦

What with all the commotion, Janie and I had taken more than an hour's lunch, which annoyed Dr. Nielsen. I stayed late to make up for it, then headed over to Ben's house. It was something I hadn't done in years—just drop by unannounced. Justine had made it clear she didn't appreciate it.

But this time I actually wanted to see her, not Ben. Maybe if I surprised her with the photo, she'd admit to engineering the prank. Or at least I'd see a hint of guilt or embarrassment on her face.

The late afternoon sun was casting deep shadows across the front yard when I got out of my car. It made Justine's decorative lawn tableau of deer and garden gnomes around a wishing well look sort of sinister.

I rang the doorbell. In my hand I held the folder containing the three photos, now stained by a greasy fry I'd dropped on it during lunch.

Lia, my five-year-old niece, answered.

"Aunt Beth!"

"Hi, sweetie."

"Mommy! Aunt Beth is here! Are you here for dinner? Daddy said Susie could eat with us, so I guess you can too."

"No, honey, I just need to talk to your Mommy for a minute. Who's Susie?"

"She's my dolly, *duh!*"

Good lord. Glad to see my nieces were learning good manners.

Justine appeared behind Lia and shooed the girl away.

"What do you want?"

She didn't open the screened door. I bent the folder open to the cemetery picture and held it up against the screen.

"What do you know about this?" I asked.

She glanced at it and shrugged.

"It's a picture. Looks bad, so I guess it's one of yours."

"Look at it."

She sighed elaborately.

"That what I have to do to get rid of you? Fine."

She opened the door, took the folder, and thumbed through the three pictures with an obvious lack of interest. Then she stiffened. I could see her knuckles turn white, hear her stop breathing. Slowly she looked up at me. Long seconds passed. She just stared.

It wasn't guilt I saw on her face. It was confusion and fear. No, not fear—terror.

Finally she snapped back to life, as though someone had hit her play button. Without saying a word, she threw the folder at me and slammed the door in my face. The pictures scattered across the front porch. One of them landed in a puddle where the porch roof had leaked.

For a few seconds, I stood there amazed. It hadn't been the reaction I was expecting. At all. I rang the bell again, then knocked on the door when no one answered.

"Justine? Justine?"

I couldn't hear anything at all from inside the house. No voices, no footsteps, no TV. It was as though the whole place had gone to sleep. Strange. I knew at least two people were in there. I went from knocking to something closer to pounding.

"Justine! Ben? Ben! Lia?"

This was weird. Why had Justine freaked out like that? Was she afraid I'd get her in trouble for the prank? Surely not—playing a joke on someone wasn't illegal. I gathered the photos up and walked around the side of the house. The lights were on, but the shades were drawn. I stopped to listen.

It wasn't just quiet. It was still. Utterly still.

The hair prickled on my arms and my pulse sky-rocketed. My mouth went dry and a wave of dizziness sent me staggering against the house. Terror engulfed me. Without even thinking about it, I turned and lurched back to my car, piled in, and locked the doors. Then I sat there, gasping for breath, chest aching. Snapping my rubber band didn't help. I couldn't get enough air. I grabbed the little wastebasket I kept on the passenger side floor and threw up. Then I clawed at my shirt collar, trying to loosen it.

I must've passed out. I came to sprawled awkwardly to the side, clumps of hair sticking to my sweaty face. I sat up, dazed and sick, and did what I always did after an attack—looked around to see who'd witnessed it. In this case, no one. A small favor.

I thought briefly of just going back and knocking on the door like a normal person, but even considering it made my pulse shoot up. I profoundly did not want to get out of the car. I couldn't shake the sense that if I got out, something terrible would happen.

I started the car up and headed home. It was either that or have back-to-back attacks.

My hands trembled on the steering wheel the whole way.

What had been so scary about that situation?

I sighed. I always asked myself that after an attack, and it was almost always a pointless question—there was hardly ever a rational explanation. Hardly ever an irrational explanation, for that matter. They came out of the blue.

Just thinking about Justine and Ben's place made my heart speed up again. I tried to put it out of my mind and focus on my driving.

By the time I parked and got inside my house, the adrenaline rush was fading. It left me exhausted.

I should call Justine.

That thought made the panic begin to rise.

The phone's all the way upstairs, I told myself, *and I'll have to look up the number*. I never called Ben at home, anymore, and didn't remember it. *I'll call her later*, I thought. Tomorrow was soon enough, especially after she'd been so rude.

Plus, if I went upstairs, I'd check the answering machine to see if Matt had called, and that would be pathetic. I knew he wasn't going to call.

Besides, I had stuff to do. I needed to clean up the darkroom and make some dinner. Then I'd watch TV and go to bed early—tomorrow was a workday. I tried to push the memory of Ben's house and the attack into the background.

After getting a drink of water, I headed down to the basement to neaten up. I'd left the darkroom a mess the night before, when I'd freaked out about the monster-foot trick. Looked like I'd even left the basement lights on.

I was most of the way down the stairs when I looked up and saw a man standing in the darkroom, going through a sheaf of prints. I froze, not really processing what I was seeing.

After what seemed like ages, he looked up at me. He didn't look at all like a burglar caught in the act—there was nothing surreptitious or guilty in his manner. He just stared at me, then set the prints down on the counter.

That motion jogged me out of my paralysis. I turned and ran back up the stairs, trying to remember where I'd set down my keys.

I'd only made it a few steps when my left foot was jerked out from under me and I fell, banging my forehead on a step hard enough to make me dizzy. I lay there, feeling confused and tangled up in my own limbs.

As though from a distance, I felt the man step over me and heard him close the door at the top of the stairs. Then he dragged me back down the steps and into the darkroom. He leaned me up against the back wall. I promptly slid over onto my side, feeling sick. He closed the darkroom door and went back to what he was doing—looking through stacks of prints. I closed my eyes for a while and just listened to the slippery rustle of photographic paper.

Slowly, the spins and nausea receded. I collected my thoughts a little. It occurred to me that he was probably going to kill me. I'd gotten a good look at him. I'd be able to ID him in a line-up.

My head ached fiercely. It was like I could actually hear it hurting. I thought about pretending to be unconscious, but that didn't seem useful. If he was for sure going to kill me, he'd do it whether I was awake or not. If I talked to him, maybe I could help myself.

I opened my eyes. The man was now going through my shoebox of negatives, holding each strip up to the light and studying it carefully. All my prints were out on the counter in piles—not only those I'd made myself but also those I'd had done professionally before I set up the darkroom.

Something about him nagged at my brain. It took me a minute, but then I realized he had thick scar on his left wrist. And a blue sweatshirt. And jeans.

I stared at him. He had brown hair, but otherwise he looked nothing like the man who'd been with Callie in the restaurant. Whereas that man had been bland enough to fade into a white wall, this guy was anything but. Instead of neat and conservative, his hair looked shaggy and none too clean. His features were severe. He looked a lot bigger, and he was the opposite of unnoticeable. "Dangerous" just roiled off him. If this guy had walked into Pete's Eats, Pete would've reached for his shotgun.

And yet, the scar looked just the same. And the clothes were so similar. Was it the same shirt, or just one very like it? His sleeves were pushed up, so it was hard to be sure. But did it matter? Two men could dress the same, but they wouldn't have the same scar. This must be the same person—a master of disguise, or something.

My god, had "Moral Crusader Callie" gotten herself involved with terrorists?

I took a deep breath. "What do you want?"

No response.

"Are you looking for money? My purse is upstairs."

Silence.

"What are you going to do with me?"

He didn't bother looking up.

I thought about how close my neighbors' houses were. My basement was mostly underground. The few windows were up near the ceiling and only a foot high. Would anyone hear me if I screamed?

As if he'd heard what I was thinking, the man said, "No screaming." He had a slight accent, and his tone was flat, affectless. It sounded unnatural.

He continued going through the negatives, ignoring me. It took quite a while—I had many more negatives than I had prints. I sat there watching, too terrified to think of what to do.

When the task was done, he crouched down in front of me and studied my face.

"Where are the pictures you had at the restaurant?"

I hadn't really believed, not completely, that this was the same guy. Taken by surprise, I blurted out the truth.

"Upstairs. On the kitchen counter."

Then again, I couldn't think of an advantage to lying. He'd already seen them.

"Have you taken pictures of any other Seconds?"

"What?"

"Seconds," he said flatly, as though I were being evasive. "Beings of the Second Emanation."

Oh my god, Callie had convinced him that "hellspawn" were real and that I was passing around pictures of them. Or maybe he was the one who'd convinced her. That thought brought a wave of nausea. Callie's moral crusades were annoying, sure, but they were basically harmless. If this guy was the one launching the crusade, there'd be harm. Lots of harm.

"Look, I'm sorry, but I don't know what you're talking about. I photograph places, people I know, pets—that kind of thing. There's nothing special about my pictures. Someone was just playing a joke on me, sticking that foot in there."

He looked bored, waiting for me to finish talking.

"Why did you photograph the green man?"

"Green?"

He looked at me, silent, waiting.

"Come on, this is crazy. Those pictures show a black guy walking in front of a bar."

He reached back and grabbed a big handful of my hair, close to my scalp. Then he twisted it.

It might seem like a pretty small thing, almost schoolyardish—someone pulling your hair. But no one had ever intentionally hurt me before. It hurt so much more than I would've thought. It was like, in that instant, I knew I was at the mercy of someone who cared nothing about me, maybe someone who enjoyed hurting me. I had no control over what was going to happen to me. Panic surged through me, and I thrashed and flailed, screaming. I would've told anyone anything. Resistance was unthinkable.

I think he only hurt me for a few seconds, but it seemed to go on forever. It was a while after he stopped before I could get any words out.

"Take the pictures! Take the negatives. I don't care. I won't tell anyone. Just leave me alone—please!"

"Tell me why you photographed him."

"I didn't! I was just taking pictures of the bar. I didn't see him!"

For the first time, an emotion crossed his face: surprise. Then he looked thoughtful.

"You never saw it?"

I shook my head. Big mistake—it hurt.

"Did you see the one in the cemetery with your own eyes?"

"No! There was nothing there."

He stood up and leaned back against the counter, thinking. I slumped back against the wall and took deep, shuddering breaths.

"Have you ever taken any other pictures that showed weird things?"

"No."

"You sure?"

"Yes. I only started taking pictures last year. Everything I've taken is in this room."

"How old are you?"

"Twenty-three."

"Why did you start taking pictures?"

My fear started receding a bit. It wasn't that the situation seemed better. I think it's just not possible to maintain that level of terror for very long. In its place came exhaustion. I sensed it was almost over, maybe that *I* was almost over.

I looked up at him, not really focusing.

"Tell me why you started taking pictures."

"I don't know."

His eyes narrowed.

"I mean, I don't know why it makes me feel better. I get anxious." I seemed unable to get my ideas in the right order.

He was silent for a while. Then he rubbed the back of his neck and said, "Fuck."

He knelt down and grabbed my chin, forcing me to look at him. For the first time, I really saw his face close up. It was harsh and heavily lined. No, a lot of those were scars, not lines. His eyes looked too dark. He was terrifying.

"Someone'll come talk to you about this soon. For now, don't tell anyone I was here. Don't take any more pictures. Don't show your pictures to anyone. Don't talk about them with anyone. Don't leave town. Don't attract attention to yourself in any way. If you do any of those things, you'll die. You understand?"

I couldn't have spoken for the world. I just jerked my head.

He stared at me for another few seconds, maybe to make sure I really got it. Then he stood up and left.

For a long time, I just sat there on the darkroom floor, staring at nothing. I had no idea what to do. I felt oddly listless and distant, as though most of me was far away, connected to the rest of me by a thin tether.

What was I going to do?

The first thing was to move. I shifted against the wall, and my body came alive with sensations. None of them was pleasant. My head swam and pounded, my scalp hurt, and my right hand ached where I must've slammed it against the wall. Plus, I was cold and wet. I'd pissed myself.

I thought, *This is the worst moment of my life.*

I had no idea what to do. He'd said someone would come for me. Someone like him? Who was he? Some sort of religious vigilante? What was going to happen to me?

A single thought crystallized: get away. I had to get far away and never be found. Not by him or anyone like him. Once I realized it, I was completely clear on this point. It was essential.

But no … was that really right?

He'd said I'd die if I told anyone about him or if I tried to leave. I believed he meant it. He would do it himself. It didn't matter what his motives were. It didn't matter that I hadn't done anything wrong. Dead is dead, even if you're killed by a crazy person for a crazy reason.

But he'd also said someone would come for me. I couldn't sit here and wait for *that* to come again. I could not. It was a terrible struggle not to run screaming from the house that very moment.

It occurred to me that I probably wasn't being rational. I tried to take a step back. *What if I sleep on it and decide in the morning?*

The very room reacted to the thought, closing in on me, crushing me. My breath came in gasps, and all the strength left my muscles. Black spots rushed at my eyes from the far wall. I flopped forward, trying to claw my way to the door. I didn't make it.

I woke up on the darkroom floor, not sure how long I'd been there. There was no more question about staying in Dorf. All I needed was a head start. I needed time to pack some things, get my money out of the bank, and put gas in my car. Then I was out of there.

I would call the police. I'd say I'd walked in and found Callie McCallister's boyfriend rifling through my stuff. He'd assaulted me, then run off.

I could make it believable. Billy and Doyle had heard Callie accuse me of photographing "hellspawn" in Pete's earlier. He'd been with her and had shown an interest in my pictures.

It could work. I had a big lump on my forehead as evidence of assault. He hadn't been wearing gloves, so he'd probably left fingerprints all over. Maybe one of my neighbors had seen him getting in or out of his car—even when he left, it wouldn't have been dark yet.

But would anyone have recognized him? He looked so different.

My mind skittered away from that thought.

Even if the charges didn't stick, I'd have a chance to get out of town before the cops let him go. Doyle was a good guy. He'd be willing to call me with a warning if they were about to release him.

I got up slowly, testing my legs. They worked. I went upstairs and dialed 911. Then I sat down to wait.

During the many hours that followed, the police were

unable to find the folder with the three photos. The man had taken them.

Chapter 4

"BETTY? HEY, IT'S Doyle. Honey, the charges aren't gonna stick. Turns out the guy's FBI. Paperwork's going through now. He'll probably be out within the hour."

"He's in the FBI?"

I couldn't believe it.

"Yep. Apparently he's up here investigating a meth ring."

"A *meth ring*?"

"Yeah, you know, it's this drug ..."

"I know what it is, Doyle. I'm just having trouble believing it. I mean, if he's an FBI agent, where's his partner? And why's he living with Callie McCallister?"

"Beats me. Maybe he was undercover or something. Guess we blew that."

God, was he really in the FBI? Was that who the government was hiring now—thugs who broke into people's houses and beat up women?

"You guys checked this out with the FBI directly, right?"

"Sure thing. The chief called Washington and talked to his supervisor. Who was pretty damn pissed, actually."

Suddenly I felt very alone. Very alone and very scared.

"You believe me, don't you, Doyle? About what he did to

me, I mean?"

"Sure, Betty, I believe you. All of us do. I mean, you had that knot on your head."

Did I imagine a little bit of doubt in his voice? Maybe he was thinking about other explanations for that so-called evidence. They hadn't found any way to confirm my story. None of my neighbors had noticed the man's car, and somehow he hadn't left any prints. It was just my story and my injury.

"Okay, Doyle, thanks. And thanks for calling to let me know. I really appreciate it. I owe you one."

"No problem. You hang in there, okay? Just give us a call if something seems funny. Hey, maybe have Janie come stay with you for a few days."

"Good idea, Doyle, thanks. Bye."

I gave myself exactly one minute to sit in my car and cry.

Callie's boyfriend's name had turned out to be John Williams. The cops had picked him up early that morning, after spending the night going over my place and hearing my story. Now it was a bit after 2:00 in the afternoon. What with the things I'd had to do before leaving town, I'd gotten less than six hours' head start.

I wiped my face on the back of my sleeve and got out of the car. I was parked in an interstate rest stop, where I'd pulled off to get gas. Heading over to the parking area for the big rigs, I took a moment to tuck my cell phone behind the cab of one of them. It was an ultra-cheap pay-as-you-go model I'd bought that morning, just so I'd be able to get updates from Doyle. I couldn't risk keeping it now—they could track a cell phone's location, right? It had served its purpose, anyway.

I got back on the road. I was glad I'd gotten most of my money out of the bank before leaving Dorf. If Williams was in the FBI, he'd have a lot more resources at his disposal than I'd imagined. I probably shouldn't use my debit or credit card.

Then again, if he was in the FBI, he wouldn't be pursuing me, right? He'd stay in Dorf, investigating meth dealers.

Somehow I didn't believe it. Maybe he wasn't really in the FBI but had contacts in the FBI who would lie for him. That sounded more like it. It also sounded a lot more frightening.

I stayed on 90 westbound for another hour, then turned south and headed down into Iowa on county roads. Hopefully the semi with my phone would keep heading west.

I kept driving until I couldn't stay awake any longer. It was the middle of the night. I stopped in a small town in the southeastern corner of Nebraska. I found a sleazy-looking motel and paid in cash. When I told the clerk I'd lost my wallet and didn't have ID, he just rolled his eyes.

I showered, then made a dinner out of some granola bars and peanut butter I'd brought with me. The sheets were scratchy and the room was cold. My head still ached fiercely from its impact with the stairs. It didn't matter—I hadn't slept in a day and a half, and for a good chunk of that time, I'd been scared to death. I was out as soon as I lay down.

🖌

Morning gave me my first good look at America west of the Mississippi. I'd always thought of Nebraska as flat, but in this part, at least, it was hilly.

I felt a lot better than I had the night before. Calmer, clearer. My head only hurt a little.

Standing at the window looking out, I also felt a lot less certain I'd done the right thing. I'd planned my getaway, yes, but I hadn't really thought about it in a bigger sense. In fact, I dimly remembered deciding *not* to think about it.

Where exactly was I going to go? If I just kept moving, I'd run out of money pretty fast. I needed to settle some place and get work. But how could I do that without getting found? I didn't know the first thing about getting a job without ID, or about getting fake identification, for that matter.

Did I even have enough to rent a place somewhere while I looked for work? I emptied my wallet and the envelope of cash I'd gotten at the bank. It came to $1,264, plus change. That wasn't much when you factored in a security deposit. Could I get a place here in——I looked at the phone book——Sway Creek for that? And wouldn't any landlord want my social security number?

I drummed my fingers on the bedside table. No solutions presented themselves.

What about Ben? I hadn't told him I was leaving, much less where I was going or how to get in touch with me. Ben and his girls were all the family I had. Was I prepared to never see them again?

I'd called him Monday night right after I called the police. He'd come and met me at the hospital, where they'd taken me to make sure I didn't have a concussion. Ben wasn't the most emotive guy, but that night he looked pretty scared. I'd always known how much I needed my brother. It was a big part of why I resented Justine——she kept him from me. But the reverse hadn't really occurred to me: maybe he needed me, too.

I sat still, holding my breath as an awful new thought tried to crawl to the surface.

What if I wasn't there to hurt, and John Williams hurt Ben instead? Or the kids?

Horror settled over me. It was the feeling of having

screwed up. Big.

Should I go back?

No, I couldn't. Williams had given me a direct order not to leave town. He'd also ordered me not to tell anyone about him. If he found me, he'd kill me. Twice.

I needed to call Ben and make sure he was okay. I'd tell him to take the family on a little trip. I could do it from a pay phone, then drive in a random direction for the whole day. It was chancy because it might let Williams track me, but it was the best I could do.

❧

"Beth? Oh my god, where are you?"

Ben sounded panicked.

"It's okay. I'm okay. I'm just getting out of town for a while, until that Williams guy leaves. You heard they didn't charge him, right?"

"Beth, Justine's gone!"

It so was not the response I was expecting that it took me a moment to grasp it.

"What do you mean, gone? She left you?"

"No, I don't know, she's just *gone*! She didn't pick the kids up from school yesterday. No one's seen her. Beth, I know something terrible happened to her. She might leave me, but she'd never leave the kids."

I stood there in shock.

"Beth? Beth?"

"I'm here. When's the last time someone saw her?"

"The security camera at the Cenex caught her getting gas a little before noon. That's it. She was supposed to be at the school at 3:30, but she never showed."

Doyle had called me at 2:15 to say Williams would be out soon. "Within the hour," he'd said.

Oh god, oh my god.

He hadn't been able to get at Ben. Ben had been at work, surrounded by people. So he'd taken Justine instead.

"Beth?"

"Did you call the police?"

"Of course! Beth … they want to talk to you about it."

It took me another few seconds to understand what he meant.

"They think I kidnapped Justine? Ben, you can't be serious!"

"I know. They're wasting their fucking time when they could be looking for who really did it. But people saw you two fighting at church." His voice slid from angry to defeated. "I think it's the only lead they have. Could you please just talk to them? Maybe once they let go of that idea, they'll get a better one. Beth, we have to find her. I need her."

"Ben, I'll call you back in just a sec."

"Beth—"

I hung up on him. Then I stumbled to the curb and threw up my breakfast beside someone's junky pickup. I was in the parking lot of a 7-Eleven—the first place I'd seen a pay phone. What a place to be when you find out you're going to die.

❧

Even taking the most direct route, it took me more than twelve hours to get home.

That morning, I'd bought a bottle of water and rinsed out my mouth. Then I'd called my brother back and told him I'd be there to talk to the police as soon as I could.

Things had been pretty clear to me after I talked to Ben. I'd made a bad mistake when I left Dorf. If I went back now, maybe Williams would let Justine go. Maybe taking her was his way of sending me a message: come back, or else. If he'd already killed her, at least going back now would keep him from hurting anyone else. What he did to me was out of my hands, but maybe I could keep him from doing anything to anybody else. That idea had brought a measure of calm.

That calm was still with me when I pulled into the parking lot in front of the small brick building that served as Dorf's police station.

I sat for a minute, enjoying the warmth and familiarity of my car. It was a '91 Le Mans. It had been my mother's. When I'd gotten the job with Dr. Nielsen, Mom had offered it to me sort of offhandedly. We were cleaning up after dinner one night, just the two of us. She'd said she thought she'd get herself a newer car, but maybe we should hang onto this one for a while so I could drive to work.

I'd been so ashamed, back then, of failing at college. She'd saved for years for me to be able to go. It's not like you make that much, working at a supermarket. She took extra hours whenever she could, even did some house-cleaning on the side. With my scholarships and financial aid and her loans and savings, we'd just been able to make it work. But I'd thrown her money away and all her hopes for me, too, because I was too crazy to do what billions of eighteen-year-olds did every year.

And there she was, still trying to help me.

I should've gotten in her lap and cried like a baby; instead I shrugged and said, "Sounds good," as if it didn't mean the world to me, how much she cared.

She never got that new car, either. Instead, she got run over crossing Center Street.

I sighed and got out. It was uncomfortably cold. The nights still have a lot of bite in early April in northern Wisconsin. I stood next to the car, wondering if Williams was already hunting me. Maybe he'd shoot me from a distance, and I'd never feel a thing.

After a minute, nothing had happened. I gathered my courage and headed into the warmth and light of the station.

"Yes, Justine and I don't like each other. No, I didn't do anything to her."

I was repeating the same basic information I'd been giving the chief for the last hour. I'd been scared at first. Then fear had faded to nervousness. Now I was just annoyed. Why was he being so dense?

"So, let me get this straight," he said, consulting his notes. "Right after we brought in Agent Williams on Tuesday morning, you left Dorf, even though we'd asked you to remain available."

"That's right."

"And you did this why?"

"I was afraid of him. He told me he'd kill me if I told anyone what he'd done."

I might be a dead woman walking, but like hell if I wasn't going to let people know who killed me. Well, who was going to be responsible for killing me when it happened, that is.

"Betty, do you really think we're going to accept this story of yours again? John Williams is an agent in good standing. He's never been reprimanded. In fact, he's been decorated three times—I have his file right here." The chief patted one of the folders on the table. "You expect us to believe he broke into your house, assaulted you, and tried to steal your photographs?"

"I don't care what you believe. Fact is, I was afraid of him, and I left town at about 8:00 on Tuesday morning. I drove to Nebraska. When I heard from my brother that Justine was missing, I headed back. That's it."

"Problem is, you have no proof of that, which means your whereabouts are unaccounted for during the time that Mrs. Ryder went missing."

This was infuriating—so not helpful to finding Justine. Well, so be it. I guess it's true that no good turn goes unpunished.

"Actually, Officer Shumaker's phone logs should support my story. Since I was so scared Monday night, he was kind enough to call and let me know when Williams was getting out. I talked to him at about 2:15 Tuesday afternoon, and I was already in western Minnesota when I received the call."

The chief looked like he'd bitten into a lemon. I couldn't have kidnapped Justine between 11:45 and 3:30 and also been in Minnesota at 2:15.

"What's the number on your phone?"

I got out my wallet and handed him the scrap of paper where I'd written down the number.

"Where's the phone?"

"I left it in Minnesota after I talked to Officer Shumaker."

"How come?"

"I thought Williams might be able to trace where it was."

The chief looked at me as though he were realizing for the first time that I was the saddest, most pathetic lunatic in Dorf.

"Wait here."

He got up and left the room with the phone number. I felt

bad about ratting out Doyle, but I thought he'd probably be okay. The chief was his brother's godfather, so they were family friends.

I sat there for quite a while, twiddling my thumbs. Then, curiosity getting the better of caution, I reached over and opened the folder with the FBI logo on the front. On top was a personnel page, complete with photo. I picked it up.

Special Agent Christopher Duncan resided in Bethesda, Maryland. His middle name was Carlos. He'd been in the FBI for eight years. The picture showed a handsome African American man with short dreads. He was wearing a dark suit and a muted green and burgundy tie.

What was this?

I shifted through the rest of the pages in the folder. They all belonged to this Duncan person. I was totally confused. The chief had definitely pointed to the folder I'd picked up.

At that moment, the chief walked back in. Unfortunately, Williams came in right behind him. The bland Pete's Eats version of him, anyway.

"You shouldn't be looking at that," the Chief said. "It's confidential."

He reached down and jerked the personnel page out of my hands. I saw him glance at it as he was putting it back in the folder. I sat there, stupefied. What was going on here? Was the guy blind?

"Agent Williams, your suspect," the chief said, gesturing at me disgustedly.

Finally I found my voice. "But that's not his file!"

The chief glared at me.

I shot a glance at Williams, who was standing quietly by the door.

"Chief, that file belongs to someone named Duncan."

"Nonsense," the chief snapped. He jerked his head at me. "She's all yours. I'll be in touch if her alibi doesn't pan out."

"Wait, you can't give me to him," I protested, all my calm evaporating. "What do you mean I'm 'his suspect'?"

The chief eyed me with displeasure.

"Should've known you'd be wrapped up in something like this."

He stalked out.

Williams's blandness seemed to vanish. Suddenly he looked a lot less like a milquetoast and a lot more like a murderer. He grabbed me by the upper arm and proceeded to drag me out of the building.

Not too long before, I'd been pretty cool with the idea of surrendering myself to get Justine back, but self-sacrifice suddenly seemed a good deal more concrete and terrifying. I did a fair amount of screaming on the way out of the station. No one came to help me.

❧

Williams had a full-sized van. Not surprising for someone who probably had to dispose of dead bodies regularly. He lifted me into the back of it and cuffed me to a ring in the floor near the front seats. I had to hunch there awkwardly on my hands and knees.

I knew I was past help. I stifled the impulse to beg.

He drove for about an hour, then pulled off the pavement. I flopped around like a Raggedy Ann doll as the van lurched over the hardened ruts of some dirt road. I realized we were driving to a place where he could dump my body.

I wished I'd stopped to see Ben before going to the police station. Why didn't I think of that? Now I'd never see him again.

Finally we stopped. Williams unlocked and relocked my cuffs so I wasn't chained to the floor anymore. He went around and opened the back doors and pulled me out onto the ground. Then he stepped back.

I ended up on my side in half-frozen mud. Slowly I got up onto my knees, eyes averted. I wasn't ready to look at him, yet.

I was at the edge of a corn field. Last year's dried, broken stalks stretched out to my left. To my right was a dark copse of trees. Probably a little stream down there. I looked straight up and saw stars. It was a clear, cold night. Everything was washed in dim silver from the bright half-moon.

Finally I looked at him. He was leaning on the van with his arms crossed, looking down at his feet. He was completely still.

"Why," he finally said, "did you do that?" I could tell from his voice that he was just about as angry as it was possible to be. He actually growled.

I figured "that" encompassed everything I'd done that he'd told me not to do. I didn't know what to say. Couldn't he figure it out?

"I was scared. I thought I could get away."

He stared at me, silent, for several minutes.

Finally he said, "You are a lot of trouble." The words came out at long intervals, as though he were squeezing each one through his teeth with great effort.

"I'm sorry. I'm here now. Could you please just let Justine go?"

He jerked me to my feet.

"I'm going to show you something, and you're going to take a good long look at it."

He pulled me into the trees. When I fell, he just kept walking, dragging me over roots and dead bracken until I managed to scramble back to my feet.

After about five minutes, we reached an outcropping of large boulders. They were bunched at a low point in the land, like cattle pressed together at a watering hole. Williams threaded between them, pulling me along by my cuffed hands. The space in the midst of them was filled with the detritus of the forest—dead branches, leaves, twigs. There was a slight smell of decay, as though some small animal had crawled into the pile and died. We stood there in front of the wreckage.

At first, I wasn't sure what I was supposed to be looking at. Then the shadowy shapes began to resolve, taking on new meaning. The shards of wood became bones; the dead leaves became twists of dried, shredded skin. The smell of decay mushroomed. It was overpowering. I gagged.

Dead people. I had no idea how many. They were jumbled together, as if each new body had been dumped on the pile and had slowly broken down into pieces and fallen through the mass as it decayed.

"This," Williams said slowly, "is what I do. Every one of those, I put here."

He gave me a shove, and I fell into the pile. The remains weren't as dried out as they'd looked. The stench was everywhere; it was like someone had soaked a wool blanket in week-old blood and stuffed it in my mouth. Things squished under me as I thrashed around in the dark, trying to get my feet and cuffed hands to work together.

I finally managed to get myself clear of the bodies. I lay there on my side, gasping and retching. Williams nudged me with his foot. I looked up at him. He was just a vague silhouette against the starlit sky. I absolutely hated him.

"Do not fuck with me, Ryder. Not again."

He pulled me back to the van and ran my cuffs through the ring again. We drove. I lay there, shocked and exhausted. That terrible smell was in my hair and on my clothes.

I was too afraid to ask again about Justine. Justine could deal with her own problems.

It was some time before it occurred to me that he hadn't killed me.

*

When Williams dragged me out of the van a second time, it was at Callie McCallister's house. Unbelievable. I could not imagine two people who seemed less likely to hook up.

He frogmarched me up the walk. As we approached the front door, Callie opened it. At first she looked apprehensive. Then, when she recognized me, she looked frightened.

"No. No, no, no. We can't shelter her. The order's gone out."

She blocked the door with her body. I expected Williams to shove her aside, but instead he stopped a respectable distance away.

"Let us in, Callie. I'll explain."

He spoke with the kind of gentle, soothing tone a parent would use to calm a scared kid.

Amazing. I wouldn't have thought he had it in him, even for the purposes of manipulation.

"John, this isn't a good choice."

Williams said, "Callie. Trust me."

Callie stared at him for a long while, then nodded slowly. She stood aside.

Williams only took me in as far as the foyer. Callie closed

the door and edged around me, wringing her hands nervously.

Williams leaned over and growled "Don't move" in my ear. Then he took Callie's elbow and led her farther into the house for a private conversation.

Williams couldn't see me, so I risked looking around. The house was a rambler with an open floor plan, so I could see much of the living space: a large living room to my left, with a dining area just beyond. The kitchen was straight ahead of me. Beyond the kitchen, I could see a den with a fireplace. The bedrooms must be down the hall to the right.

The place was extremely clean and orderly, which didn't surprise me. It was also really nice, which did. I'd never thought about what Callie's house might look like inside, but if I had, I'd have predicted a wall of kitschy porcelain shepherdesses, some Jesus paintings, and a bunch of lace doilies. It wasn't like that at all. The furnishings were simple and modern, very tasteful. Lots of pale colors and wood tones. It was nicer than my place, that's for sure. Mom's decorating had been less Scandinavian Designs, more St. Vincent de Paul.

I stood there, not moving, until my captors came back. Williams told me to go with Callie. She looked nervous but gave me a tentative nod and headed down the hallway. Just as I went to follow her, Williams caught my arm.

"Do not hurt her."

I could tell from his tone of voice that this was a different category of forbiddenness than "don't move" had been a few minutes earlier. The fact that he squeezed my arm hard enough to leave bruises added to that impression. As soon as he loosened his grip, I jerked away, heart racing. His touch was unbearable.

Callie took me to the master bathroom. She told me I could shower, but that she had to stay in the room with me for now. She sat down on the toilet and discreetly looked away as I stripped.

I turned the water on as hot as I could stand it and scrubbed myself. Then I stood there, just letting it wash over me. Slowly, the muscles in my back and shoulders began to unknot.

As my body relaxed, all the weirdness, disruption, and terror of the past few days came welling up. Oddly, I didn't have a panic attack. Instead, I started crying and couldn't stop. I just stood there and sobbed, minute after minute.

Finally, Callie reached in and turned off the water, which had gone cold. She helped me out and dried me off, making cooing noises, as though I were a baby. She sat me down on the edge of the bed. By that point, I was so tired I could barely move. I was just done. I let her put some sweats on me. They were warm and soft. Then she pressed me down into bed and pulled the covers over me. I slept like the dead.

Chapter 5

IT WAS EARLY afternoon when I woke up. I felt better physically. A lot better.

Mentally, things weren't so good. I had to sit there and figure out what day it was: I'd fled Dorf Tuesday morning, returned Wednesday night, and it had been early Thursday morning by the time Williams had brought me to Callie's. So, now it was midday Thursday.

Shit. I was supposed to have been back at work today.

I went to the bathroom and found that Callie had left a new toothbrush on the sink for me. I brushed and thought about my situation.

First, a group of religious nutcases had kidnapped me and seemed to have some future plans for me that I probably wouldn't like. Second, my sister-in-law was missing. And then there were some ancillary issues. If I didn't show up for work, I was going to lose my job. I'd seen a huge pile of murdered people but didn't know where they were, exactly. Williams was pretending to be an FBI agent, and the police chief seemed to be in on it.

When I got to thinking about it, it was really a bit much. I felt the panic coming on, so I sat down on the bathroom floor and snapped my rubber band, focusing on my breathing. I had to calm down and figure out what to do.

It didn't work.

❦

Twenty minutes later, I lay on the floor, recovering from the attack. The cool tiles felt good against my sweaty cheek. I stayed down until the nausea receded and my heart rate slowed.

Slowly, my ability to think came back. I tried again to consider the situation.

It all went back to the three photographs and the interest they'd generated. If I could convince Williams and Callie that I didn't go around photographing "hell-spawn," maybe they'd cancel their plans for me and let Justine go. Once Justine and I were safe, I could worry about the other stuff.

So, how could I convince Williams and Callie that there was nothing demonic about the pictures I'd taken?

The one showing the naked guy in front of J.T.'s should be easy: all I had to do was find that guy. No one could claim there was anything weird about the photo, then.

But what about the monster foot? Unfortunately, I still hadn't come up with an explanation for it myself. It looked so real. If I couldn't explain it to myself, I'd never be able to convince others it was nothing special.

I retrieved my toothbrush and finished brushing. Then I lowered the toilet seat and sat down to think about it. I wished I had the photo to look at. Damn Williams for taking it. I called the picture up in my mind's eye, which wasn't too difficult, considering how much I'd looked at it. I remembered how you could see the ankle tendons flexing.

What if it was real?

I sat very still. Where had that thought come from? Of course it wasn't real.

I needed something to eat. I checked myself over. No piss or barf this time, thank god. Callie's sweats were too short in the arms and legs, and too tight all over. I wasn't a particularly big woman, but I wasn't tiny and delicate like her. Whatever. I was covered.

When I opened the bedroom door, I could hear a washing machine running somewhere. Maybe my clothes were in it. Frankly, I'd rather have thrown them away.

I stood there, finding it hard to leave the room. I'd felt relatively safe inside.

I reminded myself that was an illusion: I wasn't really any safer in one room than another. Squaring my shoulders, I headed down the hall.

Callie was in the kitchen. No Williams, thank god.

Callie looked up nervously. She blurted out, "You can't leave," then flushed and seemed to remember her manners.

"Would you like some tea?"

"That'd be great, thank you."

Callie made me a cup of tea and then a sandwich, which was nice. She sat down across from me. There followed an awkward silence of several minutes. It felt increasingly weird to eat while she alternately looked at me and stared down at her hands. Finally I couldn't bear it anymore.

"Did Williams go out?"

"Yes, he had something to take care of."

Torturing a puppy to death, maybe.

"Will he be back soon?"

"I'm afraid I don't know."

Well, so much for the questions I really cared about. I

wracked my brain for small talk.

"Where did you two meet?"

Callie seemed to be considering whether to answer me.

"I had been taken by Satan's minions," she said at last, "some years ago. They did wicked things to me, sinful things. John rescued me. He told me I could be a warrior against that kind of evil. He has friends who taught me what to do, what not to do. I've been fighting evil ever since."

Right, momentarily forgot about the crazy thing.

Well, maybe I could get a better handle on the way these people thought.

"So, how do you fight evil?"

Callie flushed and looked down at her hands.

"Well, I'm not much of a fighter—not directly. I'm more of a watcher, like a sentinel. When I see evil, I let them know. Sometimes they don't do anything. But sometimes they send John. He's one of the fighters. Sometimes they send others."

I took another bite. It was a good sandwich—chewy, seedy whole-wheat bread and everything.

"Who's 'them,' exactly? Some kind of secret society?"

"I don't know how much I should tell you about that," she said, uncertainly.

I hadn't really expected a clear answer.

"So why don't they always send a fighter when you tell them you've seen evil? Don't they believe you?"

I sure was hoping they didn't.

"No, they believe me. I don't know why they ignore the demons sometimes. I don't understand it, really." She paused, looking troubled. "That creature in the cemetery—it's been there for as long as I've lived here. I keep telling them it's there, but they always say it's okay so long as no one knows about it. I don't see how that could be. It's on holy ground, even."

I stared at her. Maybe my photograph had prompted a full-on psychotic break.

"You could fight it yourself," I suggested.

She looked at me like I'd grown a second head.

"It's eight feet tall and has teeth like a shark. And claws. And horns. It would kill me."

"Ah. Well, it's probably best to leave it alone, then."

Callie nodded, and a few moments passed in silence.

"John says you can't actually see it?" she asked, cocking her head at me.

It was an oddly birdlike gesture. But then, she was vaguely avian—slender and tiny, with a long neck and pale, sharp eyes.

"No, I've never seen it."

She nodded, looking pensive. "That's really unusual, I think."

"Oh?"

She nodded. "I've heard of people who can photograph demons, but not without seeing them first. It's like you make music you can't hear. Well, not exactly."

She drifted off a bit, thinking.

Whoever these people were, they hadn't done Callie any favors on the sanity front, filling her head with this stuff. I felt sort of angry on her behalf, which was surprising since I didn't even like her. Then again, I'd never talked to her at length. There was something childlike about her. I'd always assumed she was nasty, what with all the moral crusading, but maybe she wasn't. Nutty, but not nasty.

"Callie, did you hear that my sister-in-law is missing?"

"No," she said. After some hesitation she asked, "Do you think she's in trouble?"

"I really don't know." Damn, no help there.

"Well, I hope she's all right." She stood up. "Excuse me, I'll just switch the laundry."

She left the kitchen. After a few more bites of sandwich, I followed her. The laundry was in a small room at the end of the hallway. The dryer was running, and she was folding a load of lights.

"Can I help?"

"Oh, no, that's all right. I like folding laundry."

I leaned in the doorway, formulating a plan of attack. I knew I couldn't leave. There was no way I'd try it. Go ahead and call me a coward, but I wasn't going to cross Williams again. I was viscerally afraid of him in a way that made it impossible.

"Callie, I should probably call Ben. I haven't talked to him in more than two days. And maybe my workplace. Would you mind if I used your phone?"

She glanced up at me, unhappy. "I'm sorry, but John said you couldn't."

"He said I couldn't call Ben?"

"He said you couldn't use the phone at all."

"Oh."

I thought for a minute. Maybe there was a way around this.

"He's probably afraid I'll try to tell someone again, but now I know I can't."

She nodded, not looking at me.

"So I won't tell Ben anything, okay? I'll just let him know I'm all right."

"I'm sorry, Elizabeth. I'd let you if I could, but the phone won't work for you. You just can't make any calls."

"What do you mean the phone won't work for me?"

"There's a barrier around the house. It's something John can do, a gift from the Lord. You can't leave or make calls or wave at someone out the window or anything like that. I'm sorry."

I stared at her. I went to the kitchen and tried the phone. It was dead. I went to the front door, my skepticism momentarily overcoming my fear. I opened it and tried to step out.

There was something in front of me that I couldn't see. It was like running into a massive blob of invisible gelatin. I stepped back from it. The world swayed.

From behind me, Callie said, "You really didn't believe any of it, did you? He said so, but I wasn't sure."

"No," I said, my voice sounding weirdly calm and normal, "I really didn't."

Callie sat me down in the living room and tried to explain things to me, but honestly, it all sounded like a jumble of crazy. Hell as a vast world full of demons. People like her and Williams as protectors of our world from demons who came here to sow evil and reap souls.

I listened with a fraction of my attention, catching random tidbits. With the rest, I focused on my breathing.

We were still sitting there when Williams got home. He stood there for a second, taking in the tableau—me hunched over, pale and shaking. Callie holding my hand, speaking to me quietly.

"Had a come-to-Jesus moment?" he said nastily.

I stared back at him, too shell-shocked to respond.

"I don't think I'm getting through to her," Callie said. "Can you explain it to her?"

"Nope. Not my job."

He headed into the kitchen, then called out, "Come with me tonight, Callie? I still can't get it closed. Must be stuck on something."

She stiffened slightly beside me.

"Is it safe?"

"I just need you to take a look. No need to leave the barrier."

She nodded but didn't say anything. I wondered what sort of demon they were going to send back to Hell that night. The thought struck me as so ludicrous, so cliché, that I got the giggles. Lord help me, I couldn't stop. Even Williams growling "shut the fuck up" didn't do it. I laughed until I cried. Eventually I got up and wandered into the den and turned on Callie's TV. I channel-surfed until I found a dour episode of *Law & Order*. Even then, I kept having to stifle laughter. It kept bubbling up, as though it were washing something away.

At last, I curled up on the couch and went to sleep to the drone of the TV.

❧

Sometime in the wee hours, the front door crashed open. I got into the kitchen just as Williams was setting Callie down on the floor. At first he was in the way, and I couldn't see. When I did, I couldn't make sense of what I was seeing. Her face, neck, and upper chest were a dry, grayish white. I couldn't see her features. I could only tell it was her by the gray slacks she was wearing. I didn't understand. What had happened to her?

I came closer and smelled cooked flesh. She had no hair. She had no ears. In a rush, comprehension came—she was burned to char. What I was seeing was ash.

"Not in here," Williams said without looking up.

I rushed out but didn't make it to the bathroom before vomiting. I crouched at the end of the hallway, heaving, for several minutes. Then I gathered myself and struggled back to the kitchen. I was shaking so badly it was hard to walk.

Williams was speaking quietly into a cell phone. He had brought in some couch cushions and put Callie's feet up on them. I looked at her. The unburned parts I could see were a clammy white. Her fingertips were bluish.

When he hung up, I said, "Was that 911?"

He didn't say anything.

"She needs a hospital. Right now."

He turned to me. I cowered, expecting rage, but his face was strangely blank.

"You want to be useful? Hold her hand."

That was it. Even though I knew I was colluding in Callie's death, I didn't say another word.

I sat down on the floor beside her and took her hand. It was unnaturally cool to the touch, and sweaty. I listened to the harsh crackle of her breathing. Her airway must've been burned as well. Williams sat on the other side of her with his back against the cabinets, looking down.

There we waited. For hours.

Callie did regain consciousness briefly at one point. Her hand tightened on mine, and she stirred. I saw the opening that used to be her mouth moving and bent down to hear. I couldn't really understand her. She might've said, "Doesn't hurt."

*

Around dawn, I heard the rumble of a motorcycle outside.

Moments later, someone entered the house—a woman. She paused in the kitchen doorway.

"Is she alive?"

Williams didn't answer, so I nodded.

"Thank god. Move over."

I glanced at Williams again for guidance, but he was still looking down.

I got up and stepped back. The woman took my place. She was young—in her late teens, maybe twenty, tops. She was quite a bit shorter than me, five-foot-one or -two. Her curly hair was shaved close on the sides and bleached almost white. Her skin was the color of coffee with cream. I wasn't sure of her ethnicity. Latina, maybe. She had several facial piercings, and the edge of a tattoo showed above her collar. But for all the tough-chick fixings, she looked nervous.

She picked up Callie's hand and closed her eyes. As I watched, ash began to slough off Callie, first in a drift of fine, airborne dust, then in chunks. Her chest and face seemed to inflate gently. The ash was followed by bits of flesh—a mixture of black and raw, angry red. Then larger chunks. As the char fell away, I could see new skin underneath. It was bright red and blistered, but it was there. New ears began to emerge, pushing out the blackened nubs that had been there before, like an adult tooth pushing out a baby one. Eyelids and lips formed as well.

Callie was recognizable again—definitely still burned, but recognizable.

The blond woman moaned and slumped back against the cabinets.

Callie began to stir and whimpered in pain.

The blond woman tried to say something. She was shockingly pale. A sheen of sweat stood out on her face. On the second try, she managed to say, "Bag."

I noticed the small duffle in the kitchen doorway only when Williams stood up and fetched it. The woman must've dropped it there when she came in. Williams had to unzip it for her. It was full of medical supplies. Following her directions, he prepared a syringe and injected it into Callie's arm. After a few seconds, Callie's body relaxed, and her breathing slowed. She was unconscious.

She was also largely healed. I mean, she still had serious burns, but the difference was night and day.

If I'd needed further convincing that there was more to the world than I'd believed, I'd just gotten it.

The blond woman sat with her head between her knees and taking deep breaths for about fifteen minutes. Then she looked up at Williams.

"Can you move her to a room where I can sleep too?"

Williams nodded and picked Callie up carefully. He took her down the hallway.

When he got back, the woman said, "Let's take a look at those hands."

Williams knelt in front of her and held out his arms. I noticed then that the backs of his hands and forearms were burned pretty badly. The woman examined the wounds, probing gently at bits of burned cloth that had stuck to the skin.

I watched, expecting to feel sick. It didn't happen. I guess what I was seeing was small potatoes compared to Callie's burns.

The scar I'd noticed before on the back of Williams's left wrist caught my eye. As the woman turned his arm, I saw that it actually went all the way around. It looked like his hand had been cut off and reattached. Was that possible?

"These burns need healing, but it'll have to wait 'til tomorrow. I'm shot."

Williams grunted. When it came to languages, he sure had "Thug" down pat.

The woman directed him to a small aerosol can in her bag. She told him to spray his burns, which he did, then pointed to some pills he could take for the pain. He nodded, then thanked her in a serious tone for healing Callie. The blond woman looked a bit surprised. I was glad I wasn't the only one. Then he got up and left the room. A few seconds later, I heard the front door close.

I felt myself relax marginally. I had no idea who the blond woman was, but at least she wasn't him.

She looked up at me and said, "I'm Kara. Who're you?"

"Beth. I'm new."

"New, huh? Bummer. Well, we can talk about it tomorrow." She struggled to her feet. "Right now, I need to sleep. That's the biggest healing I've ever done."

She shambled off down the hallway. I heard a bedroom door close.

I stood there, looking down at the ash and charred flesh all over the kitchen floor.

The house was quiet. I felt alone. I'd been reborn into a world that looked like the one I knew, but wasn't. Terror surged through me, dank and suffocating.

A two-attack day. Not good.

When I could move again, I just crawled into bed and lay there shaking until sleep came.

Chapter 6

I SLEPT EVEN later than I had the day before—well into the afternoon. The house was quiet. I lay in bed for a while. Very irrationally, I was hoping what I'd seen in the last twenty-four hours would somehow just go away. My mind kept poking at this heap of impossible experiences, as though it might hop up and say in a funny accent, "Why, excuse me, I seem to have wandered into the wrong universe! I'll be on my way now."

Instead, the pile of impossible just sat there, refusing to leave or be integrated with the rest of my psyche.

I knew I couldn't function that way. But deciding to tackle the situation might've been the hardest thing I'd ever done. Every cell in my body resisted the idea.

I understood why. It was in my nature to withdraw. Maybe my panic disorder had made me that way. In the past, new places and experiences had made it flare, so I tried to stick to routines as much as possible. And when something new and scary did happen, my impulse was to get the hell away from it.

It could have been worse—some people with panic disorder end up prisoners in their own homes, too afraid of triggering an attack to go out. That hadn't happened to me, maybe because I had attacks at home, too. But I did try to avoid the new. I mean, photography was literally the only new thing I'd tried since I was eighteen.

But now "the new" was overrunning me, and I was going to have to confront it. If I didn't start trying to make a place for myself in this new world, it would shred me.

Maybe it wouldn't be so bad. After all, what I'd seen the blond woman, Kara, do—that was miraculous. What if I could do something like that?

I showered, then went hunting for my clothes in Callie's dryer. Someone's snoring was audible in the hallway, even though all the bedroom doors were closed. I hoped it was Kara, not Williams.

When I got to the kitchen, there was someone new there. A man. He was drinking coffee. He looked up at me, and his face shifted into what appeared to be a friendly smile.

"Hi. You must be Elizabeth. I'm Graham. I'm here to show you the ropes."

This was it. I had to confront the new. I seized my courage in both hands and made a bold first move.

"Um. Hi."

Good lord, I was going to have to do better than that.

"Um. Coffee?"

He grinned and motioned toward a can of grounds and some filters on the counter.

I turned my back on the scary stranger and made myself a cup of coffee. Then I brought it over to the table and sat down with him to drink it. It was really good. I didn't usually drink the caffeinated stuff.

"Well," he said, "you seem to be handling all this pretty well."

"Thanks."

He smiled again. Big smiler, this guy.

"Want some breakfast?"

"Okay."

He got up and made enough eggs and toast for two. I watched him. He was good-looking—tall and slender, with brown eyes, blond hair, and a TV anchorman's even, chiseled features. He was wearing khakis and a fitted pale green sweater made out of some fine material. He was at least a few years older than me and carried himself with confidence. I wondered if he was a lawyer or a doctor. He seemed professional, sophisticated.

He brought me a plate, and I thanked him. We ate in silence.

When we were both finished, he pushed back and sat there looking at me, smiling a little. I looked back at him.

Confront the new, I reminded myself.

"Can you explain things to me?" I said.

He nodded. "That's what I'm here for. I oversee the Upper Midwest. New talent is part of my responsibility."

"Oversee? So this is an organization of some sort?"

"You could say that. Basically, we look out for things that shouldn't be happening and try to fix them. We have a territory with different regions. Each region has an overseer."

"What are you called?"

"What, like the 'League of Justice,' or something?" he said, laughing. "We don't have a fancy name for the organization."

"Oh. Okay." I felt dumb.

He sat for a minute or so, drumming his fingers on the table softly.

"It's always a bit hard to know where to start with newbies," he finally said. "It's particularly hard with you, since you're so much older than most. You have the capacity to understand a great deal—you know, unlike a seven-year-old."

This happened to little kids? God, how horrible.

"But if we get into too much detail right off the bat," he continued, "it's going to be overwhelming, and we also won't get to working on your abilities. As I understand it, your development has been a bit unusual. Figuring that out should be our first priority."

"Okay," I said, "so give me what you think I need for now. I'll ask questions if I need to."

He nodded, looking a little impressed. I was sort of impressed with myself, actually.

"Well, the first thing to understand is that there's more than one world," he said, sounding like he'd rattled this stuff off before. "We call the world you see around you right now the First Emanation. That's all the vast majority of people ever see. But there's also a Second Emanation. You can think of it as another world that overlaps or coexists with this one."

"Like a parallel universe?"

"Sort of. They're not so separate as that phrase implies. Some things, like major geographic formations, exist in both worlds at the same time. Some other features are shared, too—usually things that are old for their kind, like big trees, ancient buildings, that sort of stuff. But people and animals only exist in one place or the other."

I nodded and tried to look like I was getting it.

"So, the F-Em has a large population of creatures—animals and people."

"FM?"

"As in 'First Emanation.' Big 'E,' little 'M,' as in 'Emanation.'"

"Oh. Right."

So much for getting it.

"The S-Em has a population as well. We call those beings

'Seconds,' for short. Sometimes you'll also hear people refer to 'Firsts.' That means the people and animals from here."

"Why are these places called 'emanations'?"

"That's probably more than we need to get into right now," he said. "It comes from what the Seconds believe about how they and their world came into being."

"Okay."

"Right. So some Seconds look just like you or me, and some look different. The essential distinction between Seconds and the beings of this world is that they can see and manipulate something we call essence. Working essence enables them to do things that aren't possible for most human beings. They can reshape reality itself in different ways. Usually the effects are small, but they can be substantial."

"Are you talking about magic?"

"Not really. It might seem magical to humans, but to Seconds it's not mysterious or illogical."

He stopped to think.

"You know how our bodies can generate heat and keep themselves warmer than their surroundings? Well, their bodies can touch this other level of reality. To them, it's all very normal and reasonable, just as our bodies' ability to stay the same temperature seems ordinary to us."

"So essence is energy, like heat?"

"No, it's more fundamental than that. It's what lies under all matter and energy—the core of existence itself."

He must've seen my mystified expression.

"Human science can get you part of the way there. See all the things around you? They're all different, right? This is cloth," he said, pointing at a dish towel, "and the table is wood. This plate is ceramic. If you look at them, touch them, they seem different. But those differences are misleading. Actually these things are all made out of the tiny particles that make up atoms, right? Science tells us everything in this room—including us—is just particles and electromagnetic fields and empty space."

I nodded, but that stuff wasn't a big part of high school physics. Building a bridge out of spaghetti I remembered. The more theoretical stuff was foggier.

"Okay, well if you follow me that far, just imagine essence as what makes up the particles and the empty space."

Right. Okay. I guess.

"Are you sure it's not just magic?"

"Yep, I'm sure. Look, what if you went back in time and showed some stone-age people a TV with a remote control? It might seem to them that you were controlling the TV with magic, but to us it's just a piece of technology."

It occurred to me that I didn't really know how a remote control worked. I felt myself blush.

Graham smiled. "Even if you can't explain the details of how a remote works, you know there's a scientist somewhere who could. You don't think it's magic."

Okay, so people on this other world had some kind of amazingly advanced biotechnology, so advanced it seemed like magic. I could accept that. It was like a sci-fi movie.

But what Graham was saying didn't seem to jibe with what Callie had told me.

"Callie described the other world in religious terms."

"Ah." Graham paused for a few seconds. "Callie has her own way of understanding these things. It's what works for her, given her beliefs and experiences, but based on what I know, it's not an accurate picture. What I'm telling you is what everyone else understands to be true."

For some reason, that was a big relief, maybe because all

that judgment and hellfire stuff didn't seem to be part of the equation.

"Given your potential," Graham continued, "it would be better if you had a more precise and nuanced understanding of how the S-Em works."

I nodded, but the thing about "potential" didn't sound good. My feeling of relief dissipated. I didn't want these people to have any more interest in me than was absolutely necessary.

"Okay, so like I was saying, beings from this world are called 'Firsts.' The ones from the other world are called 'Seconds.' Firsts can't travel to the S-Em, but some Seconds can travel here. That's where people like us come in—we police the Seconds who come to the human world. If they break the rules, we take care of it."

So, these people were basically a secret branch of law enforcement? Maybe Williams really was in the FBI—some secret X-Filesy part of it.

Then I thought about the place Williams had taken me.

"By 'take care of it,' do you mean you kill them?"

Graham looked a little uncomfortable.

"Most Seconds don't intend any harm to humans. If they come here, they don't cause any problems. But a few of them are dangerous. Sometimes, the only solution is termination."

What he was saying was rubbing me the wrong way. Or maybe it was the pile of decayed corpses I'd rolled around in a couple nights ago that had rubbed me the wrong way.

"Do they get a trial?"

"I'm sure there's a process in place."

Huh. That was pretty vague.

As though feeling the tension, Callie's glass tea kettle cracked with a loud pop. We both jumped. I let out a nervous laugh, and Graham smiled. Steam billowed up from the hot burner as the water drained onto the range.

"I'll get it," he said, standing up and grabbing a dishtowel.

"Weird. These things are supposed to be just about indestructible," he said, mopping up hot water. "Anyway, we're able to deal with troublesome Seconds because we're actually like them: some human beings are also born with the ability to sense and manipulate essence. Those of us with the right abilities can meet Seconds on a more level playing field, especially if we team up. And since a number of powerful Seconds support our activities, they can back us up if we get in trouble."

Wait a minute, said an alarmed little voice in my head. *Am I included in that "we"?*

"What did you mean when you mentioned 'my potential'? Am I going to have to—"

Just then, Graham's cell phone rang. He pulled it out and looked at it.

"I'm sorry, Elizabeth. Please excuse me."

He headed into the living room and began a conversation I couldn't quite hear. It lasted a while and seemed to prompt several other calls. Finally he wrapped it up and came back to the kitchen's entrance, pocketing his phone.

"Sorry about that. Hey, why don't we do a few tests to see exactly how your development is coming along?"

"Um, you don't think I can 'reshape reality itself,' do you? 'Cause if so, I have some bad news."

"Hold on," he said, laughing. "Working essence can take a lot of different forms. Most of it isn't so spectacular as that phrase makes it sound. Let's just see what you might be able to do."

I could've told him right then I didn't have any special

abilities, other than possibly taking weird pictures. But I followed him to the living room. We settled on one of Callie's comfortable white couches. Graham opened his mouth to say something, then froze, looking over my shoulder.

I turned to look. Kara was standing at the end of the hallway, looking as surprised to see Graham as he was to see her. He recovered first.

"Kara. It's good to see you. What brings you here?"

Kara looked down at her hands, which were gripped together.

"Williams called me early this morning. Callie got hurt. I came to heal her."

"Is she okay?" Graham said, sounding concerned.

"Yeah. I did some more work on her just now. She'll be up and around soon."

"Good, good. So, you'll be heading back to the Twin Cities today?"

"I guess."

"Best not to leave your area unguarded for too long."

She nodded quickly and vanished into the kitchen.

Hm. Kara was afraid of Graham. I studied him a little more carefully as he began to explain the testing process to me. He didn't seem scary. Maybe I was missing something.

❧

Two hours later, I was well and truly shaken.

Graham had asked me to report whatever I saw. Then he'd changed from one person into another as I watched—a heavyset middle-aged farmer, a schoolmarmish old lady, a slinky beauty, a broken-down old man. Each time, I had to describe the person I saw in detail.

Seeing Graham change like that reminded me of Williams, with his Blandy-McBlandsville disguise. I didn't want to be reminded of Williams.

Afterwards, Graham picked up a decorative bowl from Callie's coffee table, and I watched as it shifted from bowl to football helmet to soccer ball, and finally to a living armadillo, which turned its head and looked right at me. I had to describe each one of those things, too.

Apparently finished with the special effects, Graham sat back with a sigh.

"Well, this has got to be pretty unusual. I haven't seen anything quite like it."

"Is something wrong with me?"

My tone seemed to get his attention. He leaned forward and caught one of my hands, giving it a reassuring squeeze.

"Elizabeth, I know this must all be very unsettling. It's always like that at the beginning. I promise, it'll start making sense. You'll adjust, and it'll get better."

"Okay," I said, trying not to sound so quavery.

I reminded myself that I was supposed to be confronting this stuff, not just reacting passively and letting my fear of it rule me.

"I'll explain what's going on, as best I can. Remember how I mentioned earlier that all Seconds and some humans can sense and manipulate essence?"

I nodded.

"There are two ways to manipulate essence. One is called a 'working.' A working changes essence from one state into another. And remember, essence is the substance of everything. That's why I said we're capable of reshaping reality itself—if you change the building blocks, you change the building."

"Right, okay."

"The other kind of manipulation is called a 'half-working' or 'halfing.' When you make a half-working, you don't change essence fully from one state to another. Instead, you let it oscillate really fast between its original state and what you'd like it to be. So long as the essence has the shape you want more than half the time, that's the shape people are going to see."

"Why would you want to do that?"

"It saves a lot of energy. When you make a disguise, like I was doing just now, you might have to keep it up for a long time. Halving your energy use can make all the difference."

"And that's what you were doing just now?"

"Yeah."

It was hard to believe. I hadn't seen any sort of flickering or blurriness. One moment he'd been himself, and the next he'd been someone else.

"So, moving on to how you're developing," Graham said, "when people like us come into our abilities, it happens in four stages, which we call 'castes.' There's actually a little ditty to help kids remember the order: 'sense a working, get a gift, handle essence, learn to work.' It goes to some nursery-rhyme or other."

He thought for a moment, but apparently couldn't dredge up the tune.

"Anyway, 'sense a working' means becoming able to perceive workings and half-workings. Once you can see a halfing, it won't fool you anymore. You'll still see the worked shape, but you'll also see the original. Full workings are different. They change reality completely, so there's no 'original' state of things left to see. Sensing them just means being aware what you're perceiving is the result of a working.

Think of the way a jeweler can tell a natural pearl from a cultured one, whereas to most people, a pearl is a pearl—it's like that."

"Okay," I said, trying to commit workings and half-workings to memory.

"Here's the thing: typically, when people hit the first caste, they start seeing halfings and workings all at once. It's an all-or-nothing thing, like throwing a switch. If the essence has been disturbed, they're aware of it. It isn't happening that way for you. You're getting little glimpses, but it's mostly still hidden."

"I don't think I'm seeing either of those things. Workings or half-workings," I said.

"But you are—partially. Most of the halfings I just showed you, you didn't see at all. You perceived the illusion as real. But with a couple, you described something that was part of the original, not the halfing. For instance, the young woman I created had black hair, but you said she was a blonde. That means you saw my real hair color instead of the illusion. I bet you've gotten glimpses of reality through other halfings, too, and just not realized it."

"But I've never seen anything unusual, except in that picture I took."

"Williams led me to believe there was more than one photograph."

"Well, there were three he seemed interested in, but two of them just showed a regular person. I thought so, at least."

"Huh. Can I see them?"

"You'll have to ask Williams. He took them."

Graham frowned. I guess Williams had neglected to tell him about that bit of thievery.

Suddenly I remembered Williams's FBI file. Maybe when

the chief had looked at those pages, they hadn't looked like they described some other person. Maybe I'd been seeing through a half-working Williams made.

"Okay, never mind." Graham said. "We can look at them later. For now, take a look at this."

He handed me a boxy and somewhat beat-up camera. It was a Polaroid.

"Is this an instant camera?"

"Yep," he said. "We're going to visit your spooky cemetery and take a picture or two."

A spasm of fear clutched at me. I reached down and gave my rubber band a couple hard snaps. *Confront the new*, I reminded myself. Exploring what was going on with my pictures was a good step forward.

"So you think the weird pictures are part of this seeing-bits-and-pieces thing?"

"Yeah, I do, and I want to see it in action. Let's wait until dark, though. It'll be easier to disguise our presence."

While we waited for the sun to set, I checked out the Polaroid. It was a straightforward point-and-shoot—you couldn't even disable the flash. So the camera shouldn't be a problem. We'd see how much trouble my subject matter posed.

After I'd examined the camera, I thought I might ask Graham some more questions. Unfortunately, he was on the phone.

I wandered down the hallway, curious about how Callie was doing. I found her and Kara in one of the bedrooms. Kara motioned me in. Callie was still deeply asleep. Her skin looked much better—still red and inflamed, but no longer blistered. I wondered if Williams had been back to the house for healing as well, maybe while I was sleeping away the morning. The thought made me shudder. I didn't want him nearby when I was asleep.

I felt awkward standing there gawking.

"Will I wake her up if I talk?" I whispered.

"No, she's drugged," Kara answered in a more normal tone.

"Is she going to have scars?"

"No. The burn's superficial, now. Even if I left it this way, it wouldn't scar. But I won't leave it this way—it's too painful. I'll do a little more tonight."

I nodded. "What you can do, it's really amazing. If I hadn't seen how bad it was, I would never believe it."

Kara shrugged and looked uncomfortable.

"So," she said, "Graham's here training you?"

"Yeah, I guess."

She didn't follow up, so eventually I took my leave and headed to the room I'd been using, which I thought was Callie's. I wondered if she'd given it to me because the en suite bathroom meant I didn't have to go out into the hallway if I didn't want to. If so, that was really thoughtful. Maybe she understood about being terrified, even if she wasn't scared of Williams herself.

By 9:00, Graham and I were sitting in his sedan behind St. Mary's. It was quite dark—the sun had set more than an hour earlier.

He said, "Stay here a sec," and got out of the car. He walked into the cemetery. I could vaguely see him moving through the gravestones for a few seconds, and then the dark claimed him.

Before long, he came back to the car and gestured me out. I followed him through the dark cemetery. He led me toward a big maple in the back.

"You see that tree?"

"Yeah, sure."

"Do you see anything near it other than grave markers? Look carefully."

I let my eyes rove around the trunk and the surrounding area. Several stones were close enough to be under the tree's canopy, but I couldn't see anything else. There was only the tree and a bunch of gravestones between us and Gil Jensen's southernmost field, which abutted the church property.

"No, there's nothing else there. Not that I can see, anyway."

"Okay. Take a picture of the tree," he said.

"This little flash isn't nearly enough to light it."

"Just get the trunk."

Feeling a bit silly, I walked to within about ten feet of the trunk, close enough for the flash to do some good, and snapped a picture of it. Then I returned to Graham as the camera was spitting out the developing print.

"Here you go. One tree trunk," I said, holding it out to him.

Instead of taking it, he handed me a little flashlight.

"Look at it. What do you see?" he asked.

I looked down at the print. It had finished developing. It did show a tree trunk. It also showed a standing figure.

"There was no one there!"

"Oh, but there was," Graham said, grinning. "That's Bob."

In the picture, a large creature was standing in front of the tree. He was furry, had long arms, and was very obviously male. He was smiling toothily and waving.

Goosebumps ran up my arms. My heart rate kicked into high gear, and my lungs seemed to close. An attack was coming. I sat down on the ground and snapped my rubber band. Surprisingly, Graham settled down beside me and put his arm around my shoulders, making soothing noises. That startled me, which actually helped. The oncoming panic paused and hovered, then receded. Thank god.

Once I relaxed, Graham scooted away from me a bit, giving me space. I looked up at him and found him watching me with a little smile. A number of seconds ticked by. I really didn't know what to say.

"So," I started, and then cleared my throat. "So, the abominable snowman lives behind St. Mary's?"

Graham laughed. "Pretty close, actually. Bob's a good guy. Never causes any trouble. But some of his people who aren't so law abiding do crop up in the Himalayas."

Yet another thing for which I really had no response. I looked at the photo again. Bob was heavily furred on his torso, but the fur thinned out on his limbs, giving way to leathery skin. That skin was pale green and marked with gray rings. His fur was white with gray rings. Doyle Shumaker had looked at my photo and joked about a "bagel monster." Pretty accurate, actually.

I looked into the darkness beyond the flashlight's glow. Bob the non-abominable snowman might be standing right next to me. He hadn't just disguised himself as something else; he'd made himself invisible. So what else was out there that I couldn't see?

"Elizabeth, it's okay." Graham was looking at me with sympathy. "It's a big adjustment, I know, but it'll be okay."

"Wait," I gasped, and put my head between my knees. I cupped my hands over my mouth and breathed into them, trying to head off hyperventilating. Several long minutes passed before the nausea and dizziness passed, and I could speak.

"Why can't I see it? Why can I take a picture of it but not see it?"

"I don't know. I've never heard of someone photographing Seconds but not being able to see them. I'm guessing it's another way you're glimpsing through half-workings, like I was talking about before. But why your development is working this way, I'm frankly not sure."

He rubbed his face, thinking.

"You know, it might have to do with how late your abilities are manifesting. Most of us reach the first caste as little kids. About twenty percent get there as teens. Your abilities are appearing so late that you already have a set view of the world—what's possible and what isn't. Maybe your mind is resisting the 'impossible' things your eyes are taking in."

"Okay," I said, taking a deep breath, "I want to start seeing what's in front of me. How do I do it?"

"Well," Graham said, "let's go have a chat with Bob."

I followed Graham back under the maple. It was nerve-wracking to think that a creature like the snowman was out there, and I was blind to it. I kept expecting something to take a bite out of me.

Graham positioned me about ten feet from the tree's trunk and suggested I sit. Then he sat down right next to the tree and proceeded to have half a conversation with nothing. It was bizarre to watch.

"How's it going, Bob?"

"Really? Well, I'm sorry to hear that. When did you last hear from her?"

"Ah. No, that doesn't sound promising."

"I don't think that would be the best approach, no."

This went on for some time. Apparently Bob was having troubles in the love department. It added new meaning to the word "incongruous." It seemed so absurd, it was hard not to get the giggles. I bit the inside of my lip and tried to sit still.

"Maybe she'd appreciate a small present," Graham was saying.

"No, that'd be too big. It'll make you seem desperate."

"It makes you look needy instead of confident," I said. "That's sort of a turn-off."

Graham stopped and looked at me. The weird thing was, I could sort of feel someone else looking at me, too. Someone big and sad.

Graham said, "Can you see him? Or hear him?"

I shook my head.

"Then why did you answer his question?"

"I don't know. I don't think I actually heard anything."

"You must've on some level. Before you spoke, Bob had just said, 'What's wrong with seeming desperate if you are?'"

It was such a plaintive, naked question that hearing it took some of the absurdity out of the situation. Poor Bob. I could identify.

But I still couldn't see him.

"You getting anything?" Graham asked.

"I have this vague feeling that someone else is here, but that's it. I can't see or hear him."

"Huh. Any ideas, Bob?"

Graham listened.

"He says you won't see him unless you really want to."

"I do want to!"

"Some part of you doesn't, he says."

Great. I was being psychoanalyzed by a walking piece of deep shag.

"Well, it's not a part that's listening to the rest of me. I don't know how to want to see him more than I already do."

Graham looked pensive. "Hey, let me go make a call, okay? Someone who's been around longer than I have might have more ideas."

"Wait! You're not leaving me here, are you?"

"I'll just be a few feet away. Don't worry—Bob wouldn't hurt a fly. A stray cat, maybe, but not a fly."

Graham grinned at me, then got up and walked toward the car, sliding his cell phone out of his pocket. He faded into the night. I started to feel very afraid. I couldn't see Bob, but Bob could see me, and he was huge. I reminded myself that Bob seemed more like a schlemiel than a monster. *Sure, a schlemiel with big teeth,* some other part of me answered. I shivered. I swear I felt him looming over me, reaching for me with ragged claws, breathing dead-cat breath on me.

I started to feel another attack coming on and scrambled up.

"Graham? Graham!"

Graham didn't come.

I felt sick and dizzy. I tried to run, but my legs wouldn't hold me up, and I flopped back down to the ground.

Just as my vision started to tunnel, I glimpsed a face, more like a remembered image than the face itself. Then an impression of color—a silvery white. Then a sense that someone was speaking just a bit too softly for me to hear.

Clutching my chest, I stared at the place Bob had seemed to be when Graham was talking to him. It was like looking at that duck-rabbit illusion. I always saw the rabbit and had to force myself to see the duck.

Finally, I saw the duck.

It's not that he shimmered into view. He was just suddenly there. All eight furry feet of him. I sat there staring at him until I could get enough air in my lungs to speak.

"Wow. Um. Hi, Bob."

I could also see his not-thereness, which was bizarre. As I thought about him being invisible, he started being more not-there than there. I quickly focused on his thereness, and he came surging back.

He was smiling strangely. I realized he was probably trying to keep his teeth covered.

"Hello, Elizabeth Ryder. You have nothing to fear from me," he said.

Bob's face was definitely humanoid—a somewhat flattened nose, red lips, and large, dark eyes. But the whole thing was covered with short, white fur. He didn't have eyebrows, exactly, but there were large tufts of curly fur above his eyes. Starting on the top and the sides of his head, the hair got longer, blending with the fur on his body to form a thick, shaggy coat. His mouth looked a bit too large for his face. It probably had to be to fit all those teeth inside. Short, sharp horns stuck straight out from the sides of his head. I could imagine him disemboweling a horse with them.

Graham emerged from the dark, grinning broadly.

"Excellent! Great idea, Bob!"

I turned on him.

"You guys did that on purpose?"

"Yup," Graham said. "Bob wondered if needing to see a danger might overcome whatever part of your mind was blocking your sight."

Graham looked pretty pleased with himself.

"Great. That's great. Thanks a lot. You can take me home, now."

I stalked back toward the car. Graham trailed after me.

"Hey, don't be that way. You really did want to see, right?"

I didn't say anything.

"Elizabeth," he said, catching my arm.

"Get off me!"

I think my anger surprised both of us. We just stood there, me seething at him, him looking at me with a mystified expression.

"I don't understand why that upset you so much," he finally said.

I suppressed the urge to just let fly with something nasty and instead let the silence stretch until I calmed down a little.

"Look, I've been getting really scared of nothing all my life, but the last few days have been way worse. Now it's not nothing that's scaring me. It's you people. And you're doing it on purpose. I'm sick of it. I didn't have you pegged as someone who was going to do that to me."

His expression softened, then tightened again in anger.

"Williams."

I looked away so he wouldn't see the fear wash across my face.

"It's unfortunate that he found you. Most unfortunate. He's not cut out for dealing with emerging talents."

"Glad to hear you think so," I said caustically.

Graham looked down. Then he said quietly, "He's very good at what he's assigned to do. That's because he's a sadist."

I shuddered. "Yeah."

"Look," Graham said, "I'm sorry. I shouldn't have played that trick on you. I didn't know you'd been treated so badly."

He looked very sincere.

"Thanks." I forced a laugh I didn't quite feel. "I guess it worked, right?"

In truth, I wanted to be able to forgive him. I very much wanted to like at least one of these people I'd been thrown in with.

"Yeah, but working isn't everything," he said with a little lopsided grin.

After a few seconds of more companionable silence, he said, "Hey, mind if we go back and chat with Bob a little more? I don't want to leave on a bad note."

"Yeah, sure, I guess."

The snowman still made me nervous.

We headed back to the tree. Bob was looking dejected, but he perked back up when he saw us. We spent fifteen minutes making somewhat awkward small talk. He did seem like a nice enough … person? I wasn't sure how to think of him. Definitely not an animal, though it was beyond weird to converse with something so large and furry. He did have beautiful eyes—big and dark and expressive.

He asked me to come by and talk with him again soon.

"I look forward to getting to know you, Miss Ryder," he said. "I have lived here a long while, watching but never mingling. Sometimes I grow forlorn."

"Why don't you go home?" I asked.

Graham gave my arm a little squeeze, as though I shouldn't have asked that.

Bob didn't seem offended, though. He just sighed and said, "There are reasons I cannot."

Poor guy. He was lonely. The idea of visiting him alone sort of gave me the willies, but I said I would and that I was looking forward to speaking with him again.

We said our goodbyes, and he trundled off into the darkness. Graham and I headed back to the car. He told me I'd handled the conversation well.

"You notice how he didn't call you by your first name? Seconds tend to be pretty formal, compared to contemporary American manners. It isn't wise to be impolite when speaking to them, even if it's a friendly one like Bob."

Yeah, thanks for telling me that beforehand, I thought to myself.

"If they're so formal, why is it okay to call him 'Bob'?"

"We couldn't possibly pronounce his real name—his species is capable of making a number of sounds we can't. He probably chose an F-Em name that was short and simple out of courtesy to us."

We got in the car and headed back toward Callie's.

"Okay," he said, "I think we can feel pretty darn good about the day's work. We figured out where your development was stalled, and we got it moving again. Since you've probably been blocked for a while, the second stage might come quickly. We'll have to do some testing to see if that's the case."

"Can I ask you something first?" I said.

Suddenly I felt nervous. Graham seemed to be an okay guy, but I didn't really know that. Still, I got the sense he wasn't a Williams fan. That might work in my favor.

"Sure, what is it?"

"Do you think Williams could've kidnapped my sister-in-law?"

I could tell I'd taken him completely by surprise. He actually pulled over and turned to face me.

"Why would he have done that?"

"When he first came to talk to me, he told me not to leave town and not to tell anyone about him. But I was so scared that I went to the police. Then I took off. I was gone about a day. When I came back, my brother's wife had gone missing. She disappeared just after the police let Williams go. I thought he might've taken her to get me to come back here. That's why I came back, actually—I called my brother from the road and he told me she was gone and that the police suspected me. They were interrogating me about it when Williams came and got me—they think he's with the FBI."

Graham stared at me, apparently at a loss for words.

Finally he said, "Well, I've never heard of him using quite that kind of tactic. He's usually more direct. What you're describing sounds like it would take some planning, and he's not the brightest bulb. Then again, I don't think there's much he's not capable of."

He paused for a minute, thinking.

"Why don't you let me look into it quietly for a few days. I have some contacts in the organization that don't care much for Williams. Let me get in touch and see what I can find out."

"Thank you," I said, and really meant it. "I'd like to be able to talk to him soon—my brother, I mean."

"Of course you can talk to him," Graham said. "Go see him, if you like. We'll just have to discuss some basic ground rules beforehand."

"What ground rules?"

"Why don't we talk about it tomorrow? It's certainly too late to call or visit anyone tonight, right?"

He pulled the car back out. It was almost 10:00.

"Okay," I said. "Tomorrow."

Chapter 7

WE WENT TO check on Callie when we got back to the house. She was resting comfortably in the guest bedroom. Kara didn't seem to be home, but she'd clearly done more healing. Callie now looked fine. I spent a while standing there marveling at her skin as she slept. It was perfectly restored. In fact, she looked a little younger, as though Kara had taken away some of the years' wear and tear along with the burn.

The memory of what she'd looked like when Williams carried her in rose up powerfully in my mind. The thought twisted my feelings from wonder to anger.

"What was it that burned Callie?" I asked, when I went to sit down in the living room with Graham.

He glanced up at me but didn't answer.

"Graham?"

He sighed. "Williams originally came up here to deal with an S-Em incursion Callie reported—a large fire nearby."

"You mean the old mill up at Bilford Crossing?"

I remembered that you could still see the column of smoke on Sunday, more than a day after it had caught fire.

"Yeah, that's the place."

"So Callie got burned in that fire?"

"I imagine so."

"I don't get it. What does the fire have to do with the other world?"

Graham looked uncomfortable. "There's no reason for you to worry about that kind of stuff, yet. Let's just focus on your development, okay?"

It was nice that he was trying to protect me, but it wasn't going to fly. I needed a better picture of what I was facing. He must've seen it on my face.

"Okay, okay. You remember how I said that some Seconds can travel from their world to this one?"

I nodded.

"There are several ways that can happen. One way is the opening of a strait. A strait is a place where it's easier to pass between the Ems. You might think of the worlds as having skins that are thicker in some places and thinner in others. I've also heard it described as rippling, so that in some places the Ems bulge out and can touch, but in others there's a lot of distance between them."

That confused me. "Well, which one is it?"

"Neither, really. Those are just metaphors. No one really knows how the worlds coexist. There are different theories."

I nodded, feeling a bit dense.

"The mill is built on a strait, which seems to be stuck open. The human fire fighters can't put out the fire because it's actually coming through the strait from the S-Em. They can't get at what's really burning."

"That sounds bad."

"It's actually not too big a deal. It takes a major working to open a strait. You're supposed to design the working to close the strait after you go through it, but sometimes they get stuck. It's not good to have them sitting open, so closing them manually is something we have to do on occasion."

"So, Williams came up here to get it closed, and just happened to find out about me because he saw my pictures?"

"Yes, as I understand it."

So I'd been an added headache from the get-go. And then I'd kept him tied up with the police for hours. No wonder he'd been so monumentally pissed off. Not that I felt bad about that. Well, not so far as he was concerned. I guess I'd feel pretty bad about it if the result was something dangerous coming into our world through the opening.

Then again, he can't have been working on it too hard, not if he'd been having a leisurely brunch with Callie at Pete's Eats on Monday.

"If closing one of these things is no biggie, why'd he take Callie? You should've seen her when he asked to go. She was scared. She told me she's not a fighter, more of a watcher."

"Absolutely right. He should never have taken her," Graham said angrily. "It's ridiculous. Apparently, he very nearly got her killed."

We lapsed into silence. I realized I still didn't have a clear sense of what threat the open strait posed.

"So," I said, "the worry is that something dangerous might come through the opening and start, I don't know, eating my neighbors, or something?"

Just as Graham started to answer, the front door opened and Williams walked in. A shudder rippled over me.

He stopped short when he saw us on the couch. There was no mistaking his anger.

"You're finally showing up? I called you a week ago."

"I expected you to handle the situation on your own," Graham said evenly. "I'm here to work with Elizabeth, not do your job for you."

He showed no sign of being afraid of Williams.

The big man looked like he wanted to put his hands around Graham's neck and squeeze. A tense couple seconds passed before Williams turned and stalked down the hallway.

Graham watched him go, then turned back to me with an expression of patience, as though he often had to deal with difficult underlings.

"Why don't you get some sleep, Elizabeth. It's getting late, and this must've been a tiring day for you."

I nodded and trundled off to bed, trying to feel smug about having seen Williams get the smack-down. Unfortunately, I was still deeply afraid of him, so my satisfaction was half-hearted.

*

I showered and got in bed. It was after midnight, but since I'd slept until well past noon, I wasn't all that tired. I lay there, unable to go to sleep.

When Callie woke and went out to the living room to talk to Graham, I heard their voices. I couldn't quite make out what either was saying. I crept to the bedroom door and cracked it open.

"… has to go," Callie was saying. "I'm certain."

"She's not ready for that, Callie," Graham answered, "not any more than you were. I don't want to risk her without more information."

Was he talking about me? I had to be the most unready person here.

"You say she can see the truth, now. If so, it won't be dangerous. Not if she pays attention," Callie said. "If she doesn't go, things are not going to work out."

Graham made a frustrated noise. "Why does she have to go? How are things not going to work out? Can't you be more specific?"

"I assume she'll be able to see better than I could, but I'm not certain. You know the Lord doesn't show me everything. He gives what he gives, and it's up to us to use it for good, with faith that it will be enough."

There was a pause, then Graham said, "All right, I'll think about it."

"It has to happen, Graham," Callie said more insistently. "She must go. I've seen it."

Graham made an angry sound, but didn't say anything further.

I eased the door closed. Callie seemed to have some precognition. At least, she thought so, and Graham hadn't dismissed it.

I quietly got back in bed and pulled the covers up to my chin.

I had a bad feeling the place she wanted me to go was the old mill. That thought made sleep a very long time coming. I mean, confronting the new was all well and good; doing something incredibly stupid wasn't.

🍂

I slept briefly and badly. When I woke, it was about 9:00 in the morning. The house was quiet, and I wondered if everyone else was asleep. Callie was up, though. I found her in the kitchen, cooking something. I stood awkwardly in the doorway, not sure how to interact with someone who'd basically risen from the dead.

"Hi, Callie. How are you?"

"I'm fine," she said, turning and smiling at me. Then her smile faded, and she studied me for a while. Finally she spoke again.

"I was wrong about you, Elizabeth. You do the Lord's work, even though you don't recognize it."

I flushed. It was phrased in Callie-speak, but it was a genuine compliment.

"Thanks, Callie. I don't know that I entirely deserve that, but I appreciate it. And please, call me 'Beth.'"

"Beth," she said, as though trying out the name.

We smiled at each other.

"Callie, I heard you talking to Graham last night about me needing to go somewhere. Can you tell me about that?"

She looked a little worried, so I hurried on.

"It's great that Graham wants to protect me, but I think decisions about where I go and what I do are mine to make. Right? So what is it that you think I need to do, exactly?"

It wasn't really that I wanted to make a decision. I already knew I didn't want to go anywhere near that fire. But I did want to get a sense of what these people were planning for me.

Callie still didn't answer. Instead, her eyes shifted over my right shoulder.

From behind me, Graham said, "Let's you and I discuss this privately, Elizabeth."

Damn it, how had he come down the hall so quietly? I turned and looked at him. He was freshly showered and looked rested. He turned and headed back to his room.

I glanced at Callie. She'd been watching me, but her eyes skittered away. She turned back to the stove.

"Come on, let's talk about it," Graham said over his shoulder.

I followed him back to the other guest bedroom. I wondered in passing where Williams had slept the night before.

Graham sat down on the edge of his neatly made bed and gestured me toward the armchair in the corner of the room. As I turned around to sit, I noticed his eyes were aimed a bit low. Was he checking out my ass? It really sort of looked like he was. I was so surprised that it took me a few seconds to regroup and get my mouth moving.

"I heard some of what you and Callie were talking about last night. I'd like to get the full story."

He nodded. "That's fair enough, Elizabeth." He paused. "I take it you may have guessed at Callie's gift."

"She can see the future?"

"After a fashion. She doesn't see the future in a specific way. It's more like a sensation, a feeling about what we should or shouldn't do. It's not an exact prescription, and there are generally no details."

"Thinking I have to go to the mill, if that's what she was saying—that's pretty specific."

"Yes and no. Where exactly are you supposed to go when you get there? And what are you supposed to do there? Exactly how bad will the results be if you don't go, and how much better will they be if you do? She couldn't or wouldn't tell me any of that."

I nodded. That did leave a lot up in the air.

"Worst of all," he continued, "she doesn't know what the cost will be to you. I wouldn't like it if something happened to you." He paused. "I mean, you're my responsibility. It's my job to protect you until you're really ready for what we do."

"Does she have any sense of *why* I need to go to the mill? Does it have to do with some ability I might have?"

"She doesn't know, which is part of the reason I think it's a bad idea. I think we should wait and see if she can offer any more information before we take you there."

I nodded. I was still worried, though, because it sounded like Graham was open to the possibility of taking me there later, depending on what Callie came up with.

Graham must've seen I wasn't comfortable with the situation because he added, "The other reason I don't want you there is that we haven't prepared you for that kind of encounter with the S-Em. You've seen firsthand how dangerous that fire is, right? Let's keep you away from it, if we can."

"Yeah, okay," I said, trying not to show how much better that made me feel. I hated to look like a coward, even if that's what I was.

"Hey," he said, "you wanted to see your brother, right? Why don't we do that this morning?"

My mind flew to Ben.

"That'd be wonderful! Also, I should really call my boss. He was expecting me back at work on Thursday."

"Okay, let's go. You can use my phone on the way."

A minute later we were in the car, and I was happily giving him directions to Ben's house. I was so glad Graham recognized that I had no business going near the mill. I mean, I had no idea what I was doing, no idea at all. *Thank god*, I thought to myself, *at least one of these people is sane.*

❧

"Okay, so I said there are ground rules," Graham said as we turned into Ben's neighborhood. "They're pretty simple: don't tell anyone about the S-Em or about the Seconds living among us. Not anyone, for any reason. No exceptions. Don't tell anyone about your abilities or about anyone else's you happen to know about. Don't talk about essence or workings or anything like that."

I waited for him to go on, but apparently there wasn't any more. I was surprised.

"That's it? I would think rules like that would be commonsense. Otherwise you'd all be in mental hospitals, or maybe top-secret government research labs."

"Yeah, you'd think," Graham said. "But we take these rules very seriously, so it's important to make them explicit."

He gave me a searching look.

"It means you can't tell your brother, all right? If you get married one day, you can't tell your spouse. You can't even tell your priest."

"I hadn't thought of that," I said.

A small loneliness washed over me.

"Sounds like the rules would make marriage and family pretty hard."

"That might be why we tend to pair off with one another," he said, and gave me a little smile.

Was he flirting with me? No, he couldn't possibly be.

"But seriously," he continued, "you have to be really careful. Don't keep any photos or negatives that show Seconds in their true form—burn them right away. Don't do internet searches on terms like 'Second Emanation' or on the names of any Seconds you get to know. Don't keep a diary. Not an accurate one, at least. Always be certain a person is one of us before saying anything incriminating—at least a few governments around the world have suspicions about this stuff, and you don't want to give information to an undercover agent by accident."

I nodded. I hadn't really thought about how many ways there were to slip up. It occurred to me that I'd already broken the rules in a big way by showing the picture of Bob's foot around Pete's, but if Graham didn't bring it up, I sure as hell wasn't going to.

"So," he said, "why don't you make that call to your boss. Let's think about what you're going to tell him."

As Graham coached me, I realized I was going to have to get used to lying a lot more. His advice was to keep it simple—a straightforward excuse or explanation was easier to remember and often more convincing. It could also be helpful, he said, to blame yourself. That way people spent their time being annoyed at you instead of questioning your story.

"The thing is, I don't know if Dr. Nielsen will have found out about how I left town and then was questioned by the police about Justine. If he knows about that, it's going to get complicated."

Graham pulled into a space a few houses down from Ben's.

"How could he know about that? It's a police matter."

I rolled my eyes. "Clearly, you're not from a small town."

He laughed. "Well, let's think of how you might handle either situation. That way you'll be prepared to follow the conversation wherever it goes."

After some discussion, I called Dr. Nielsen at home and told him I still wasn't feeling well and might need to take another sick day on Monday.

"Beth, that's fine," he said. "Head injuries are unpredictable that way. But why didn't you call earlier? I was expecting you back on Thursday. I've been worried."

"What, really? I thought I said Monday, not Thursday."

"Janie and I both thought it was Thursday. She was really worried, by the way. You should call her."

"I must've been so out of it that I said Thursday when I meant Monday. I'm sorry."

"That's all right, Beth. You did seem a bit disoriented when we spoke. Please let me know how you're feeling Monday, so we know whether to expect you Tuesday. In the meantime, Judith is happy to fill in."

I thanked him and hung up. When Graham nodded his approval of the conversation, I went ahead and called Janie.

"Oh my god, Beth, I've been so worried about you," she said. "When you didn't come in Thursday, I called your house. By the end of the day, I was tearing my hair out! I went to your place and knocked and knocked, but you didn't answer. Friday, too. Where have you been?"

I gave her my story, explaining that I'd been home but must've been on pain meds and sleeping heavily when she called and dropped by. I apologized profusely and tried to sound embarrassed instead of guilty.

"Jeez, don't worry about it. I can totally understanding doing something like that. And," she said, lowering her voice, "I think Mrs. Nielsen is sort of enjoying being back at the helm."

"Yeah," I said, "I bet."

Judith Nielsen had been her husband's receptionist from when he opened his practice in the early '80s until four years ago. That's when she'd decided she wanted more leisure time, and he'd hired me to replace her. She was sort of a dragon lady, so I suspected Dr. Nielsen had been a little relieved at her decision. He certainly got away with being a lot more crotchety with me than he had with her.

"Hey, is it really true that Justine up and left Ben without even telling him?" Janie asked. "I heard it from Suzanne yesterday. I've been dying to ask you."

"Well, I don't really know what happened between them. I guess she might've left him."

"Wow." She paused. "Are you psyched or what?"

I laughed. "No, not really—she sucks, yeah, but Ben loves her and the kids must be so upset."

"Yeah, yeah, you would take the high road," Janie said. "Mama always said you were too nice for your own good."

I laughed again, though the compliment wasn't justified—I might be the reason Justine was gone, after all. She might even be dead because of me.

"Okay, I'll see you next week. Feel better, okay? Let me know if you need anything."

"Will do, Janie, thanks."

I hung up and looked at Graham.

"Very good," he said. "The one thing I'd change is that you said, 'I've been at home' when you were explaining yourself. But if you were really making the call from home, you probably would've said, 'I've been here,' right?"

I looked at him, surprised at his recall of what I'd said.

"Yeah, I guess I would."

"Also," he said, "a pronoun like 'here' is more flexible. If you get caught in the lie somehow, you can always say you meant something else by 'here'—not your home, say, but a friend's house."

"Wow, you've really thought about this stuff."

"In our line of work, it's an unfortunate necessity. And it's often the small stuff that catches you up—stuff you say without thinking because it seems so unimportant."

He waited until I nodded my understanding.

"Okay, we should talk about how you're going to handle your brother. That's going to be a more challenging situation."

But the visit with Ben turned out not to be so challenging

after all, at least not in the way Graham meant. Ben was too wrapped up in his own fear and sadness to be interested in what I'd been up to for the last few days. He was just angry that I hadn't been there for him. He did say the police had told him I had an alibi for the time Justine disappeared. Beyond that, it was all about his situation—whether their fight on Sunday might've driven Justine away, where she might've gone, whether someone might've kidnapped her, whether she was dead.

There was also a lot of focus on how the kids were handling their mother's absence. The short answer was "not well," but I didn't get the short answer.

We both did a lot of crying, Ben from grief, me from guilt. It was awful. Worst of all was glancing up and seeing Tiffany peeking around the banister to watch her father crying. The look on her face was unbearable.

⋰

"Denny's?" I asked, confused.

After leaving Ben's, I'd gotten in Graham's car, and he'd kindly left me alone with my misery. I hadn't paid attention to where we were going. He'd driven most of the way to Wausau, and I hadn't noticed.

"Sure. Thought we could get a bite to eat."

As soon as I thought of food, I realized I was starving.

"Okay, yeah."

We were seated and got our pitcher of coffee. It occurred to me that Graham might be able to help with Justine, beyond just asking his contacts if they knew anything. He talked about Williams as if he'd known him a while. Maybe he could make some educated guesses on places the bastard would stash someone he'd kidnapped.

Unfortunately, we'd been seated in the center of the main dining room and were surrounded by people. Asking about it here would probably break the rules.

The main course passed pleasantly enough. I could tell Graham was trying to distract me from my worries. He asked about my family and my experiences growing up in Dorf. He touched on a sore spot when he asked about my father, and I had to admit I'd never known him. But he recovered artfully and quickly steered the conversation onto safer ground. He really was quite charming. I sure didn't have the social graces he did. I mean, I could eat a meal without dropping food on myself, but that was about it.

I asked Graham about himself and found out he'd been born in North Carolina and had grown up on the Outer Banks. It seemed like an exciting place to be a kid. When I said as much, he got to talking about shipwrecks and hurricanes. And also beach parties, where "all the girls ran around in bikinis." I could've sworn he glanced at my chest during that story.

Dessert arrived—a piece of cherry pie each. After a few bites, Graham sat back and eyed me. Then he asked if I minded a personal question.

"I guess not," I said. "I mean, you can always ask it, but I might not answer it, if it's too personal."

I flushed. I really could find the most awkward way to handle anything.

He just nodded. Then he said, quietly, "Have you been diagnosed with panic disorder?"

I leaned back, surprised. True, I'd had that near-attack at the cemetery, but most people had never heard of panic disorder.

In answer to my unspoken question, he pointed at the rubber band on my wrist. I fingered it self-consciously. It had been the suggestion of one of the shrinks my mother took me to when I was a kid. When an attack started coming on, the pain of snapping the band was supposed to disrupt whatever chain reaction was causing it. It only worked for me sometimes, but sometimes was better than never.

"Yeah. I was diagnosed when I was six."

He nodded. "I think you'll find you don't have it, after all."

"That sounds like wishful thinking to me. So far, it's pretty much dictated my life."

"Yeah, I bet." He paused and looked around. "Let's talk about it in the car."

Curious but guarded, I followed him out. He opened the car door for me, then got behind the wheel and turned to me.

"People like us are in a terrible position before we begin seeing what's really out there," he said. "Even before we can see Seconds and workings, many of us are able to sense them on some level. Fearfulness, anxiety, panic attacks—that kind of stuff is common in the pre-sighted. The mind doesn't react well to getting contradictory information from the senses, especially about something that could be a threat. Do you see what I mean?"

"So you're saying that every time I have a panic attack, there's a Second nearby that I can sort of sense, but can't see?"

"Maybe. Or it might not be a direct cause-and-effect thing—a Second gets within a hundred feet of you and, bang, you have a panic attack. It is that way for some of us. Others just live in a state of heightened anxiety, and panic attacks are sprinkled in randomly. But in general, the more we're exposed to things we can't see—Seconds, workings, even someone like me, if I'm using a halfing disguise—the worse the effect. It's very lucky you live in such a small town, where there aren't many Seconds. If you lived in a more populous area, your mind would've been destroyed by now. Late bloomers just don't survive unless they grow up in the boonies."

I sat for a long time, mulling it over.

Finally I said, "Have you ever been to Madison?"

"I live there. It's regional headquarters for the Upper Midwest."

"Are there lots of Seconds there?"

"Tons. They like college towns. A transient population makes it easier to blend in."

I sat there, totally at a loss. I didn't know what to say. I didn't even know how to feel.

My life had had two central constants—my mother and my illness. I'd already lost my mother. Now the other constant was being rewritten, maybe erased. Losing a bad thing should be a good thing, but instead it was profoundly disconcerting. Like I was losing who I was.

After a few minutes, Graham said, "Elizabeth, I know this is very difficult. You've had to deal with being pre-sighted for far longer than most of us do. It's a testament to your strength that you're as sane and stable as you are."

I nodded dully, not really feeling the compliment.

"But just think," he continued, "real panic disorder can be treated, but sometimes it doesn't go away. If that's what you had, you might've struggled with it all your life. But that's not going to happen to you. Your problem was situational, not biochemical. Your panic attacks are going to stop, now that all your senses are on the same page."

"They're going to stop?"

"Yes, almost certainly."

"They're going to stop."

It was starting to sink in. They were going to stop.

I could date. I could go back to school.

I could leave Dorf.

Lost in a reverie of what my new, panic-free life might be like, I didn't remember to broach the issue of Justine until we were more than halfway home.

"Graham, I know you're checking with your contacts about my sister-in-law, but I wanted to ask you something else about that."

"Yeah, what is it?"

Just at that moment, someone rear-ended us, hard. I was pressed back into my seat, and the fields around us lurched backwards. Then we slowed suddenly, and my seatbelt cut into me. Finally, there was a crunch-bang as we hit a highway sign post and the airbags deployed. We ended up in a ditch. The road sign, which helpfully told us that Dorf was fifteen miles away, was on our windshield.

I looked over at Graham, who groaned and rubbed his head. I saw he'd been wearing his seatbelt as well, thank god.

"You okay?"

"Yeah, I think so," he said. "You?"

"I'm okay. We'd better check on the other driver."

Or drivers, plural, I thought. The road between Dorf and Wausau was four lanes. The moron who hit us could've caused a real pile-up.

Fortunately, the other driver wasn't hurt, and hers was the only other car involved. Some witnesses had pulled over and gotten her out of her car. By the time we walked up, she was sitting in someone else's back seat, babbling about her accelerator getting stuck.

"Yeah, sure," a guy standing next to me said under his breath. "Probably drunk."

"In the middle of the day?" someone else said.

"Couple of years ago, everyone's accelerator was getting stuck. Remember that?"

"Dang foreign cars," a fourth person said.

The conversation continued as we all waited for the police.

It took more than an hour for things to get sorted and for Graham to get a tow truck. I watched his car being winched out of the ditch. It looked totaled to me. Graham was sitting in the back of a police car, rubbing his neck—whiplash. I seemed to have gotten off lighter.

Graham had the car towed to Dorf. One of the cops gave us a ride back to town. It was nice of her. Or maybe Graham was also a super-secret FBI agent, like Williams. That'd explain why none of the police on the scene looked twice at me, even though I'd been the prime suspect in a possible kidnapping a few days earlier and was now thought to be part of a meth ring. Christ almighty, how was I ever going to get my reputation straightened out?

As we drew into town, Graham asked if I had a car. I told him I did, but that I'd left it parked in front of the police station on Wednesday.

"Mind if we go pick it up?" he asked. "I think we need to have one on hand, and it'll take me a while to get a rental delivered."

"Sure, no problem. Hopefully they haven't impounded it."

Unfortunately, they had. It took more than two hours of dealing with a pretty surly Dorf PD, plus a fine, to get my car out of lock-up. As far as the local cops went, I clearly hadn't been forgiven for allegedly getting mixed up with drugs, making false charges against an FBI agent, and worst of all, wasting their time.

"Hey," Graham said as we finally pulled out of the police impoundment lot on the edge of town, "if you haven't been home since you left town, maybe you'd like to spend the night there instead at Callie's house?"

"Oh my god, that'd be great!"

"Cool." He turned left and headed toward my place. "This is good. Not only can you relax and get some fresh clothes, but this'll keep Callie from starting another argument about taking you to the fire."

Boy, did that sound good to me.

Chapter 8

GRAHAM WALKED ME up to my door, which surprised me a little. Before he left, he gave me a warm smile and stroked my upper arm affectionately, which surprised me even more. The vibe I'd been getting all day from him was a little more than friendly. I hoped I was reading too much into his behavior. Graham seemed nice, and he sure looked good, but I shouldn't get involved with one of these people. There were too many unknowns.

Being on my own was a firmly established habit, anyway. Before Matt had asked me out, I hadn't been on a date in more than a year and a half.

But maybe it doesn't have to be that way, now, I thought. If it weren't for the panic attacks, things would've gone differently with Matt, right? Maybe I wouldn't drive away the next guy who asked me out. Or maybe I could even get back with Matt.

If the panic attacks really did stop. *And if I want to have to lie to someone all the time*, I thought, remembering Graham's warnings.

Well, no sense in worrying about that right now.

I let myself in. It felt good to be home. I hadn't been gone all that long, but the house had that just-home-from-vacation feeling—the smell was a little off, and it was oddly quiet.

I curled up on the couch with a hot bowl of soup and a cold soda. It seemed like a million years ago that I'd last done this very normal thing. It was great.

I'd only slept a few hours the night before, so I went to bed at 8:00. My own worn, mismatched sheets had never felt so good.

🍃

I came wide awake in the wee hours, certain that something was wrong. I slid out from under the covers, then smoothed them quickly, making the bed look unused. Opening the top drawer of my bedside table, I pulled out my mother's old .38.

When Mom was alive, she always stored the bullets separately. Ben's kids came to the house back then, so loaded guns were a no-no. I no longer bothered with that precaution. I checked by feel to make sure the cylinder was full, then moved as quietly as I could across my bedroom and crouched in the corner behind the door.

Mom had made me go shooting at the range in Frederick a couple times a year. I hadn't done it much since she passed. It just didn't seem like a priority. Dorf was pretty darned safe. I carefully settled my finger outside the guard and thumbed back the hammer. It had been long enough since I'd used the gun that these actions were no longer automatic. I couldn't remember when I'd last cleaned the thing. Damn.

There were footsteps on the stairs. Surprisingly, the intruder didn't sneak into the room. Instead there was a soft knock and a pause before the bedroom door swung open. The light flipped on, and a female voice said, "Beth?" I peaked around the side of the door and saw bleached-blond hair. Kara.

She looked back out the door. "She's not here."

"She's here," Williams said.

Fuck.

I waited until Kara left the room, then stood and moved quickly into the doorway, gun leveled. Putting all the steel into my voice that I could, I said, "Stop."

Kara and Williams stilled. They both had their backs to me and seemed to realize I was armed, maybe from my tone of voice. They'd been about to check the second bedroom, which was right across the landing. Both slowly looked over their shoulders at me. Kara's face was very surprised. Williams's was blank. I took a slow step back, so that I'd be out of lunging range, and shifted the gun toward Williams. The three of us stood there for a few seconds, staring at each other.

It occurred to me that I wasn't feeling a panic attack coming on. I was scared, but I was also angry. I'd had it with these people, especially Williams. A sadist, Graham had said. I could believe it.

I realized I might very well shoot him. A strange sense of calm descended on me.

Williams's expression changed fractionally. A finger on his right hand twitched. He didn't strike me as a twitchy sort of person. I wondered if he'd just put up some sort of force field to protect himself. It would be just my luck to get killed by my own ricochet.

The moment of distraction helped me get a handle on my anger. Good as it'd feel to shoot Williams, he hadn't actually made a move in my direction, yet. I took two more steps back and pulled the gun back and up to my shoulder, still holding it with both hands.

"What do you want?"

"We just want to talk," Kara said.

I waited.

"You need to come out to the mill. We're not getting anywhere with it. Callie says we need you there."

"What, nearly burning one woman to death isn't enough for you?"

If the jab bothered Williams, he didn't show it. In contrast, Kara seemed genuinely upset at the thought.

"That's not going to happen to you! Look, I know it's really fucking scary—it is, totally. But it's also really important. You've got to come."

"How long have you guys been doing this? A year? Ten years? Huh? I come along and join your little freak show, and two days later, you can't do it without me? Bullshit."

"I know it's weird. But Callie's never wrong. She doesn't see all that often, but when she does, it's right."

"No."

Williams made a small, exasperated noise and pushed past Kara. Without hesitation, I brought the gun down and fired at him. I only got off one shot before he slammed me back against the wall with one hand and took the gun away with the other. God he was fast.

Either I was right about the force field, or my aim had really gone to shit—he'd been a yard or two away and coming right at me, and I hadn't hit him.

No ricochet had come back at me. I was sort of sorry for that. I'd rather die by gunshot than be burned to death.

Williams dragged me out of the room and down the stairs. Kara followed, looking scared and swearing under her breath. He hauled me around the corner and into the living room, then froze.

Graham was standing in the middle of the room. His

expression was only mildly annoyed, but I got the sense he was madder than he looked.

"You're kidnapping my trainee?"

Williams didn't say anything.

From behind us, Kara said, "Graham, we need her out there. Callie says."

Graham cocked his head. "I don't think so."

He brought one hand up and looked at it. At first I thought he was checking out his fingernails. Then I realized he was holding a cell phone.

"How fortunate you just happened to call as you were leaving the house, Kara. I was able to follow along with your progress quite nicely."

Kara blanched. She pulled her own phone out and ended the call she clearly hadn't known was going on.

"Look …," she said.

"Get out." Graham sounded almost bored.

Amazingly, Williams dropped me and stalked out of the house. Kara followed, squeezing to the side, as though she wanted to stay as far away from Graham as possible.

I have to admit, it was sort of weird. They were afraid of him. Well, Kara was obviously afraid of him, and Williams was at least unwilling to challenge him. I still hadn't seen anything particularly scary about Graham. He seemed like a middle-management type—sending people here and there, training people, that kind of thing. What had I missed that Kara saw?

He watched them leave. Once they were gone, he turned back to me, looking concerned.

"Elizabeth, are you all right?"

"Yeah," I said.

I sat down on the couch and reached back to rub my back where it'd hit the wall.

"Just need an ice pack or two. That's getting to be standard with you people."

"Not all of 'us people' are the same," he said quietly, sitting down beside me. "Of course, you have no idea if that's true or not," he added wryly, as though he could read my mind.

He put an arm around my shoulders but must've felt me stiffen, because he just patted me, then let me go.

"Seriously, are you okay?"

"Yeah, I am. Thanks for the save. I'd probably be on my way to dead right now if you hadn't shown up."

That got a big smile.

"Did Kara really call you by accident?"

He grinned. "Yep."

"Man. What a loser kidnapper, eh?"

He laughed. "I don't normally want my people to be losers at anything, but in this case I'm delighted. Now," he said, his expression softening, "why don't you take some Tylenol and try to go back to sleep. I'll hang out here, just to be sure they don't come back."

That didn't exactly make me feel better, but what could I do? Saying I'd be fine alone and he should leave would sound silly, considering what had just happened.

Which reminded me that my neighbors had probably all called the police. A .38 makes a big noise on a quiet night.

But the night was still silent—no sirens, no Suzanne at her front door, hollering to find out if I was okay. In fact, when I went to the window, I didn't see lights on in any of the surrounding houses.

Graham seemed to know what I was thinking.

"They were keeping things quiet. None of your neighbors heard anything."

When I still looked perplexed, he said, "We haven't talked

119

much yet about workings. One thing you can make quite easily is a noise-dampening field. Most of us learn to do that. I'm sure you'll be able make one yourself, once you get to that stage."

"Wow," I said. "That must come in handy. What else can I learn to do?"

He smiled. "Well, lots of us can open locks." He gestured at my front door. "See? They didn't have to break in. One of them did a working to unlock it."

"Huh. I'm surprised more of you don't take up lives of crime."

He laughed a little too hard—it hadn't been that funny. Maybe Graham was a notorious cat burglar on the side.

"Okay," I said, yawning. "I'm going to try to get a little more shut-eye. There's a blanket and an extra pillow in that cabinet over there. Or you can watch TV in the den. Help yourself to whatever's in the fridge. Which isn't much."

"Great, sounds good. When you're up and about, we can discuss that second-caste testing I was talking about."

"Okay. Good night."

"Good night. And Elizabeth," he said as I turned toward the stairs, "I'll be having a talk with the others. This won't happen again."

I nodded. I hoped I looked grateful enough. The way he'd said it gave me a little chill, so I had a feeling the talk would be effective.

I headed up to my room. After a moment's hesitation, I locked my bedroom door. After all, what if he'd told me that thing about opening locks just to make me think there was no point in locking my door? Probably dumb, but hey, it couldn't hurt.

I flipped off the overhead and turned on my bedside lamp.

Then I got in bed. Lying back, I noticed a bullet hole in my ceiling near the door. So there had been a ricochet, and it went straight up. I guess bulletproofing was par for the course, too.

Not good. The gun had given me a moment's confidence, had let me put anger ahead of fear, however briefly. If I couldn't even shoot these people, I really was helpless.

*

I woke at around 7:00 and trundled directly into the bathroom. Callie's place was nice, but I wanted to shower in my own bathroom, with my own shampoo, my own conditioner, and my own shower pouf. I also needed to make serious use of a razor.

When I was clean, I dressed in a sweater and fresh jeans, trying hard not to think about which pair would be most flattering. I was probably wrong about Graham's interest, and even if I wasn't, getting involved with him was out of the question.

When I went downstairs, I found Graham cooking breakfast. He must've actually gone shopping first, since breakfast included bacon, eggs, toast, bananas, and OJ, none of which I'd had on hand. He'd also made coffee. It was all delicious.

After eating, I felt like crawling back into bed for a nap, but instead we got in my car and headed east. I think I dozed part of the way. Big meals early in the day always made me sleepy.

Our destination turned out to be Rib Mountain, a four-mile-long ridge just west of Wausau. It took more than an hour to get there, since we had to wend our way up through the state park that surrounded the mountain.

On the way there, Graham told me a little more.

"You remember about the four castes? 'Sense a working, get a gift, handle essence, learn to work,' right? Okay, so we've got you into the first caste, now—you're seeing worked essence for what it is, instead of getting glimpses while remaining blind to most of it."

I guess I could see, now. I'd seen Bob, at any rate.

"In the next caste, you get what we call a gift. Kara's ability to heal, Callie's ability to sense future events—these are examples of gifts."

"Does Williams have a gift for shields?" I asked, remembering the bullet hole in my ceiling and how I'd been trapped in Callie's house.

"Yes, but we call that sort of thing a 'barrier.' The word 'shield' is too restrictive for what can be done with a barrier."

Good lord, just want I didn't want to hear.

"So," Graham continued, "what we're going to do today is see if your gift has emerged. Usually people spend quite a while in the first caste before reaching the second, but since you were stalled for an unknown amount of time, maybe your gift will come quickly."

"What's the difference between workings and gifts?"

"The word 'gift' is shorthand for a working you can do automatically, without having to actually learn how. Most of us have at least one thing we can just do, without even thinking about it. Sometimes gifted working can be fine-tuned through practice, but the basic ability is always just there from the get-go."

"What about the things you were mentioning last night—making disguises, unlocking doors, and such?"

"Right now you can sense essence that's been disturbed by a working—that's the first caste. In the third caste, you gain the ability to see essence in its natural state. Once that happens, you can begin to do workings aside from your gift. We called that 'learned' working. You can also learn to do half-workings at that point—mainly disguises and false images. Some people devote a lot of time to learned workings and become very adept. Those people are said to have reached the fourth caste. People who rely mostly on their gifts, even though they're capable of learned workings, remain in the third caste."

"So even if I don't have a gift for healing, I might be able to learn to do it?"

"Exactly. People who aren't gifted healers can still learn to do healing work. Their abilities will probably be much more limited than those of a gifted healer like Kara, but it would still be very useful."

We pulled into the parking lot at the top of the mountain. Our car was the only one there. It was too late in the year for skiing, snowshoeing, and other winter sports, and too early to do much else besides slog through cold mud.

That last seemed to be what Graham had in mind. He got a backpack out of the trunk, and we headed into the woods. I think we covered less than a mile, but it took the better part of an hour, since there was no trail to follow.

I realized at one point that Graham must've been telling the truth about the sound-containment thing. I could certainly hear us crashing along through the dead leaves and brush, but nothing else seemed able to—several times we startled wildlife at close range.

At least I wasn't the only one who suffered. About half an hour into our hike, Graham tripped and fell in a pretty substantial mud puddle. He stood up, brushing pointlessly at his pant legs, which were drenched and muddy up to the knees. Then he shot an annoyed look at the snag he'd tripped over.

"You okay?" I asked.

"Yeah. Darn rock."

We continued on. Finally, Graham motioned to stop. He stood still for about a minute with his eyes closed, concentrating on something. Then he nodded to himself and said, "This is good."

He opened his backpack and got out two large trash bags, which he unfolded and laid on the ground. We each sat on one. My butt instantly got very cold.

"Okay," he said, "I'm going to test you for some common gifts. If nothing shows up, that's no big deal. It just means you haven't hit the second caste, yet."

"Is there something about this place that makes it good for testing?"

"Yeah. This mountain's made out of very hard rock, so it's much older than the surrounding land—approaching two billion years. It exists in both emanations, and its essence has been worked and reworked so many times that it's thick with all the echoes and remnants. That makes it a place of power for people like us—the essence is easier to grasp, and sometimes you can build on the remains of someone else's working, which increases what you can do."

"So, the older things are, the more powerful they are?"

"Age is often associated with thickness, but it's not consistent. Sometimes relatively new sites can get pretty thick. It depends on how much working has been done there and how much of it sticks in the essence. Some places seem to be naturally sticky."

Graham spent the next two hours trying to figure out what I could do. He had me see if I could turn myself into mist, which involved trying to "feel transparent," in his words. That didn't go anywhere. He had me try to change into an animal by visualizing it. I remained stubbornly myself.

From that point, the list of failures just grew. I couldn't communicate with him telepathically. I couldn't heal a tiny cut he made on his finger. He pricked my finger with a pin, and I couldn't heal that, either. I didn't seem to have any effect on water or fire or stone or metal or the weather. I couldn't move things with my mind. I wasn't unusually strong or fast. I couldn't speak or understand foreign languages. I couldn't go invisible. And I couldn't fly.

Which of course made me ask if they really had people who could fly. Graham's response—"none living"—wasn't particularly encouraging.

At the end of the session, he sat back with a sigh. A few moments passed.

"Remember, just because you aren't demonstrating a particular gift now doesn't mean you won't be able to do it later."

"Yeah, okay."

I told myself that was good—the less I could do, the less interest this group would have in me.

"So there are other abilities some people have?"

"Yeah, sure, there are lots of different gifts. The stuff I've been testing you for is big—the things that tend to be too impressive to go unnoticed. But there are tons of subtler, more unusual gifts. Sometimes you hear them called 'quirks.' The word's considered pejorative, though, so I try not to use it. Really, every gift is a gift."

I nodded and wondered if he had a so-called quirk himself. I sensed it would be rude to ask, so I kept my mouth shut.

"At any rate, I suspect you just haven't come into your gift, yet. There's a rule of thumb for figuring out how long someone's going to keep developing: you take the person's age at the time they enter the first caste and divide that number in half. Then you add the two numbers together. When the person reaches that number of years, they probably aren't going to develop much more raw power, though they could keep learning and refining their skills."

"So, if you start sensing workings at age ten, you keep developing up to age fifteen?"

"Yes, exactly. There are certainly exceptions, but it holds true for most."

"So if I'm starting at twenty-three …"

"You have a lot of developing to do," Graham finished. "It's possible you'll be able to fly, but not until you're thirty," he said, and winked.

Great. It was all well and fine to develop slowly, but if I could do something now, I'd like to know it. I felt like a guppy who's just realized its aquarium is full of piranhas.

"Is there a way to test for the more unusual gifts?"

"Not specifically. There are literally thousands of them, and some of them are pretty hard to pin down. It's possible that many of us have one or more that we never find out about. For instance, one guy I knew could put anything up his left nostril, so long as he could pick the item up and push it in that direction. But he didn't know about it for the longest time. I mean, who really tries to put a chair up their nose, right?"

"Yeah. Wow."

I hoped that if I had any quirky gifts, they didn't involve bodily orifices.

"Anyway, this last test is open-ended. It might allow an unusual gift to show up. What I'd like you to do is just open yourself to the energy of this place and see what might come to you."

I sat there, feeling dull. "I don't know how to open myself to the energy of a place."

"It's a bit like meditating. Have you ever done that?"

"Nope."

"Well, try closing your eyes and relaxing all your muscle groups one at a time. Then allow yourself to focus on your surroundings—what you feel, what you hear, what you smell. If your mind wanders, just bring it back to those things. Try to notice as much sensory information as you can, but don't think about it. Just notice. That's all you have to do, really."

I sighed and closed my eyes, certain the exercise would be pointless and boring. I tried to focus on my senses. My rear end was going numb, and that occupied all my sensory input at first. Slowly I began noticing other things—the sound of the wind in the bare tree limbs came first. It actually was quite loud, though it had been background noise a minute earlier. The breeze touching my face was obvious, but I found I could also feel colder and warmer spots on my legs, depending on how the wind was striking them. The smell was what I think of as not-quite-spring. It was wet, and that was springlike, but it was still dead, like old leaves. When spring really came, in a few more weeks, it would start to smell like fresh dirt and earthworms in a place like this. Far off I heard a bird call, though I had no idea what kind.

I sat there, just taking those things in. It actually wasn't boring at all. It was interesting and sort of stimulating. I felt energized, more awake to the world than I had in ages. My hands grew warmer, and I could feel my pulse beating in them, which was weird.

After a while, I felt sure there was something in front of me that I needed to pick up. My internal editor immediately pointed out how dumb that was, but I shushed it. Graham was trying to teach me. I'd always been a conscientious student, and that wasn't going to stop now.

Without opening my eyes, I reached down to the ground in front of me. For a moment, it felt strangely slick, as though all the texture had gone out of things. Then my fingers found the dead leaves, dry on top and damp beneath. I brought my hands together in the leaf litter and felt something soft and warm in them. I raised my hands and opened my eyes to see what I had.

It was a small golden-brown mouse. It crouched in my cupped palms, then sat up on its haunches, looking at me and sniffing. It had impressively thick whiskers on its snout. They quivered charmingly. It didn't seem scared at all.

I'd never been afraid of little critters—even snakes and rats and spiders were fine by me. I actually thought this little guy was really cute. Was it a "he"? I checked the back—yup.

"Hi, buddy. What're you doing out this early in the year, huh?"

I looked up at Graham, half expecting him to be repulsed by the fact I'd picked up a rodent. Instead he looked … well, it was hard to describe. There was an element of surprise there, but the word didn't do it justice. Maybe it was a mixture of several feelings. He looked from the mouse to me and back, and didn't say anything at all.

"Um … so, I can tame wild animals?"

He kept staring at me and the mouse, apparently at a loss for words.

Finally he said, "That's really unusual. It's been a long time since I've seen someone do that." He paused. "It's definitely a good ability. Very good."

"Really?"

"Yes," he said firmly. "Definitely. Just think how useful it could be."

I was dubious. I mean, what was I going to do, sic a hoard of mice on Williams the next time he came to kidnap me? Maybe Graham was trying to make me feel better about a not-very-useful gift. Come to think of it, maybe the mouse wasn't wild at all. Sometimes people dumped their unwanted pets in places like this.

He got up and opened his back pack to put his trash bag back in.

"You'd best let Mickey there go back to what he was doing."

"Okay." I set my hands down in the leaves, expecting the mouse to hop off, but instead he ran up my arm and into my hair. Like I said, I wasn't afraid of creepy-crawlies, but a mouse in my hair was a bit of a surprise, even for me. I reached up, then hesitated. If I dug around in there, he might bite me.

"Graham …"

The mouse wiggled his way into the collar of my coat and promptly curled up there against my neck. He was so warm and soft. Suddenly, I really wanted to keep him. He just had to be someone's pet—he was so friendly.

"What? Did it take off?"

"Yeah."

I just didn't say where. I got up and handed him my trash bag, and we headed back to the car. The mouse seemed content to sleep all the way home.

❧

When we got back to my house, Graham walked me up to the door and gave me a kiss on the cheek. When he started bending over to do it, I was a bit worried he'd touch my neck and squash the mouse, but he touched my shoulders instead.

It turned out to be sort of lingering, for a kiss on the cheek. I felt my body sit up and take notice, against my better judgment.

He pulled back and looked at me, then leaned in again and brushed his lips against mine once, twice. His breath touched my lips, and I tipped my head up to him. He kissed me slowly, tracing a fine line along my lower lip with the tip of his tongue. I opened my mouth, and he deepened the kiss gently until our tongues were stroking together. His hand slid down to my lower back and pressed my body into his. I could feel the hardness in his groin, and felt a warm tightening deep in my belly in response.

It had been a long time.

It would have to be a little longer.

My hormones shouted and waved angry placards, but I pulled back anyway. Getting together with Graham right now just wasn't a good idea. He leaned his forehead against mine and gave me a little smile. Instead of pressing things, he looked pleased I'd let him kiss me at all. That was a nice ego boost. Made me want to kiss him again, actually.

I needed a cold-shower line of thought.

"Do you think Williams will come back?" I asked.

"Not a chance," Graham said firmly, giving me a little hug and then letting me go. "They know I'm onto them."

He looked completely confident on this point, so I accepted what he said. Still, I wish I'd managed to tame a wolf instead of a mouse.

He gave me a warm smile, then said he'd come by that night at about dinner time, if that was okay. I said it was, then immediately thought, *Why did I say that?* I was going to get myself in trouble.

I stepped inside and leaned against the door for a few minutes, gathering my wits.

Chapter 9

FROM THE SILENCE, Ghosteater watched me kiss Graham. He could smell our arousal. It brought back ancient memories from the time before his difference truly emerged, the time when he still ran with his pack, hunting the great lost beasts of that age, the time when he still hungered to breed and make young. But no she-wolf would have him, even then. They feared him.

He didn't realize, at first, that he was unlike his kin—bigger and stronger, perhaps, but not truly other.

At some point, though, the hunts began to bore him. Leaping from the tall grass upon a bison or sloth—such creatures presented no challenge. They smelled of rank terror and tasted of it, too. When his kin would not follow him against other, more equal creatures, he left them and wandered alone, hunting the great cats and bears. When he returned at last, his kin ran from him, as terrified of him as any other animal would be.

He grieved, then, afraid he would always be alone, a terrible thing for a wolf. And so he had, mostly. But he had been wrong to fear it. Solitude had its rewards. And he wasn't a wolf, after all—not really.

He scented the air again.

Graham was unfamiliar, but he recognized me as blood kin to the other humans the wind had shown him. That made sense—it was me the wind had brought him there to see.

The wind spoke incessantly, and it liked to be heard. Few things could understand it, so it often sought him out. Usually it simply told him about what it had touched, of late—a months-dead doe just emerging from melting snow, cold drops of water falling toward the forest floor, the line of harder rock protruding from an exposed peak.

But now, for the third time in just a few days, the wind spoke not of what it had touched, but of what it might touch in days to come. When he gave it his attention, it fractured into a thousand competing voices, each running down a different path. Rapid and fleeting, the whispered stories avalanched over him like mist, there and gone before they could be grasped. In the end, he understood only their common thread.

She-pup, she-pup, she.

Intrigued, he crept closer, watching as I went inside.

Then he studied Graham. He sampled the air and tasted anxiety.

Graham walked down the path to his car and got in. Then he sat for several minutes, drumming his fingers on the steering wheel. Ghosteater could tell his anxiety had to do with me—it was blended with lingering notes of desire. Perhaps he feared for me. But why? I whom the wind had named.

Finally, Graham came to some decision and started the car. He smelled of risk and purpose. When he pulled out, Ghosteater followed him. He loped through the silence behind the car, but only so far as the eastern edge of town. He could not run fast enough to keep up on the highway. Curious, he settled down to see if Graham would return.

Chapter 10

FIRST THINGS FIRST: I needed a home for Mr. Mouse.

There was an old ten-gallon aquarium in the basement from one of my brother's childhood pets. I brought it up to the kitchen and shredded some newspapers for the bottom. I added a little bowl of water and a slice of bread. Then I carefully scooped the sleeping mouse out of my collar and settled him in a corner of the tank. I put a couple heavy books over the top, leaving some cracks for air.

I made myself a quick sandwich, then went and knocked on Mrs. Gunderson's door and asked if I could borrow her car to run an errand. I would've asked Suzanne, but I knew she'd never be satisfied with the explanation that I'd loaned mine to a friend. She'd want details, and I'd end up lying and getting caught.

Mrs. Gunderson, on the other hand, was getting a little vague. She was happy to loan me her car, no questions asked, so long as I picked up a few things for her at the supermarket while I was out. That was no problem—I did that for her most weeks, anyway.

There was a pet store in Frederick, and it was open on Sundays. I got a lid for the aquarium, a water bottle, some rodent kibble, a tiny bowl, a little wooden house, and a wheel. I also got a bag of paper bedding—I'd hate for the little guy's nice golden fur to get all newsprinty.

After dropping off Mrs. Gunderson's groceries, I went and got the mouse out of his tank. He was awake by that point and seemed glad to see me. He ran up my arm again and snuggled in my hair while I dumped out the newspaper and arranged his new home. When I put him back in the tank, he ran around sniffing everything and quickly settled on the food bowl as the most interesting item. I left him holding a kibble in his cute little pink hands and nibbling away.

I made a cup of tea and settled on the couch in the den to think about Graham.

That kiss had been really nice, but his attention confused me. I just didn't understand why he would be interested in me.

He was older than me—approaching thirty, maybe—and seemed so sophisticated. He didn't speak like I did, didn't dress like I did.

I was a young, uneducated small-town girl. In fact, I had barely been outside Wisconsin. I couldn't see that my personality was the big attraction. I was nice enough, but I wasn't vivacious or incredibly funny. Similarly, I was smart enough, but smarts didn't make up for ignorance. If I'd turned up with some amazing ability, like flying, maybe that would draw his interest, but that hadn't happened either.

I wasn't trying to be down on myself, just realistic. I thought I was reasonably attractive—not stand-out beautiful, but pretty enough. I mean, a guy like Matt wouldn't have asked me out if I didn't look okay. But no way was I attractive enough to overcome what would undoubtedly be a lot of deficits in the eyes of a worldly older man.

I realized I was overanalyzing Graham, probably because it was titillating to keep thinking about him. The long and the short of it was that I didn't trust his motives, and it wasn't the time to be getting involved with someone, anyway. I needed to draw a firmer line the next time I saw him. Hopefully I could do it without having to say something directly, since that would make things uncomfortable.

The phone rang. I thought about letting the machine pick up—I didn't much feel like getting off the couch, which was now nicely warm. It rang again. With a sigh I unfolded myself and climbed the stairs to answer it.

"Beth?"

It was Ben. He sounded distracted and annoyed.

"Ben. What's wrong?"

"It's Tiffany—she's run off. We're at the mall. I know she's in here somewhere, but I can't find her. The mall people are looking for her, and they've called the cops, too. Can you come and pick the rest of the kids up and take them home?"

I was relieved. It didn't sound like a serious situation, just the kind of minor rebellion an upset kid would stage. Tiff was probably hiding in a dressing room somewhere, starting to feel silly.

"Yeah, of course. Tell me where to meet you."

"We're at security. It's by the Younkers."

Also right by T.G.I. Friday's. Great. I'd get to relive my most embarrassing recent memory.

"Okay, I'll get there as soon as I can."

"Yeah, okay. Thanks, Beth."

The mall was south of Eau Claire, more than an hour's drive. I grabbed my wallet and coat and headed back to Mrs. Gunderson's. I explained that I needed her car again for a family emergency. She didn't mind, though she did ask me to go to the grocery store for her on the way home. Along with the keys, she handed me the same list she'd given me earlier that afternoon. She didn't seem to have noticed that all the items on it were crossed out. I didn't bother mentioning it, just pocketed the list and started driving.

I made it to the mall. I didn't make it inside. Just as I was getting out of the car, the van I'd parked beside opened up, and someone pulled me in. I bet you can guess who it was. I struggled, but it didn't help. I ended up bound and gagged on the floor.

Williams shifted to the driver's seat, and we pulled out. Kara leaned over me worriedly. I tried to put my outrage into my stare, but she didn't seem interested in what I was feeling. Something else was worrying her. Maybe it was Graham. I had a moment of satisfaction, but then I remembered Graham didn't know where I'd gone. Shit.

❦

We drove for about half an hour, then pulled off onto a dirt road. After a few more minutes, the van lurched to a stop. It all seemed sickeningly familiar. At least we hadn't gone far enough to have reached the old mill. Not unless we'd gone twice the speed limit.

Williams went around and opened the back door, then grabbed my feet and hauled me out. Kara held my head so that it didn't bounce along the metal floor on the way. Maybe they were setting up a good-cop, bad-cop routine.

I was surprised when I heard the passenger door close, and Callie appeared. Her eyes widened when she saw me.

"Beth! Are you all right?"

She knelt down beside me and reached for the gag.

"Callie, please get back in the van," Williams said.

She looked up at him, clearly torn.

"She's frightened. Why did you have to frighten her?"

God, what an innocent, I thought. She seemed to have no idea what sort of people she was involved with.

Williams was looking at her with an expression that suggested he might be thinking the same thing. It was probably the only time we'd ever be on the same page. He bent, helped her up, and walked her around the van, speaking quietly.

I took a look at my surroundings. We weren't on a farmer's access road, this time. I found that only marginally reassuring. Williams could have corpse piles scattered all over the Upper Midwest, for all I knew.

We seemed to have pulled into an abandoned homestead overgrown with trees and bushes. A ways to the left stood the ruins of a small house, and behind that a pile of warped wood that might once have been a shed or lean-to. Lone fence posts stuck up here and there, and the ground was littered with rusted pieces of metal. We were completely out of sight of any road. The sun was touching the line of trees on the horizon. It would be dark in less than an hour.

I heard the van door shutting again, and Williams came back alone. I guessed he'd convinced Callie to hang tight in the front seat. That brought a surge of fear—Callie's gentle presence might've restrained the man's violence.

He lifted me up and set me down on a stump. Cold moisture from the wood immediately started seeping through the seat of my jeans. I cringed away from him, but he didn't seem to notice—just looked at Kara and nodded, then backed off a little ways and sat down to watch.

I was mystified. What was Kara going to do to me? She didn't look like she had it in her to beat me, physically. She was quite short, and though she wasn't delicate, like Callie, her mass came from a curvy figure, not muscle. Then again, who knows what havoc she could wreak with her ability— maybe healing was only the positive side of what she could do.

Surprisingly, what she seemed to want to do was talk to me. A whole lot.

"We brought you out here because we need to explain some things to you," she said. "I'm sorry it went down like that. We had to make it fast, and it had to happen out of Graham's range. Callie sensed an opportunity, and we thought it might be our only chance to reach you. We figured you wouldn't come willingly."

She'd figured right. I just stared back at her, which she seemed to find a little unnerving. She shot a glance over at Williams, but I could've told her he wasn't going to help her out with this. The guy wasn't much of a talker.

Kara took a deep breath and squared her shoulders. She looked sad. She also looked a lot older than her years, sort of worn out.

"Graham trained me too," she said. "He told me that we protect the world from dangerous Seconds. Sound familiar? It's not true. Our job is to keep humans from finding out about the S-Em. He also told me that we have the support and protection of some powerful Seconds. That's misleading. The real story is they control us. Totally. We're basically slaves. The Seconds tell us what to do, who to fight, who to kill. We don't have any choices."

I felt my body go still, like the world had stopped but only I realized it.

"They don't care if humans are killed, so long as it's kept quiet. I've never been sent on a mission that was supposed to protect humans. The only thing we protect is the secret. I've been sent to kill Seconds that were as harmless as kittens just because they slipped up once, and someone might've seen something funny. And I know of one back in New York that kills a human every couple weeks, but they leave her alone because she's discreet."

I thought about it. Had Graham ever actually said his organization protected humans? Maybe not. He'd said some Seconds were dangerous. Maybe I'd jumped to conclusions.

"He tell you about the open strait?" Kara said.

I nodded.

"I bet he gave you the idea we were trying to keep something dangerous from coming through. That's not true. The only thing that matters is getting the thing closed. A fire that can't be put out is too weird—it might lead to discovery."

"You know, they don't even think we're human," she said.

Now that she'd gotten going, the words just kept coming. Every time I thought she'd reached a conclusion, something new spilled out.

"They call us 'Nolanders.' They basically think we're retarded Seconds—like we were supposed to be Seconds, but we were born stunted and can't work essence well enough to open a strait and enter the S-Em. They used to actually hunt us. We moved up from game animals to slaves because they realized that humans pose a threat, and that we could be useful on that front. They use us until we fail at some task they give us. Then they figure we're not useful anymore, and we die."

She took a few shaky breaths. I honestly didn't know what to think. If she was making this stuff up, she was a great actress. But maybe that's what she was. If this group included receptionists, why not actresses, too?

"I bet he's been coming on to you. Yes? That's what he did with me. I was so stupid. Probably stupider than you are. I mean, I was fifteen fucking years old. Why would some hotshot older guy want me? I was so cocky, I couldn't see how absurd it was." She laughed bitterly. "That's how he works. Gets you all starry-eyed and pumps you full of bullshit, then uses you to get ahead. Makes you do the most fucked-up shit, then takes all the credit. By the time you realize he's using you, he's ready to move on to his next mark."

She stopped.

I sat there, staring at her. My fear had faded. Kara and Williams weren't going to kill me. They were trying to recruit me.

The fear was replaced by frustration. Now I had two versions of things that were completely different. I was supposed to be confronting my new reality instead of being a passive victim. But how could I do that if I couldn't get a handle on what was actually going on?

How the hell was I supposed to decide who was right? I had nothing to go on except what two different people had said.

I risked a glance over at Williams. He had his elbows on his knees and was looking at his hands. No help there—I couldn't even see his face. Callie wouldn't be any help either. I already knew her version of things, and it didn't match Kara's or Graham's.

I wanted to believe what Graham had told me. It was neater, simpler, nicer. He hadn't made it sound like I'd be a slave, subject to the death penalty if I couldn't get something done. Plus, he'd made it sound like we did something noble, protecting humanity from monsters.

But maybe his story was too good to be true. Shouldn't I be more suspicious of the nice story than the horrible one? And just a couple hours ago, I'd decided I didn't trust Graham's romantic interest. That resonated with what Kara had said.

Jesus, had he really seduced her when she was fifteen? That would be rape.

But suspecting Graham was one thing. Throwing in with these people was another. Especially Williams. My tendency was to think that any side he was on was the wrong one. At least Graham had never hurt me.

But had he hurt Kara? It seemed like something had damaged her. The hair, tats, and piercings said "bad ass," but her body language said "broken." She reminded me of Callie, in a way, even though one woman was a conservative Christian adult and the other was a slightly foul-mouthed teen.

I looked down at the long, weedy grass in front of me.

I wasn't sure. I just wasn't sure.

I made a noise to attract Kara's attention, then jerked my head, trying to tell her I wanted the gag removed. She looked at Williams.

He said, "No screaming or running, Ryder," without looking up.

Nervously, Kara came over and cut the gag off me.

"I don't know who to believe."

"Yeah, I know," she said, looking discouraged.

"Do you have any evidence? Anything concrete?"

Kara shook her head, looking miserable.

Williams said, "Graham put the hit out on Bob."

We both turned to look at him. He was still studying his hands.

"Abominable snowman Bob? At the cemetery?"

Bob who was pining after a girl.

"Yup."

I felt cold. "But why? He was nice."

Then Williams did look at me. His stare was icy.

"Dozens of humans saw his foot. Think you were there."

"But … how could he have known he'd show up in my picture? It was just an accident."

I shook my head. It didn't make any sense.

"That's just like I said, Beth," Kara chimed in. "The point is to keep the S-Em secret. That's all they care about. They send us to take out anyone who creates a risk of discovery, human, Nolander, or Second. It doesn't matter how or why."

I said, more to myself than to them, "I don't *know* that Bob's dead."

Bob the bagel monster.

Williams said, "Want to see him?"

Then I knew where Bob was and who had put him there. *Oh god*. I fought back nausea, remembering. I put my head down on my knees, struggling.

Things shifted in my mind, and the weight of my belief scraped and groaned over to Kara. I couldn't have told you exactly why. Graham had been so nice to me. But I just knew. Maybe it was because no world that gave Williams a prime place could be as bright and orderly as the one Graham seemed to live in.

As I sat there, my new reality was replaced by an even newer one. It sucked. I'd been wasting my time on pretty lies.

By the time I was able to straighten up and look the latest version of my world in the face, it had gotten pretty dark. That seemed fitting. I had no idea what lay ahead of me. Before, I'd been imagining some combination of my old aspirations and something new—I'd go back to college and protect humanity on the side; I'd eventually be able to afford a new car, but sometimes I'd decide to fly instead. I know that sounds ridiculous, but those were the kinds of combinations my mind had been trying on for size.

Now I realized the rest of my life was going to bear no resemblance to what had come before. I no longer had a likely future stretching before me, a comfortable path through the streets of Dorf. Nor would I be following any of the getting-out-of-Dorf dreams I'd once nurtured. Instead, there was yawning blackness all around. And I was part of that dark unknown. What was I going to become?

I guess I was someone's slave.

And Graham. Goddamn it, I'd liked him. I could almost still feel his hand pressing into the small of my back. Damn.

I felt small and sad and used. And very alone. I was nothing to these people. They only wanted me for what they thought I could do for them. Which made sense, if the punishment for failure was death.

"What do you want from me?" I asked Kara.

"We need you to come to the mill," she answered instantly.

I could've guessed that one.

"Graham thought I wasn't ready. He thought I'd get hurt, like Callie."

Kara sighed. She went and pulled a milk crate out of the back of the van and sat down on it near me. Williams didn't move. He was little more than an area of darker darkness.

"Beth, you have to quit thinking that he has your best interests at heart. Graham has Graham's best interests at heart."

"So why wouldn't he want me there? Doesn't he want that strait thing closed?"

The question was met with silence.

"I don't get it. Why would he want it left open? Won't he get in trouble, too?"

"We don't know," Kara said. "It doesn't make a lot of sense. A strait sitting open can attract human attention in a number of ways. But it really seems like that's what he's doing. I mean, you know Callie's predictions are almost always accurate, right?"

"That's what you keep saying."

"I mean, our lives are on the line. So why didn't Graham rush you out to the strait the minute Callie told him your help was essential? It's weird."

I opened my mouth to object.

"Look," Kara cut in, holding up her fingers to count off her evidence. "First of all, he didn't send anyone up here to close the thing. Callie called him first, but he didn't do anything, so she called Williams. Williams called me. It's like Graham was just going to ignore it. Now he's been here three days, but he says he's here for you, and he hasn't tried to do anything about the strait. The fucker hasn't even gone out to look at it. He's the overseer for the Upper Midwest. Getting it closed should be the Number One priority for him. Instead, he's fucking around with a trainee."

"No offence," she added belatedly.

We all sat there for a moment, digesting. It did sound pretty damning.

Finally I said, "I don't understand how I could help with the strait. I mean, Callie's much more experienced than I am, and it nearly killed her. What could I possibly do?"

"Callie's so strong she can see pretty deep into an open strait. That's why Williams took her there—to see what it was stuck on. She tried, but she couldn't see the snag in this one. We're guessing you'll have better luck."

I felt like laughing, it seemed like such a random hope.

"Why on earth would you think that?"

"Did Graham tell you that the later your abilities manifest, the stronger you're going to end up being?"

She must've heard me stop breathing.

"Yeah, I was guessing he skipped that bit."

That was what Graham had meant when he mentioned my "potential." Kara was kind enough to let me sit there a while and come to grips with what she'd said. Again.

I wondered if it was too late to run. If I moved far away, then I could ignore any Seconds I saw and just live as a normal person. Right?

I thought about it and decided my best source of information was right in front of me.

"Could I get away from all this?" I asked, "Go somewhere far away and keep my head down?"

"It's probably too late for that," Kara said.

Her voice held a note of sympathy.

"You have to understand that they'll want you back really bad, since you have a lot of potential. We all know what you look like, and if they sent one of us after you, we'd have no choice. And if they know about your friends and family, they'll use them to bring you back."

Well, there went that idea. I might as well sign death warrants for Ben and the girls. Janie, too.

Still, it didn't mean I had to go to the mill. Burned Callie flashed through my mind. I could still refuse.

Or maybe not. If successfully following orders was the only way to stay alive, maybe I had to throw my lot in with Kara and Williams and help them do what they'd been ordered to do.

Or I could stick with Graham. But getting wrapped up in whatever game he was playing seemed more dangerous than fire. If I had such potential in these people's eyes, I might become a bargaining chip as Graham tried to meet his goals, whatever they were.

"If I go to the fire with you, how will you keep me safe? I'm, you know … defenseless."

I hated to say it, but it was god's own truth.

Kara's voice brimmed with relief. "You'll be safe if you pay attention and do what Williams says."

Williams. Damn it. "Williams" and "safe" didn't belong in the same world, much less the same sentence.

"What happened to Callie, that was an accident," Kara continued. "She was trying to get a better look, and she walked through his barrier. She's stronger than he is, so it didn't hold her in."

"It was definitely my fault. I just wasn't paying attention," Callie said from behind me. I started, then wondered how long she'd been standing there listening. If she heard that her colleagues understood the other world in non-Christian terms, would it bother her?

"Williams can make different kinds of barriers—it's his gift," Kara said. "A protective one should be strong enough to withstand the fire at the mill. If he doesn't have quite enough juice, I'll be there to feed him some of mine."

So Kara would be coming with us. That made me feel marginally better.

"Okay," I said. "Okay, I'll go."

I felt like I was choosing the slower method of suicide. I hoped we left soon. If we didn't, I was going to chicken out.

Chapter 11

ONCE WE WERE in the van headed toward the mill, Callie started coaching me on what to look for in the open strait. She said openings sometimes "got snagged," which kept them from collapsing after use. The snags were generally visible in the opening, and once located, they could be unhitched from this end if you "grabbed the strait and shook it just right." No kidding, that's what she said.

Snags generally looked to her like a fold or wrinkle in fabric, she said, but some people thought they looked like spots of irritation on skin or like knots in a piece of wood. Basically, I should look for an anomaly. Once I found it, I should tell Williams exactly where the problem was and how big it looked, so he could grab the strait and close it.

When I asked exactly what caused the snags, she said it was "demons who had escaped Hell and were at large in the primordial deep." Neither Williams nor Kara contradicted her, but I suspected they would've offered a different explanation in private.

Even minus the religious stuff, none of it made a great deal of sense. I had trouble envisioning the physical relationship between the worlds and exactly how straits and openings connected them. I'd settled on an elevator-shaft analogy, with the worlds as different floors in a building, but when I ran it by Callie, she explained that the strait here didn't open into S-Em northern Wisconsin, or whatever this part of this continent was called over there. It might open into S-Em London or S-Em Antarctica—there was no way to know. Some straits could connect to just one location, and some could connect to more than one, but they were never just a straight shot between the same spot in both worlds.

I just nodded along and hoped it would suddenly make more sense when I actually saw it. If I actually saw it. I was still unconvinced on that front. They all seemed sure about my "potential," but I sure hadn't seen much sign of it. Maybe I'd luck out and the strait would be caught on a mouse.

"Do you have a phone I can use?" I asked the car at large. "I should call my brother. I was going to meet him at the mall."

"Yeah, sure," Kara said. She handed me a little flip phone. I had to call 411 to get Ben's number, which was sort of embarrassing. I rang his house, but no one picked up. He must still be trying to get the thing with Tiff sorted out. I left a message for him, telling him that my car had broken down on the way and apologizing.

Poor Ben. He was really having a rough time. Speaking of which ... Williams was driving, so I seized my courage in both hands and addressed his right shoulder.

"I want to know if you took Justine."

"Who's she?"

"My sister-in-law. She disappeared about the time you were getting out of police custody."

"Wasn't me."

He sounded thoughtful, though. Beside me, Kara perked up immediately.

"Is she a Second?"

"Of course not! She grew up right near me in Dorf."

Neither one of them replied, but Kara was clearly thinking.

Annoyed, I said, "Why would you even ask that? She's a normal woman. A great big bitch, yeah, but normal."

Kara answered. "Well, one thing we've wondered is whether the green man you photographed might be what came through the strait. Green men are bounty hunters—fucking good ones, too. If your sister-in-law took off right about then …"

"No, the picture I took …"

"Did you show her your pictures?" Williams asked.

That stopped me, and not just because it was a complete sentence.

"Yeah. I did."

It was hard to say the next words because I knew they'd latch onto them.

"She freaked out."

"What do you mean?" Kara said. "Don't leave anything out."

Exactly what I was afraid of: Kara sounded as keen as a hound on a three-legged squirrel.

I described my visit to Justine's house, how frightened she'd seemed, and how I'd gotten scared myself and had driven off.

"Damn," Williams said.

"Yeah, totally," Kara said.

"What?"

"That's textbook pre-sighted stuff—you couldn't see what she was, but you sensed her otherness, and it scared you. Used to happen to me all the time until I started sensing workings."

That was the kind of thing Graham had been talking about

on the way home from Denny's.

But seriously? Justine?

"Look, I know this stuff seems to fit together, but it's just not possible. I mean, I've known her as long as I can remember. She lived around the block from us. She babysat me when she was a teenager."

"A lot of Seconds can create very convincing disguises. Pretending to be a child wouldn't be hard."

I shook my head. "But I've never had that kind of reaction around her before, even though I have panic attacks constantly."

Kara shrugged. "That is strange, but I still think there's a good chance she's a Second."

"Callie," I said, "I'm sure you've met Justine plenty of times. You'd have noticed if she was different, right?"

Everyone in the car looked expectantly at Callie. She shifted uncomfortably.

"Beth is right—I've met Justine, and I never saw anything strange. If she's a demon, her true form is beyond my sight."

"Huh," Kara said. "Well, Callie's one of the strongest seers out there. If she didn't see anything, I guess there was nothing to see."

She didn't sound convinced, though.

"Well, I'm sure there's nothing weird about her. She's the most conventional person you could imagine. She's a house-wife. She never misses church. She goes to the gym four times a week and gets her hair highlighted once a month. She makes the nastiest-ass tuna casserole ..."

Suddenly the van lurched and started shuddering.

Williams said, "Blow-out," and pulled over onto the shoulder. For a few seconds, everyone sat stiffly in their seats, as though afraid. I didn't get it. These country highways did cause flat tires occasionally—sharp stuff sometimes fell off farmers' trucks.

We all got out and stood around while Williams changed the tire. Then we got back in. There was still a tension to the air that I didn't quite understand.

We started up again but hadn't gone more than twenty feet when another tire blew with a bang. This time Williams didn't pull over. Instead he put the van in reverse and hit the gas, even though we were obviously riding on the rim. He only paused once, putting on the hazards to let to another vehicle go around us. The other three were clearly worried, so I kept my mouth shut. After about a quarter mile, Williams did a U-turn and continued back the way we'd come. We went another mile before he finally pulled over.

"What was that about?" I asked.

"That was Graham," Kara said. "He must've gone to the mill."

"Graham can blow out tires?" I said, incredulous. I figured he had one of those so-called quirks, but the ability to cause flat tires was even quirkier than I'd imagined.

"Not exactly. Graham's gift is luck. He's the luckiest sonovabitch who ever lived. We just drove into his range, which is about a mile. He doesn't want you at the mill, and his luck is going to keep you from getting there. Goddamn it."

"You must be joking. Come on—that was a coincidence. Or not even: a box of nails probably fell out of someone's truck back there and scattered all over the road."

"Yeah, that's probably exactly what happened. But it happened because of Graham."

I shook my head. "Callie, are you on board with this?"

"Oh yes, Beth. What they're saying about Graham is absolutely true. I used to think it was a sign of his godliness, but I have my doubts, now. Perhaps he bargained with the enemy."

She shuddered.

"I'm sorry, but this sounds really paranoid."

"Didn't you have any weird experiences when you were with him? Like just happening to pocket-dial your boss while you're going behind his back?" Kara asked. "Cock-cankers, that sucked."

"Kara, don't be disgusting," Callie said.

I thought about it. I had tended to get interrupted by one thing or another when I tried to ask Graham questions. By his phone, for instance, or a cracked kettle. Or a car accident.

Sticky accelerator, the other driver had said. I felt cold.

"A couple years ago," Kara said, "I was on a job with this other Nolander named Kyle. Nice guy, but sort of dumb. Turned out he'd been doing half-workings to make fake lottery tickets. At first he was careful and just gave himself little wins. Then he got greedy, made himself a Powerball ticket. It was a big jackpot, and he got on the news. The boss got wind of it, put the hit out on him. Graham took it on. Anything to make himself look good, the bastard."

Kara made a disgusted sound, then continued.

"So, I didn't know about any of this, right? I'm with Kyle on this job, and Graham catches up with us in Des Moines. Now, Kyle might not have been the smartest guy, but he was strong. Double gifts: flight and fire. So the two of them square off, right? And Kyle comes rocketing at Graham with a fireball in each hand. Looks like he's moving way too fast for bad luck to catch him. Graham's just standing there like a dope. You know what happened?"

Kara paused for effect.

"A fucking 1959 Cadillac Eldorado fell out of the sky,

landed right on top of Kyle." She shook her head. "Right out of a blue sky. Damnedest thing I ever saw. When the police found him, they called a weather guy. Weather guy said the car must've been picked up in a tornado they'd had earlier that day a hundred miles away. Sure enough, it was registered to some old guy in Omaha. That's the kind of thing that happens when Graham's around."

"But you said his range was a mile, not a hundred miles."

"Kyle wasn't a hundred miles away, right? That's what counts."

"But he had to influence an event a hundred miles away to get the car up in the air."

Kara shrugged. "Yeah, I know. That's how it works, though. It's like he controls everything without even meaning to. There's probably something happening in Timbuktu right now that will end up helping him next week."

It was hard to believe. Really hard. But all these people believed it, and there was that car accident. I shuddered. Jesus.

"Well, this boss guy you mentioned will just have to come out here and take care of things himself," I said.

Kara snorted. "Come on, seriously? The Seconds never 'take care of things themselves.' If they went around doing workings all the time, they might get discovered, and you know what would have to happen then. That's why they have us. We're expendable."

"So what you're saying is that Graham's won? He's unbeatable?"

"Maybe not," Kara said. "We've thought before that someone with significantly more power might be able to evade the bad luck he sent their way, but we've never tested it out."

"Maybe now's the time for me to see if it's true," Callie said, sounding nervous.

"No," said Williams.

There was a finality to his voice that I sure didn't want to contest. Kara didn't say anything either.

We all thought about Graham for a while.

"So he's at the mill, and we can't get any closer to him—not in a car, not on foot, nothing?"

"That pretty much sums it up," Kara said. "He left Dorf for a while this afternoon, and Callie saw it was going to happen. Otherwise we never would've made it out of town ourselves to come get you. We were hoping he'd stay away, but I guess his luck brought him to the mill. Or maybe he figured out what we were doing and knew we'd try to bring you there. Unfortunately, he's not dumb."

We all sat there thinking again. Finally, I had an idea. The kind of idea you have when you're a new set of eyes looking at an old problem, maybe.

"What we need to do is change something so that it becomes lucky for him if we make it to the mill and unlucky if we don't," I said.

"I guess that would work," Kara said dubiously. "But how on earth could we do that? What he wants is the opposite of what we want."

"Well, you mentioned your boss—the guy who wanted Kyle killed? He sounds plenty dangerous. What if we called your boss up and told him that Graham might be trying to keep us from closing the strait? Then, if we close the strait after all and tell him Graham helped, maybe he'll be reassured. We'd be doing Graham a good turn by getting him out of trouble. His luck should be on our side. Maybe."

"So," Callie said, "we would get him into trouble, then try to get him out of that same trouble?"

"Yeah. And during the getting-him-out-of-trouble part,

we'll actually be on his side. Even if he doesn't know it."

There was a thoughtful silence.

Kara said, "Lord knows I hate Graham, but ratting him out ... I don't know. He's still one of us, not one of them."

Callie nodded. "He's a human being, with a chance at redemption." She paused. "However slight."

Williams said, "We have to close the strait," and everyone looked down.

I could see the writing on the wall, then—their own skins were on the line, and no one was going to make that kind of sacrifice. *And why should they?* I reminded myself. Graham was putting them in danger by making their task impossible. If he didn't care about their safety, why should they care about his?

"We could call Graham and threaten to rat him out," Kara suggested.

I thought about it.

"I don't think that'd work," I said. "If we're a threat to him, his luck will try to eliminate us, once we get in range. It doesn't really matter if he agrees to cooperate with us—he'll still be safer if we're not alive to tell tales, and his luck will act accordingly. The only way it works is to go ahead and change the game on him while we're out of his range."

Another silence followed, but I could tell it didn't have to do with thinking of other approaches.

Finally Kara said, "We'll have to call Lord Cordus," and shuddered.

"I will not speak to that creature," Callie said flatly. "Not for any reason."

"Well I sure as fuck am not calling him," Kara said.

"I will," Williams growled.

"No way," Kara said. "We'll all end up dead if you talk to him."

"Whatever. I'll do it," I said.

In for a dime, in for a dollar, right? I was going to be on the boss's radar soon enough, if I wasn't already. Why not get off on the right foot with him by warning him of a possible traitor?

"Beth," Kara said, sounding uncomfortable. "He's not like a human being. Talking to him—it's not easy."

"What do you mean?"

She squirmed in her seat. "He can play with your mind, make you feel what he wants. He goes in for sex games. It's pretty sick. God, even thinking about it is awful."

"That sounds like rape."

"Oh yeah. It is, totally. Except you want it while it's happening."

Jesus H. Christ.

"So how do you resist him?"

She looked like the thought had never even occurred to her.

"You'd have to have enough power, I guess. A shitload more than I have." She paused. "Sometimes you catch him on a good day. Then he's okay."

"He's never okay," Callie said flatly. "He's a demon among demons. I've never understood why he's involved with us."

I figured it couldn't be that bad. I wasn't sure where this Cordus guy was, but he wasn't close enough to rape me, even if he made me want him to.

"Look, let's just get it over with. If he makes me do something, you guys can handle it, right?"

I tried to leave the "something" as vague as possible in my mind.

There was a resounding silence.

Finally Kara said, "Yeah, sure we can. No problem."

She handed me her phone again, then undercut her own words by getting out of the van as fast as humanly possible.

An entry in her address book was highlighted. It read "Boss Man." I made the call.

"Kara Dolores Sanchez."

My god, his voice. I was instantly aroused. My hand slid toward my crotch. The urge to touch myself was overwhelming.

"It's Beth," I forced out.

There was a pause, during which I managed to drag my hand back. I might be able to imagine more embarrassing things than getting myself off in a car full of people, but not many.

"Elizabeth Joy Ryder," he said in a different tone. He still had a super-sexy voice, but not in a paranormal way.

"Yeah," I said, relaxing a bit. I heard Callie let out a breath, and even Williams's shoulder shifted, as though some tension were leaving him.

"I have been looking forward to speaking with you but did not expect the conversation to occur so soon. To what do I owe the pleasure of your call?"

I took a deep, steadying breath.

"Well, we think we're running into a little problem with the open strait near my town. We're not certain what's going on, so we thought we'd better seek your advice," I said as deferentially as I could.

"I see. What seems to be the problem?"

"A couple days ago, Callie had a premonition that I needed to go to the strait to help. She believes it's essential."

I had to stop myself from getting into how unlikely that seemed to me.

"So she and Williams and Kara have been trying to get me

out there, but we think Graham may be trying to stop us."

I tried to suppress the feeling that I was betraying a friend. *God, why had I kissed him? So stupid.*

I could feel the surprise on the other end.

After a moment, Cordus said, "What evidence can you offer to support your accusation?"

I got the sense that I'd better have some, and it'd better be good.

I reported the conversation I'd overheard between Callie and Graham, and my own conversation with Graham the next morning. I also said Graham had moved me back into my house in part to keep Callie from pressing me. Lastly I described Graham's intervention when Kara and Williams had tried to take me the night before and the two blow-outs we'd just had. I left out the fact that Graham hadn't been out to the mill himself since arriving. That seemed too damning. I didn't know if Graham's luck would help us if he was beyond saving.

"And how long has this strait been open?"

"Since last Friday, so nine days."

The silence on the other end was ominous.

Finally Cordus said, "Please wait a moment," and I heard him set the phone down.

A minute later, he came back on the line.

"I have tried to contact Mr. Ryzik. Apparently, he does not see fit to answer."

His voice was still sexy, but now it also made all the hair on my arms stand up. I realized I had hunched down in my seat, as if someone was shooting at me.

"We may have misunderstood his actions," I said hurriedly.

"I hope that you have, Miss Ryder. I will look into this matter. In the meantime, please do not endanger yourself by trying to approach Mr. Ryzik."

"We'll stay safe," I assured him.

"Good-bye, Miss Ryder. Thank you for calling."

He hung up. I closed Kara's phone and sat there a moment. I never wanted to meet that man. I'd rarely felt so certain about anything. Too bad I probably wasn't going to get my wish.

Williams rolled down his window and motioned to Kara, who got back in.

"How'd it go?" she asked nervously.

I described the call.

"I think we all need to put it firmly in our minds that we are going to the mill to save Graham. Graham is in big trouble with his boss, so we have to get there and help him."

There was a pregnant pause.

"Having a little trouble really feeling that one," Kara said.

Williams grunted, and Callie sighed.

"We have to do it, right? Otherwise a car's going to fall on us, or something."

Callie said, "What's the worst thing you've ever seen the demon do?" After a pause, "Now imagine him doing that to Graham."

Williams grunted.

"Yeah, got it," Kara said. "Good one, Callie."

Wow. And I knew how much Kara hated Graham. Now I really didn't want to meet Cordus.

Graham-saving thoughts firmly in mind, we started up and headed for the strait. Williams looked straight ahead and drove. The van groaned, squealed, and shuddered. He'd probably need a new one after the abuse we were heaping on it. The rest of us sat there swiveling our heads, looking for weird dangers bearing down on us. The yards ticked by. Nothing happened. Soon enough we were pulling into the mill parking lot.

We got out of the van. The parking lot was a jigsaw puzzle of broken asphalt and dead weeds. Flood lights, powered by a noisy generator, illuminated the area. Hoses crisscrossed the lot. It looked like the firefighters had uncovered the mill's old well and were pumping water out of it. Several fire trucks were parked in front of us, and a handful of firefighters had a hose trained on the smoldering pile of wreckage. Occasionally a gout of fire would erupt from the pile, and the hose would be trained on that area, only to be moved to a new spot a few minutes later.

"Aren't they going to see us?" I said.

"Williams has a barrier around us," Kara said. "Can't you feel it?"

I shook my head. Kara looked shocked.

"She wasn't seeing fully a few days ago," Williams said.

"But I am now," I said. "At least, I thought I was."

"Graham said he took her to St. Mary's, and she saw Bob," Callie said.

"Look at me," Williams said.

I looked at him. His Blandy McBlandsville disguise suddenly appeared. It wasn't quite as disconcerting as seeing Bob's disguise along with the real Bob—with Williams, at least there wasn't simultaneous presence and absence.

"You see it?"

"Yeah."

Williams held up his right hand.

"Can you sense this little working?"

"I don't know. I don't think so."

"What the hell?" Kara said, looking freaked out.

"What the fuck has Graham been doing with you all this time?" Williams said.

His sudden anger reminded me how much he scared me. I shrugged, trying to project submission.

"Today he had me looking for gifts."

"Goddamn it."

"John," Callie said, "you mustn't talk that way."

"Could someone please tell me what's going on?"

"Graham explained about seeing reality—workings and half-workings?" Kara asked.

"Yeah."

"You're seeing half-workings, but not the other."

An obvious answer occurred to me.

"Maybe that's because I'm really weak."

"No," Kara said. "That can't be it. No matter how weak you are, you always see both. The first caste means being sensitive to essence that's been worked."

Was I just ignoring something I should've noticed?

"What does the barrier look like?"

"Well, it's more a feeling than a seeing," Kara said. She glanced at Williams, uncomfortable. "This one's for protection as well as invisibility, so it feels like an area of safeness. Sort of warm and cozy. Like a bubble bath. No offense, Williams."

"I think it's like being buried in puppies," Callie said.

"Jesus Fucking Christ," Williams said.

"John!"

"I definitely don't feel anything like that," I said.

"So what do we do?" Kara said. "Give up? If she can't see workings, she can't see the strait."

"No, we still have to try," Callie said. "I know it doesn't make sense, but somehow she's going to help. I saw it."

"What if she walks through the barrier, like you did? She doesn't know where it is. Can you make one that contains as well as protects?"

"That'd weaken the protection—too risky. Fire turned out to be stronger than I thought it was, last time."

Williams turned and began rooting around in the back of the van. He came up with a rope, which he had me tie around my waist. He tied the other end around himself, leaving about five feet of slack between us.

"This'll keep you inside the barrier," he said. "Don't untie it."

He gave me a look that might've been stern on another face. On his, it looked like the wrath of god.

I was shaken. Obviously something was still wrong with me, and it was a big deal.

Taking a deep breath, I pushed the new issue to the back of my mind. Confronting was good, but I couldn't confront everything at once.

We turned back toward the wreckage and stood there for a minute, just taking it in. Slowly, my nerves settled. Kara had said Callie's gift was infallible. There must be some purpose to my being here, even if I was still broken.

"Anyone see Graham?" Kara asked.

"I don't," said Callie.

"We don't need to talk to him," I reminded them. "We just need to do what we can to help him."

Callie nodded and stepped forward. I caught Williams and Kara sharing a look behind her back.

"Callie, why don't you stay here and keep an eye on the van," Kara said.

Callie turned back to us, and I realized she was pale and shaking. Why hadn't I thought of it? She must be terrified. After what had happened to her, she shouldn't even be here.

"Thank you, Kara, but I need to come with you."

"You just think that, or you know it?" Williams asked.

"I know it."

He didn't look happy, but he said, "Okay. Let's go."

As a group, we moved toward the wreckage. We got within about a hundred feet of the pile before Graham stepped out from behind a fire truck. He looked angry. Maybe a little scared, too. My bet was that he'd never expected us to make it this far. He planted himself in front of us, clearly thinking his best offence was to force us to do something he didn't want us to do—walk past him.

But that's just what we did. I said, "We're here to help you," as we went by. He didn't respond but just watched, amazed, as we trooped past.

We stopped about twenty feet from the edge of the wreckage that used to be the old mill. I wasn't sure whether I should focus on Graham or the fire in front of me.

Callie said, "Can you see anything, Beth? The strait's right there."

She pointed at a cavelike area near the center of the wreckage, where some part of the structure hadn't collapsed completely.

"Try focusing really hard. It looks to me like a dark blue tube sock, all stretched out like a hose."

A tube sock? Seriously?

I took a couple steps forward and stared at the spot she'd indicated.

My movement seemed to shake Graham out of his paralysis. He made an angry sound and ran right at me.

Things happened fast. Callie lurched toward Williams, her hand stretched out. Before she could reach him, he grunted like he'd been punched and went down. Graham jumped over Williams and tackled me. I fell hard with Graham on top of me and hit my head on the pavement. A second later, I heard a loud sound, and Graham collapsed on me. Something warm and wet washed down the side of my face.

There was a moment when nothing moved. Dazed and terrified, I tried to figure out what was going on. Then I heard voices from my left—the firefighters, shouting. Graham's limp body was rolled off me, and I sat up, holding the back of my head. Kara knelt beside me and took my hand. My head stopped hurting. I looked around.

Graham was lying beside me. There was a pool of blood forming under his head. He was either unconscious or dead. A little bit to my right, Callie was helping Williams sit up. The big man was as white as a sheet. He looked sick and shaky. Cool.

"Fuck," he said. "No way he should've been that strong. That was as strong as I could make it, and he still broke through."

I looked at Graham, who hadn't moved. I touched the side of my face, and my fingers came away bloody.

"Did someone shoot him?"

"I think his own luck zapped him," Kara said, and laughed a little crazily. "There was an explosion in the wreckage. This thing flew out and hit him in the head."

She toed a dark hunk of metal that was lying at her feet.

"A fireman got hurt too."

Sure enough, the crew had dropped the hose and was helping one of their own across the lot toward the road. The injured man was hopping along. Maybe some debris had hit him in the leg.

"Come on. We still have to try with the strait," Callie said.

I looked around, trying to gather my wits.

"What should we do about Graham?" I said.

"Leave him," Williams said angrily.

"No, we're supposed to be helping him, remember? If we leave him to die of his injury, we're not helping him. The luck will turn against us."

"Not if he's dead, it won't," Williams said.

Kara sighed. "Too big a chance—he could do a lot of damage before he dies. I can heal the head injury but leave him unconscious."

She put her hands on him for a few seconds, then leaned back. I couldn't see any difference.

I had to admit that I didn't really want to see him wake up. Not right then, at any rate. His attack had really rattled me. He'd seemed like a pretty suave guy. I'd have expected some complex and nuanced assault—manipulation, a trick, something like that. Instead he'd just knocked me down like a schoolyard bully.

I gave myself a mental shake. It was dumb to spend time being disturbed about the specific way someone attacked you.

We got ourselves together. Williams staggered up, and Kara and Callie each took hold of one of his hands.

"What are you doing?"

"He needs help making a new barrier," Kara said. "Getting your working busted that way really takes it out of you."

"We can share our strength with others this way—skin-to-skin contact, plus intent," Callie said. "Kara and I don't have John's gift for barriers. Kara's keeping us unseen right now, but she can't protect us from the fire. John can, but he'll need to pull on our strength to do it."

"You should only do this with someone you trust," Kara added. "Once you open yourself to someone, it's pretty easy for them to pull more than you want them to."

Even thinking about doing that with Williams made me feel ill.

When they gave me the go-ahead, I stepped toward the wreckage. The fire was picking up again in the center, now that the firefighters had stopped hosing it down. I peered into the fire, trying to see past it.

"Don't try to look *through* it," Callie said from behind me. "Look *into* it. Look deep, not long."

I nodded, though the difference between looking "deep" and looking "long" didn't make a lot of sense to me.

"Remember, you're looking for a catch or hitch—an anomaly of some kind."

I tried to do as she said. I stared at the mound of twisted metal, trying to make out the shapes and colors, the lumps and cavities. I didn't see anything shaped like a tube, much less a tube with a hitch in it.

Fire sprang up in the spot I was studying. I watched it leap and shimmy like a living creature. I noticed its yellow and orange, and the pale white at its heart. There was more to it than what I was seeing, I realized. What I saw was a tiny outpost of a whole world of fire. It drew me. I wanted to see the whole. It was just a little ways away.

"That's good, Beth," Callie said shakily. "I think you're seeing it. When it pulls you, let your sight follow. It will probably look like a tunnel to you."

"It doesn't look like a tube or a tunnel. It doesn't look like anything."

"That's okay," she said. "Whatever it looks like, just try to find something out of place."

I again focused on the fire until the pulling feeling happened. I looked deeper. Flames suddenly engulfed me, but they didn't burn. Distantly, I could hear voices, but what held my attention was what I saw—not a tunnel, but an expanse of black, craggy ground, sloping gently upwards toward a low hump that convulsively spewed white-hot fire. Red embers spouted up from the white heat, settling in graceful arcs, and pale gray smoke drifted up against a black sky. Long tendrils of orange wound down the slope toward me, pooling here and there like fire-licked mirrors. A distant sound caught my attention—a clattering roar punctuated by sharp pops and booms. It swelled until I couldn't hear anything else. I began to feel heat on my face.

Was this what the strait looked like inside?

I was supposed to look for an anomaly. I glanced right and saw more of the same—blackness and fire. Then I looked to the left and saw the most surprising thing. A folding lawn chair was perched on the jagged rocks. In it sat a man, or rather, a man-shaped creature. His surface was similar to the black rock all around me, except it seemed to be riding on a molten core, which occasionally blossomed through a crack, then cooled and darkened. He was sizzling softly. Impossibly, he was reading a paperback. As I watched, he shifted and crossed his legs, then glanced up. His eyes narrowed and swept over and around me a few times before catching my gaze. A look of astonishment spread over his face. The book in his hands combusted in a puff of ash and smoke.

Frightened by the realization that he could see me, I pushed the heat and sound away and then pushed harder, reminding myself that I wasn't actually standing in that landscape. *It's just a picture in the fire, a picture in the fire*, I chanted in my head, *Go away, go away, go away*. Slowly the scene shrank and lost its sensory richness until it was just an image. I closed my eyes for a long second, and when I opened them, all I could see was smoldering wreckage. I couldn't see any flames.

I looked away and saw that things around me had changed.

Callie was still standing next to Williams, holding his hand, but Kara was lying at his feet. Williams himself looked pretty damn wobbly. The asphalt was slagged in an arc around us. I shivered. The fire had come for us, but Williams's barrier had held.

"Is Kara okay?"

"She will be," Callie said. "When the fire surged, John pulled enough to drain her. She'll be back to normal in a few days. Until then, she'll be weak and ill."

It was a damn good thing Callie had come with us, I realized. Williams had needed more than what Kara had.

"We need to back off," Williams said.

It took a while. He gripped Graham by the front of his shirt and dragged him along while keeping a hold on Callie with his other hand. I pulled Kara along by the ankles. She wasn't big, but I wasn't strong, so it was hard. We moved back about a hundred feet before Williams seemed to feel safe dropping the protective barrier.

I was bagged, and Williams looked even worse. Callie might not have been so tired physically, but I could see she was mentally exhausted. I didn't blame her—I couldn't imagine facing that fire again after what had happened to her. I went and sat next to her and took her hand.

"You were really brave to come back here," I told her.

She smiled and squeezed my hand.

Williams said, "What'd you see?"

I described it to them, including the guy in the lawn chair.

There wasn't a moment of stunned silence. There was a full minute of it.

Williams said, "Limu."

Finally Callie said, "You saw *through* the strait. You saw through and ..."

"Talk about that later," Williams interrupted. "We have to tell Cordus about Limu."

"Who's Limu?"

"That's who you saw," Callie said, sounding shaky. "Lord Cordus controls this part of the world. Lord Limu holds the Pacific Rim."

Williams said, "Call Cordus. Now."

"Graham has to do it," I said. "This was all supposed to be helping him, remember?"

"Fuck Graham. It's over. It doesn't matter."

"Oh my god, don't be so dense!" I said, my exhaustion making me forget who I was talking to. "If we were faking it, his luck wouldn't have helped us. But it did help us. That means we really were helping him. Now is the point when we can actually give that help, so we have to do it. From how the luck shook out, we already know what decision we make at this point. We're just following through with what we already know happens. Got it?"

Williams stilled and focused on me. I felt like one of those red dots from a laser sight had appeared right between my eyes.

Callie interceded. "I don't really understand it either, John, but I think we should let Beth decide. It was her idea, and it did work."

If looks could kill, the one Williams gave me would have. It also would have cremated me and scattered my ashes at sea.

I didn't realize I'd tightened my grip on Callie until she started saying my name and patting my arm with her other hand.

"Sorry," I said, letting go.

Don't make him angry, I reminded myself. Maybe he wouldn't hurt me with Callie right here, but she wasn't going to be with me 24/7.

After an uncomfortable silence, I said, "So, any ideas on how to wake Graham?"

Williams hauled himself up and, ignoring Callie's protests, came over and gave Graham a couple kicks. Jesus, what a monster.

Graham groaned and rolled over, holding his side. Then he saw us, and froze. He looked entirely different than the person I'd come to know over the past few days. The confident, friendly, flirty guy was gone. What I was seeing now was a man stripped of everything—horrified, desperate, like an animal in a trap. It hurt seeing him like that, however much of a liar and user he might be. At that moment, for the first time, I really wanted to protect him.

"Here's what's happening," I told him. "Lord Cordus suspects you of scheming to keep the strait open. You are so deep on his shit list I'm surprised you can breathe. We looked into the opening and saw the other end. We're going to let you call and tell Lord Cordus about our success. You can take credit for managing the operation."

"Tell him it's closed," Williams added.

Was it really? I hadn't realized. I looked back at the wreckage. I couldn't see any flames, but the firefighters were dousing it again. Maybe they'd finally knocked it back.

Graham knelt there silently for a while, eyes shifting back and forth among us.

"Why are you letting me call him?" he finally said.

"Because we're just that nice." No reason to clue him in on his gift's loophole.

He thought about it, then nodded. Clearly he didn't see a way out. Being on Cordus's shit list must be very bad indeed.

I rolled Kara over, got her phone out of her pocket, and

scrolled down to "Boss Man."

"Tell him you were waiting for us here, and that when we got here, you coached me on looking into the strait. Then hand the phone to me, and I'll tell him what I saw."

I hit "send" and handed him the phone.

Pale and shaking, he put it to his ear. When Cordus answered, though, Graham's voice was steady. I watched, a little nauseated, as he smoothly constructed a version of events in which he'd done no wrong. He mentioned the green man, as though he'd seen my photo and made the connection himself. Then he brought up Justine. Clearly he'd been thinking along the same lines Williams and Kara had—bounty-hunter shows up in town, local woman disappears, bingo. All that stuff about checking with his contacts had been bullshit. He'd never believed Williams was the kidnapper.

When he was done, Graham handed the phone to me without meeting my eyes.

"Elizabeth Joy Ryder," a super-sexy voice murmured in my ear.

My pulse went through the roof.

"I am most impressed. You seem to have found a way to turn Mr. Ryzik's talent against him."

Huh. Cordus had a pretty good bullshit meter.

"I will give Mr. Ryzik a second chance, but only because your strategy has obligated me to do so," he said. "I must ask you not to thus obligate me again. The consequences of such an action would not please you. In addition, I directed you not to approach Mr. Ryzik, and yet there you are, within arm's reach of him. Reliability is as important to me as results, Miss Ryder. Do you understand?"

I squeezed a "yes sir" past the lump in my throat.

"Now," he said, "please describe to me exactly what you

saw."

I gave him a detailed account of the place I had seen in the flame. I also described the guy in the lawn chair. I added that Williams said the strait was closed.

He absorbed what I said in silence, then asked, "You heard the sound of the volcano and felt its heat. Is that correct?"

"Yes, especially toward the end. The experience seemed to be getting ... I don't know. Richer. Closer. Also, the guy there saw me. I'm not sure how, exactly, but he knew I was there."

"Did he speak to you?"

"No. He seemed surprised, though. He burned up his book."

"Most interesting," Cordus said softly.

"Miss Ryder," he said after a few moments, "Mr. Ryzik's identification of the green man's quarry is likely correct."

"Oh," I said, shocked to my depths. "So it's true? She really might be ... one of you?"

"In the sense you intend, yes."

He paused. He certainly had a measured, careful approach to conversation.

Finally he asked, "Has Mrs. McCallister received any premonitions regarding Mrs. Ryder's status or location?"

Mrs. McCallister? That was news to me.

"Not that she's mentioned. Do you want to speak to her?"

"I do not believe that would be productive. Should her ability shed additional light on the situation, however, I would appreciate a call."

"Okay," I said, already feeling like an informant.

"Your team may retire and rest. I will be in touch soon with further instructions. Before we disconnect, however, I must speak with Mr. Ryzik once more."

"Okay. Here he is."

"Thank you, Miss Ryder."

I passed the phone to Graham, who paled noticeably. He said, "Yes, Lord Cordus?" then held the phone to his ear for about thirty seconds, just listening. At last he said, "Yes, I do," then closed the phone and sat there staring out into the darkness and shaking. I was really glad not to have been privy to whatever Cordus had said. I had a feeling it would've made "threatening" sound like a day at the beach.

Once we'd recovered a little longer, Williams drove the damaged van into the brush at the edge of the parking lot and set a barrier around it that, according to Callie, would keep it invisible to regular people for at least a few days.

"How're we going to get home?" I asked.

"There's a working over there," Callie said, pointing to the other side of lot. "It's probably a barrier hiding Graham's car."

She glanced at Graham, who nodded, looking a little confused. He must've been wondering why I hadn't noticed it myself.

Williams picked up Kara, and we all walked to the other side of the lot. As we approached the edge, my car appeared right in front of us.

We got in and headed back to Callie's.

When we arrived, Callie had Williams put Kara in the center of her king-sized bed. Then she and I crawled in on either side of her and slept like stones until morning.

Chapter 12

UNFORTUNATELY, BY "MORNING" I mean "very early morning." That's when Kara woke up, lunged over me, and vomited. She got most of it on the floor. Then she flopped back with a groan.

"Fucking Williams. Goddamn fucking Williams fucking asshole ..." She drifted back to sleep.

From the other side of her, Callie propped herself up and frowned at me. "I wish Kara didn't use language like that. Taking the Lord's name in vain is wrong."

I nodded, filing away for future reference that "goddamn" was a big no-no around Callie. Then I wormed my way out of bed, trying not to touch anything Kara might've hit.

I ended up touching it anyway when I cleaned it up a few minutes later. Whatever. Kara'd probably cleaned up what I left in the hallway a few days back.

When I was done showering, Callie had gone back to sleep. I quietly headed for coffee.

Graham was sitting in the kitchen. Damn. Why was he still with us? I'd have thought Cordus would've wanted to keep an eye on him or something. It seemed impossible that he was just going to keep hanging out with his old crew. Talk about painful and awkward for everyone.

He looked up at me with dead eyes. It took him a while to speak. It was like he'd forgotten how.

"It was your idea, wasn't it? Calling Cordus."

I didn't see much point in lying.

"Yeah."

I waited for him to react, to get angry, but he didn't say anything.

"Kara said they could be killed if they failed to close the strait. You seemed to be putting all our lives at risk."

Again he didn't say anything for a long time, just looked at me. Then he looked down at his hands.

"Callie finding the strait and calling Williams, Williams finding you, Williams calling in Kara—none of that should've happened. No one was supposed to know anything about it. No one was supposed to come here. No one was supposed to be in danger. That's how it should've gone. Things always go the way they're supposed to. Well, almost always."

Huh. Maybe Callie had ended up testing that Graham-luck-evasion hypothesis after all, without realizing it.

"Why were you trying to keep the strait open?"

Graham shook his head. Some secrets were staying secret.

"What're you going to do now?"

He shrugged. "Same thing I was doing before."

But the look he gave me was so empty my throat tightened. I guess he'd gotten the same sense from Cordus that I had: second chances were pretty much in name only.

I really wished I hadn't kissed him. I wondered how many more times I'd have that thought.

I made coffee for both of us and sat down. He took a sip or two, then seemed to forget about it and just sat there. I watched him. The day's first sunlight came through the crack between the window blinds and touched his hair.

"Why did you lie to me?"

I hadn't meant to ask that. It just popped out.

He looked up at me. For a moment, he looked much older than his years. When he finally spoke, he sounded tired.

"What we do, it's ugly. It's easier if you ease new people into it instead of dumping the whole truth on them in one go."

"Oh yeah? Easier for who?"

He looked away, effectively silenced.

"Graham …"

"Just let it go, Elizabeth. There's nothing I can say to you that'll make it better."

I sat there, surprised and saddened. I wished I understood.

"Beth," I said.

He looked up at me, confused.

"No one who really knows me calls me 'Elizabeth.'"

He smiled a little, accepting my olive branch, then looked back down at his cup.

Seeing an opportunity to escape, I took my coffee out to the living room and curled up on the couch to look out the window.

Now that I had no trainer to ask, I was full of questions.

Why would Graham betray Cordus? If we were all little more than slaves, it seemed like a huge risk.

What about the lava man on the lawn chair? Limu. The boss of another region, Callie had said. One of Cordus's rivals, maybe. Was Graham working with him?

Was Justine truly a Second, and was she being hunted by the person I'd photographed? Cordus seemed to think so, and he should know, right?

If she was, did Ben know? What about the kids? Were they really Ben's children?

And what was wrong with me, anyway? One moment I couldn't see some basic thing the others expected me to see, and the next I saw more than I should—all the way into the other world, if I'd understood Callie right.

Trailing along like someone's forgotten kid brother, one last question came into my head. Was Bob really dead?

Well, there was one I might be able to answer.

I got my car keys and headed out the door, moving cautiously until I was sure Williams's barrier was gone.

Okay, Bob, I thought, getting in the Le Mans, *I'm coming for that chat, like I promised.*

🌿

I sat down on a slanted stone bench near the sad "Daught." monument and took a deep, steadying breath.

Time had paid no attention to my personal drama. Early April had shaded into middle of the month. Today was the first day we'd had where I really smelled spring. It was earthy and wet and promised renewal.

I'd made several full circuits of the cemetery. There was no sign of Bob.

I felt a strong sense of loss—far more than what I'd feel for some human citizen of Dorf I'd met once and talked to for a few minutes. It was mixed liberally with guilt and anger. If he was dead, it was because of me.

I reminded myself that while Bob's presence would've proven he was alive, his absence didn't prove he was dead.

Then again, Williams didn't strike me as the kind of person who'd bother lying.

It'd been silly to come. I'd wanted to escape Callie's house, with all its tensions and sadness, but really, escape was impossible. The whole situation was dreadful.

I looked down at my hands. My nails had gotten too long. Despite the hot shower I'd taken an hour ago, there was crud under them. I set about cleaning them with my thumbnail. Depressing thoughts crowded into my mind.

When I'd looked into the strait, I'd done something that had surprised the others. Unless it turned out to be something bad, it would probably make me more desirable to Cordus than I had been before. And I got the idea that my late development had already made me a hot commodity.

So, what would happen to me? What would they try to make me do?

What we do is ugly.

How ugly?

I didn't just need a bunch of questions answered, I realized. What I needed was good advice. Even if Graham hadn't turned out to be a liar, I still wouldn't have trusted him to advise me, not when I'd only known him a few days. Kara seemed nice, but maybe not stable and seasoned enough to give clear-eyed guidance. Callie couldn't help me either. Because she read all this stuff through her own religious beliefs, she had no idea what she was actually participating in. Maybe that's what she needed to do to survive, but it wasn't going to work for me.

That left me with no idea what my goals should be.

For instance, what should I do about Justine? I felt responsible for her because she was my nieces' mother. But if she was bad news, then trying to save her might be the wrong choice. On the other hand, if she was an innocent person being hunted by this green-man creature, then I had to try to help her. Then again, if what Kara said was accurate, I wouldn't really have any choices to make about Justine, anyway. I'd be doing whatever Cordus told me to do.

I'd decided to confront my new reality, but really I was still just reacting to what came down the pike. I felt like a victim, and I didn't know how to change that dynamic.

I was sitting there cultivating a headache when someone spoke my first name, and I just about fell off the bench. Looking over my shoulder, I found an African American woman standing behind me. She had long black hair gathered in a ponytail and was dressed in a flattering pair of dark jeans, a tan tank, and a jaunty little jacket that came down to just below her breasts. It was made out of some kind of exotic-looking brown fur. She was older than me and extraordinarily beautiful.

I stood up nervously. She was a few inches taller than me, but then again her boots had heels. I realized I was staring and flushed.

She looked me over with a neutral expression. Then she said, "I'm Zion. Lord Cordus sent me up here to join your team. I'm a tracker."

"Oh," I said.

Then, because I couldn't think of an indirect, non-embarrassing way to ask, I said, "What are you supposed to track?"

She looked at me like I was the slow kid in class. "A Second who's been living in this town under the alias of Justine Ryder, née Jenson."

"Oh, right. Of course."

I stood there wondering why she was talking to me instead of looking for Justine. Zion looked like she was just managing to keep herself from rolling her eyes.

"I'm told Justine Ryder's been masquerading as your sister-in-law. I need to you take me to her home so that I can get her scent."

"Her *scent?*"

What was this woman, a magical bloodhound or something?

Annoyance blossomed on Zion's face, and I quickly ran my memory backwards to make sure I hadn't said the "bloodhound" part aloud.

"Excuse me," she said in a carefully polite tone, "Given your age, it's hard to remember you're … uninformed. 'Scent' is trackers' shorthand for someone's essence trace."

"Okie-dokie, then," I said, getting annoyed myself.

It wasn't my fault I was "uninformed." If these people could get their act together and send me a trainer who did his job, I'd get informed as fast as I could.

"Your car or mine?" I said, probably a little snappishly.

We ended up in her car, but only after she'd taken a good long look at mine and found it wanting. Admittedly, the Le Mans was a little worse for wear. In contrast, Zion had a Porsche Panamera. I couldn't even imagine how much it cost.

❧

Ben was upset with me. He thought it was terrible that I hadn't shown up at the mall. I was suddenly glad I hadn't pulled up in my own car, since it was supposed to be in the shop. Ben also thought it was shockingly insensitive that I'd just left a message the night before and hadn't called back to make sure Tiff was okay. She was, fortunately, though she had made it out of the mall, after all. The cops had picked her up trying to hitchhike southeast on I-94.

Clearly, the situation had been a lot more serious than I had assumed. I was retroactively terrified. "Kidnapped, then out 'til 11:00 p.m. ogling a lava-man," was unfortunately off-limits as an excuse. I couldn't think of a reasonable substitute, so I spent a long time apologizing and talking about what an idiot I was.

The whole time, Zion wandered around the first storey, touching things. She was using a half-working disguise, I realized: I could see the weird doubleness of presence and absence about her, and Ben was clearly unaware of her. I had a hard time not glancing at her—getting chewed out by my big brother in front of a gorgeous and ultra-competent stranger was excruciating.

Eventually, Ben headed upstairs to hurry the girls along, since they'd have to leave for school soon. Zion drifted over to me.

"I'm having a hard time getting her scent. What I'm sensing seems human to me. Has another adult female been living here?"

"Not so far as I know. No, Ben would've mentioned it to me."

"I need to visit her bedroom. That's where her scent will be strongest."

"Okay. Let me offer to stay here with the youngest while Ben takes the other three to school."

Zion's eyes widened and darted toward the stairs.

"She has children? Why didn't you tell me that?"

"I'm sorry," I said sweetly, "I assumed you'd been fully briefed."

She glowered at me. "They may well be Nolanders. If so, they'll see through my disguise. I'll have to hide."

The thought of Ben's girls being like me came as a shock. I guess it made sense—if Justine was a Second, her kids would be half. That might mean they inherited some weirdness. It just hadn't occurred to me.

I headed up the stairs and told Ben I could stay with

Madisyn while he took the others to school. That pleased him, since Madisyn was still in her PJs and was ignoring the order to get dressed.

When she saw me, her face lit up.

"Aunt Beth! Nanny Hansen's doggie says you can find Mommy! I wanted to come tell you, but Daddy wouldn't let me."

I glanced at Ben, who was rubbing his forehead. Actually, he was rubbing his eyes.

"Oh, Ben," I said, and put my arms around him.

We stood there for a good while with Madisyn looking up at us and occasionally tugging on my pant leg and saying "doggie" in a loud whisper. The other kids gathered at the door and peeked in, looking sad and a little scared. Finally Ben pulled away from me and throatily told Tiff, Jazzy, and Lia to go get in the car. He followed them out without speaking to me. I didn't hear any shrieks from downstairs, so apparently Zion had gone unnoticed.

Once I heard the car pull out, I knelt down in front of Madisyn.

"Sweetie, do you think I should meet Nanny Hansen's doggie?"

"Yeah, okay!"

She took my hand and led me downstairs and out into the back yard. She looked around carefully, then crossed over to the fence separating Ben's yard from the neighbor's land to the west.

Whoever lived there—Mrs. Hansen, I guess—had a large, overgrown piece of property. Last year's dead grass was thigh-high in places and all gone to seed. In other spots the snow had packed it down into wet humps. A huge stand of sumac had taken over the back of the yard, and a thicket of honeysuckle covered another part. A big maple and a pine loomed over the small house itself, looking like they could take it out completely, given a big enough storm. Compared to Ben's neatly groomed lawn, it was a jungle.

Madisyn gathered herself. I half expected her to display some strange ability, but all she did was holler.

"Doggie! Doggie! Doggie!"

For several minutes, nothing happened. Just when I was sure nothing was going to happen, the sumac swayed gently, as though touched by wind. The honeysuckle rustled, then parted to expose the biggest dog I'd ever seen. It was at least as tall a wolfhound, but massively boned instead of leggy. It must've weighed more than three hundred pounds. I recalled that Madisyn had said its fur was glass. That could be the case, if glass were flexible and floaty. Whatever the animal's coat was made of, it was translucent and shone softly in the morning light. The creature's eyes were golden, like a wolf's.

It studied me for a while in silence, then approached the chain-link fence. Madisyn gave a little squeal and ran over, completely unafraid.

"Doggie!"

"Madisyn," the creature said.

I noticed that its mouth didn't move. I felt like I was hearing it in the normal way, though—not like it was speaking inside my head.

Madisyn stuck her little arms through the fence and buried her hands in the beast's coat.

"Hi, doggie. You're a good doggie. Good doggie."

The dog nosed Madisyn's arm. It seemed friendly enough. Slowly, I came over.

"Hello. I'm Madisyn's aunt. My name is Beth Ryder."

"I know you. You are interesting."

The look it gave me out of its unblinking golden eyes was unreadable.

"Madisyn told me you think I can find her mother, Justine."

"Yes," the creature said.

Madisyn didn't react to the dog's confirmation. She just ran her hands through its fur and murmured "doggie" under her breath.

"Madisyn, would you mind if I spoke to ...," and I hesitated. It hadn't introduced itself, and I was pretty sure it wasn't a dog. I decided to go with a pronoun and glanced down. "If I spoke to him alone for a minute?"

She looked up at me. "Grown-up stuff?"

"Yeah. It's important."

"Okay," she said with a sigh, and retreated to the back stoop. I watch her go, then turned back to the not-dog.

"I've told you my name. May I ask yours?"

"Call me Ghosteater."

I suppressed a shudder. Why couldn't this one have gone with something like "Bob"?

"Ghosteater, I'd like to ask you a question, but I'm afraid I'll offend you."

"You will not offend me."

I nodded. He didn't seem to have Bob's formal impulses.

"Do you know what my sister-in-law is, exactly? There's a tracker here with me, and she's having trouble sensing anything special about her. She says Justine feels like a human woman to her."

Ghosteater cocked his head.

"She is unfinished. Your tracker must seek fragment. That is how she will taste her quarry."

"Okay. Thank you very much."

The idea of "fragment" having a particular smell or essence

trace or whatever seemed weird to me. I hoped it would be enough to help Zion.

"I will ask you a question, now," the beast said.

That worried me a bit.

"When the man left you yesterday, where did he go?"

It took me a few seconds to compute.

"Do you mean Graham?"

"The one with golden hair."

How did he know about Graham? Had he been watching me? I wrestled down the impulse to ask. He'd answered my question. Fair's fair.

"I'm sorry, but I don't know where he went. One of the others, Kara, said he had left town, but that's all I know."

"He went east in a car."

That wasn't very helpful. Half the state was east of here.

"Well, we'd just come back from Rib Mountain when he dropped me off. Maybe he went back there. Maybe he'd accidentally left something behind."

Ghosteater looked at me for so long that I was sure he knew I'd given a bull-shit answer and was considering eating me. Finally, he just turned away.

I hurriedly added, "Thanks for being so kind to my niece."

Ghosteater paused and looked back at me over his shoulder.

"I am not kind."

Then he turned away again, and I saw that he had no paws. His massive legs just faded out at the bottom. He melted silently into the bushes.

Well. You couldn't get much higher on the creep-o-meter than that.

Suddenly the idea of Nanny Hansen living in that little overgrown house seemed unwise. I thought for a moment about knocking on her door and telling her to move the hell out because a monster was living in her backyard. But no. She wouldn't move. Instead, she would call the police and tell them a crazy woman was on her doorstep. Then Cordus's people would kill me for breaking the rules.

Sighing, I headed back to Madisyn. I took her hand and led her into the house. I turned on *Sesame Street* for her, then hurried upstairs to find Zion. I told her about Ghosteater and what he had said about looking for the scent of fragment. She looked at me like I was losing it, but she did sit down on Ben and Justine's bed and give it a try. After a few minutes, a look of surprise and comprehension washed across her face. She spent a minute just soaking it in with her eyes closed. Then she nodded, satisfied.

Just then, Ben got home, so I hurried downstairs with Zion following behind. I apologized again and took my leave. He nodded and patted me on the arm, clearly too worn out to keep chastising me, even though I deserved it. I left him trying to cajole Madisyn into taking off her PJs, the feet of which were now all wet. Hopefully he wouldn't notice and realize I couldn't even watch one of his kids for twenty minutes without muffing it up.

Chapter 13

GHOSTEATER WATCHED ME and Zion drive away. Then he slid back into the silence and began moving east. He wasn't the fastest of beasts, but he could run a very long way without tiring. His nose would tell him if Graham had gone to the ancient rock twice the day before. If he had, there was the interesting question of why.

Chapter 14

ZION AND I headed back to the cemetery to pick up my car. The Porsche purred grumpily through Dorf's little streets. I could almost hear it muttering, *I'm a supercar, not a golf-cart, damn it!* What did Zion do that she could afford a car like this? I'd never been in anything so nice.

"So, what do we do now? Get the others and go find Justine?"

"Yes. Then we take her to Lord Cordus. Her and you," she added, glancing over at me appraisingly.

Great. That was just great.

"Where does he live?"

"His court's in New York. He has an estate north of the city."

Dread washed through me. I didn't want to take Justine to Cordus. Who knows what he would do to her? And more importantly, I didn't want to see him myself. Meeting that man, or whatever he was, and spending time in his home was at the absolute bottom of my to-do list.

Damned if I could see a way out of it, though. If I tried to run, Williams could easily overpower me, and if I did manage to slip past him, Zion could find me. She'd already found me once—I hadn't told the others I'd be at the cemetery.

Ten minutes later, I pulled the Le Mans into Callie's driveway behind Zion's Porsche and then sat for a moment, watching her walk inside. I got out and followed her, feeling ignorant, poorly dressed, and anxious.

"... south-southeast, about fifty miles," Zion said as I came through the door and almost fell over some luggage. She was speaking to Williams, who was standing in the living room. Graham was sitting in the kitchen, toying with a coffee cup. I wondered if he'd moved at all since I'd left him there.

"Let's go," Williams said. He looked at me. "Get Kara."

I obeyed without even thinking about it. Callie was in the bedroom with Kara, who was sitting up in bed, looking ill.

"Hey, guys. A tracker named Zion showed up. She has a line on Justine, so we're leaving."

Kara groaned. "So long as I don't have to ride with Williams. I'm gonna fucking kill him."

"I'm sure he didn't mean to drain you," Callie said, looking upset. "The fire just came so suddenly."

"Yeah, well, he should've drawn more from you and less from me. Goddamn it. I feel like three-day-old shit." She sighed. "Okay, help me up."

Callie and I supported her out to the living room and set her down on the couch.

I thought about our travel options. There were six of us, and Justine would make seven, if we found her. Kara's ride was a decrepit motorcycle. Williams's van was back at the mill, trashed, and Graham's car was out of commission. If he'd gotten a rental replacement, I hadn't seen it out front. The

Panamera seated four. We'd have to take my car as well.

"Who wants to ride with me?"

"Me," said Kara immediately.

"I will," said Graham, getting up.

Great. Many, many hours of guilt and awkwardness. I looked at Callie.

"Oh," she said, looking uncomfortable. "I couldn't possibly go. There's far too much to do here. I have to get the Big Screen boycott up and running. I haven't put any time into that for the last week."

I stared at her in disbelief. She got to just stay here and pick back up with her normal life as Dorf's moral gadfly? I looked around the room. No one else looked at all surprised. Instead, Williams stepped forward and touched her arm.

"Thank you for letting us stay, Callie. And for helping with the strait."

I wouldn't have thought the man had one and a half vaguely gracious sentences in him.

"Yeah," Kara said, "Thanks. And it was good to see you."

Everyone trooped out. Over her protests, Williams just picked Kara up from the couch and carried her towards my car. I was left standing there with Callie.

"You're really not coming?"

I felt bereft. Callie might be a little nutty, but I was pretty sure she was a genuinely good and brave person. She might be the only one who was. I wanted to have her with me.

She looked down.

"I don't go to New York." She paused. "I suppose Lord Cordus regrets his fall, and that's why he works with us. But he still feels evil to me. I won't go near him."

I didn't understand why she got to make that choice. I said my goodbyes as graciously as I could, but I felt resentful.

✿

"So why does Callie get to stay home?" I asked, once we were on the road. "Why doesn't she have to suck it up and go deal with Lord Cordus, like the rest of us?"

No one said anything for a few seconds. I glanced over at Kara and saw her slumped against the door. She'd fallen back asleep.

Finally, from the back seat, Graham said, "Lord Cordus makes allowances for her."

"Why?"

"Her ability is very unusual. It's also quite useful, as you've seen," he said bitterly.

I realized he probably blamed Callie for his downfall—she was the one who'd called Williams, and Williams was the one who'd found me, and I was the one who'd ratted him out.

"But she's fragile," Graham continued. "If he wants to be able to use her, he has to be careful with her."

I guess that made sense. I wondered if I could masquerade as fragile and get away from Cordus that way. Probably not. I'd never been very good at pretending. Besides, most "fragile" people he probably just got rid of. Head cases were a lot of trouble, and it's not like I could see the future.

I chewed on it for a few minutes, then decided it was dumb to spend time envying Callie, even if she got to stay home. After all, I sure didn't envy whatever experiences had damaged her. It had sounded like rape and torture the one time she'd mentioned it. I shut up and drove.

✿

"Almost due west from here," Zion said.

We were all standing on the side of a small road a few miles north of Stevens Point, on the east side of the Wisconsin River. Well, not Kara. She was still asleep in my car.

Zion squinted. "She's less than half a mile away. She's asleep, I think. At least, she hasn't moved in a while."

Asleep or dead, I thought with a shudder. What on earth was Justine doing out here? The area was all marshland.

When we left Callie's, I'd followed Zion to the old mill. There were no firefighters in sight—I guess the strait really was closed. Williams had transferred some stuff from the back of the van into the Porsche. Then he'd set the van on fire. After that, we'd driven over to Wausau and headed south on 39. About fifteen minutes ago, we'd gotten off the highway and onto the small local roads. We'd gone as far west as they could take us. The rest of the way would have to be on foot.

For the first time I could remember, I wished it was still winter—wetlands were a lot easier when everything was frozen.

Zion and Williams opened the Porsche's trunk and started to suit up. Zion donned a chainmail vest. That was an eye-opener. Did she do her shopping at Renaissance fairs, or something?

Both armed themselves with knives and handguns. I would've guessed Williams would go for some big-dick gun like a Desert Eagle, but he had a pretty standard looking 9mm. Then he slid a scabbard onto his back and picked up a riot shotgun. Maybe that's where he kept his big stopping power.

"Graham," he said, as he started feeding cartridges into the shotgun. "No weapons."

Graham shrugged, as though the idea was beneath contempt.

"I don't carry weapons. Never needed them."

Williams shot him a look that said something like, *A real*

man *would carry anyway*. Or maybe, *Bet you never needed your cock either*.

There certainly was no love lost between those two.

"Mandatory pause for male posturing: check," I murmured. Then I asked aloud, "Is Kara going to be all right if we leave her here?"

Zion shot me an amused look. Guess my murmur was louder than I realized.

"Yeah. Williams will leave her shielded."

She stepped into the brush. Williams gestured for me to follow her. He came next, with Graham bringing up the rear.

First came a roadside ditch with almost a foot of icy-cold standing water. It came in over the tops of my boots. Then came a field of impenetrable waist-high bushes that seemed to have talons instead of twigs. Then a series of marshy oxbows. It sucked. I couldn't imagine why they hadn't left me in the car with Kara. I had no weapons and no abilities, and I wasn't particularly outdoorsy.

At least all the crashing around and swearing I did weren't audible—we passed several large flocks of ducks that ignored us completely. Apparently they couldn't see us, either. But whatever the others were doing to shield our presence, I couldn't sense it. What had happened at the mill hadn't fixed me.

Eventually Zion stopped.

"In there," she said, pointed to a small stand of aspens. The trunks were slender and densely packed. I had no idea how we were going to get through them. Or how Justine had.

We moved forward another twenty feet or so. Then Williams came to the front. He lifted a finger and drew a horizontal circle. Nothing happened, so far as I could tell.

"What did he do?" I asked Graham in a whisper.

"He put a barrier around the trees. She won't be able to get out."

Wow. Useful trick.

Graham was looking at me, puzzled. "Can't you sense it there?"

"Nope. I still can't see workings."

The look of consternation on his face bothered me. I turned away.

We advanced on the stand and almost reached it before something crashed out the far side. I couldn't see what it was at first, but eventually a terrified deer came running around toward us. It kept charging forward and then trying to leap away from the trees, only to hit some invisible wall, then picking itself up and trying again. Poor thing.

"Can't you let it out?"

Williams glanced over at Zion.

"I think ..." Zion hesitated. "I think that's actually her. Yes. Yes, that's her."

Justine could turn into a deer? I turned back to look again, then leaned over to Graham. Guess he was still the go-to guy for questions, in this crowd.

"That's a working, right? She's changed herself fully into a deer—that's why I can't see through it?"

"No," he said, watching the animal's increasingly desperate escape attempts. "It's not a working." He glanced at me, clearly at a loss. "So far as I can tell, it's just a deer."

"Me too," Zion said, "but that's what I've been tracking. It's her. How do we catch her?"

Williams pulled his shotgun out of its scabbard.

"Hey!"

He ignored me. I didn't have time to take more than a couple steps toward him before he raised the gun, aimed, and fired. The deer went down, bawling and thrashing. Then he waved a hand, and she stilled.

I stood there in disbelief. Why had he done that?

Williams walked over and began trussing the deer up with a coil of rope he produced from his jacket. I advanced slowly and saw that the deer was still alive. Her large, shining eye looked up at me, panicked. It took me a few seconds to speak without letting out the sob that was lurking somewhere inside.

"Why'd you shoot her? We're supposed to bring her in."

"Beanbag ammunition," he said, without bothering to look up at me.

I looked the deer over more closely. Her left shoulder was twitching violently, but I didn't see any wounds. Thank god.

I knelt down and took her head in my lap. I stroked her face, speaking softly to her.

"What are we going to do with her? We can't travel with her this way."

Williams sat back on his heels.

"Beats me."

He waved a hand over the deer, apparently releasing whatever barrier she'd been inside. She thrashed a few times, but all her legs were bound together, so she wasn't going anywhere.

"She knows you," Zion said. "See if you can get through to her."

Calling the deer "Justine" and asking her to change back didn't do anything. Telling her that her husband and children missed her didn't have any effect, either. Saying that we were there to help her wasn't any better.

We were all just gathered there, wracking our brains, when we heard a strange noise. Something like a laugh, but weird.

Williams drew the shotgun and turned to face the direction

we'd come from. Graham turned the other way. Looking perplexed, Zion drew her gun and faced out as well. I stayed down with the deer, out of the line of fire.

"There," Zion said, pointing into a tree about a hundred yards east. I could see something dark and hunched clinging to the trunk.

"Green man," Williams said.

"Son of a bitch," Zion swore, bring her gun around. "Why do I always get the FUBAR assignments?"

Suddenly the hair all over my body stood up. There was a flash and a deafening roar. The tree the green man was on exploded into burning splinters.

My god, had that been *lightning*? Out of a blue sky? I looked up and saw the leading edge of a massive, anvil-shaped storm cloud thousands of feet above us. It must have been moving really fast—it hadn't been visible a few minutes earlier.

Zion started shooting. The green man was skittering toward us on the ground, unharmed. It ran on two legs, but strangely hunched forward. Its movement had a spastic, random quality that turned my stomach. Lightning struck twice more. Each time the thing contorted itself out of harm's way.

I could finally see why it was called a green man—it looked dull black most of the time, but when the light caught its skin just right, it flashed brilliant green. The effect was like a hummingbird's gorget.

Zion came up empty and started reloading. Williams, who'd held back, started firing the shotgun. The green man evaded, twisting and moving bonelessly. Williams switched to his pistol.

The thing was really close. A huge, protuberant mouth full

of small, sharp teeth took up half its face. A thick gray tongue hung out, bobbing to the side of its head. Its nose was almost non-existent—just nostril slits. It was laughing, its eyes gleeful and insane.

Williams got off one last shot, and the thing jerked to the side, and then screeched and fell. Trying to dodge the bullet, it had stepped in a leg-hold trap. I processed the metallic clang a few seconds after the fact.

A big-game trap? Set out in the middle of a field on public land? What were the odds?

The thing lunged at us, slavering and cackling, but the trap jerked it back.

Williams said, "Stay together."

He scooped up the deer and started backing off. We all followed him, staying in a bunch. We got a couple hundred feet away before the green man stopped its mad dance long enough to bend down and figure out how to open the trap.

Williams dropped the deer and grabbed my hand.

I understood. He wanted to use my strength.

The green man or Williams? It should've been no contest. Nevertheless, fear surged through me. I fought the urge to struggle and tried to calm myself.

I felt him reach into me somehow. It was like I was a dog-food can, and a big, filthy mutt was sticking its tongue way down inside to get the last bits at the bottom. It was horrible. I held my breath and tried not to fight it. I felt him drag something out of me. Whatever it was didn't want to go. It hurt tremendously, like he was ripping part of my insides out.

He gestured. This time, I could feel the barrier. It materialized around us like an infinity of cobweb knotted together with extraordinary complexity. It throbbed with weight and menace, almost like a living thing. I'd never perceived something so extraordinary.

A second later, the green man launched into the barrier and rebounded explosively. Through Williams, I could feel the impact as physical pain, though I couldn't tell what part of me hurt. The green man landed about twenty feet back and flopped on the ground, clearly injured. It never stopped its crazy cackling. I bent over, feeling sick.

Williams jerked on my hand. "Offer it. Don't make me drag it out."

"I don't know how!"

"Let me do it," Zion said.

"You don't have enough."

"I'll do it," Graham said.

There was a heavy pause, as we all considered. Graham wasn't safe from the green man. Otherwise his luck wouldn't have come to bear, and it surely had—the leg-hold trap had to be him. He also wasn't strong enough to defeat it alone. The failed lightning strikes had to be him, too. Therefore, he needed us.

Apparently coming to the same conclusion, Williams reached for him and let me go. Thank god. The barrier faded from my perception.

We started moving again. Zion and I wrestled the deer along, which wasn't easy—it wasn't a big one, but it certainly weighed a hundred pounds. There was no sign of the green man pursuing us, but maybe that's because Williams kept the shield up the whole way.

When we reached the cars, we dragged Kara out of mine and put her in Zion's backseat. Then we stuffed the deer into my backseat. Williams took shotgun in my car, and we peeled out. I drove as fast as that little Le Mans would go.

The wheel vibrated in my hands. The temperature gauge was near the red. I'd been going between eighty and ninety for six hours. Even so, Zion kept surging ahead and then slowing down when we dropped too far behind. I was afraid the Le Mans wouldn't last much longer—if it had ever been built to go this fast, it wasn't up to it now.

I wished Graham was still in my car. I had some questions I wanted answered. No way was I asking Williams, who hadn't said a word.

As though he could hear me thinking about him, he turned from the window and leaned over toward me. My heart rate sped up, and I shrank away. He looked at the dashboard in front of me, then sat back. I relaxed.

I wish I weren't so scared of him, some part of my brain said. *I wish he weren't so scary*, the other part answered. Good point— it wasn't like I was being a wuss. He was genuinely terrifying.

He got out his phone and placed a call. Up ahead of us, I saw Zion bring her phone to her ear.

"Get off at the next rest stop," he said, then hung up.

We were somewhere in western Ohio. The next rest area came up in about fifteen miles. Zion exited and parked at the very edge of the lot. I pulled in beside her. She and Williams both opened their windows. Hers glided down smoothly. His squeaked as he cranked it open in fits and starts.

"Go get another vehicle," he said to Graham.

Graham got out. He looked a little pale. It had taken us almost fifty minutes to get back to the car with the deer in tow. Maybe he was feeling the strain of having helped power that strong a shield for that long. He walked slowly across the parking lot toward the building.

I saw with a pang that this stop had a Wendy's. When I was a kid, one of the things I'd wished for at every birthday was a Wendy's in Dorf. Mom explained that Dorf was just too small for a fast-food franchise, but I didn't really get it. I mean, I would go every day, right?

Graham was gone for about fifteen minutes. When he came back, he was driving a late-model minivan. He also had a big pile of Wendy's bags.

Well, that was one small upside.

"I am not leaving my car behind," Zion said.

Williams shrugged.

Knowing there was no way to argue for my car, I pulled it off onto the grass at the edge of the lot and got into middle row of the minivan with Kara. Williams settled the deer in the way-back, then got behind the wheel. Graham got shotgun. We pulled out, and Zion followed in the Porsche.

I wondered if Williams had put an invisi-shield around my car. Either way, I doubted I'd ever see it again. The maintenance people would start mowing the grass in a month or so, and when they did, they'd find it the hard way.

Kara, who'd woken up for the change of vehicles, glanced over at me.

"Tomorrow you should call and report it stolen."

"Yeah."

She and I rooted through the food and chose our poisons. I got a cheeseburger and fries.

"Kara, did Zion fill you in on what happened back there?"

"Yeah. In between all the swearing, I think I got most of the story. I'm glad I missed it. She's usually pretty cool about stuff, but she was shitting herself."

She grinned lopsidedly and looked a little like her old self. She must've needed the food.

"Do you think the green man is still following us?"

"Oh yeah. They never give up. Best trackers out there."

I couldn't suppress the shudder. "So what do we do?"

"Hope it was hurt bad enough that we got a good head start. It's not like they can fly or something. It'll have to follow us by car."

The thought of that spastic thing driving was unsettling.

"Can you tell me anything else about them?"

"Sure. They're body-snatchers. When they catch you, they spread themselves all over you like a second skin and sink right in. Once they're in you, they can control you. This one probably planned to catch Justine that way and then walk her right back through the open strait. At least, that's my guess." She shrugged. "I've never actually seen one. You're getting the textbook version of things."

She turned to the front seat.

"Anything to add, fuckface?"

Both men glanced back, which I thought was pretty funny. Neither one said anything.

"So it would've found the nearest person with a car and taken them over, then followed us?"

"Yep. And before you ask, switching cars like we did won't help."

"How can we get away from it, then?"

"We can't. We need to reach Lord Cordus or a Second allied with him who's strong enough to capture or kill it."

She settled back in her seat and shot an angry glance at the back of Williams's head.

"All right, seeing as how I was *drained*, I'm going back to sleep, now."

Someone touched me, and I jerked awake. It was Williams.

"Your turn," he said, holding out the keys.

Groggily, I got out. How long had we been driving? It was pitch black out. I checked my watch. It was after 10:00. The minivan's GPS said we were in central Pennsylvania, so we were pretty close.

"I have to pee," I said, embarrassed.

Williams jerked his head at the side of the road. I hesitated.

"I'll go with," Kara said, sliding gingerly out of her seat. "You'll probably have to help me."

For some reason, that made it less embarrassing.

It didn't make it any less scary, though. As soon as I went around the cars, all I could see ahead was darkness. Which I now knew contained monsters. You might think turning my back on all that night and dropping trou would've been a great "up yours!" moment, but instead it just scared me.

By the time we got back, people had shuffled around. Now Williams was driving Zion's car and Graham was riding with him. Zion had claimed shotgun in the minivan and was already almost asleep. Kara stretched out in the middle row, and I climbed into the driver's seat. I hoped there wasn't too much farther to go. From up here I wouldn't be able to check on the deer.

We started up. The Porsche pulled out first, and I followed. Driving the minivan hardly felt like driving. It was more like floating along on cloud. I had no problem hitting ninety and keeping it there.

Unfortunately, my enjoyment of the vehicle was short-lived. We went under an overpass, and something hit the roof with a crash, denting it way in, then swung down hard against the passenger side. The van rocked wildly to the right, and everything slowed down as the world tilted. Then the roof crunched again and we crashed back down onto all four wheels. Zion shouted something, but I couldn't understand her.

The roof peeled away with a weird tearing noise, and the air rushed in. Instinctively, I jammed both feet down on the brake. The antilock brakes kicked in with a stutter. Something large and dark flew off us and skidded down the road in front of me.

The green man.

"Go, go, go!" Zion shouted.

She wanted me to run it down.

It righted itself. Its dark form was hard to distinguish from the road, but I could see its teeth glimmering in the headlights, and patches of its skin blazed green as it moved.

I noticed it had talons. Rip-the-roof-off-your-car talons.

No way was I driving at that thing. It would tear the van apart. I cranked the wheel left and drove into the median. The minivan took it like a champ, bouncing over the uneven ground without tipping. We came out on the westbound side and I hit the gas.

I thought we'd made it. Then the van lurched and green man's head popped up outside what was left of Kara's window, like some sick jack-in-the-box, grinning and cackling. It was clinging to the side of the van. Kara yelled and brought her gun up, but the creature ducked and climbed back along the side. I could hear its claws ripping through the metal. Kara took a couple shots at it, then Zion started shooting toward the rear. The inside mirror was hanging broken, so I couldn't see where the thing was.

I yelled, "Don't shoot the deer!"

We were coming back to the underpass. I thought the green man had climbed around to the passenger side—I could see a dark shape in the outside mirror. I veered back into the median and aimed for the underpass's central pillar.

Zion looked forward and shouted, "Shit! Ryder!"

We reached the pillar. I was a little closer than I'd planned to be, so we not only lost the mirror, but also some paint.

"Did I get it?" I shouted.

"I don't see anything in the road," Zion shouted back.

"I think it's still on us!" Kara yelled, sounding panicked.

"Can you see it?"

"No!"

Shit. Plus we were driving the wrong way on the interstate. Good thing it was the middle of the night. A truck barreled past us, horn booming. No one was keeping up our invisi-shield, I guess.

I slammed on the brakes and turned the wheel, aiming to do one of those powerslide turns you see in the movies. Instead we spun out and ended up sideways, halfway off the shoulder. Heart pounding, I turned back onto the road and gunned it.

"Where is it?" I yelled.

Zion and Kara were huddled toward the center of the vehicle, one watching the passenger side and the other the driver's side. I glanced in the only mirror we still had, on the driver's side. Nothing along the outside of the car, there.

"It's in! It's in!" Kara shrieked.

"Get down!" Zion shouted, and opened fire.

Ears ringing, I risked a look back and saw the horrid thing flowing over the ruined rear window, right into the space where the deer was lying. I jerked the minivan into the median and stopped. We all piled out and ran around to the back of the van. Zion had her gun trained on what was left of the rear door. Kara gave her gun to me and got out her phone.

"Zion. Don't shoot her."

"Like hell I won't," she said, her voice shaking.

"I'm serious. That's my sister-in-law. Don't."

The Porsche roared up, and Williams and Graham jumped out.

Something moved inside the van, rocking it slightly. Then a dark shaped leapt out and hit the ground running. Williams reached out and the shape tumbled to the ground.

We all approached. It was the deer, but now it was the color of the green man—dull black, like a chalkboard, with shimmering patches of green where a passing headlight caught it just so. Williams had it encased in a sort of globe. I couldn't see the barrier itself, but the deer was all balled up.

Kara sat down heavily.

"Girl, that was some sick driving. Sick."

I hoped she meant "sick" in a good way.

Oddly, I didn't feel frightened. I remembered I hadn't felt afraid after the thing at the mill, either. Maybe it was because I'd been the one doing things instead of getting things done to me.

Graham and Williams turned to survey the minivan. They were holding hands. Oh my god, hilarious. I put both hands over my mouth to hold in the laughter. It was so not the time for that. If I pissed Williams off right now, I'd get to play battery instead of Graham.

The van was trashed, so we abandoned it. Williams stuffed the green-man-covered deer, still in its barrier, into the Porsche's trunk, which was already pretty full of gear. Then he and Graham got in back. I perched in between them, though there wasn't actually a seat there, just a space for drinks and doo-dads. Kara took the front passenger seat, and Zion drove.

"Sure not falling asleep anymore," she said, shaking her head. "Goddamn."

❦

Graham lasted about an hour. Then he started to look sick and faint. I held my hand out to Williams, absolutely dreading it.

"Just relax. Let it happen," he said impatiently.

I nodded, but the advice didn't really help. If anything, realizing that he was already annoyed with me made me tenser.

Some part of him slid into me and pulled something out. The barrier he was working sprang into my awareness, small and dense and rigid in the trunk of the car. He pulled more out of me. It hurt just as much as last time, only this time it didn't stop.

"Goddamn it," he growled, frustrated.

I tried to allow it, tried to be open. Lord knows, I didn't want Justine to get away any more than he did. But it seemed wholly out of my control. I couldn't tell what he was taking, so I couldn't release it to him.

It was beyond horrible—the pain, the sense of violation. Soon enough, I was sobbing uncontrollably.

Kara leaned back between the seats.

"Beth, I'm going to sedate you, okay?"

I nodded, hiccupping and gasping. She took the arm Williams wasn't holding and injected something. Almost immediately, I loosened. I slumped back against Graham and drifted, only vaguely aware of what was happening to me. I knew it was something bad, but it didn't seem to matter much anymore.

Chapter 15

I SURFACED SLOWLY. I was lying on a hard surface. Something was buzzing. Someone was bending over me. Focusing was a struggle. Annoying. I turned my face away. The floor was pleasantly cool and solid. My arms and legs felt heavy, immobile. There was a touch. Someone was touching me. I didn't want to be touched anymore. No more invasion, no more pain. I pushed away, whimpering. I felt myself held and began to struggle.

Suddenly, my head cleared. A strange man was bending over me, touching my face. He was the single most arresting person I'd ever seen. He had a languid, almost bored expression, but I also got the sense of tremendous energy running beneath the surface.

He was astonishingly beautiful—to the point of unreality. He was more like a work of art. Every lock of glossy black hair hung just so around his face. His mouth looked sculpted with light in mind, so that shadows would offset its shape. His nose was bold, faintly aquiline.

I looked into his eyes. Each brown iris contained a tawny starburst pattern, which shifted as his pupils contracted. His complexion was olive and completely even, like he'd not only never aged, but never had a pimple, never scratched a bug bite, never gotten razor burn.

He was no more human than the green man.

This must be Cordus.

I stared up at him, awestruck.

Finally, he looked away, releasing me.

"Have you stolen her capacity?" he asked.

That was definitely the super-sexy voice I'd heard on the phone. His tone reminded me of the one Graham had used when he confronted Williams and Kara in my living room—barely interested, yet menacing. So this was what Graham had been imitating. Palely.

"No, my Lord," Kara said from behind me. "She consented, but she didn't know how to share. It was hurting her, so I sedated her. She consented to that, too."

You couldn't mistake the fear in her voice.

There was one of those long pauses I remembered from talking to him on the phone. Then he looked back down at me.

"Is this true?"

I nodded.

I couldn't have spoken for the world. He terrified me in a way Williams didn't. With Williams, I was frightened of getting hurt, getting killed. Those were terrible things, but at least I could conceive of them. Cordus made me aware that I could suffer the unimaginable.

"Very well," he said.

Kara let out a shaky breath.

He straightened and moved away from me. I stood up and did a quick survey. I was in the grand entryway of what seemed to be a large, opulent house. Everything was white marble shot with pale gray. The central space was at least six-ty feet across. Matching staircases swept up either side. A massive silver chandelier sparkled above us, its tiny lights irregularly spaced. It was a beautiful room, but cold and impersonal.

Kara and Zion were standing behind me. Williams and Graham were standing behind them. Neither man looked happy to be there, but the similarity stopped there. Graham was trembling and looking down, clearly frightened. Williams, in contrast, was tracking Cordus like a wolf watching its prey for weakness. Boy, talk about getting things mixed up. Like a wolf stalking a T-rex.

The deer, still wearing the green man, was standing behind everyone, as though it had bolted for the door. It was clearly immobilized. Cordus walked over to it.

"A green man, hunting one of my people, within my territory. How singular. Your ambassador will have much to explain."

He gripped the loose skin at the deer's throat and just tore the green man off of it. The deer collapsed and lay still. For a few seconds, the green man hung there like a flayed deerskin. Then it shivered into its familiar shape. Cordus had it by the neck. It dangled from his fist, for a moment, then began squirming and snapping and hissing.

Its talons caught Cordus in the side.

He flinched, then smiled and said, "That was ill-advised, young one."

The green man brought its right hand up and flexed its clawed fingers. They were tipped with Cordus's blood.

Then the creature reached across its body and, screeching, dug a chunk of flesh out of its own left arm. It dropped the tissue on the floor with a wet plop and dug out another piece.

I watched, horrified.

"Why is Lord Limu hunting this individual?" Cordus asked,

drawing the green man's face close.

It continued mutilating its own arm, writhing and scream-ing as it did so. With a terrible shock, I realized Cordus was forcing the creature to injure itself. I swallowed convulsively, struggling not to throw up on that nice marble floor.

Cordus gazed into the green man's crazed eyes for several long minutes as it tore away chunk after chunk of its arm, until only bones and ligaments remained. He seemed wholly unbothered by its agony.

Then it started in on its belly. Cordus set it down on the floor, and we all stood there, watching it kill itself. It ripped away almost its entire abdomen before it finally died, its hoarse screams fading into whimpers, then gurgling breaths, then silence.

The stench of blood and feces was overpowering. I couldn't believe what I'd just witnessed.

Cordus said, "Mr. Williams."

Williams made a gesture, and the green man's remains drew together into a ball. He bent and picked the mass up by whatever invisible netting was holding it together, and headed outside with it.

Cordus turned to us. If he'd found something out from the creature, he didn't share it.

"You may refresh yourselves and rest in your quarters. I shall speak with you in the morning."

Just as I was about to breathe a sigh of relief, he turned to me.

"Miss Ryder, you will attend me now."

❦

I stood watching Cordus examine the deer. He'd had it

carried to what looked like a guest bedroom and laid on the bed. He'd spent some minutes passing his hands over its body without actually touching it.

I found myself mesmerized by his fingers, which were long and graceful, like a pianist's. I was terrified of him but couldn't stop looking. My eyes strayed to his side, where his shirt was ripped and a little bloody. I wanted to touch him.

"She is alive, but weakened," he said, jolting me back to attention. "I assume her trip here was neither easy nor pleasant."

He turned to me.

"Miss Ryder, do you believe this animal to be your sister-in-law, Justine Jenson Ryder?"

God, I was going to have to talk to him.

"Um, I don't know."

I searched for something else to say.

"Zion was sure it was her."

"I sense only an animal. *Odocoileus virginianus*, to be exact."

He tilted his head to one side and studied me.

"Why was Zion so certain?"

Haltingly, I told him about taking Zion to Ben's house, and about her inability to sense anything other than a human woman there until I passed on the advice from Ghosteater.

Cordus observed me again in silence.

Finally he said, "'Unfinished' and 'fragment'? The beast used those words, specifically?"

"I think so. That's what I remember, anyway."

"Fascinating," he murmured, turning back to the deer.

He passed his hands over it once more without touching it and then reached down and cupped its nose in his palm.

The reaction was sudden and violent. The deer's eyes shot open and it took a great, shuddering breath. Then it exploded into hundreds of small blue spheres that looked soft, almost fluid, like globules of paint. A few more spheres popped into existence, then all of them regrouped and became Justine. She lay naked on the bed, moaning groggily. The entire transformation took maybe three seconds and made no sound whatsoever.

Slowly, I got up off the floor. I didn't feel too bad about my reaction. Even Cordus had taken a quick step back when the deer exploded. He stood there, looking down and rubbing his chin. No more bored look—I could see his eyes tracking back and forth. He was thinking furiously.

After a few seconds, he went to Justine and touched her arm. She relaxed into unconsciousness. Then he turned to me.

"Elizabeth Joy Ryder, I charge you to reveal nothing of what you have seen here. You will not speak or sing of it or depict it in a work of art. You will not encourage another to guess at it. You will not allude to it indirectly through the use of analogy or any other figure of speech. You will take no action that you suspect might violate this charge, even if I have not specifically forbade that action herein."

All that seemed to call for a formal response, so I said, "I understand."

He stared at me. "You must not only understand the charge, Miss Ryder, but agree to abide by it."

"Right. Yes, I agree," I said, flustered.

He looked around. "I shall have a second bed brought to this room. I am certain Mrs. Ryder will be confused and frightened when she wakes. Perhaps it will help if she is greeted by a familiar face."

"Okay," I said, "but she doesn't like me. I don't know how helpful it'll be to have me here."

I flushed and looked down, annoyed with myself. Why had

I told him that? I didn't want him to know any more about me than he already did.

"Why does she dislike you?"

I shrugged. "Jealous of the time her husband spends with me? I don't know. It doesn't matter."

He did the head-tilt thing again.

"Perhaps she recognized you for what you are and feared you would reveal her."

That hadn't occurred to me. Huh.

"I shall leave you for the night. Members of my household will see to your needs. Until tomorrow."

He inclined his head, then turned and walked out.

I let out a long breath. Well. That hadn't been nearly as bad as I thought it would be.

Then again, the green man probably would have disagreed.

🍃

Cordus wasn't entirely right about Justine. She was confused when she woke up, all right, but "angry" would have been more accurate than "frightened." She basically just sat up in bed and started screaming at me—since I was right there, clearly the whole thing was my fault. The central points of her tirade were that I was going to jail for kidnapping and that she was going to sue me.

I wasn't surprised. I also wasn't upset—with what I'd seen in the last week and a half, Justine in full threat display just wasn't disturbing anymore.

"So," I said, when I could finally get a word in, "you don't remember turning into a deer and running off into the woods?"

She stared at me, seemingly speechless.

"You're crazy. Oh my god. You've gone crazy."

Bunching a bed sheet around herself, she got up and backed toward the door, then felt around behind herself and turned the knob without taking her eyes off me. When it opened, she darted down the hall, yelling for help.

Too bad I couldn't scare everyone else off that effectively. It'd be nice to be feared instead of fearful, for a change.

I didn't bother going after her. I had a feeling people didn't leave Cordus's home without permission. For the moment, Justine wasn't my problem. Thank god.

I swung my legs over the side of the bed but jerked my feet up when they touched cold marble. I looked around the room, which I'd been too tired to take in the night before. It was large—big enough to hold two queen-sized beds, a large sitting area, a standing mirror, a desk, and several bookcases without feeling cramped. Daylight streamed through three tall, sheer-draped windows, giving the pale carpets and bedding a soft glow and making the quartz veins in the floor glitter. The dark woods of the furniture stood out richly against the pale fabrics.

In addition to the exit, the room had two doors. Padding over to one, I found a spacious walk-in closet. The other revealed a bathroom with two sinks and a tub separate from the shower. It also had something I guessed was a bidet. The floors, counters, and walls were marble.

I stood in the entrance to the bathroom, looking around and feeling uncomfortable. The place was luxurious, yes, but it felt impersonal, like a hotel. I noticed a thermostat on the wall and went over to kick it up a few degrees, but it was already set above room temperature.

A hot bath or shower would do the trick. And since Justine was busy running around shrieking, I got first use of the bathroom. I guess there are some benefits to having people think you're nuts.

I locked myself in, then drew a bath and eased in. The water was hot and the shape of the tub was perfect. Slowly, I warmed up. I can't say I totally relaxed, but it did feel nice.

My mind bounced around and settled on Graham. He'd been so scared the night before, standing in Cordus's foyer. I remembered the look on his face. He didn't think Cordus was going to give him a true second chance. You could see it.

But he'd really helped us on the way here. Without his weird luck, the green man would've caught Justine north of Stevens Point, maybe killing one of us in the process. If it'd gotten her then, Williams never would've been able to keep a shield on her long enough to reach Cordus. Apparently I could give him enough power for an hour or two, but for twelve? Surely not.

And Graham had nearly let Williams drain him, too. Well, maybe he didn't have a choice. Kara had said it was hard to limit what someone took, once you let them in.

I sighed and shifted in the tub. I felt bad about Graham. Yeah, he'd been up to something, but after what I'd seen Cordus do to the green man the night before, I wasn't sure I blamed him. If you worked for a monster, betraying your boss was understandable—maybe even laudable.

But the way Graham went about the betrayal endangered others, I reminded myself. That was profoundly selfish. I shouldn't make him out to be some noble freedom-fighter.

Then again, he hadn't intended to endanger anyone. He'd assumed no one would find out about the strait.

But what about lying to me and trying to seduce me? If he'd been on the up and up with me, the thing with the strait might seem more like a one-time lapse, less like a larger pattern of deceitfulness.

Damn.

The bath had relaxed me too much—it had let some stuff come up that I really would rather not have thought about. After all, what could I do?

There was a fluffy white robe hanging on the door. I got out and put it on. The fresh scent was comforting. I wondered if Graham had a fresh, fluffy robe in his room.

Jesus, my brain needed an "Escape" button.

When I came out, Justine was sitting on her bed, looking scared. A tall, muscular white woman was guarding the door. She looked to be in her late thirties, and I could see she'd lived through some serious injuries. One particularly nasty scar ran from her jaw up into her hairline, pulling her left eye a little askew. She was almost as tough-looking as Williams. Maybe she did the same kind of work. No wonder Justine looked scared.

When she spoke, though, she sounded calm and rational—not exactly friendly, but certainly not psychotic.

"I'm Gwen. You're Elizabeth?"

"Yeah. Hi."

She nodded civilly. "The staff brought both of you some breakfast and some clothes that should fit. Lord Cordus will visit you soon, so you'd both better eat and get dressed."

She gestured at the untouched breakfast tray on Justine's lap. A similar one was waiting on my bed.

"Cordus?" Justine said in a strange tone.

Gwen and I both turned to look at her. She'd visibly relaxed, and the expression on her face was sort of vacant.

"You know Lord Cordus?" I asked.

She frowned. "I don't know." Her eyes roved around, as though searching for some lost thing. "No," she decided, "but he sounds trustworthy."

She started tucking into her breakfast.

"Mmm, this is good."

I looked back at Gwen. "Did you tell her anything about Lord Cordus?"

She shook her head, looking a little perplexed.

Well, whatever. Cordus could work it out.

🖋

As it turned out, he couldn't. Justine seemed perfectly relaxed in his presence, even happy to see him, yet maintained that she'd never laid eyes on him. She claimed to have no memory of running away or of turning into a deer. The very idea clearly struck her as ludicrous. Such things were simply impossible, and even if they weren't, she was a normal woman—they were impossible for her.

And yet, when Cordus mentioned returning to Dorf, she blanched and said she couldn't.

On the other hand, she couldn't come up with a reason why not.

"I just can't," she said, shaking her head and trembling.

The three of us were perched in the suite's sitting area. Cordus had shown up about half an hour after I came out of the bathroom. Gwen had opened the door for him, then left. He'd questioned Justine extensively, while politely declining to answer any of her questions or to let her call Ben.

"Would you feel safer," Cordus said slowly, "if I were to tell you that the green man is dead?"

Justine again visibly relaxed but at the same time said, "Who's the green man?" A second later she said, "I still can't go home."

Then she accused me again of having kidnapped her and flirtatiously asked Cordus to have me arrested.

He sighed, then reached over and casually brushed his fingers over the back of Justine's hand. Instantly, she slumped over, asleep.

Okay, that was unnerving.

He sat back, legs crossed, and gently bounced his foot, thinking.

Finally he said, "I do not know what to make of Mrs. Ryder. I believe she is telling the truth when she denies any knowledge of me or of what she calls the 'supernatural,' yet her own body gives signs of the very knowledge she denies." He looked up at me. "What are your thoughts?"

"You're asking me?" I couldn't help sounding incredulous.

"Miss Ryder," he said with patience, "you are the only other person who witnessed Mrs. Ryder's transformation early this morning. Thus, you are uniquely positioned to help."

He leaned back again, waiting for my response.

I didn't think the transformation had told me anything except that Justine really was a Second, but I tried to put on my thinking cap. It was either that or sit there staring at him, and if I did that any longer, I was going to have to start thinking about why I was staring.

"Well, it sort of seems like someone erased her memory but didn't get everything. Is that possible?"

He steepled his fingers and watched me. Suddenly I felt like I was being tested.

"There are those who can manipulate memory," he said, "but none I know would do so incomplete a job."

I thought again.

"Well, she seems to be made of those blue ball things. What if they got put back together in the wrong order, and it messed up her memory?"

"An intriguing possibility," he said. He kept bouncing the foot, though, so I guessed I was expected to come up with a third idea.

"Maybe she's hypnotized herself not to remember certain things."

That sounded pretty lame, even to me, but Cordus looked thoughtful. He tapped his index fingers together in time with his bouncing foot for a while.

The way he used his body was striking. He seemed to cycle between rhythmic motions and intense, pointed stillness. The motion hypnotized me. Then I'd get pinned by the sudden, unexpected focusing of his attention.

Even as I had that thought, he uncrossed his legs and leaned forward, freezing me in place.

"None of your suggestions account for all the facets of the situation, Miss Ryder, but they are useful nonetheless."

I shifted uneasily under his gaze. Talk about lukewarm praise.

"So," I said, taking the bull by the horns, "what sort of being is she, exactly? I mean, the green man could spread itself all over someone like a second skin, but even it had flesh and blood inside when you ... um ..."

I just stopped, unable to come up with a phrase that didn't sound judgmental.

He looked at me for quite a while. I started to worry.

Finally he said, "Miss Ryder, you will need to learn that it is considered impolite to ask 'what sort of being' a Second might be. We are, each of us, what we are. Some of us are unique in our persons and abilities, while others, such as the green men, breed true and have produced a group of similar individuals."

I must have looked chastened, because he dismissed my

faux pas with a wave.

"I know that you do not yet understand such issues of etiquette. I sought to educate, not to criticize. To answer your question—which is, of course, quite relevant—Mrs. Ryder is likely among the unique. I have never encountered another like her."

"That said," he continued, "I am not old, even among human-derived Seconds, so there may be much I have not yet encountered."

I was surprised by his candor.

"Is it rude to ask someone's age, too?"

"Yes. Extremely."

An uncomfortable silence ensued.

After some time, he said, "Do you have cause to believe Mrs. Ryder is the biological mother of her children?"

"Maybe. Her youngest might be one of us," I said, remembering how Ghosteater had sought out Madisyn.

"By 'one of us,' do you mean the child is a Nolander?"

I nodded and tried to suppress a grimace. Kara hadn't made it up—they really did think of us as homeless floaters. The realization immediately shifted the dynamic between Cordus and me, reminding me that this was not a conversation between equals, or between teacher and student, or even between employer and employee. He was the master, and I had no rights.

"Nolanders account for slightly more than one in one hundred thousand human births," he continued, "so for another to appear in your small town is statistically unlikely. That said, the potential can run in families, so perhaps your brother is the source of your niece's ability."

"I guess."

I doubted it, though. I was pretty sure Ben couldn't do

anything out of the ordinary. If he could, he'd sure kept it quiet. But maybe the curse could skip a generation or only appeared in the family's women. Who knows?

After another bout of quiet thought, Cordus stood and told me he expected me to make a court appearance that evening. At first my mind jumped to the idea of legal proceedings, but then I remembered Zion mentioning he had a court, like a monarch. It would be hard to imagine something less up my alley.

"That sounds great, but I don't have anything to wear," I said, hoping for an easy out.

"My staff will prepare you appropriately."

I nodded, trying not to look grim.

"What about Justine?"

"She will be moved to another room and will remain there, under guard, until I understand why she prompted the green man's incursion into my lands."

What about Graham? I thought to myself, but I didn't say it.

He touched Justine to awaken her, then inclined his head politely to me and left.

Surprisingly, I only had to listen to Justine's accusations and complaints for fifteen minutes before Cordus's staffers showed up to move her out and get me ready. That didn't strike me as a good sign—he'd said I'd be going to court in the "evening," and it wasn't quite 2:00 in the afternoon. How much preparation did I need?

☙

The answer: a lot. Cordus's staff was more like an army. At least five people had been working on me, and it had been hours. They wove around one another like needles, darting in and out, stitching together a new me.

Six hours later, I had been given another bath. My hair had been cut, styled, and pinned in a loose up-do. My brows had been plucked. My finger- and toenails and cuticles had been shaped and, oddly, oiled lightly rather than polished. Every inch of my skin had been gone over with tweezers, exfoliators, and moisturizers.

I had been made up meticulously. My pale skin was completely even. Every blemish had been eradicated, not with makeup but by an actual healer—I guess Kara wasn't the only one with that gift. My lips were a muted pink, only a little different from their actual color. What at first seemed like an odd combination of smoky and light pink eye shadow made my gray eyes look arrestingly pale and strange, instead of boring.

The dress they put on me was like nothing I'd ever seen, much less worn. It was made mostly of muted black silk that hugged my upper torso, was belted loosely with a ribbon, then fell in a soft sheath to the floor. A high side slit showed a substantial amount of leg. The thin shoulder straps and the breast were a creamy sliver color and were finely detailed with delicate crystal-and-pearl florets. The unadorned black body of the dress made the decorative top stand out beautifully. The top, in turn, made me stand out quite nicely, pressing up my modest breasts and making the most of them with a tastefully small v-shaped central slit. It didn't so much show cleavage as suggest it.

The dress was matched with a pair of open-back black satin pumps with a slender t-strap. Small leaves created from tiny white gems were scattered down the central strap and across the tops of the toes. The shoes put me within a couple inches of six feet, which was cool. So long as I didn't fall down.

Despite the obvious expense of everything else, the sheer black thigh-highs were somehow the biggest shock. I'd never worn that kind of stocking before. They felt perverse—like they'd been invented for the sole purpose of letting you have sex without taking off a scrap of clothing.

The stockings exemplified how strange I felt as I stood in front of the mirror, ogling myself. If I'd seen yesterday, hanging on a wall somewhere, a framed picture of what I was seeing now, I truly wouldn't have recognized myself.

It was disconcerting.

In the last few days, I'd found out that I was someone different on the inside than I thought I was—potentially powerful but flawed, not free, maybe not mentally ill but maybe not quite human. Now who I thought I was on the outside had vanished as well. I mean, even if I came back to my room tonight, showered, and put my jeans and sweater back on, I'd always know I *could* look like this.

I turned this way and that. Maybe my womanly sensuality and power had been brought to the fore, giving me a whole new set of weapons.

Or maybe I'd just been gussied up into high-class arm candy.

I thought the latter was a lot more likely.

I heard a low whistle from the doorway and looked up. Kara and Zion had come to collect me. Both were gawking.

"You look really different," Zion finally said.

I wasn't sure it was a compliment.

Kara elbowed her.

"What Zion means is you look totally hot."

Zion shook her head. "Not 'hot.' 'Hot' sounds trashy. That isn't trashy."

A tailor was still on his knees making the last alterations to my dress. Zion and Kara stood there watching him work.

I could tell that neither of them had had the benefit of the full "staff" treatment. Kara was wearing a pretty little black cocktail dress and heels. The dress had a slender line of white ribbon running along the neckline. It looked really nice on her, showing off her great curves without revealing too much, but even I could tell it wasn't an expensive outfit, and it hadn't been custom fitted.

Zion had probably sunk quite a bit more into her vintage black flapper dress and strappy heels. Plus, she was wearing a truly extraordinary diamond barrette in her long hair. Given the Porsche, I was guessing the stones were real. The dress hung beautifully on her tall, lean frame. Strings of tiny black glass beads tinkled all over it as she moved. It was really striking. She also had a fur coat, whereas Kara's was wool.

But I had a feeling what I was wearing could buy the best house in Dorf. Maybe the second- and third-best houses, too, with the Porsche thrown in as a bonus. And there was all the special attention to my skin, hair, and makeup, too.

I started feeling like some 4-H kid's hog going to its first county fair. I'd been washed and brushed like crazy, and now I was going to be paraded around so the judges could assess the depth and leanness of my ham. I was Cordus's latest acquisition. He was going to show me off to my best advantage—or rather, to his best advantage.

Zion must've noticed the look on my face.

"Court appearances get easier after the first one."

I nodded, appreciating the effort. Zion was a tough customer. She probably didn't put on the comforting hat very often.

I noticed Kara didn't say anything, though she did give me a little smile and a shrug when I caught her eye. She looked pale, actually.

"You okay, Kara? Are you back to normal now?"

"Not really. I mean, I'm okay to be up and around, but I need another day or two to be a hundred percent."

The tailor finished working on the dress and went over to the huge rolling wardrobe he'd brought with him. He pulled out a coat made of some short, glossy black fur.

"Let's get this show on the road," Kara said, squaring her shoulders. The tailor helped me into the coat, and Zion, Kara, and I headed down the hall. After a few steps, I realized Kara was shaking. Either she was less well than she'd said, or she was terrified.

❧

I had imagined Cordus "held court" in some ballroom in the huge house we'd been staying in, but the coats suggested otherwise. Kara and Zion walked me down three floors, into an underground basement, through a tunnel, and then up into a massive garage. We found the Porsche and headed out. Several other cars had left just before us. I could see their tail lights winding downhill as we drove away from the house.

The drive was pleasant—mostly woodlands, with an occasional development or shopping center on the right.

As we drove, Kara gave me some pointers. Some seemed like commonsense: don't stare at Seconds; don't touch them; be polite and deferential. Some were less obvious: don't ask any questions, not even in making small talk; don't withdraw from a conversation without leave; never show surprise; don't eat or drink unless they do; don't turn your back on them unless you're at least ten feet away; don't agree to do anything for them.

"What if they ask me to point them to the bathroom or to get them a drink?" I said.

She shook her head. "Definitely don't get them anything to eat or drink. And they can find the bathroom on their own. Just say you don't know."

Zion added, "Say something like, 'I'll just ask Lord Cordus which of his wines he thinks you would like best.' That tells them you're onto their game. Unless they're looking for an excuse to get into it with him, they'll back down."

I'd never felt more like a rube. *If I get out of this alive*, I thought, *I'll be surprised*.

The traffic didn't seem heavy, though I knew we must be close to New York City. After about fifteen minutes, we crossed what Kara said was the G.W. Bridge, then took a highway that put the river out our right window. Unfortunately, I couldn't see much—just the twinkle of lights on the far side.

We went around a traffic circle and dove into the city proper. I'd never seen anything like it. The buildings pressed in on us from all sides, and there were cars everywhere, especially taxis. They seemed to have no sense of a safe distance from other vehicles. I was constantly sure one was going to clip us.

Although it was night, the streets were brightly illuminated. Everyone here must have to get black-out curtains for their windows.

Perhaps strangest to my eye was the lack of greenery. Small trees dotted the sidewalks, or lined the center median, but mostly it was stone atop stone, punctuated with metal. It all looked hard and alien.

Our destination turned out to be an imposing building, massive and boxy on the bottom, but topped with slender matching towers. It curved partway round a big traffic circle. The many lighted rectangular windows gave it a stacked look that reminded me of Legos.

We turned onto a street that ran along one side of the building. I'd thought from the front that it contained commercial space, but the entrance we pulled up to looked residential.

A valet, a buff young Asian guy, was waiting to take the car. He gave me an appreciative look as I stepped out. I felt myself blush.

"Hey, Koji," Zion said as she got out of the car. "Not going to scratch her up, are you?"

Koji eyeballed the Porsche. "Fugly car like that, you should thank me if I did."

"Huh. I hear envy."

"Not even. That thing looks like a station wagon."

Zion snorted. "You get your GT-R yet?"

"Naw. Almost ready to take the plunge, though. Any day now."

"Perfect car for you, Koji—a ricer for a ..."

"Don't say it, woman. Your hotness will not save you."

She grinned.

"Hey," she said, sobering up, "anything we should know?"

Koji glanced around, then said quietly, "Lady Innin's up there."

"Seriously?" Kara asked.

"Yep. Keep your heads down."

Zion grimaced. "Thanks."

At that point, Koji looked at me over Zion's shoulder, so

she turned and introduced me. I put my hand out to shake and blushed all over again when he swept it up dramatically and kissed it, then winked at me.

A doorman let us in. Zion and Kara seemed to know him, too, but didn't stop to chat. He took us into an elevator, using a special key to send it to a top floor.

After he stepped out, the doors closed and the elevator began to rise sluggishly. To pass the time, I asked if Koji and the doorman were Nolanders.

"Yeah," Zion said. "Couldn't you feel it when you touched Koji's hand?"

I shook my head.

"That's ... strange," Zion said, looking appalled.

"She also can't see workings," Kara said. "Halfings, yeah, but not workings. Weird, huh?"

"Yeah," Zion said. "I've never heard of that happening."

She looked me over, eyebrows knit. I felt like someone with a rare disease surrounded by astonished medical students.

"Graham didn't even try to do something about it—just tested her for gifts. As if she'd get a gift before seeing workings. Can you believe that?"

"I don't think he knew ..."

Zion cut me off. "Sure I can believe it. He didn't want her looking into that strait you had sitting open up there, right? You can't see workings, you can't see a strait—simple as that."

Kara looked stunned. Then her surprise turned to anger.

"That bastard! He really was trying to get us killed."

"What does seeing workings have to do with knowing someone's a Nolander?" I said, feeling uncomfortable and hoping to get them off the subject of Graham.

Still steaming, Kara explained that normally you can get a general feel for someone else's capacity to work essence by touching them.

"It's like your power senses their power. You can definitely tell if they're a Nolander or not. Sometimes you can tell how strong they are, especially if they're weaker than you. That's why you won't see Seconds touching each other very often—not skin to skin."

"I guess that's another way my development's screwed up."

"I'm sure it'll be okay," Kara said.

"Do you think I'll get a replacement trainer?"

Zion cleared her throat. "I heard Lord Cordus wants to teach you himself."

Kara shot me a glance that was pure horror, then quickly looked away.

"As for telling who's a Nolander," Zion said, filling the uncomfortable silence, "just look for black clothes. Seconds don't like wearing black, so that's what we wear at events where we'll be mixing with them. Those of us with significant power wear a little silver or white, like my barrette or the trim on Kara's dress, but that's it."

Koji and the doorman had both been wearing all black. I looked down at the beautiful beaded top of my dress. Not only were the straps whitish, but the top four or so inches of the dress were, too.

"Yeah," Kara said, following my gaze. "That's a lot of white."

"Am I going to get in trouble?" I would've thought Cordus's staff knew the rules.

Zion shook her head. "If that's what Lord Cordus's staff put on you, that's what he wants you to wear." She paused. "It just means you're very strong—the more white, the more power. He's decided to advertise your potential."

"I wonder how much white he'd put on Callie. If he ever got her down here, I mean," Kara mused, looking at my dress.

Before I could think of anything else to say, the doors hissed open. The elevator, along with several others, emptied onto a marble hallway. There were attendants waiting at one end to take our coats. They both looked like tough customers, so I guessed they functioned as guards, too.

After handing off my fur, I followed Zion through a short hallway into a large room, with Kara trailing behind.

I'd been vaguely imagining some medieval scene— everyone standing around watching Cordus sitting on a dais at the end of some ornately decorated hall. Maybe he'd even be on a throne, like a king.

What I'd walked into looked more like a hoity-toity cocktail party. We were in what seemed to be a very large living room. It stretched dozens of feet to both the right and left. The floor was carpeted, and people were standing around in clusters, chatting and drinking. Some were seated at various furniture groupings. Some stood alone or with just one other, near the walls. A few were standing at the floor-to-ceiling windows, taking in the cityscape. I couldn't see much, with all the people in the way, but it seemed we were up pretty high.

The good news was that no one paid us the slightest attention when we came in. The bad news was that the room was full of Seconds. Most had a human shape, but some were bizarre, and a few were terrifying.

I saw a green man standing off to the right. The fact that it was holding a glass of wine and talking to someone made it all the more disturbing. Something in the room's lighting made its skin fluoresce green all over, as though it were made of foil. Or maybe it could control the effect and was showing off.

I saw a snowman that reminded me, with a sharp twinge, of Bob. The snowman was speaking to something that looked like a small dragon.

Across the room, a towering, pale pink, batlike creature hulked near the windows. I could see its grossly long folded arms, pouchy with membranous wings, jutting up above the heads of those standing nearby. I was staring at it, so of course it looked my way. Incongruously, it had the face of a jowly old man, complete with rheumy eyes and a thin, gray comb-over. I quickly looked away.

"Big crowd," Kara said softly at my shoulder.

I nodded. Zion moved away, into the press, but I stood there frozen.

Even the human-shaped Seconds were clearly *other* to my eyes. As with Cordus's impossible beauty, there was something about each of them that was off. The more I looked at them, the more disturbing they became. They were the non-human stuffed into almost-human packaging. It was eerie, wrong. The idea of walking among them was frightening.

Kara moved forward and took my arm. Again, I could feel her shaking.

"Come on, let's get a drink," she said.

We threaded our way through the crowd to a small bar set up in one corner. Kara introduced me to the barkeep, a pleasant-looking middle-aged white guy dressed all in black. His name was Hank. He too gave me an admiring once-over. My feeling of being on display intensified.

Glasses of white wine in hand, we moved to the windows. The view was stunning. Directly ahead, we looked down on several smaller skyscrapers, then a mixture of tall buildings and smaller ones. Looking slightly left, far taller buildings marched away for blocks and blocks, including some that looked familiar, even to a girl from small-town Wisconsin.

"That's the Empire State Building," Kara said helpfully.

I could see the top of it clearly, bathed in white light. We stood for a few minutes in silence. Kara kept bringing her glass to her lips, then lowering it. I imagined she really wanted to down it, but kept reminding herself it wouldn't be a good idea. That was certainly what I was thinking.

The reflection of movement behind us caught my eye. I looked back to see the snowman I'd noticed earlier looming over us.

"You are Elizabeth Ryder, are you not?" it rumbled.

"Yes," I answered, bowing my head in a way I hoped looked respectful. I felt Kara draw closer behind me.

The snowman observed me quietly for several seconds. It made me uncomfortable, but at least there was nothing overtly sexual in its perusal.

"I have heard that you brought death to one of my people," it said at last.

I looked up at its face. Its expression was not as neutral as its voice had been. Despite the inhumanity of its features, I could see sadness there.

I teared up. I couldn't help it.

"I guess I did," I said. "I'm sorry."

"Will you offer no reason?"

I explained about the photograph I'd taken of Bob's foot and how it'd been passed around in Pete's Eats.

The creature sighed. "A more absurd cause of death can hardly be imagined. Who ordered the execution, and who carried it out?"

"With all due respect, Lady Ambassador," Kara said from behind me, "that's something you should probably take up with Lord Cordus."

The snowman's eyes flicked briefly over my shoulder at her, then focused on me again.

"I certainly shall. But for now I am asking Miss Ryder."

I took a deep breath. "All I've heard is hearsay. I won't pass that along as though it were fact. I'm sorry."

Kara stopped breathing. I felt her take hold of my elbow.

"Perhaps this is an issue we should discuss privately, Lady Ambassador," a super-sexy voice said from behind the snowman.

The creature stepped aside with surprising grace, revealing Cordus.

"Gnaeus Cornelius Marci Filius Cordus," it said, and bowed. "I will look forward to discussing the fate of my kinsman, at your convenience."

It nodded at Kara and me, inclined its head to Cordus, and moved away.

Cordus turned toward us.

"Elizabeth Joy Ryder, you look quite lovely," he said, looking me slowly up and down.

You'd think I'd have been used to it by that point, but I blushed hotly. His eyes dwelt on my face and neck, perhaps enjoying my evident embarrassment. Usually I looked down when I blushed, since it made me so self-conscious, but I couldn't take my eyes off him. I just stared back.

Finally, his eyes shifted over my shoulder.

"Kara Dolores Sanchez," he said in a different voice, one that tugged at my insides even though it wasn't directed at me.

Kara gasped, and her hand tightened painfully on my arm. I felt her press her face against my bare shoulder. Cordus let the moment hang. He seemed to be enjoying it.

Then he smiled slightly and said, "I would speak with Miss Ryder alone."

Cut free, Kara wrenched herself away from me and stumbled off into the crowd.

Cordus watched her go, then turned back to me. He was wearing a slim-cut white shirt and dark pants. I absolutely was not going to look down to get more specific than that on the color. My heart was still racing from catching the edge of what he'd directed at Kara.

"You handled your interaction with the Lady Ambassador reasonably well, Miss Ryder," he said. "However, the death of the ice man in Wisconsin is not your responsibility. You had no cause to apologize."

Burgundy. His pants were burgundy.

God, what was wrong with me?

"On the next such occasion, it would be best simply to refer the matter to me, as Miss Sanchez attempted."

Huh. It would've been nice if he'd complimented Kara, rather than tormenting her and then praising her once she was gone.

"Come," he said, holding out his arm.

I really didn't want to touch him, but there wasn't much choice. I settled my hand on his forearm—which was covered by his shirtsleeve, thank god—and followed along as he led me through the crowd.

Over the next two hours, he stopped and spoke to at least twenty guests. He greeted each one formally, but the long names quickly blended together in my mind. Not a single one of them addressed me, but most seemed to notice me. Several gave my dress a pointed look. A few others revealed displeasure before schooling their features.

They all made me nervous, but the last—a tiny, caramel-complexioned woman with curly black hair and pretty, delicate features—was the only one who really scared me. She was wearing a pair of loose blood-red pants and a matching sleeveless top. The female Seconds seemed to prefer gowns, so her look stood out. They also seemed to like height, but this one was making no effort to look taller than her five-foot-nothing: she was wearing red beaded flats.

She studied me very directly as Cordus greeted her, which the others hadn't done. Finally she turned to him and nodded, greeting him by name.

Then, apropos of nothing, she said, "I will give you Florida for this one."

I was shocked, then flooded with horror. I didn't want to go with that woman, whoever she was. I glanced at Cordus and saw that he was quite surprised himself. He'd actually arched an eyebrow.

A pained silence ensued. Was he considering it? Surely it was a good deal—I couldn't really be worth a whole state.

Finally he said, "Thank you for so handsome an offer, my Lady, but I must decline."

Then he stood there chatting with the woman. She wasn't much of a small-talker, so the conversation was a bit stilted. Maybe she just had trouble keeping up her end because she was so busy staring at me like I was a prize steer.

Cordus finally moved on from the tiny woman. Instead of greeting another guest, he steered me to a dark corner, where a large someone in all black was standing. It was Williams. Great.

"Miss Ryder needs to rest," Cordus said to him. "Keep her company."

Cordus smiled briefly at me—*Good girl*, I imagined him saying—and moved back off into the crowd. I was left standing there awkwardly.

Well, whatever. At least Williams was human. Sort of.

"Do you know who that small, black-haired woman is?" I asked him.

"Lady Innin."

Shit, the one Koji'd mentioned.

"Is she someone important?"

"She controls the Caribbean and the Gulf—Florida, eastern Mexico, Central America, northern South America."

Wow. I wondered if she was more powerful than Cordus. I felt chilled.

"She just offered to trade Florida for me."

Williams turned and looked at me. Perhaps I'd actually surprised him. Or maybe not. After a few seconds, he shrugged and said, "Florida's gonna be underwater in fifty years, anyway."

No doubt he was trying to be an asshole, but it struck me as funny. Or maybe laughter was just my response to stress. Whatever the reason, I had to clap my hands over my mouth and turn to the wall until I got a handle on myself.

Not much happened for the remainder of the evening. Kara found her way back to me, and we hung out quietly near Williams. Gwen and Zion both drifted by, drinks in hand. Just to be sure, I asked Kara if Graham was there.

"Are you kidding? That sonovabitch is in a world of hurt. No way Lord Cordus is letting him out to play."

I saw the memory of our elevator conversation flit across her face. She frowned.

"Ratfink bastard."

I stifled the impulse to defend him. What did I know? Maybe he'd been negligent not to realize I didn't start seeing workings along with halfings.

After another hour or so, guests began to leave. Eventually, only Cordus and his people were left. Cordus headed into his study to make some calls, and the rest of us hung out in the living room while our cars were brought around.

I got to put names to some new faces. In addition to Hank, there were two other bartenders, Hortensia and Bud. Kristin,

James, and Rafiki had been circulating with drinks and hors d'oeuvre. Mary and Valerie had been working in the kitchen. The bruisers taking coats were Andy and Theo.

Looking around at everyone, I started to get a sense of how things worked. Nolanders with less strength or power, or whatever you called it, did lower-status jobs: the waiters, caterers, and bartenders were all wearing all black. Koji and the doorman, who was named Grant, had been too. I'd bet Cordus's estate staff were in the same category.

In contrast, Kara, Zion, Gwen, and I, who were all wearing some white, had been circulating freely among the guests. Andy and Theo, the coat-checkers-slash-guards, were also wearing white—folded pocket handkerchiefs and silver cufflinks. Maybe we were the security detail, or maybe we were just assets to show off.

Though everyone seemed to know one another and be friendly, I noticed that people tended to group according to clothing color. Maybe the members of each group worked with one another more often and had gotten to know each other better.

As the rest of us talked, Williams leaned against the far wall, looking down. He seemed to be profoundly antisocial.

I realized as I watched him that he was an exception to the color-coding—he'd been circulating, but his clothes were all black.

Grant called up to let us know the Porsche was ready, so Zion, Kara, and I got in the elevator. It went down a lot faster than it had gone up.

When we saw the car, it appeared to have a big scrape along the driver's side. It turned out to be masking tape—Koji had put it there to see Zion's reaction. Everyone had a good laugh except Zion, who cuffed Koji on the back of the head.

Not hard, though. I could tell she was only pretending to be mad.

As we crossed the bridge out of the city, I asked Kara and Zion whether they ever hung out with any of the dressed-all-in-black people.

"I'd sure like to hang out more with Koji—he's hot," Kara said. "But I guess it can get a little weird with them sometimes. They're all pretty nice, though," she added.

"How about you, Zion?"

"I don't 'hang out' with any of you people. We're coworkers, not friends."

"Fuck you," Kara said. "That's stupid. There's no one else for us to be friends with."

Zion shrugged. Kara chewed her out a little more, then lapsed into resentful silence. After a minute or two, she said something else pissy.

Zion lost her temper. "You know what, Kara? You need to grow the fuck up."

"What does that mean? You think you're too good for everyone else?"

"What do you think this is, high school? Like we're in different cliques or something? You people are fucking blind."

I was more curious than offended.

"Blind? What do you mean?"

Zion rolled her eyes. "Lord Cordus gives some of us higher status and makes us advertise it to the others. That breaks us into groups that resent each other—we resent the weaklings for not doing the dangerous work, and they resent us because they're menial labor and get paid a lot less. So now there're factions instead of unity. That makes us all easier to control. See?"

The resulting silence was profound.

Finally Kara said, skeptically, "He pays us more?"

"He pays you more if you ask, dumbass. You should be making twice as much as me—you're at least that much stronger. Instead you're probably making what Grant makes."

The genius of Cordus's system started to become clear to me.

"So," I said, "to get the extra pay, you have to ask to be treated better than the others. That means you're the one who has to go to him and claim they're not your equals."

"Got it in one. Bonus for the new girl."

"But why?" Kara said, sounding choked up. "Why would you do that? We're not better than them. I'm not better than you. Beth's not better than me."

"Seriously. That part of the system would fall apart if no one asked him for the raise," I said.

"Who should I answer first," Zion said angrily. "The woman who drives a twenty-year-old Pontiac, or the one who can't afford a car at all?"

"Zion, that is so fucked up. I don't even know you. Jesus Fucking Christ."

Kara slumped back in her seat.

I was still thinking through Cordus's system.

"He gives the strongest people the most perks. That makes them feel more invested in the status quo. That makes sense, since they'd be the most dangerous to him if they rebelled."

"'Rebelled'? We can't rebel—don't even think about it," Zion said. "He would crush us all without lifting a finger."

We stopped at a light, and she turned to give us both a hard stare.

"You two need to get it through your heads that there's nothing we can do about our situation. Lord Cordus can do whatever he wants with us. At least the weak ones live to be old. The three of us are going to live short lives, and we're going to die hard. We'll be lucky to make it out of our twenties. All we can do is try to enjoy what we can, while we can. There's nothing else."

Kara didn't say anything. She'd crossed her arms and drawn her knees up to her chest, physically withdrawing from the conversation.

I thought about Williams. I wondered if he was resisting the system by not wearing white. Maybe he was a little smarter than he looked. Or maybe he was just contrary.

"It seems like Williams gets away with ducking the clothing thing," I said. "He's got to have enough strength to wear white, but he wasn't tonight."

"Yeah, well, Williams is Williams," Zion said. "I don't know why Lord Cordus lets him get away with that shit. He sure wouldn't stand for it from me. Wearing white isn't a choice."

"Is his ability with barriers rare and useful, like Callie's precognition?"

Zion frowned. "I don't think so. He's great with barriers, and that's definitely useful, but most of us can do at least a little barrier work, and there are some others with real strength in that area, like Andy. Callie's literally one in a thousand. Williams isn't."

She thought some more. "He does have a lot of raw strength. Second only to Callie, probably. Maybe that's it."

Third is more like it, I thought, remembering how Graham had broken through Williams's barrier to attack me.

I sat back and let the Porsche's muted rumble seep through me.

I could understand Kara's horrified reaction. What Cordus was doing was so wrong that it was hard to put into words.

But I could also understand Zion's position. I'd seen what had happened to Callie, and I'd noticed how scarred up Gwen and Williams were. And how young everyone seemed to be—Gwen was definitely the oldest person wearing white. The lives of those who hunted Seconds were probably nasty, brutish, and short. Why not enjoy what small pleasures you could?

It all hinged on whether Cordus really was as unbeatable as Zion said. If he was, then resistance would be nothing but a symbolic sacrifice, and no one was likely to do that. But if he wasn't unbeatable, then colluding with him wasn't nearly so forgivable.

Chapter 16

THE NEXT MORNING, I received a letter from Cordus. I could tell from the initialing that it had been typed by a secretary for his signature. It informed me that I was to consider myself a member of his household until further notice. I was not allowed to leave the premises without permission. I was being given that day to wrap up my pre-existing affairs. My wages would be $32,000 per annum, from which my monthly room and board of $2,000 would be deducted. My household membership came with a credit card and a fancy cell phone, which were attached to the letter in a padded envelope. The card was for pre-approved work expenses only. A list of recommended clothing items was also attached—mostly things I'd put in the "business casual" category, though I noticed with a chill that black undergarments were included.

Cordus had added a hand-written note at the bottom: he would be conducting my formal training, and it would begin the following morning. Gwen would be in touch with me about the specifics of my schedule.

I put down the letter and its attachments and just sat there. I'd kept repeating to myself that I had to confront my new reality. But now that reality had been given paper form and slipped under my door, and it clearly had no room for any part of who I'd been—not my house, my job, my family, my friends, or even my existing wardrobe.

I resented it profoundly.

Also, it scared me.

I sat there, expecting the thought of my future to trigger a panic attack, but it didn't. It occurred to me that I hadn't had one in a while. I hoped that Graham had been right and that I didn't have true panic disorder after all.

That's a pretty big silver lining, I told myself. *Maybe I'm losing a lot, but that's a huge gain.*

It was hard to think positively, though. The losses were too big and too new.

Sighing, I picked the letter back up, wondering how much I could get done today. I turned it over and jotted down a to-do list that started with "quit job" and ended with "black panties."

If I knocked enough things off the list this morning, maybe I could go shopping. The letter said a percentage of my salary could be advanced if I needed funds for clothes or other essentials. I thought of the $1,200 I'd been carrying around in my wallet for the last week. If I spent it carefully, hopefully it would be enough. I didn't want to ask Cordus for an advance. He might decide to treat it as a request for a raise.

Okay, top of the list. I sat there for a while thinking about various lies I could tell the people back in Dorf, especially Ben and Dr. Nielsen. It was hard to come up with something that sounded even vaguely reasonable. In the end, I decided to keep it as simple as possible—I was very upset about having been attacked in my own home and had decided to leave Dorf for a while until I got over the experience. I didn't know where I was going to go, and I'd rather not have people contact me.

Given my well known mental illness, an extreme reaction

like that might seem plausible, at least to some people. I went over the story several times in my head, then decided to let it sit for a while, while I did other things.

Cordus's letter had included a mailing address I could use—a post-office box. I used the cell phone to file a mail-forwarding order online. Then I stopped my home phone service and changed the mailing address for my gas-and-electric bill.

I called the Ohio State Highway Patrol and reported my car stolen. I got a call back twenty minutes later: my car had already been found. Maybe Williams hadn't bothered with an invisi-shield, or maybe it had expired. I thanked the trooper and told her I wouldn't be reclaiming the car. I could tell she thought something fishy was going on when she asked why I hadn't reported the theft earlier. I just played dumb. In the end she told me they'd keep the car for ninety days, then donate it to a program that provided job training for at-risk youth.

So much for my mother's last gift to me.

I went back over my story. It still seemed like the best thing I could come up with, so I called Suzanne and tried it out on her. Not surprisingly, she was brimming with questions, but I just kept repeating the party line—I'd be away for a while, I wasn't sure where or for how long, I'd prefer not to be contacted unless it was an emergency. I gave her my cell number and asked her to turn my thermostat down and keep an eye on my house.

Then I remembered the mouse. How could I have forgotten? Poor little guy. I thought quickly about just asking Suzanne to let him go in the backyard, but there were so many cats running loose in the neighborhood. Instead I asked her to hire a trustworthy kid to feed and water him once a week and clean his cage. I told her I'd send her some money to cover it.

After she agreed, we said our goodbyes, and I hung up. I took a deep breath. That had been relatively easy.

Calling Dr. Nielsen was a lot harder. He was intensely worried about me and quite unwilling to let me "just disappear following a traumatic experience," as he put it. I stuck to my guns but had the feeling he'd be calling the police when we hung up. Well, that would come to nothing—I was pretty sure the Dorf PD had written me off.

The next call was Ben. That conversation was awful. He was worried about me, yes, but he was even more worried about his family. How could I just disappear, right when he and the girls needed me most? Sticking to the party line didn't do any good. It just infuriated him. It was horrible. In the end, he hung up on me in disgust.

After about fifteen minutes, the cell phone rang. The caller ID showed Ben's number, but when I answered, it was Tiffany. Jesus, it was really my day for punishment.

"Aunt Beth?"

She spoke in a low, muffled voice, as though she was crouching in a corner and whispering into the phone.

"Hi, sweetie. How're you doing?"

She ignored my question. "Ghosteater said you could find Mom. Did you?"

You'd think, after the last two weeks, I'd have stopped getting caught by surprise. Unfortunately not. I sat there holding the phone, wondering what on earth to say. Just as I was about to answer, Graham's and Kara's warnings about the rules came back to me. I shut my mouth and thought some more.

"Beth?" Tiff whispered, sounding desperate.

I decided I had to take a hard line. Tiff was twelve and had a good head. She could take it.

"Who else is going to find out what I tell you, Tiff?"

"I won't tell anyone except Ghosteater."

"Not Madisyn?"

Tiff paused. When she spoke, she sounded sad.

"No. She's not old enough to keep the secret. It's started too young for her."

Maybe that was a good thing, I thought to myself. If I understood what I'd been told, it meant she had very little strength. If Cordus got a hold of her, she'd get one of those low-paid but safe household positions.

"Are Jazzy and Lia like you and Madisyn?"

"Not yet. It only started for me last year, though."

She'd have been eleven. I wondered where that put her, strengthwise.

"Tiff, do you know how serious the rule is about keeping the secret?"

"Mom said I could never tell anyone about anything special I could do."

"Did she tell you that there are people who will come and kill you if you do tell anyone? Anyone at all, even your Dad?"

From the silence on the other end, I guessed Justine hadn't been that explicit. Maybe she didn't know it herself. She seemed pretty out of it.

"I understand," Tiff finally said in a shaky voice.

"Okay. The good news is that I did find your mother. She's not hurt, and she's staying someplace I think is safe for her. The bad news is that she's not going to be able to come home right now, and there's no way you can visit her or speak to her."

"Why?"

"Honey, that's in the can't-talk-about-it category. I'm sorry."

"Are you with her?"

"I'm staying at the same place she is. I'll try to see her as often as I can."

I paused. "I'm sorry I can't give you better news. You know, I didn't find out about the special stuff until just the last couple weeks. It's all new to me, and I don't understand a lot of it. I don't know what I can do for your Mom, but I'll try my best to help her and keep her safe."

Tiffany took that in. Finally she said, "Okay," in a small voice. She sniffled, then cleared her throat.

"Can I call you?"

"Absolutely. If I don't answer when you call, leave a message telling me when I should call you back and at what number, okay?"

"Okay," she said, sounding marginally better. "I love you, Aunt Beth. I want you to come home."

"Oh sweetie, I love you too, so much. I hope I'll be able to come home soon."

There was a big sniffle, then, "Bye."

I set down the phone.

Damn.

❦

I took a long, hot shower, trying to rinse away the aftertaste of having lied to and disappointed everyone I cared about.

When I was done, I put on the same clothes I'd been wearing when Williams, Kara, and Callie grabbed me at the mall, days back. The house staff had been laundering them each night, but I was getting pretty tired of them.

I opened my phone's address book. It was programmed

with numbers for all the Nolanders I knew so far, and quite a few I hadn't met yet. I called Gwen and told her I'd like to use the afternoon to find some of the clothes on my list. She said she'd check with Cordus and that if it was all right with him, someone would take me shopping. Half an hour later, Kara and I were on our way in a generic black sedan.

Not surprisingly, the area turned out to have a variety of shopping options. Despite Kara's objections, I started at Kohl's.

"There's no reason to pay a lot for bras and panties," I said as we rooted through the lingerie section. "I don't have that much to spend, and there's a lot on this list."

"Yeah, but …" Kara paused awkwardly, a black bra in each hand.

"What?"

"The lingerie is the most important stuff."

I lowered my voice to a hiss. "Lord Cordus is *never* going to see it."

"He will, Beth. I'm sorry, but it's going to happen. There's nothing you can do about it."

She turned away before wiping quickly at her eyes.

I felt absolutely cold inside and tried not to think of Tiffany and Madisyn. I waited until I could speak firmly.

"Then look for the cheapest stuff. A rapist doesn't deserve to see a $13.99 bra."

Kara laughed weakly. "You're a braver woman than I am. Here're some on sale, two for $9."

"Perfect."

Kohl's provided not only all my new black underwear, but also some in lighter colors. I found several pairs of jeans and a bunch of black clothing: three pairs of slacks, two sweaters, and a slinky blouse. I was careful to make sure each item was entirely black. I also got three pairs of slacks in other colors and a handful of nice knit tops in muted tones that Kara labeled "tasteful."

Kara insisted on Saks for one item on the list—a black suit. While there, I also got what she identified as a "nice" pair of jeans. Those and the suit knocked me back as much as everything I'd bought at Kohl's.

For shoes, I put my foot down—Saks was out of my league. Kara took me to Nordstrom. Still a lot of sticker-shock for small-town me, but not quite so bad. I left with heeled boots and a pair of pumps, both in black.

Our last stop was a sporting-goods store, where I got most of the other things on my list: sweat pants, running shorts, sports bras, socks, and athletic shoes. That stuff gave me a bad feeling. I'd never tended to put on weight, so I'd never gotten into working out. I didn't particularly want to start.

Then I remembered trying to haul unconscious Kara along by her feet at the mill. Maybe getting a little stronger wasn't such a bad idea.

We didn't have time to buy the one thing left on the list, a black coat. I'd just have to hope spring came on quickly.

We headed back to the estate.

"So," I said to Kara as we drove, "Do you live here most of the time?"

"Thank god, no. I'm based in Minneapolis. Me and Williams and Callie are part of the Upper Midwest group. Graham too. He was in charge of it, actually. I'm sure that's going to change, now."

"Oh. Does that mean you'll head back there, soon?"

"I sure hope so." She must've seen the expression on my face. "I'm sorry, Beth, but I couldn't stay here with you if I wanted to. And god, I don't want to. I'm sorry."

"I know. I understand."

I did understand, but I felt very alone. I liked Kara, but liking someone only mattered so much. Real friendships must be hard when any of us could be sent anywhere, anytime, and where fear was such a dominant force. Another part of Cordus's control system, maybe.

"You'll get to know the New York people. They're good folks. Maybe you'll get to hang out with Koji."

She gave a half-hearted whistle as tribute to his hotness.

"Yeah, maybe so," I said, and tried to smile.

Gwen knocked on my door at 6:00 the next morning. She suggested I shower and dress, then come with her to breakfast in the dining room at 7:00.

The staff had been bringing my meals on a tray, but I guess that was too good to last.

Noting that Gwen hadn't been wearing black, I put on a pair of beige slacks and a white knit top. Pairing them with the black heels wouldn't have been my first choice, but beggars couldn't be choosers—it was either that or boots.

Breakfast was served in a huge dining room on the second floor. It took up a corner of the house. Tall windows looked out over the front lawn, which swept down and away to the distant tree line. When I stopped by a window and commented on how big the property looked, Gwen said it was almost a thousand acres and had been state and local parkland until Cordus took it over in the 1970s.

"He took over a state park? How?"

Gwen looked a little uncomfortable.

"Lord Cordus is gifted at influencing others," she said.

I'd seen that gift first-hand with the green man, but that was just one mind. I remembered that it was indelicate to ask about Seconds' abilities. Still, how was I going to find out about these things if I didn't ask?

"But millions of people live around here. Can he really influence that many people?"

"He doesn't have to. A few key people needed influencing. I think they believe it's a top-secret military installation. Everyone else still thinks it's a park. But if they decide to come hiking here, they end up changing their minds at the last minute. If they notice cars coming and going, they forget about it. The roads and buildings don't show up on satellite photos. The barrier around the property takes care of that sort of thing."

At that moment, as I looked out across the lawn, it occurred to me that there might not be any meaningful limit to what Seconds could do in our world. What if one of them decided it was in their interest to assassinate a president? To cause a recession? To start a war? Maybe they'd been shaping our history from behind the scenes for a long time.

It was a shocking thought. I stood at the window, trying to collect myself.

"Come on," Gwen said. "I'm hungry."

There were between twenty and thirty people eating, and I knew fewer than half of them. The room was equipped with a variety of tables, some round, some square or rectangular. You could sit with just one other person, or as many as seven. All the tables were elaborately set with white linens and multiple dishes, glasses, and pieces of silverware. It was going to be a headache figuring out which things to use.

Gwen steered us toward Andy and Theo, the guys who'd been taking coats at court. They were alone at a four-top near the edge of the room. Once we all sat down, the three of them made me feel wispy. Gwen was very tall, and she looked like a bodybuilder. Andy and Theo were big men, both tall and brawny. I felt like a reed in comparison.

A waiter came and began serving us. Coffee and tea were offered, as well as water and a selection of juices. We placed orders for one of a handful of available entrées. I chose the omelet. Fruit and cereal, either hot or cold, were served while we waited for the main course to arrive.

It was certainly the most elaborate breakfast experience I'd ever had.

Once I felt confident I wasn't going to be approached with yet another question or offer of food choices, I relaxed a little and turned my attention to my companions. I realized, looking at Theo and Andy up close, that they looked quite a bit alike.

"Are you guys brothers?"

"Yeah," Theo said. "You got any siblings?"

"Yeah, an older brother."

"Is he a Nolander?"

I shook my head.

"Too bad," Andy said.

"Why's that?"

"Families grow best if everyone gets some manure," he said with a wink.

I laughed.

Theo and Andy might've reminded me a little of Williams when I first saw them, but they turned out to be quite friendly and perfectly capable of normal conversation.

After some questions about Dorf and life in rural Wisconsin, Andy asked what I was doing for the rest of the day.

"I guess Lord Cordus is going to start training me today," I said.

Both men's forks stopped halfway to their mouths. They glanced at Gwen, but she was looking down at her plate, concentrating on mopping up her egg yolk.

"He's training you himself, is he?" Theo said.

"Hey, don't worry about it," Andy said, recovering himself. "It'll be fine. Just listen carefully, try hard, and be really polite."

I nodded.

"And don't be afraid to ask questions," Theo added. "Just, you know, skip the dumb ones." He grinned at me, breaking the tension.

Still, it wasn't the most auspicious start to the day. By the time we finished and Gwen walked me to Cordus's office, I was scared. I felt like I was walking into the proverbial lion's den, except this den belonged to some sicko rapist lion.

She knocked on the door, then opened it and stuck her head in.

"Lord Cordus, I've brought Miss Ryder."

"Thank you, Miss Hegstrom. You may go on to other duties, now."

"Yes, sir."

Gwen opened the door a bit wider and nodded at me to go through. She even gave me an encouraging smile, which looked a little odd on her stern, weathered face.

My return smile felt more like a grimace. I blinked hard and took a deep breath. Then I headed into Cordus's office.

*

"Miss Ryder, your development is indeed anomalous."

Cordus removed his fingertips from my arm and leaned

back, studying me.

He and I were sitting in leather armchairs at one end of his office.

Actually, it was more like a library than an office—there was a desk at the other end, with several straight-backed chairs in front of it, but most of the room was given over to floor-to-ceiling shelving in some beautiful, dark wood. From what I could see, most of the books on the shelves looked old. Very old. Unlike in the dining room, there were few windows. The effect was cavelike.

It was the only room I'd seen on the estate that had any personality. I liked it. I wondered what it would be like in there on a winter night with a fire in the fireplace. Cozy. So long as Cordus wasn't in there with you.

That said, once again, Cordus's behavior hadn't matched the horror of his reputation. He hadn't tried anything inappropriate; in fact, he'd been polite.

I felt confused. Confused and fascinated. Fascinated and repulsed. It was hard not to stare at him, but when I did, I remembered that same stunning face impassively watching the green man tear itself apart.

At a loss, I'd retreated into the role of student. I was good at being a student, and I liked it. Good students didn't think much about their teachers, and especially not their teachers' looks. Instead, they thought about what they were studying.

He'd begun with exercises similar to what Graham had had me do at Rib Mountain—deep breathing and concentration. Then he'd asked if I could describe my sense of the worked-essence barrier he'd placed around us to keep our lesson private.

I'd told him I wasn't aware of the barrier at all. That was when he'd touched me.

"How is it anomalous, exactly?" I asked.

"Did Mr. Ryzik explain to you the castes of development?"

"Yes: 'sense a working, get a gift, handle essence, learn to work.'"

A trace of a smile ghosted across Cordus's face.

"And he explained what it means to 'sense a working'?"

"Being able to perceive workings and half-workings."

"Correct. And did he explain what the term 'capacity' means?"

"Someone's ability to do workings?"

"Yes. The measure of that ability is your capacity. When one is born, a tiny capacity is present, and it grows over time. When it reaches roughly two-thirds of its full potential, one achieves full sensory perception of worked essence. This is the first caste."

"What about gifts?" I asked.

"They usually remain latent for several more years."

No wonder Graham's approach to training me had struck a false note with the others.

"So why aren't I developing like everyone else?"

"I believe that your capacity lies at the root of the problem. As I said, one enters the first caste when one's capacity has reached roughly two-thirds of its full potential. I believe you began to enter the first caste significantly before your potential reached that mark. Therefore, it is not functioning typically."

"But aren't I old for all this to start?"

"Yes, you are entering the first caste at a comparatively advanced age."

"But …"

"Please ask your question, Miss Ryder."

"It seems like I already have a fair amount of capacity. I had enough to power Mr. Williams's shield for some time when we were on our way here."

He looked at me in silence for several long seconds.

Finally, he said, "Your perception is correct."

A chill ran through me. What was I going to be, when all this was said and done? He allowed me to sit in silence for several minutes, digesting. Then he started back in.

"It would be useful to know what triggered your premature entry into the first caste. Can you describe what, in retrospect, you believe to be the first signs that something unusual was happening?"

I told him how I'd started feeling more anxious a year or so earlier, and how photography had seemed to relieve the anxiety. Then I mentioned the photos I'd taken less than two weeks earlier.

"Yes," Cordus said, "I have seen them. Can you remember any event that may have triggered your anxiety or your ability to photograph Seconds?"

I shook my head.

"And how did you come to see half-workings?"

"Mr. Ryzik got me to see them. He took me to visit a Second I couldn't see and then left me with him. When I got scared enough, I saw him."

Cordus was surprised. The eyebrow went up.

"That approach was unwise," he said. "Trying to engender capacity through fear or other powerful emotions can have unpredictable and dangerous results. I shall have to speak with Mr. Ryzik about his training methods."

"I don't think he knew that's what he was doing. He seemed to think my conscious mind was just suppressing what I was seeing."

Cordus looked at me in silence. I took it to mean the subject of Graham's mistakes was not open for discussion.

Finally, his point seemingly made, he said, "I believe it is safe to proceed, so long as we move carefully. Our lessons must offer your capacity the opportunity to stabilize and grow without applying undue pressure."

"Okay," I said, stifling the impulse to ask how sure he was about the "safe" part.

He held his hand out between us, palm up.

"I have made a small, spherical working three centimeters above my hand. The nature of the working is to create heat: the air within the sphere is fifteen degrees warmer than that in the room at large. Focus your attention on that spot. Try to sense the disruption in the preexisting state of reality."

I concentrated on the air above his palm. It looked perfectly normal. I kept staring at it. Nothing happened. After about thirty seconds, Cordus closed his hand and had me relax for a few minutes. Then he had me try again, but with my eyes closed. No go. The third time, he had me reach out and touch the air above his hand. I could feel that it was warmer, but couldn't sense anything else.

After five efforts, he sat back, and I got the feeling we were done.

"Miss Ryder, please do not attempt to sense workings, except during our lessons. Gentle stimulation of your capacity should do no harm and may help. Doing more than that would be unwise. Is that clear?"

I nodded. He held my gaze for a moment, apparently to convey how very much he meant it. Then he rose and retrieved a folder and a book from his desk.

"We shall meet again at the same time tomorrow morning," he said, "and every day thereafter. In the meanwhile, please read the document in his folder. You will return it to me tomorrow. You may write on it, but do not copy it or take separate notes."

I nodded and accepted the folder. It was slender. There couldn't be more than a few pages in it.

"This," he said, holding up the book, "is a textbook of Baasha, the common language of the S-Em. You will comprehend the first chapter before our next meeting. Keep this book and any notes you make out of sight: most Nolanders do not have the opportunity to pursue this line of study."

I accepted the book with some trepidation. I'd taken French in high school and had loved it, but the idea of being given an "opportunity" others didn't get made me nervous. I took it to mean I'd end up doing things they didn't have to do.

"Lunch is served in the dining room between 11:30 and 1:30," Cordus continued. "I have asked Miss Hegstrom to accompany you to that meal today and to give you a tour of the estate afterwards. I hope you will learn your way around quickly."

I nodded and stood and, after a hesitation, thanked him for his time. It seemed the polite thing to do, even though the lessons were clearly compulsory. He nodded graciously, accepting my thanks, and I left, relieved to have gotten through the first lesson without pissing him off or becoming another unwilling notch on his bedpost.

❧

"Can you ride?" Gwen asked.

She and I were leaning on the top rail of a white wooden fence, watching a handful of horses graze.

"Yeah, sort of. I mean, I've never had lessons or anything, but my best friend grew up on a farm. They had horses, and we used to ride them a lot. Mostly just bareback around the farm."

I turned back to watch the horses.

"I really like them. They smell good."

Gwen looked at me like I had a screw loose, and I blushed, suddenly feeling like an eight-year-old with a bedroom full of unicorn posters and My Little Ponies.

"Well, different strokes, I guess," she said. "I've had to do stable duty before. What comes out of their asses sure doesn't smell good."

I wouldn't mind doing stable duty—I thought horse shit was pretty innocuous. But I didn't say so.

We'd already walked over some of the grounds, and Gwen had pointed out several trailheads for biking, running, and hiking, warning me to stay alert for the barrier that surrounded the estate. I wasn't to try cross it for any reason—doing so would be dangerous. I didn't mention that I probably wouldn't know it was there until I ran into it. I figured I'd just stay near the house.

She'd also shown me the garage, tennis court, and outdoor pool. The stable was the last stop.

After seeing the grounds, we embarked on a full tour of the house. It had four wings, one of which held Cordus's private quarters. That was a no-go zone, except when invited. The other three wings were full of suites and small apartments for Nolanders. The place could house well over a hundred comfortably and three times that number if people shared space.

Gwen had taken me to see her apartment, which was much larger and fancier than mine. It was also full of weapons—not only guns, but also blades, bows, spears, axes, and other things I couldn't have named. Apparently Gwen was a serious collector. Many of the more beautiful items were displayed on the walls, but she also had an entire room dedicated to storage.

We talked shop about some of her guns. I didn't know much about the more exotic firearms she showed me, but it's hard to grow up in a rural area and not get acquainted with rifles and shotguns—hunting is a big part of life in northern Wisconsin. And even though Mom's handgun was pretty basic, she'd enjoyed browsing the newer models whenever she took me shooting. I'd picked up enough over the years to hold up my end of the conversation, which I hoped made me seem less little-girly in the wake of the horses-smell-good thing.

In addition to the apartments, each wing contained recreation areas; a small kitchen; laundry facilities; and a walk-in supply closet full of bedding, towels, toiletries, and cleaning products. Gwen pointed out the unscented shampoo, conditioner, soap, and deodorant to me and explained that several types of Seconds had very sensitive noses. It was considered rude to wear perfumes around them, so the policy was to avoid scented products entirely. Smoking was prohibited for the same reason.

The central part of the house had several subbasements. I'd visited one of those levels briefly when we used the underground tunnel to the garage. Most of the basement space was dedicated to athletic facilities: an indoor pool, extensive weight and cardio rooms, racquetball and basketball courts, and several rooms set up for martial arts, gymnastics, and other punishing activities. It all gave me a sinking feeling that I'd soon be getting a lot sweatier than I liked.

The basement also housed a sophisticated medical facility. Doctors and nurses were present at all times to deal with emergencies and dispense routine care. Next to the "clinic," which really looked more like a mini-hospital, was a large lending library. That was a much happier discovery for me. I didn't have a chance to explore it, but I hoped they had some things I'd like to read.

Above ground, the main part of the house was all public rooms. A vast ballroom took up the center, but there were at least a dozen smaller rooms for meetings, receptions, parties, and so forth. The Nolanders' quarters had been sized for humans, but the public rooms seemed to have been built to accommodate larger creatures—all had at least twelve-foot ceilings, and the doors were oversized. So was some of the furniture.

The central part of the house also had a number of bathrooms. Some of them had facilities I'd never seen before. Gwen paused to chat with someone, so I poked around in one of the strange ones. It had a toilet that was basically a three-foot-wide sunken tub. When you flushed it, which you did with a floor pedal, a large central hole opened up and tons of water cascaded down the sides.

What sort of creature would require such a thing? I tried to picture Ghosteater squatting at the edge and pooping. It was hard to imagine.

I thought about the document Cordus had given me, which I'd read before lunch. It had turned out to be a short handwritten early history of the other world.

According to what I'd read, the world I was standing in right now was the "First Emanation" because it had emerged through natural processes. The cosmos had come into being, galaxies had formed, the Sun had been born, planets had consolidated around it, life had arisen and evolved on Earth, and so forth. All that sounded familiar.

But after that, the story diverged from what I'd learned in

school. On Earth, the document said, living things began to appear that had the capacity to recognize and manipulate essence, which was defined—more poetically than helpfully, I thought—as "the grain of is-ness." The Second Emanation emerged not from the unguided processes of nature, but through acts of creation by these new beings. That meant it was one step removed from the first world's more natural origins. Thus the idea of its being a second emanation.

At first, a few places on Earth gained echoes or shadows—pockets of duplicated space created by essence-workers reshaping their surroundings. Over time, more and more echoes were generated, and they spread and connected with one another until they formed an entire shadow world. The separateness of the S-Em increased as it became a whole. It was still essentially linked to the F-Em, but passage between the two worlds was now difficult. It took a very strong worker to open a strait.

What had surprised me most was the idea that the S-Em began to emerge hundreds of millions of years ago. Countless species had contributed to its creation. The ability to work essence wasn't limited to human beings or even to intelligent animals. Essence-workers appeared among dolphins and crows and elephants, sure, but also among bacteria and trees and goldfish. That meant the other world was the product of a lot more than the human imagination.

It also meant the S-Em had what the history called strata—some places had multiple layers created when different essence-workers reshaped the same space. Movement between strata was usually possible, if challenging. Sometimes, though, they got completely separated from the rest of the S-Em—little worlds unto themselves.

I thought about getting stuck in a bacterial stratum—not

fun. And what kind of world would a tree invent for itself? One with twenty-four-hour sunlight and no caterpillars?

I looked down at the tub-toilet and shook my head. My new reality was a strange place.

⌖

Gwen had told me when dinner was served, and I'd said I'd meet her there at 7:30. I walked into the dining room ten minutes late and didn't see her. I looked around the room and didn't recognize anyone. Except Graham. He was sitting at a table by one of the windows, looking out. No one was sitting with him. No one was even sitting nearby. He'd become a pariah.

His untouched place setting suggested he'd only just gotten there himself. After a moment's hesitation, I went over and asked if I could join him. He looked up at me, surprised. Then he nodded at the empty chair across from him, and I sat down.

An awkward silence ensued. Both of us seemed to be trying to think of something to say. Thankfully, a waiter came to take my order, which was a rather lengthy transaction. I had to choose dishes for four courses, as well as beverages. When the waiter described the entrées, I didn't recognize some of the things he mentioned. The process left me a bit flushed and embarrassed.

After the waiter left, Graham gave me the ghost of a smile.

"I wouldn't have guessed you liked snails."

"Snails?"

"The chicken breast comes with escargots."

I must've look dismayed, because he said, "Don't worry, they're on the side."

The waiter filled our water glasses.

"So, how are you settling in?" Graham asked.

"Okay, I guess. It's all …" I paused, at a loss.

"A bit much? Really, really weird? Exciting and terrifying at the same time?"

"Yeah," I said, "all that."

He asked what I'd been up to for the last few days. My first course—an onion soup—arrived as I described my experience at court and my first lesson with Cordus.

Graham nodded. "Any questions?"

I hesitated, perplexed. "Do you still think of yourself as my trainer?"

"No. But I can still answer questions."

I must've looked dubious, because he gave me a sad smile and added, "Just don't ask me something I'll have to lie about."

I gave him the laugh he was looking for, though his comment was painfully close to what I'd actually been thinking.

Well, why not ask some of the questions that had occurred to me over the past couple days, some of the things I couldn't ask Cordus himself? It's not like I had to believe his answers, if I didn't want to. I lowered my voice.

"Why does Lord Cordus let Williams get away with wearing all black?"

Graham looked at me blankly.

"I hadn't realized that was happening. He doesn't go to court, much. I guess I never noticed."

He thought about it.

"I don't know why Lord Cordus would allow that. If you qualify to wear white, you have to."

Our entrées came. My chicken breast was indeed accompanied by a dish of snails, each sitting in its own bath of melted butter. Graham showed me how to fork one out of its shell. It was actually pretty good.

"Do you know anything about the snowman ambassador?"

"No, sorry, she's quite new to the job."

"Good thing you helped with the snail, 'cause a fat lot of good you are on the questions," I said, leaning back.

Graham smiled a little.

"Is Lady Innin stronger than Lord Cordus?"

"No idea. They keep that kind of information to themselves, understandably."

"I thought you could tell if you touch someone."

"Ah, right. First of all, I've never touched Lady Innin. Second, it's more complicated than that. If you touch someone who's weaker than you, you'll probably get a pretty good sense of how strong they are. If you touch someone who's stronger, you'll know they're stronger, but you won't get as accurate a sense of what they can do. Touch someone like Lord Cordus or Lady Innin, and you'll just feel overwhelming power. The fine differences between them won't be discernible."

Okay, that was helpful.

"Do you know how old Lord Cordus is?"

"He was born in Constantinople in the 330s or 340s, I think."

My mind went blank. It was like he'd started speaking another language.

"Going on seventeen hundred years," Graham added, when he saw I wasn't getting it.

"That's impossible."

"Nope. Powerful Seconds can live just about forever if they want to. Some of them are millions of years old. Hundreds of millions, maybe."

I stared at him, amazed.

BECCA MILLS

"How can that be?"

Graham shrugged. "You're talking about beings that can rework the world itself. Reworking their bodies seems like small potatoes next to that, doesn't it?"

It made intellectual sense when he put it like that, but on a gut level, the idea living forever felt profoundly wrong. Like they were ignoring a law so fundamental that it should've been unbreakable. I mean, the world changed. That was the way of things. But mortality itself? No.

"Isn't the S-Em overpopulated?"

"Not so far as I've heard. Keep in mind we're only talking about the most powerful Seconds, here, not your run-of-the-mill S-Em shop-keeper. The stronger their ability, the longer they can live."

I popped a snail in my mouth and chewed slowly, contemplating this new wrinkle.

"I guess I don't understand why they're so worried about humans finding out about them. Remaking the world, living forever—they seem more like gods than people. Surely they don't have anything to fear from us."

Graham turned and looked out the window. At first I thought I'd strayed into something he couldn't talk about truthfully, but eventually he spoke.

"I saw a nature program a few years back. There were these big birds—toucans, or something—that laid two eggs in a hole in a tree. When the chicks were old enough to stick their heads out, some ants crawled up the trunk. The chicks killed every one of them. The narrator said that if even one ant got back to its nest with news about the chicks' hole, all the ants would come. Later in the program, they showed the nest again. One of the chicks had fledged and flown away, but the ants had gotten the other one. It was still there, sticking its head out of the hole, but it was skeletal, picked clean."

Graham turned back from the window. "The ants were so tiny, and the chick was so big, but it only took one getting away."

"And the Seconds are like that chick? Trapped in a hole? Defenseless?"

"It wasn't defenseless. It killed hundreds of ants. But in the end, when they came back by the millions, it couldn't kill them all."

I had to admit it was a shudder-inducing image.

"Okay, yeah, I get it. But what beings like Lord Cordus can do, it's way beyond having a big beak, or whatever that chick had to work with."

Graham shrugged. "You say they're godlike. Maybe so, but humans kill their gods." He looked up at me. "Humans kill everything. They're nature's own weapon of mass destruction."

The way he said it gave me goose bumps.

We sat in silence for a while as we finished our entrées. Conversation picked up again when our desserts came, but we stuck to lighter topics—the quality of the gym downstairs, what sort of books the library had, and so forth.

Graham and I parted ways awkwardly at the dining room doors. I was glad I'd made the effort to sit with him but relieved he didn't offer to walk me back to my room.

I reminded myself that even if betraying Cordus wasn't a bad thing, Graham's way of doing it had put Kara and the others at risk. That was no good. And he'd physically attacked me, too.

I did feel bad, though. Nothing he'd done struck me as deserving capital punishment, and that was probably what he was going to get. I imagined Cordus doing to Graham what he'd done to the green man. It was an unbearable thought.

Chapter 17

A WEEK OR so passed. Every day followed the same schedule, so it was easy to lose track of which day it was. Each morning I got dressed and headed down to breakfast by 7:00, often with Gwen, Andy, and Theo, who seemed to be on the same schedule. Then I had a half-hour lesson with Cordus, followed by a workout. Then lunch, followed by several hours of personal time, an hour of combat training, a shower, and dinner.

The personal time was mixed. I spent a little of it browsing the lending library, which was fun. I found plenty of good books and a bunch of movies I'd like to watch, if I ever had a couple free hours. A few times I hung out with Kara, which was nice, or poked around the stables.

On the other hand, I also used my personal time to visit Justine, who'd been given a first-floor suite not far from my room. Those visits were the opposite of fun. She still seemed unaware that she was anything but human. She swung irrationally back and forth between accusing me of kidnapping her and begging me to protect her from some unspecified threat.

She also mooned over Ben and the girls. That grated on me.

Why had she gone and married a human man, anyway? Just to make her cover more convincing? It wasn't fair to Ben or to the half-human children she'd borne.

Several times, Cordus came to see Justine while I was there. Her reaction to him was weird. She claimed not to have met him before the previous week, yet she clearly found his presence comforting.

She flirted with him shamelessly, which annoyed me. She was married to my brother, for god's sake. Couldn't she at least save it for when I wasn't around?

At least he didn't respond to it. Mostly he just asked her the same questions in slightly different ways. As the days passed, she noticed the repetition. I could see the questions were beginning to annoy her a little, though it helped that the asker was so attractive.

The fact that she remembered the questions she'd been asked earlier suggested to me that her mind and memory were working normally. I said as much to Cordus and got his version of "uh-huh" in response — "Your assessment is apt, Miss Ryder."

I also spent a fair amount of time on the phone with Tiffany, which always left me feeling like a heel. I could tell that Ben was having trouble keeping things together. I thought about telling her about Callie, so that there'd be someone in Dorf she could talk to about her abilities. But that would mean exposing her to another person in Cordus's organization, and I didn't want to attract more attention to her and her sisters than I had to. I also wasn't sure Callie's religiously inflected understanding of things would be a net gain for Tiff. It might just confuse her more. Lastly, fingering Callie as a Nolander would be breaking the rules.

I tried to phone Ben a couple times. He seemed to be

screening my calls. I couldn't blame him, but it hurt.

So that was my personal time—mixed at best. The rest of my schedule pretty much sucked.

The lessons with Cordus were increasingly frustrating. I still couldn't see any workings, and he only let me try a few times each day. Instead, we spent most of each half-hour working on Baasha, which turned out to be about a million times harder than French.

It just didn't feel like I was making any progress, even though being a student was the one thing I'd always done well.

Plus, Cordus disturbed me. Every day I half expected him to pull his mind-control trick and take advantage of me. The thought of that scared me sick, and I was always knotted up with anxiety before entering his office in the morning. But once inside, I regularly found myself staring at him, my fears forgotten.

My fascination with him was distressing. I suspected he was a monster inside a pretty shell, and I didn't want to find him attractive.

The physical fitness program was a total bummer. Gwen was in charge of that part of my day, and she was a fiend when it came to working out. She made me jog, lift weights, and try out various complicated machines that simulated rowing, skiing, and other forms of torture. It was unrelenting. I was sore all the time.

The combat training was ridiculous. My instructor was one of the people I'd met during my evening at court, Hortensia Tolosa. She was eighteen and went by "Tezzy." Cordus had gotten her in a trade of some sort with another Second soon after she entered the first caste at age five.

If Gwen was a fiend, Tezzy was an ogre. My guess was she'd studied taekwondo in the womb. She made me feel utterly incompetent. I wanted to empathize with someone who'd been traded like livestock when she was a little kid, but it was pretty hard to feel anything but resentful.

I had bruises everywhere. They weren't from Tezzy hitting me—she didn't do that. They were from me falling down while she tried to get me to hit or kick her, or rather, a pad she was holding.

By Day Four, she'd backtracked to just trying to teach me how to stand still. She'd have me assume a particular stance, then coach me on making it solid and resilient. Then she'd walk up to me and try to push me down. I always fell down. Always. I could tell she didn't know what to do with me. It was the pits.

⌘

One morning—I think it was a Friday—Andy and Theo were looking sort of worried when I joined them in the dining room for breakfast.

"Hey, what's up? Something wrong?"

"Lord Limu's in the city," Andy said. "Hank saw him last night."

Limu. That's who Williams and Callie thought I'd seen at the other end of the open strait.

"It's bad that he's here?"

"Dunno. We're trying to figure it out," Theo said. "It's definitely unusual. The regional powers don't enter each others' territories without a good reason, except for formal events."

"Maybe he was invited," I said, remembering how Cordus had asked the green man about him.

Theo cocked his head. "You know something about this?"

"Who, me? I don't know anything about anything," I said, kicking myself.

The two men sat back and studied me, then shared a look. They clearly weren't fooled.

Andy said, "Should we be worried?"

"I honestly don't know. I'm sorry. You know how new I am to all this."

He nodded, but an awkwardness came over the table that hadn't been there before.

"Can you tell me anything about Lord Limu? Just public-knowledge stuff?"

"Well," Theo said, "he controls most of the Pacific Basin. So, the Aleutians and southern Alaska; the west coast of North America; the west coast of South America down through northern Chile—that's all him. And the coast on the other side, from Russia down through Papua New Guinea, and the little islands, like Hawaii. And all that ocean."

"Australia, too?"

"No, someone else holds Australia and New Zealand."

I tried to pull a map together in my mind. Embarrassingly, I didn't know where the Aleutians or Papua New Guinea were.

"He's gifted with fire, and he's strong. Some say he's the strongest of the powers holding F-Em territories. He's a real bad-ass—aggressive, irrational, maybe unstable. Not a good guy, not safe to be around."

A fire-worker. I thought back to the lava-man in the lawn chair. No wonder Williams and Callie had recognized him from my description.

Andy said, "We heard he was holding a strait open up near where you're from."

Dorf wasn't the only place where gossip traveled fast.

"I don't know that it was him."

"Fine, be that way," Andy said, looking annoyed.

"Give her a break," Theo said. "She's a newbie. She's too nervous to gossip."

"Don't worry," he said to me. "You'll get a sense of who you can trust and what it's safe to talk about. FYI, Andy and I are definitely on the trustworthy list."

He winked at me and smiled. A lot of the tension drained away.

I rolled my eyes but smiled back. I didn't know if Theo and Andy were trustworthy or not, but they were certainly likeable.

Just then, Gwen walked in. She joined us and immediately said, "Y'all hear about Lord Limu?"

The conversation that morning had a circular quality.

❧

Cordus leaned forward, steepling his fingers.

I'd completed the day's five fruitless attempts to sense the working above his hand. I wondered if he was as sick of the exercise as I was. I'd never seen any annoyance in his manner, but that might just mean he had more self-control than I did.

Afraid to look at his face, I focused on his hands. They were as beautiful as the rest of him. Apprehension crawled over me. Just because he hadn't done anything to me so far didn't mean he wasn't going to do something right now.

My nervousness quickly got the better of me, which led to babbling.

"How come I can't tell if someone else is a Nolander by touching them?"

He glanced at me. "Your capacity is almost always dormant. It awakens only when you see a half-working. You would be able to identify another Nolander if you touched him or her during one of those brief moments of awakening."

"Oh. Okay."

Another minute or two of silence ensued. I somehow managed to keep quiet.

"Miss Ryder," Cordus finally said, leaning back, "you will appear in my court this evening."

Outwardly, I nodded. Inwardly, I groaned.

"We will be entertaining an important guest."

"Lord Limu?"

"Yes."

I hesitated, then plunged in. "I'm delighted to be there, of course, but why me? I mean, is there something you want me to do? Of all your people, I seem … uniquely incapable."

"That perception is inaccurate. Do you not recall looking into the strait near your home in Wisconsin and seeing Lord Limu at the other end?"

"Sure, but all I did was see him. That doesn't seem particularly useful. And it's not like he was trying to hide, or anything. He was right there."

Cordus pondered me in silence for at least a minute before answering. He was close enough that I could see the paler starburst pattern in his brown eyes. I found myself staring at it and jumped when he spoke.

"He was not trying to hide, Miss Ryder, because it never occurred to him that someone might be able to see him. He was in the heart of his domain, and he knew that I was here in New York. Who else in this part of the First Emanation could possibly see him through a strait? He felt as safely hidden there on his mountain redoubt as I feel sitting in this room."

I thought about it. He had looked awfully surprised.

"What does that mean, exactly? I mean, what does it mean

for me?" God, only I could use "mean" three times in two short sentences. Almost a quarter of what I'd just said was "mean." *Oh, don't be so mean to yourself*, I thought. I realized I was about to have one of my nervous laughing fits and bit the inside of my cheek.

"Now is not the time for that conversation," he said flatly. "But rest assured that your abilities are of value to this organization."

"As for tonight," he continued, "I suspect Lord Limu will recognize you. We shall see how he reacts to your presence, shall we not?"

❦

I sat in the back of the limo with Cordus, trying not to fidget.

I had gotten the full-on staff treatment again. The hair and make-up were similar, but my dress this time was more revealing. It had a plunging neckline that snaked down between my breasts, all the way to my navel. My breasts had actually been taped in place. I'd tried my best to ignore the staff-members' hands as they glued me into shape, but it had been distinctly unpleasant. The whole neckline was edged in at least two inches of pearl beading. The beading wrapped around the dress's collar, then snaked down to a point at my ass.

The dress made me feel less like high-class arm candy and more like a pricey hooker. The fact that I was going to show up alone on Cordus's arm underlined that impression. This dress also had even more white than the last one, and the fur stole they'd given me to wear was white, too. I felt highly uncomfortable.

At least Cordus was occupied on the phone. I couldn't hear

what he was saying, so I just looked out the window and tried to think of a name for a transparent barrier that blocked sound. By the time we arrived at the building, I'd come up with sound-wall, shush-shield, silenta-sphere, and hushification.

We pulled directly into an underground parking structure. The driver came around and opened the door. Cordus helped me out. I didn't want to touch him, but I pretty much had to—my dress made it hard to get up without falling.

Grant was waiting at the elevator to key us up to the penthouse. The damn thing rose as slowly as it had the last time. I swear it took five minutes. As we stood there, Cordus turned and looked me up and down. Very thoroughly. My pulse shot up, and I blushed. He didn't say anything.

The elevator opened on Williams, who seemed to be standing guard. Again with the all black. He glanced at my flushed face. His upper lip lifted slightly.

Was he sneering at me?

Like any of this was my fault! Anger coursed through me. I balled my hands up and glared at him.

Cordus didn't seem to notice Williams's lack of either manners or white clothing. He just nodded at him and walked by. Fuming, I followed.

Andy was at the coat check, and Theo was in the living room, unobtrusively watching from a corner. I saw Hank and Kristin circulating with drinks and hors d'oeuvre.

There were far fewer Seconds present than last time—sixteen, by my count. Most looked familiar from the circuit I'd made with Cordus the last time. I was relieved not to see Innin, the tiny woman who'd wanted to trade Florida for me.

A green man was lounging on one of the couches. I thought it might be the same one who'd been present at my last visit. As before, the brilliant color mechanism of its skin—scales, maybe?—was all active, so that it glittered like green tinsel. Horrifyingly, Cordus put his arm out for me and headed in that direction.

He stopped to speak with several other Seconds on the way, but all too soon he settled me on the couch across from the green man, then sat down beside me.

"We greet you with honor, Gnaeus Cornelius Marci Filius Cordus," it said in a raspy voice, licking its lips with a dry, gray tongue.

Cordus answered it with a long string of sound that must've been its name, and the two began to converse.

I studied the thing. What the hell was a green man, anyway? I couldn't imagine how I'd ever looked at the small, stooped, naked figure in my picture and seen a human being. The creature in front of me was more reptilian than human. It had no nose and a long, skinny neck with a pronounced kink. Its arms were strangely long and bumpy. And how had I missed all those claws? Each was more than an inch long and shaped like a talon.

I shuddered, remembering what they could do to flesh.

The thing sitting across from me shifted, and its skin twitched, flashing green light in my eyes. Suddenly I realized what I was seeing: feathers. They were mostly tiny, no bigger than a ladybug. The bumpiness on the arms came from an edging of larger ones.

The green man glanced at me. I realized I'd been staring and looked down, abruptly scared. Kara had warned me not to stare. Idiot.

"My Lord, why does it accompany you if it is not yet trained?"

"My apologies, Ambassador. She will be disciplined."

Cordus spoke in a cool, offhanded tone, as though my future punishment was almost too obvious and uninteresting to mention. I felt goose bumps run up my arms.

Cordus and the green man returned to a discussion of events in "the Float of Charms," whatever that was. I kept my eyes trained firmly on my hands, which I'd locked together in my lap so they wouldn't shake. I tried not to think about how Cordus might "discipline" me.

After about twenty more minutes, during which the green man moved on and several other Seconds came over to pay their respects, an expectant pause swept over the room. I looked up and saw Limu coming toward us. Several Seconds I hadn't seen before trailed behind him—his honor guard, maybe.

Cordus and the woman he was speaking to rose, so I did as well. Limu stopped a few feet from the furniture grouping and greeted Cordus by name. He sounded distracted and annoyed. I thought he left out one of the names, actually. Nevertheless, Cordus nodded cordially and greeted Limu by what had to be his full name. I swear it had twenty words.

By the end of it, Limu was practically jigging with impatience. I wondered if Cordus had added some titles, under cover of good manners, just to tick him off.

The woman who'd been sitting with us excused herself. As Limu sat down in her place, my initial impulse was to scramble back: surely the couch would ignite. Of course, it didn't— he'd been walking across the carpet a moment before, hadn't he? It wasn't like that'd gone up in flames.

He looked different than he had when I'd seen him before—less rocky, more metallic. His surface was a glowing orange-red, crusted here and there with craggy, blackened material and ash. In the center of his torso, the color shaded toward blazing yellow. When his mouth opened, I saw white fire inside.

His eyes burned with that fire. They were far too bright to look at directly, but I could tell they were focused on me. He was staring at me even more intensely than Innin had. It was deeply disconcerting. Innin had looked acquisitive. Limu looked vengeful. There was no doubt that he recognized me.

I felt a sudden surge of resentment at Williams and Kara. They'd walked me right into making an enemy of this terrifying creature.

No, to be fair, they hadn't asked me to look through the strait. They'd asked me to look into it. The rest I'd done myself, damn it.

Limu accepted a glass of wine from Hank and leaned back, slowly twirling the stem between his molten fingers. He sipped, then set down his glass, as though dissatisfied with the wine.

"You have something of mine, Lord Cordus. I have come for it."

"Do I?" Cordus said. "I was not aware of it. What is the item?"

"One of my people."

Cordus waited. Obviously that wasn't much of a description. Instead of elaborating, Limu let out a rumbling growl, flexing his hands as though they were cramping.

"Do not play games with me, Lord Cordus. Give her to me."

"My lord, so far as I am aware, the individuals standing behind you are the only members of your household in my lands at this time."

"Fool! Always the same with you—games and playthings. Give her to me. The one calling herself Justine Jenson Ryder.

Now."

Cordus leaned back, crossed his legs, and began slowly bouncing his foot.

"If Mrs. Ryder is the person you mean, then we have nothing to discuss, my lord. She has been living in my lands for at least twenty years. I have no reason to believe she belongs to you." He glanced up at Limu. "Unless she bears your stricture, of course."

"She does not," Limu said, seething.

"Then what possible claim can you have upon her, my honored guest?"

"She is my wife."

I saw Cordus's eyebrow go up. I know I was shocked. In what state of mind would Justine marry a being made of fire? I was pretty damn scared just being in the same building with him, much less the same bed.

"Is she, indeed? My congratulations. Nevertheless, marriage does not constitute ownership."

Cordus's tone suggested boredom.

Apparently Limu didn't care for it. Enraged, he threw his head back and roared. The sound was an avalanche of rocks and iron crashing down an endless slope. A fountain of yellow and white fire surged out of his mouth and flowed over the ceiling as though it were liquid. Near the living room door, Williams made a quick circular motion, then closed his hand into a fist. As he did, the fire boiled back in on itself and winked out, leaving a large scorched area on the ceiling. A wisp of smoke was left curling in mid-air.

I sat there, stunned. It was like death had come visiting, then been sent packing, all before I had time to react.

I wasn't the only one who took the threat seriously. Most of Cordus's other guests backed away, but a few moved forward. Andy and Theo advanced from the corners of the room, taking up positions behind Cordus. Williams stayed in the doorway, the shadows hiding his expression.

"My lord," Cordus said coldly, "such behavior is unproductive."

Limu was leaning forward and staring at Cordus, hands clenched, breathing out waves of heat. Cordus must've been shielding us from it. I couldn't feel it, but I could see the shimmer in the air.

Comically, the air-conditioning kicked in.

After almost a minute, Limu straightened up and sat back. Slowly, he opened his fists.

"She is a thief."

"Mrs. Ryder stole something of yours?"

I glanced at Cordus. The eyebrow was back up.

"Yes."

"What did she steal?"

"That is none of your business," Limu snapped. "It is my right to pursue a thief."

"Certainly, so long as the thief remains in your lands," Cordus said. "Once he or she crosses into another power's territory, it becomes a matter for local law-keepers. And," he added, "for possible extradition. Sadly, we have no extradition agreement, my lord, despite my repeated suggestions that we discuss one."

Limu responded with a rumbling growl.

I got the sense that Cordus was goading him. Why was he doing that? It didn't seem wise. Yeah, Williams had apparently contained that last outburst, but it hadn't been a directed attack on someone, just vented frustration.

"Even if you could offer evidence supporting your accusation of thievery, which it seems you will not or cannot,"

Cordus continued, "given the regrettably lacking state of our treaties, the criminal would remain under my jurisdiction."

"Law-keeping and treaties!"

With a disgusted sound, Limu spat a globule of fire onto the coffee table in front of us. It guttered instantly and went out, leaving a charred spot.

"You have spent too long among humans, whelp. As though power comes from rules and symbols. Power does not come from. Power *is*."

Cordus leaned forward, all pretense of indifference gone. His beauty seemed to blaze around him, inhuman, terrifying.

"As you say. So then, take her from me."

The room went silent. Not a creature in the place breathed.

Limu's eyes widened. He stared back at Cordus for several seconds. Then, with a howl of fury, he exploded into enveloping fire, boiling and seething just in front of us. I cowered away from it, pointlessly, shielding my face with my arm.

The fire seemed to grow ever denser, hotter, and brighter. Malevolence radiated from it. The fire wanted to expand, to consume. But it didn't. It was being restrained. Out of the corner of my eye, I saw Cordus, still sitting beside me, staring intently into the flames.

Was he holding Limu back? Yes, he must be.

After a standoff of about thirty seconds, the ball of fire— now so dense it shone like a mini-sun—convulsed and began to dim. Slowly the fire died down, revealing Limu's shape underneath, now pale yellow all over.

Rage and humiliation were plain on his face. Clearly, he'd been bested, and he hadn't expected it. He didn't say anything, just stared at Cordus, shot me a venomous glance, then stalked out.

I think the Seconds arrayed behind us were as surprised as he was. Everyone just stood there. With a sharp crack, the warped steel bars of the flambéed coffee table snapped, and the thing collapsed. Everyone jumped, then started murmuring.

Cordus sat silently for a moment, pondering the burned remnants of furniture in front of us. Then he turned to me.

"Miss Ryder, if Ambassador Cra of the First Kingdom is still present, I would very much like to speak with him again."

He must mean the green man, I thought.

Fresh out of words, I nodded and went to find the repugnant little bird-creature. Funny how much less frightening the prospect of speaking to Cra seemed than it would have an hour earlier.

❦

I was less uncomfortable on the ride home than I had been on the way to court. It wasn't that sitting in a plush limo with Cordus had become routine. I just had bigger things to think about.

Cordus had interrogated Cra about the item Justine supposedly stole from Limu.

I'd been only marginally less surprised than Cra when Cordus included me inside the barrier he set up to keep the conversation private.

Leaning back nonchalantly on the remaining couch and using a cool, bored tone, Cordus had hypothesized that the green men surely wouldn't have agreed to send one of their hunters on such a risky mission—risky both individually and diplomatically, Cordus pointed out—without understanding something of the stakes.

At first the ambassador had maintained ignorance, but under Cordus's silent stare, it eventually allowed as how it might've heard a few rumors—wholly unsubstantiated, of course. The scuttlebutt was that Limu had been working on a powerful weapon. Justine had wormed her way into his affections and stolen it from him. Then she'd disappeared.

After Cordus had gotten this information out of Cra, he'd spent a while circulating, but guests starting dropping away quickly. I got the feeling they all wanted to get home and hit the Second equivalent of Twitter to tell others about Limu's humiliating defeat.

I sat in the limo, pondering the idea that Justine was some sort of master thief. It was almost beyond belief.

When Cordus spoke, I jumped.

"Miss Ryder, I am remembering something the one you call Ghosteater said to you when describing the scent of Mrs. Ryder."

"That she was 'unfinished.'"

"Yes, and 'fragmentary.' I ask you again, are you certain those are the terms he used?"

"As certain as I can be, given that it wasn't something I thought I'd need to remember." I paused. "I might be able to ask him, if I went back to Dorf. I got the impression he'd been hanging out there. He might still be in the area."

Cordus didn't respond to the offer. Instead he leaned back and stretched out his legs, then studied his shoes as he tapped them slowly together.

"I begin to have an idea of what Mrs. Ryder may be." He looked up at me. "If I am right, we are facing a rather serious situation."

He focused again on his feet. Tap, tap, tap.

I sat there wondering if there was a way I could avoid getting sucked into his "rather serious situation." Unfortunately, I didn't think so.

"You read the document I gave to you."

I nodded, though it hadn't really been a question.

"Human species have been producing essence-workers for some millions of years—not only *Homo sapiens* but other members of the genus *Homo*, as well as several other genera. Some humanoid Seconds are, thus, comparatively old, though the reptiles would scoff if they heard any of us lay claim to that adjective."

I nodded, amazed for about the hundredth time in the last few weeks. So there were Neanderthal Seconds. People who'd been alive for tens of thousands, maybe even hundreds of thousands of years. How extraordinary.

"That said, many walk among us to whom the lives of our greatest elders would seem but moments. Some of these are old enough to have passed into legend, so that we cannot be quite sure whether they ever existed. They are, in effect, our gods."

Gods to the gods. What a thought.

"One such legend is known as 'Eye of the Heavens.' This ancient being is said to be made of the sky itself. As the legend goes, in times of desperation, the sky looks down upon the creatures crawling in the mud beneath it and takes pity on their miserable lives. It shapes a piece of itself into a champion and sends him down to save and protect those in need."

"You think Justine is this Eye of the Heavens?" I shook my head. "If the sky sent her down here to be our champion, the sky has a pretty sick sense of humor."

Cordus frowned. I guess it wasn't a matter for levity.

"Remember that what I have just recounted is legend," he

said. "The legend may be no more than an attempt to concretize and embody vague memories of a being that no one understands, that no one has seen in millennia. Memories, for instance, of an ability to shape-shift so fully that all trace of the original form is lost, memories of a creature whose true matter appears to be a group of sky-blue balls."

Well I'll be damned, I thought. The hair prickled on the back of my neck.

"Do you remember ..." I replayed the event in my mind. "Right after the deer exploded into those balls, just a second later, a few more balls seemed to appear out of thin air. Each one made a little flash."

"Yes, I do remember that."

I sat there trying to draw my idea into words.

"Thinking in terms of the legend, it's like the sky only needed a certain amount of itself to make a deer, but it needed more to make a person. So it reused the deer material but had to add some more, too. I mean, Justine definitely weighs more than the deer did."

Cordus nodded. "In addition to sheer mass, she is more intelligent and has a store of existing knowledge that a deer would not have."

I could've quibbled on the "more intelligent" part but let it go.

"But where did her human memories go while she was a deer? Is she really made of sky?"

"That does not seem likely, unless we think of the sky as something other than an expanse of air, clouds, and so forth."

His face was still aimed at his tapping feet, but he was looking up at me out of the corner of his eye. I realized he was waiting for me to catch up to his conclusions. I slipped into student mode and thought about what we already knew and what we still needed to know.

"You're thinking that there's even more of her somewhere, right? And that part—the part that's not in her now—it knows something. Who she is, maybe, or what she stole and where it's hidden."

"Exactly, Miss Ryder. Very good."

"Then we have to find her missing parts."

Cordus studied his feet a while before answering.

"Perhaps, but we must not move precipitously. Lord Limu presents a threat, and it is easy to assume that the enemy of one's enemy is one's friend. Unfortunately, that cliché rarely proves true. I would like to research further the legend of Eye of the Heavens before trying to trigger any changes in Mrs. Ryder."

I nodded, but my mind had doglegged down a different track.

"We should also try to figure out what kind of weapon Limu was making," I said. "Is there any way we can get more information about that?"

"You are certainly correct, Miss Ryder. That line of research must parallel my work on Eye of the Heavens, though we must again proceed with caution. And with absolute secrecy," he added, shooting me a pointed look.

I quickly nodded, afraid he might brainwash me into silence. Frankly, I couldn't quite see why he didn't—he hardly knew me well enough to trust me.

Actually, I couldn't see why he was sharing all this with me to begin with. Maybe he foresaw needing my help later. Even so, it was weird and discomfiting. Being the only Nolander Cordus took into his confidence was worse than being the only Nolander learning Baasha, by an order of magnitude.

"For the time being," he continued, "I can tell you one thing about the weapon: it is likely a thing of great power. Lord Limu seems to have put a noticeable amount of his strength into it. He is markedly weaker than he was when we first became holders of territories in this world, and he is not one who would surrender capacity lightly."

I thought about how easily Limu had let himself be goaded into attacking. Perhaps he'd assumed he could win. Maybe he'd always been the stronger of the two.

But wait.

"You can put your capacity into an object?" I asked. "How is that possible?"

"It is an ancient art, now lost—or so I believed. I can think of no other explanation for his comparative weakness."

He thought for a few seconds, then shook his head.

"Whatever this weapon does, I suspect it will perform its function ... what is the contemporary expression? 'To the nth degree.'"

"And it must be really important to him."

"I imagine so. He has made quite the sacrifice."

"So, we have to stop him from using it, right?"

Cordus turned to look at me directly, his cold gaze meeting mine.

"That depends, Miss Ryder, on his intended target, does it not?"

Chapter 18

AT THE END of my lesson the following morning, my day took an unexpectedly nice turn.

"You may now pay a short visit to Justine Jenson Ryder," Cordus said. "For the remainder of the day, you will work in the stables as a reminder not to offend the likes of Ambassador Cra."

I schooled my face, trying to look chastened. Inside, I did a cartwheel. Shoveling horse manure instead of getting hounded by Gwen and knocked down by Tezzy? He couldn't have given me a nicer surprise if he'd shopped all day. God bless Ambassador Cra.

I made a quick stop in my room and changed into jeans, sneakers, and a sweater for my upcoming stint in the stables. Then I headed down the hall to see Justine.

"Hey, Koji," I said as I approached. "You feeling okay?"

There was always a guard outside Justine's door. It was never one of the white-wearers. The guards didn't seem intended to overpower Justine, but just to guide her back to her room, should she wander too far.

This morning, it was Koji. He looked awful—ashen and sweaty.

"Hey, Beth. Touch of flu. No biggie."

"You sure? You look like you should be in bed."

"Naw, I'm fine."

He swallowed hard a few times.

I sighed and headed on in. What was it with guys? They always had to prove how tough they were. Ben had to be practically dying before he'd take a sick day.

Justine was sitting in front of her mirror, doing her makeup. She was wearing a pretty green silk dress and heels. I felt underdressed.

"Beth! Thank goodness you're here."

She hurried over to me, looking around with a frightened expression.

"Am I safe here? I just don't feel safe. I feel like I should run away. Please, can you do something?"

Oh, man. As much as I hated her yelling at me for kidnapping, I preferred that mood to this one. Now I would have to reassure her, knowing all the while that she would be as scared when I got up to go as she was when I arrived. Maybe it was because she didn't understand why she was scared, or maybe my reassurances made no sense. After all, there was so much I couldn't say. Whatever the reason, my efforts to calm her never made much of a difference.

And this terrified, pathetic Justine was so not the woman I knew. Don't get me wrong—I couldn't stand the woman I knew. But at least she was a familiar face, a remnant of my old life. Terrified Justine was just another stranger.

The suite had a nice sitting area. We settled down on the loveseat, and I held her hand while I told her how large and well guarded Cordus's estate was, how Cordus was the most powerful man anywhere nearby, how we were working hard to try and make her even safer.

I really wanted to mention Limu and Eye of the Heavens to see if she reacted, but I obediently stifled the impulse. By some miracle, Cordus hadn't touched me yet. I was going to do everything possible to keep it that way.

I heard the door open.

"What's up, Koji?" I said, turning.

"Beth?"

It wasn't Koji. It was Graham, looking surprised.

"Graham ... what are you doing here?"

"The door was unguarded. I was concerned."

"Oh. Koji did look sick. I bet he had to take a bathroom break."

Instead of leaving, Graham stood there, awkwardly passing a tennis-ball-sized rock from hand to hand and staring at Justine. He was wearing leather gloves. A bad feeling started to come over me.

"Graham, I think you need to leave. Graham."

His eyes jerked over to me.

"Stay out of this, Beth."

He rushed Justine.

I jumped up with a shout. There was a loud sound, and the floor heaved under me. With a shriek, Justine disappeared downwards, and a second later, I fell, too. I landed in mud and threw my arms over my eyes, scrabbling to keep my face clear as soil and debris poured over me. I couldn't see Justine anywhere, but Graham was above me, teetering on the edge of the vast hole I was in. Arms wind-milling, he lost his grip on the stone ball. It sailed across the pit, bounced off the top of the fallen coffee table, and came sailing down at my face. I threw a hand out to block it, and it touched my palm.

❧

I took a breath before I realized I was under water. Fluid flooded into my lungs, heavy and burning. I thrashed, found the bottom with my knees, and tried to thrust myself up. My head broke the surface, went under again, emerged again. I floundered and managed to stand, choking and panicked. Water poured out of my mouth and nose. Leaning over, I coughed and coughed as my lungs emptied themselves.

Finally I straightened up and tried to wipe the water and tears from my eyes.

I was standing in seawater up to my midriff.

What the hell?

I could see rocks sticking out of the water only a little ways off, so I started swimming that way. After just a few body lengths, the water became too shallow to swim, so I waded until I could drag myself up onto the rocks.

My brain just shut down for a while, and I lay there, panting.

Finally I sat up and looked around. I was at the edge of a rocky shoreline. It stretched a long way before the land started to rise and a dense forest took over. I was in a sort of cove. Towering headlands rose to either side, blocking my view. I looked out to sea. Nothing but water as far as the horizon.

It was raining steadily.

Had Graham's rock brought me here, wherever "here" was? Yes, it must've. Touching it was the last thing that had happened.

Was Justine here, too? She'd fallen into the hole before me, and I thought she'd been buried. I hadn't been able to see her, at any rate. So she couldn't have touched the rock, right?

God, I hoped she hadn't suffocated under all that dirt. The

thought made me sick.

Unsteadily, I stood up. I pried my phone out of my dripping jeans. When I opened it, water oozed out from around the keys. It was dead. I didn't know all that much about cell phones, but it was hard to imagine it recovering.

I began picking my way toward the trees. The rocks were studded with tide pools, which were full of anemones, starfish, snails, and small fish. Here and there, an octopus scooted into a crevice and changed colors to match its hiding place.

Eventually the pools grew more shallow and then petered out. The narrow beach beyond the pools was a mixture of gray sand and rocks. Just past the beach, a wall of huge trees rose. It looked almost impenetrable.

Where was I?

Shock gave way to anger.

Goddamn Graham. I'd gone out of my way to be nice to him. I'd felt sorry for him. I'd invented excuses for him. And all the while, he'd been plotting to send Justine to this place. Why?

I looked around, half-expecting Limu to show up and roast me alive, but I was alone.

After a while, I took my clothes off and wrung them out as best I could, then put them back on. After I'd done that, I sat down on the sand with my back against a rock and waited for someone to come get me.

🌿

It took me too long to admit that no one was coming.

I huddled on the beach, getting rained on, for the rest of that day and the whole night. By the middle of the night, I was so cold I had to get up and jog in place.

As the wee hours of the morning ticked by, my anger at Graham was replaced by fear. Fear became terror. Then I succumbed to despair. Finally, having run through all my emotions, I went numb.

Near dawn, the demands of my cold, thirsty body forced themselves front and center. The numbness receded, replaced by pragmatism. Clearly, I couldn't stay where I was. I needed water, I needed shelter, and I needed help. In comparison, my emotional life didn't matter.

I'd already seen that walking along the beach would be impossible. The cove lay between two rocky promontories, and I sure wasn't going to try climbing one of them. It would have to be the forest. Hopefully, I'd find a road quickly.

At first light, I gathered some dead wood and made an arrow pointing toward the trees. They'd probably send a tracker after me. If they didn't, at least there'd be some sign I'd been here. Then I headed in.

The forest was like nothing I'd seen before. Huge pine trees shot straight up to a canopy far above. All the branches below the canopy were needleless and coated in hanging moss. The trees grew very close together, so that the dead, mossy branches intertwined. Many of the trunks hosted brightly colored lichens. The ground was covered in moss and dense ferns. There were insects everywhere. Some were startlingly large. Several times, a massive dragonfly hovered in front of me, as though checking me out. Lizards, snails, and frogs were also abundant.

Almost immediately, I found rainwater that had collected in a pocket between two roots. I kept moving uphill and was rewarded with more fresh water. In fact, there were pools and rivulets everywhere. Check one necessity off the list.

The pools tended to be covered with tiny floating green plants, so it was easy to mistake them for dry ground. I found a long stick and began probing in front of me as I went. Progress was slow. There wasn't much underbrush besides ferns, but neither were there paths. Huge fallen trees in various states of decay littered the forest floor. Thank god I was wearing sneakers.

After an hour, I hadn't found anything I thought I could eat, but at least I was a bit warmer. I sat down against a tree trunk and took off my shoes, which were saturated. I propped them against the tree, soles up. It wasn't like they'd dry off in the rain, but maybe they'd get a little less wet. After some thought, I took off all my clothes and rinsed them with fresh water, then cleaned the salt off my skin and out of my hair as best I could. I put my wet clothes back on and settled back down to rest.

I must've drifted off, sitting there. I awoke with the uncomfortable feeling of being watched. I opened my eyes and looked around. There was no sign of any living thing bigger than a slug. Still, I couldn't shake the feeling.

When I finally saw the creature, I froze. It was on a tree trunk right across from me. It was about the size of a dinner plate and was perfectly camouflaged with the colors and pattern of the tree's bark. After some looking, I found its eye, which had a large, oblong pupil. Once I had that, the rest of the animal began to make sense. It was an octopus, of all things. I could see its tentacles coiled around it, adhering to the tree bark. It was definitely watching me.

I looked around and saw several more of the things. Once I'd gotten the sense of how they were camouflaged, I could pick them out by looking for protuberances on trunks. I twisted around to make sure there wasn't one on the tree I was sitting against. It looked clear. Then I just sat there, not sure what to do.

I'd assumed I'd been sent some place on earth when I touched Graham's stone. Somewhere in Limu's territory— coastal Oregon, maybe. But these creatures weren't like anything I'd heard of.

Could I have been sent to the S-Em?

If so, maybe these octopuses were more than octopuses.

I got up and stood there uncertainly. Then I nodded at each of the creatures I could see.

"Um … hello there. I don't know if you can understand me, but I don't mean you any harm."

Not surprisingly, no one responded.

"Okay then. I'm not sure how I ended up here, but I need to find food and help, so I'm going to keep moving."

I started walking again, still heading uphill. All along the way, I kept seeing octopuses. I nodded politely at each one I saw, though I felt sort of stupid doing it.

By early afternoon, my legs were shaking. Not only had I found nothing to eat, but I'd been climbing steadily uphill. I sat down to rest, trying to suppress the growing fear that I was lost forever in the S-Em.

Cordus will come get me, I told myself. *I'm valuable to him.*

But what if Graham got away? my pessimistic side responded. *What if Cordus can't find me?*

Then Graham will come get me, I told myself firmly. *He wouldn't abandon me here.*

Will he? He was trying to get Justine, not me, pessimistic Beth said.

Pessimistic Beth was too smart for her own good. Huddled on the forest floor, I started to cry, and once I did, I couldn't stop for the longest time.

What finally got through the sobs was the feeling of being tapped on the leg. I looked up and discovered a tree-octopus perched on the large root beside me. It had reached out a tentacle and touched me. As I watched, it reached out again.

I jumped up and backed away, hurriedly wiping my face. The tree-'pus retreated up its root a bit, eyeing me.

"I'm sorry to be rude, but what do you want?"

It didn't say anything.

"Are you going to hurt me?"

Again no response. What did it say about me that I'd thought I might get one?

Slowly, it unfurled one tentacle toward me. Nestled among the suckers was a large snail.

"Oh. Is that for me?"

The tree-'pus put the snail down on the crushed ferns where I'd been sitting and withdrew its tentacle. Cautiously, I edged forward and reached a hand out. The tree-'pus backed away a bit, so I picked up the snail. Turning it over in my hands, I saw the shell was neatly cracked. I lifted half the shell away, revealing the snail inside. It was still alive, though it didn't seem to be in good shape.

"Is this to eat?" I brought it up to my mouth. "Eat?"

The tree-'pus just looked at me.

"Um … thanks. I think this is a gift. I'm sorry if I'm misunderstanding you."

I put the shell halves back together and stuck the snail in my pocket.

"I do want to eat it, but I want to cook it first, okay?"

I sat back down, hoping the thing didn't squish. Once I was sitting, the tree-'pus started approaching me again. It came slowly, stopping and looking at me every few inches, so I held still. Eventually it touched my leg, then withdrew its tentacle and looked at me.

It was pretty, actually. When I first saw it, it had been dark gray, like its root. Now it was an iridescent blue with cream-colored blotches.

I thought about it. I really didn't see how such a small creature could hurt me. I mean, I guess it could wrap around my neck or something, but it was soft-bodied. It looked like I could hurt it pretty easily with my bare hands.

When I didn't pull back, it undulated onto my calf.

Maybe this was part of the possible animal-taming thing I'd discovered on Rib Mountain. I'd pretty much dismissed that "ability" as a figment of my imagination. Maybe I was wrong.

I reached out a finger and touched the tree-'pus gingerly. It was quite cold and had a slimy coating. Oh well, we can't all be koala bears, right?

It kept moving up my leg, which was a weird feeling. Eventually, it settled in my lap. I looked into its eye. The pupil reflected light back like mother of pearl.

"You're a very attractive octopus," I said to it. "It's nice to meet you."

We sat there for another ten minutes or so, and then I told it I needed to get up and keep moving. When it didn't move, I slowly stood. It stayed affixed to the front of me, as though I were a tree trunk. I felt its tentacles shift, wrapping around my waist and ass.

Great. Groped by an invertebrate. Well, plenty of women had that experience, come to think of it.

"All right, little fellow. I have to get going, okay? You'd better hop off."

From its station on my hip, the tree-'pus stared up at me with one funny pupil. I guess it wanted to stay where it was.

"I'm going to keep walking, okay? You want to get down,

just squeeze, okay?"

I took a dozen steps, then looked down at the 'pus. It showed no sign of wanting down. Looked like I had a passenger.

I continued up the forested slope for another couple hours. Eventually I realized it would be getting dark soon. I could worry about the big picture—where the hell I was and how I was going to get home—later. For the time being, I needed to get a fire going so I could stay warm over night. And cook my snail.

First I went looking for dry tinder. Unfortunately, nothing in that place was dry. Eventually, poking around a fallen tree, I found a bunch of dead moss that was only slightly damp. Then I tried to find dry pieces of wood to use as a board and spindle.

I'd never actually made fire that way, mind you, but I'd seen people do it on TV.

There simply was no dry wood. Not even a scrap.

I sat down and had another cry.

It occurred to me that I'd probably cried more in the last couple weeks than Madisyn had. It was pointless and self-indulgent. That thought helped me get a handle on myself.

I got up and started gathering more of the hanging moss, looking for the driest bunches. After about half an hour, I had a huge heap of the stuff piled beside a large tree. When the time came for bed, I'd just crawl into the pile. It was the best I could do. Hopefully it would keep me warm.

I reached into my pocket and pried out the snail. It had died, but it hadn't gotten squished. I never in a million years would've thought I could eat a raw snail, but I suppose serious hunger has way of clarifying the mind. Holding my breath, I picked it out of its shell and swallowed it down in a couple bites. It was slimy and left a nasty aftertaste. I rinsed my mouth with water from a pool.

"Thanks for the snack, little fellow," I said to the tree-'pus, which was still clutching me.

Then I sat down carefully and tried to think of something I could do that would make the next day a little better than this one had been. There was so much I needed—fire, dry clothes, food, a weapon, a way of signaling for help. I really couldn't think of a way to get any of those things.

Something touched my shoulder, and I just about jumped out of my skin. It was another tree-'pus. It was clinging to the trunk above me. Once it had my attention, it held out a dead slug.

"Hey, thanks, that's really nice," I said, taking the slug.

It was intensely gooey. I really didn't think I could eat it.

As I sat there, other tree-'puses approached me with offerings. By the time it started getting dark, I'd been given three large moths, a dragonfly, a lizard, two snails, and an earthworm. I thanked each 'pus profusely.

When the gifts stopped arriving, I retreated to my moss pile with my collection of food items. My passenger 'pus climbed off me and settled on the trunk over my head, changing color to blend in. I began to eat my gifts. The slug was just too huge and slimy, but the worm, snails, and moths went down the hatch. The lizard I offered to the tree-'pus who'd been riding around on me.

It just stared back at me in the dim light.

"Hey, I've taken you pretty far from your home. I think you deserve to get some dinner, don't you?"

It stared at me a while longer, then accepted the lizard, which disappeared under the fleshy skirt that connected the tops of its tentacles. I heard a muffled crunch and wondered exactly how octopuses eat.

"You can have the slug, too. I'm really full," I said, and held it out. After a short hesitation, it too was accepted and consumed.

I went and got a drink from one of the many rainwater collections around me. Then I climbed into my moss pile.

"Thanks for your help," I said to the tree-'puses, many of which were still parked on the trunks around me. "I really appreciate it. You're wonderful hosts, and you have a lovely forest. Very, um, moist."

Of course, nobody responded. I was starting to get used to talking to myself, though.

"Okay, well, I'm going to get some sleep. Maybe I'll see you guys in the morning."

Chapter 19

SOUGHT, SOUGHT, THE wind whispered.

Ghosteater lifted his head.

Run, the wind sighed.

How long had it been since the wind said such a thing?

He opened his mouth, smelling, tasting. He didn't know the one seeking him, but it was a creature of power. Male. Young.

How strange. Few sought him any longer. Interested, he rose to seek the seeker.

The wind brushed through his fur, mumbling its warnings.

🍃

Ghosteater crouched in the silence, watching Cordus walk down a street in the place the humans called Dorf. He didn't know Cordus but recognized him for what he was: an émigré, an equal.

Equals were dangerous. His hackles lifted.

Ghosteater had not encountered many dangers of late. The great predators of this continent had vanished, and truth be told, such creatures had stopped posing a meaningful threat when he learned to walk in the silence. Even the cats. How easy it had been to step out in their midst and destroy a whole pride. It had quickly ceased to interest him.

As for humans, despite their strange machines, they were absurdly easy to kill. Soft, blind—it was hard to believe they had multiplied so swiftly, driving so many other creatures from the face of the earth. One day they had appeared, roving in a few spare bands, curious and inventive, but often starving. The next they had overrun vast stretches of the continent. Now even the land they didn't occupy bore their mark in one way or another.

The same thing had happened in the other world, to a lesser degree. There were still places there where humans didn't go.

The other world. Unwelcome memories rose. Not many years earlier, enmeshed in the affairs of others, he had shed his blood there. He had met with true danger, in those days.

But now those ties were gone. Sometimes he felt the lesser for it. He told himself it was good to be free.

The wind agreed, murmuring the word back to him, *free*.

As though he too heard the wind, Cordus paused, looking slowly up and down the street.

The émigré had been seeking Ghosteater for two days. He had driven slowly through the countryside, stopping and looking. He had walked all the streets of Dorf several times, wearing different human faces.

For much of that time, Ghosteater had stalked the stalker, mystified by his actions, intrigued by his persistence. It had been hard to go unseen—the man's sight was sharp. He crouched now at the moment of decision: should he turn back into the silence and forget the strange things the wind had shown him in this place, or should he bite the matter and wrestle it down until he understood it?

The wind shifted, blowing from the north. Sharp and pungent, it tempted him with a taste of the boreal forest—the quiet of the deep woods, the crunch of late snow beneath his once-paws, the hot blood of a wolverine in his mouth.

The wind had brought him here, and now it wanted him far away.

He didn't understand it. The wind didn't lie. It didn't jest. It had no mind for such things.

Ghosteater shifted his weight, uncertain. He should probably heed its latest advice. In his experience, the wind didn't speak of danger lightly.

And yet, what he had seen in this place intrigued him: the woman Justine, who smelled like nothing he'd ever encountered; the pup, Beth, who seemed insignificant, and yet walked all the paths; the golden-haired man; and now, a human émigré, walking alone in the first world.

Ghosteater's curiosity ate at him.

Coming to a decision at last, he slipped forward, showing himself.

"Émigré."

"Elder beast," Cordus replied, stopping and bowing. "You honor me with your presence."

Ghosteater cared nothing for honor.

"You seek me."

"I do. I have come to ask your assistance."

Ghosteater cocked his head, waiting.

"One of my people, the woman Elizabeth Joy Ryder, has disappeared from my home. I believe she has been taken by a traitor, but my trackers cannot follow him. I know you met Miss Ryder, spoke with her. I ask you to help me find her."

Ghosteater sat down, tucking his tail over his once-paws.

He studied Cordus for some time.

These human émigrés weren't like him. They made rules, played games. They spoke words they didn't mean. They fought with subterfuge and indirection, not tooth and claw.

Until they did fight with tooth and claw. Then they destroyed everything. Repugnant.

The she-pup, though, she had interested him. She who walked all the wind's paths.

"A man was here," Ghosteater said. "A marrow-worker. Slender, golden hair, your smell."

Cordus nodded. "The traitor."

"He went to an ancient place. He found a carven strait."

Cordus stared at Ghosteater. He smelled astonished. Finally he gathered his wits.

"I had not thought any of those devices were still at large, in this world or the other."

Ghosteater chuffed with annoyance and said nothing. This species thought itself all-knowing. Many such workings were lost and forgotten eons before his own source species appeared, much less Cordus's.

"Elder beast, do you know where the companion strait is located?"

"No."

The man stood silently, thinking.

"Would you be willing to track the traitor for me?"

Ghosteater tilted his head. Becoming entangled with the émigré was dangerous. The wind had said so. A thrill ran through him, a pale echo of his first hunts, of his last battles.

Cordus seemed to sense his excitement.

"The man is exceedingly dangerous. Any who track him will be struck down, unless their strength exceeds his. None of my trackers are strong enough."

A hunt. A true hunt.

"If it is as you say, I will track him."

The man nodded. "The debt is mine."

Ghosteater was not, by nature, a keeper of accounts. He would help the émigré because the situation interested him, not out of benevolence or because he wanted a favor in return. Nevertheless, he said nothing. His long life had taught him some caution.

"The trail begins near the eastern edge of this continent," Cordus said. "We can get there most quickly in my airplane."

The great beast rose and came forward. Cordus stepped back, watchfulness and caution evident in his posture. That was as it should be.

*

Ghosteater stared out the small window. Cordus had warned him of the airplane's fragility, so he kept his once-paws carefully silent. He stared down at the tiny lights beneath, clusters connected by slender strings, sprinkled all over with single stars. Small pools of darkness marked bodies of water, and then a long darkness came as the airplane crossed one of the great freshwater seas the ice had left behind.

He sat back on his haunches. How strange to pass over the land from far above. How deeply strange.

The aircraft struck him as insubstantial, ephemeral. He could have destroyed it easily. Yet for all its frailty, it did something he would have thought impossible.

He felt unsettled. He had paid little mind to the humans who came to these lands mere millennia ago, thinking them a passing blight. Perhaps they deserved greater attention.

Danger, he heard in the violated wind's muted howl outside. *Run*.

Chapter 20

I wasn't nearly so cold as I had been the night before. Despite the dampness of my clothes, the heap of moss provided good insulation. I woke feeling cramped and filthy, and with a headache and a stomach ache, but at least I'd slept.

When I pushed my way out of the moss, I was met with an audience—dozens of tree-'puses covered the trunks and larger branches all around me. Several had even come down onto the ground, turning green to blend with the ferns and mosses.

As soon as I appeared, the closer ones began to hold out offerings. I didn't feel much like eating, but I collected worms, snails, frogs, moths, and other creatures, thanking each 'pus for its gift. The cache included several more huge dragonflies. I'd never seen ones so big. Their bodies were longer than my hand.

No, that wasn't quite right. I had seen huge dragonflies before—in drawings of the prehistoric Earth.

Maybe some essence-worker had made this place millions of years ago.

How many millions?

I looked at my collection of dead creatures. There were no

mammals or birds.

Well, whenever the place had been made, I still had to find help. I stood up and squared my shoulders.

"Guys," I said to the tree-'puses, "I'm going to keep heading uphill, today. I need to find a village or a road or something, someone who can help me get back to my world."

Dozens of oblong pupils stared back at me silently.

"Thank you for taking care of me. I really appreciate it."

I gathered the food offerings up and was momentarily stymied on how to carry them. Eventually I took off the T-shirt I was wearing under my sweater and bundled the creatures up in it. Hardly ideal, but it should keep them contained. I would eat them as soon as my stomach settled.

I looked for the tree-'pus who'd accompanied me the day before and found it on the same trunk. When I looked at it, it reached several tentacles out to me.

"Are you sure you want to come with me, little guy? I'm taking you farther and farther from your home."

It kept stretching toward me, detaching a few more tentacles to stretch out.

I was torn. It might be helpful to have the 'pus with me, but if I found help, I might have to leave it someplace where there was no good habitat for it.

The 'pus had seven tentacles stretched out to me and was clinging to the trunk with just one. Its skin was pulsing from blue and cream to pearly white.

"Okay, okay," I said, going over so it could climb onto my hip. "I hope you understand, little fellow."

It settled itself on my jeans. One of its tentacles snuck under my sweater, and its suckers gripped my bare skin—damp and shivery.

Waving goodbye to the other tree-'puses, I headed uphill.

As it turned out, my 'pus had nothing to worry about—I found nothing all day except massive trees, rain, and a steady incline. I stopped a few hours into my walk to eat the more bearable of my food choices, giving the extras to my passenger. Then I continued on, hour after hour.

By late afternoon, I hurt all over. Not only was every muscle in my body screaming, but as I grew more fatigued, I fell down more, so I had a lot of new bruises. Fortunately, the 'pus proved adept at flinging itself away from me when I fell, so I hadn't landed on it.

When evening approached, I assembled another moss pile for sleeping. I was again provisioned by the tree-'puses.

As I ate, I felt my mind worrying a bad thought that hadn't quite emerged from my subconscious.

Well, best to keep it buried, I thought. Likely there'd be nothing I could do about it, anyway. I crawled into my moss and went to sleep.

❦

Unfortunately, when I woke up, the bad thought was parked in the center of my mind, all touched up with fresh paint and a body kit.

Some parts of the S-Em had multiple strata, Cordus's document had said, layered versions of a single landscape, as reshaped by different workers. My thought was this: what if I was in a stratum and couldn't get from here to somewhere else? More importantly, what if others couldn't get from somewhere else to here?

I'd assumed there would be people here, even if this part of the S-Em was made before humans evolved. After all, humans were nothing if not colonizers. All of the Earth had been around for eons before humans evolved, and we'd covered the whole planet.

But what if people had never found their way to this place? What if I was the only vertebrate here bigger than a frog?

Should I have stayed down near the shore?

No, what would be the point of that? I had to look for help. It was either that or hunker down and wait for a rescue that might never happen. And hope the tree-'puses remained generous. That was no way to confront my situation. I'd be back in passive-victim mode.

It was better to try to find help. If Cordus had sent a rescue party, they'd be tracking me and would probably catch up to me quickly.

I just had to keep looking for people—a village, a shack, a road, anything.

Resolved, I gathered up my 'pus and the morning offerings, and headed uphill.

*

By the end of the day, I still hadn't reached the summit. The mountain seemed to go on forever.

As I bedded down for the night, I watched the 'puses on the trees around me. There was a period every evening, right around dusk, when they abandoned their camouflage and put on a short symphony of color. It started as I lay there—pulses and flashes of color lit up the trunks and branches all around me. They hit all the shades of the rainbow, and then some, the colors moving across the forest in vast waves, one after another.

The display was completely silent and quite beautiful. Exhausted and frightened as I was, it was hard not to be filled with wonder. How many people got to see something like this? *Not many*, I thought.

Let's just hope you're not the only one, ever, pessimistic Beth chimed in.

Chapter 21

"A SINK HOLE formed, here, without warning," Cordus said. "Apparently an underground spring shifted and began to saturate the soil some months ago. The earth liquefied just as Mr. Ryzik joined Miss Ryder in the room. That is the kind of event Mr. Ryzik's gift creates."

Ghosteater tasted the air in the room and was surprised.

"The woman Justine was here."

"Yes. She was staying in this room."

Ghosteater circled the hole, then jumped down into it, sniffing carefully. Justine had been under the dirt. The scents had been trampled by those who came to dig her out, but he could still read them—her burial beneath falling earth, the place where I'd lain, the carven strait falling toward the bottom of the pit, the moment of contact between it and my hand. He tasted the slightly burned scent of my passage through the strait. He smelled Graham's scramble down into the hole, his brief effort to uncover Justine, his terrified flight with the carven strait in his pocket.

"I will track him. You cannot keep up with me. I will track alone, then return for you."

"If you carry this device with you, I can follow you by car."

Cordus held out something small. Ghosteater didn't recognize it, but I can see it in his mind's eye—a GPS unit.

The beast understood. The émigré wanted to be there at the end of the hunt to best the prey and claim it for himself. Ghosteater didn't object—he had no use for the man. He permitted Cordus to put a loop of rope around his neck and clip the unit to it. He could slice it off in an instant, if need be.

He stepped into the silence and loped out of the house, allowing Graham's scent to guide him over the lawns to the edge of the property, where he went through Cordus's barrier with an uncomfortable tingle. He passed the blood the barrier had cost Graham, smelled his pain.

The trail led to a highway, where he could tell the man had entered a vehicle. He followed more carefully, then, since human habitations were thick.

He found that the car had passed over a river by bridge. Would the silence truly hide him on that slender span of rock and metal, teeming with cars? He wasn't sure. Best not to take a chance. Quietly, he slipped into the water.

*

Ghosteater slid into an alley at the last moment. The runaway city bus careened past him and struck a building. He moved away from the stink of gasoline and the screams of the injured.

He'd been working his way through the great city for more than a day. The unusual gift of the one he tracked created havoc all around him. Accidents befell him at every turn—cars ran up onto the sidewalk, air conditioning units fell from windows, utility poles came crashing down, hordes of rats emerged from sewers, shootouts broke out between police and armed suspects, scaffolding collapsed, gas mains exploded, riots blocked streets.

Each time, he had avoided injury, but the delays mounted. The man was still at least an hour ahead and had kept moving.

He wondered where the émigré was. Perhaps he had rethought his desire to follow by car. It wouldn't surprise him. Trailing this strange man was far more challenging than Ghosteater had thought it would be, and the human powers were known for caution.

*

The beast leapt sideways, avoiding a small avalanche of falling masonry. At long last, the man had stopped moving. Ghosteater had tracked him to the basement of an old building in the southern reaches of the island. The falling stone had blocked the window he had been about to slide through. He circled the building, looking for another way in.

There were no other windows into the basement. Instead, he used the building's main entrance, drawing his claws from the silence to carve through the locked door. He padded around the ground level until he found the stairwell leading down. He pushed the door open and paused. With a shudder and crash, the staircase collapsed.

Turning away from the heap of rubble, he found another shaft leading down. He cut his way in, then jerked back just in time as the building's elevator came hurtling down. Once it hit bottom, he jumped down onto it and dug through to the basement. His claws were strong, but they were not meant for steel. The process took a while, but the man's own luck had trapped him down there.

When he at last saw his quarry, he was saddened. The man

lay against a wall, exhausted, filthy, trembling, covered with wounds. Ghosteater understood—humans were not designed to run, without sleep, for four days. Nevertheless, it was a depressing end to a challenging hunt. The man had proven far worthier than the beast had ever expected. Dangerous indeed.

He advanced, then jumped aside as a heavy pipe fell from the ceiling.

The man's eyes opened halfway.

"Saw you cut them down," he whispered. "Shadows of Marshwren. Only thing that made them bleed."

Ghosteater paused, surprised. If this man had been at Marshwren, he was older than expected. Older than the émigré knew, perhaps. He approached the man and nosed him, inhaling, searching for the subtlest of clues. Yes, from the other realm and quite old for his kind.

"Why are you here, native?"

The man touched Ghosteater's foreleg.

"Strong," he whispered.

He was drained and close to losing consciousness.

"Native, why are you here?" Ghosteater repeated.

"Fugitive."

Ghosteater understood, then, to some degree. The humans made laws, snared one another in them, punished those who transgressed. Sometimes the transgressors escaped. This world had long provided a hiding place for fugitives from the other.

It was such a one who had ensnared him in years past and led him to the rending fields at Marshwren and elsewhere.

Ghosteater pushed the memory away. The man here before him was another.

He thought instead about laws. Their virtue escaped him. Beasts had a different way—the strongest ruled until a stronger one emerged. To structure and bind existence in a system of laws and submit oneself to them—this was repellent to him. A law had no claws of its own. It had no teeth. Thus it should have no sway.

Whatever rules this man had broken didn't matter to him.

Ghosteater thought about the situation.

Initially, the man had not interested him enough to squabble with the émigré. Now he did—so worthy an adversary. Looking down at the crumpled figure, the beast laid claim to him as prey taken. Now he alone had the right to kill him, and that he chose not to do, at least for the time being.

"Rest, fugitive. I will guard you."

❧

Two hours later, someone used an essence-worked barrier to punch through one of the basement walls. Ghosteater raised his head and watched Cordus and several of his people climb through the hole. The fugitive was sleeping behind him. Ghosteater yawned expansively, showing off his teeth.

"Émigré."

"Elder beast," Cordus said, "I am sorry to have been delayed. The device I gave you stopped functioning before you reached the city."

Ghosteater looked back at him, not feeling a response was needed. Cordus's eyes shifted.

"I see you have found him."

"Worthy prey," Ghosteater said. "He is mine."

An uncomfortable silence fell. The beast studied the people Cordus had brought—Zion, Gwen, and Williams. The last of them was the barrier-worker. He had some strength. Nevertheless, none of them was a threat. The émigré, of course, was.

Finally Cordus said, "I recognize that you claim him as prey, but Miss Ryder must be recovered. You will not prevent me from doing so, even at the cost of his life."

Ghosteater thought about it. In his eyes, Cordus had no particular right to me—he could find what he was sharp enough to track, keep what he was strong enough to hold. Other claims didn't matter.

On the other hand, I interested him even more than Graham did. He wished to see me again.

"Agreed," he said, and moved aside.

"Miss Hegstrom," Cordus said, "examine Mr. Ryzik, but do not go through his clothing."

Gwen went forward and checked Graham over.

"He's drained, exhausted, and dehydrated, and the barrier did some damage. I don't see any mortal injury."

Cordus nodded.

Ten minutes later, Gwen and Williams had propped Graham up in a corner. He was semi-conscious, and Gwen was spooning broth into his mouth. Cordus and Ghosteater stood back, waiting.

"Mr. Ryzik," Cordus said.

Graham mumbled something unintelligible. Gwen gripped him under the chin and forced his face up. His eyes blinked blearily.

"Yeah," Graham said, slurring.

"Where is Miss Ryder?"

"Carven strait. Dunno where it took her."

"Where is the strait?"

"Pocket."

"Mr. Williams, bring the strait to me. Do not touch its surface."

Williams shot him an I'm-not-an-idiot look and pulled on a pair of gloves before taking the stone ball out of Graham's pocket. He brought it over to Cordus, who examined it while Williams held it. Eventually, Cordus reached out and took it, not bothering to cover his skin. Everyone in the room felt the strait grasp at him, but with a concentrated expression, Cordus overpowered its pull.

He held the ball for a while, studying it.

Finally he said, "The corresponding strait is in an ancient stratum or isolate of the S-Em. It is functional."

"Fresh water? Predators? Food supply?" Gwen asked.

Cordus shook his head. "That I cannot tell."

"I'll go," Williams said. He smelled annoyed.

"Perhaps," Cordus said.

"It's been four days," Williams said. "If she's not dead already, she's probably hanging on by a thread."

"Nevertheless, this situation requires some thought and planning before anyone enters the strait. Elder beast, I suggest we return to my home. Mr. Ryzik can be cared for there, and we can consider how best to retrieve Miss Ryder."

Ghosteater stood, assenting.

About six hours later, Ghosteater, Cordus, and a handful of Cordus's people were gathered in a small room.

Graham was sleeping off his ordeal in the estate's infirmary, across the hall. Going forward, Cordus would have to keep him drained him by force. It was an unpleasant prospect, but it was the only way to detain a powerful worker.

Cordus had decided that Williams, Zion, and Kara would enter the fragment. Zion could find me; Kara could heal me, if I needed it; and Williams could protect the group. The team had been equipped with weapons and survival gear—tarps, ropes, dehydrated food, and so forth.

Ghosteater surveyed the rescue party.

He did not like company. On the other hand, the idea of entering an ancient stratum piqued his interest. It was often difficult to pass between strata. In fact, some of them—the isolates—were entirely disconnected from the main body of the S-Em. There was a good chance he'd never seen this place.

"I will go."

Cordus turned to him, surprised.

"You care for Miss Ryder?"

Ghosteater just looked back at him, silent. He knew better than to reveal his motive. His inclination to curiosity had been exploited before.

"Will you help track Miss Ryder? Her retrieval must be your first priority."

"I will track her and guard your people."

"Very well, elder beast," Cordus said, still looking perplexed. "Zion, you will work with the beast to track Miss Ryder."

Zion nodded, smelling wary.

Williams went first. Gun drawn and barrier already in place, he approached the strait, which was sitting on the floor. He crouched down and touched it, disappearing with a smell of burned space. Kara followed after thirty seconds, also with her weapon ready. Zion went next.

Ghosteater walked to the stone ball and lowered his nose to touch it. He felt the strait open and try to grip him. He resisted, inhaling. Saltwater. Oxygen-rich air and life, abundant life.

"The companion is under water," he said to Cordus.

Then he let the strait take him.

☙

Fifteen minutes later, the rescue party stood on the rocky beach. Ghosteater shook himself and looked over his shoulder at the three humans. Williams had not crafted his barrier to keep out water, so they were wet.

Ghosteater lowered his nose and quickly found the place I had huddled all night, then followed my scent to the edge of the forest. He sat down to wait for the humans, who were still wringing the seawater out of their clothing and packs.

Once the party was ready, they entered the forest.

"Look at that," Kara said, pointing to a tree-'pus. "There are tons of them here."

Ghosteater approached to sniff the creature and was met with a punch in the nose. He backed away, shaking his head. The animal was a powerful worker, and he knew by scent that there were millions of them in the forest.

"Water-worker?" Williams asked.

"Yes," Ghosteater said.

The creature had created a small wall of water, then propelled it into his face at high speed. The effect was like being hit in the nose with a rock.

"What do we do?" Kara said, looking around nervously.

"Wait 'til they decide we're not a threat," Williams said, settling on a root.

Ghosteater lay down in the ferns, then stretched out on his side, exposing his belly. Kara and Zion sat down next to Williams, smelling nervous.

After about an hour, one of the 'puses approached them. It reached out a tentacle and touched Kara's hand.

"Ugh, gross!"

The 'pus withdrew.

Zion made a disapproving sound.

"Be nice to them, dumbass."

"Easy for you to say." Kara wiped her hand on her pants. "It touched me, not you."

Williams slowly held his hand out to the 'pus, which had bunched itself up defensively.

"Hello, little one."

Tentatively, the 'pus touched his hand. When Williams didn't react, it coiled a tentacle around his wrist and began moving up.

"Oh my god, you've got to be kidding," Kara said.

"Shhhhh."

"Fuck off, Zion."

Ghosteater thought the tree creatures recognized him as a predator, so he lay still and said nothing. The humans' bickering annoyed him. Perhaps he could eat one of them. It depended on how powerful Cordus actually was and how much he would mind losing a lesser minion.

Williams now had the tree-'pus in the crook of his arm and was explaining to it that they were here to find me and bring me home.

"Do you really think it can understand you?" Zion said.

"Dunno," he said.

After another half an hour, Williams shifted the 'pus onto a tree and gave the order to proceed. The 'puses didn't react as the group got up and moved out.

Half an hour later, they found the place I'd napped on my second day.

"I think she stopped here a while," Zion said.

"She slept," Ghosteater said. "Then she went on."

"Goddamn it," Williams said.

"What?" said Kara.

"She should've stayed put."

"She was probably trying to find help."

"There's no help, here."

"How do you know?"

"Just do." He looked around. "This is an isolate."

Ghosteater looked up the trail, impatient with the humans' conversation and the slowness of their travel. He could cover this terrain ten times faster than they could.

As they moved out, the females fell back to sniping at each other. He had spent too long alone to tolerate such annoyances.

"Tracker, I will find her. Follow my trail."

Not waiting for a response, he trotted away through the trees, picking up speed in increments when the tree-'puses didn't react. Soon he was racing through the forest, leaping pools and fallen logs with ease. In ten minutes, he found the place where the tree-'pus had befriended me. Ten minutes later, he reached the place I'd stopped for the night and noted that the tree-'puses had fed me. Then he ran on through the dim forest.

Chapter 22

ON MY FIFTH day in Octoworld, as I'd started to think of it, I finally reached the summit. I didn't realize it at first. There was no pointy top where I could stand and survey the land for miles around, just a gradual flattening out of the terrain.

I stopped and looked around. The trees had changed, I realized—they were shorter and more spaced out. Instead of the clutter of pools and mossy fallen logs, the ground was dry and covered with pine needles. Dense patches of tall ferns grew here and there. For the first time, it wasn't raining.

As I stood there, the tree-'pus gave me a hard squeeze. I looked around and didn't see any other 'puses.

"What's up little guy? Do you need to get off?"

It looked up at me out of its oblong pupil. As usual, it had nothing to say, but it did squeeze me again.

Sadness welled up. Okay, it was an octopus. But it was my companion and provider. Now I was going to have to leave it behind. I'd be well and truly alone.

Afraid it would be too dry for the 'pus where I was, I headed back the way I'd come. After ten minutes, the ground began to slope down again, and the rain picked up. I found a big tree with a nice pool near its roots.

I sidled up to the trunk to let the 'pus transfer itself. Instead it detached several tentacles and waved them in the downhill direction. When I didn't move, it added a few more, stretching insistently. It pretty clearly wanted me to keep walking back into the rainforest.

"Your forest is really nice, little guy, but I can't stay there. I'm pretty sure there's no one there who can help me get home."

It kept waving.

"I'm sorry, buddy, but I have to keep looking. It's either that or just give up. There might not be anyone coming for me."

Finally it stopped waving and flowed from my hip onto the tree trunk.

"Bye, little guy. Thanks for all your help. I really appreciate it. I guess I probably won't be back this way, but I hope I'll see you again, somehow."

The 'pus didn't pay any attention to my farewell speech. Instead it moved down the trunk, lurched over the roots to the pool, and plopped in. After a few seconds underwater, it climbed out, shimmering strangely. I knelt down to get a better look. It was covered with a thick shell of water.

The 'pus crawled over the ferns to my foot and started to climb up my leg. Instead of soaking into my clothes, its coat of water stayed intact. It seemed like magic to me, but it was probably a working.

"Wow, portable fishbowl. That's some trick. So, you want to come with me? Is that it?"

It stared up at me, the water making its eye look even stranger.

I stood there, ambivalent. It obviously couldn't live unassisted in the terrain beyond the rainforest. How long would it be able to sustain itself with its water jumpsuit? If it ran out of water, it would probably die.

"I really appreciate the help, but I don't think you should come. It's too dangerous. Besides, I might not come back this way."

It didn't move.

"Why don't I just put you on this nice trunk, here?"

I pried one of its water-coated tentacles off my waist. At that point, I learned just how tenacious an octopus can be. Try as I might, I couldn't get it off me. Every time I broke a tentacle's grip, the slimy thing would whip out of my hands and wrap back around me. In the end, I gave up, afraid I was going to hurt the 'pus if I kept pulling at it.

"Okay, little guy. Thank you. I really hope I'm not going to get you killed."

With its thick coating of water, the 'pus weighed a lot more than it had before, so I urged it to climb onto my upper back, like a living backpack.

Then, at last, I headed out of the rainforest, trying to feel hopeful about what lay ahead.

🍃

Two hours later, I stood on a ledge and surveyed the land beneath.

Walking down the dry side of the mountain, I'd noticed a rocky outcropping jutting out to my left. I'd backtracked up to its highest point of contact with the main slope, then walked out along the top of it, trying to get a view over the trees.

I'd had great hopes of seeing a city, a village, even a column of smoke—anything that would suggest human habitation. My hopes were disappointed.

All around me, the land fell away sharply, the pine forest thinning out as the mountain gave way to a lush, green river valley. On the far side of the valley, I could see more wooded hills. I stood there scanning the terrain for some time but couldn't find any sign of people.

I thought about what to do. The rainforest was a known quantity. If I went back, I could use the moss to stay warm, and the tree-'puses would probably provide me with food, at least for a while.

But whatever the rainforest had going for it, I just couldn't make myself turn back. Sitting there and doing nothing, day after day, waiting for a rescue that might never come—no. The thought made my skin crawl.

Waiting for whatever happened to me to happen—that's what I'd been doing ever since I ran home from college. I couldn't afford to be that person anymore. Whatever I might've lost, at this moment, I had the power to make a choice, and I was going to choose action, not passivity.

I could follow the river. People often built cities and towns along rivers or where rivers met the sea. Maybe that would be my best bet. The river would be good for the 'pus, too— plenty of water.

Decision made, I walked back along the outcropping to the main slope and continued down the mountain.

❧

After about forty-five minutes of easy downhill walking, I heard movement off to my right. Since leaving the rainforest, I hadn't seen any creatures larger than a dragonfly, so I crept closer to investigate. When I got near enough, I peered cautiously around a tree trunk.

What I saw could only be a dinosaur. It was small—its back might've come up to my knee—and walked on its hind legs. It had a narrow, snakelike head, which it was using to root around in the thick carpet of dead pine needles. Everything about it looked light and agile, from its long neck and tail to its small body to its slender limbs. As I watched, it used its clawed hands to shift a small fallen branch, then snapped up a lizard that had been hiding underneath.

The creature pumped its head, gulping down its prey like an owl swallowing a mouse. Then it caught sight of me and froze, staring at me with large, yellow eyes, a bit of lizard tail sticking comically from the corner of its mouth. Then it whirled and darted off. The dark-brown-and-rufous pattern of its skin blended perfectly with the surrounding forest, and I quickly lost sight of it.

"Well, what do you know about that?" I said to the 'pus. "I guess there are some larger vertebrates here, after all."

But except for one mini-dinosaur, the forest seemed strangely empty. Maybe I'd entered mini-dinosaur paradise—all the bugs you could eat and no competition.

After about another hour of walking, the tree-'pus gave me a hard squeeze. I stopped and surveyed the terrain before me. I couldn't see anything. It squeezed me again, harder, and I turned a slow circle, looking behind and to the sides. Nothing.

I walked on, spooked. The 'pus kept squeezing me, but every time I stopped to look around, there was nothing there.

Finally, about twenty minutes later, I caught movement out of the corner of my eye. I turned quickly and saw a patch of ferns swaying, as though something had just darted into them. I saw another movement to my left and spun around, this time just catching a bit of reptilian tail as it disappeared behind a fallen log.

Minis-dinos. They were following me.

My heart rate shot up, and I quickly reached for my rubber band. It wasn't there. At some point it had come off, and I hadn't even noticed. I took several slow breaths, reaching for calm.

I hadn't been afraid of the one I'd seen. It'd be like fearing a housecat. Sure, it had teeth, but it was quite small. It might bite me, but do serious damage? No. Furthermore, it had seemed afraid of me.

A whole pack of the things was a different matter, though. I backed away slowly, picking up a few fist-sized stones as I went.

Over the next few minutes, they grew bolder about showing themselves. Finally, one darted at me, feinting at the last moment and retreating. Several more emerged from the ground cover. They came forward slowly, crouching a bit, heads held low and weaving slightly. It sure looked like stalking behavior to me. Not good.

"Okay, 'pus, hold on," I murmured.

I gathered myself and rushed them, shouting and throwing stones. They immediately spun around and raced back into the ferns. Once they were out of sight, I turned and sprinted downhill, hoping I'd scared them off.

I wasn't counting on it, though. After a few minutes, I slowed and began looking for more rocks. I pulled off my T-shirt and knotted it into a little bag, which I filled with stones.

Within half an hour, they were back on my trail—I could tell by the 'pus's squeezes. They trailed me for about an hour before they began getting bold enough to show themselves again. Several times I drove them off by shouting and throwing stones, but eventually that tactic lost its effect, and they began darting in, nipping at my ankles or jumping to snap at my hands.

I knew I was in trouble. Now that they were getting close, I could see they had a formidable array of teeth—small but sharp and numerous. Their claws also looked perfectly capable of cutting skin.

I considered climbing a tree, but what if they didn't lose interest once I was up there? I couldn't stay in a tree forever.

Afraid to keep my back to them, I turned to face them, walking backwards slowly. I was taken by surprise when one rushed in from behind me and bit my calf. I shouted and lost my balance. I twisted and swung my arms wildly, trying not to fall. By sheer luck, my bag of rocks caught the mini in the head as it let go of me and feinted to my right. It weaved around, disoriented. I lost my battle with gravity and fell right on it.

I scrambled to my feet. My attacker lay there, twitching. I'd crushed it.

Heart racing, I backed away as at least a dozen other minis advanced. But when they pounced, their target was their dying comrade, not me. I turned and ran.

Five minutes later, I had to stop. The stitch in my side made it impossible to breathe, and my leg hurt. I could tell it was bleeding from the squishy feeling in my shoe.

I stood there, bent over, gasping. If I got out of this situation, I was never going to complain about Gwen's workouts again—clearly, I needed them.

Only after a couple minutes did I realize I was lucky not to have left the tree-'pus behind. Usually it bailed out when I fell. This time it hadn't, but I hadn't stopped to think about it before I ran.

"Sorry, buddy," I said, reaching through its watery casing to pat the limb it had wrapped around my chest.

Feeling very shaky, I limped downhill. Hopefully the minis

would be satisfied with their meal. If not, I didn't think I could escape. There was nothing at the bottom of the mountain but fields of grass. Nowhere to hide.

*

The dead mini bought me more than an hour. I pushed as fast as I could with my injured leg. By the time they caught up with me, the slope had begun to flatten out. The trees were growing sparser, and the patches of ferns came more often. I was leaving a trail of bloody footprints.

This time, they came on without hesitation. I heard the rustling in the ferns and didn't even get fully turned around before they were darting in all around me, clawing and biting. I swung the sack of stones and connected a few times, but there were too many. They started leaping up at me, aiming at my face and neck. I staggered back and fell, and they swarmed me. Instinctively, I threw my arms up to shield my face and neck, even though it was pointless.

Something wet shuddered past me with a deep *whump*, and a force pressed me down into the ground for a split second. The biting stopped.

After a few moments, I raised my head. Everything within a forty-foot ring around me was destroyed—there was nothing but flattened ferns and downed trees. A few minis were lying some distance from me, moving feebly. The others were out of sight.

I looked for the 'pus and found it a few feet behind me. Its watery coating was gone, and it was coated in pine needles.

Painfully, I rolled over and stood. I'd been bitten many times and could feel blood running down my legs. I gathered up the 'pus and staggered on.

Half an hour later, the ground leveled and the trees petered out. The lush, green valley I'd seen that morning stretched out ahead of me. The greenery wasn't grass, as I'd assumed—it was ferns, a dense sea of ferns.

I limped out past the last of the trees, moving toward the river I remembered seeing. I badly needed water, and the 'pus's skin had taken on a dry, sticky feel that couldn't be good.

Once out in the ferns, I looked back.

There were the minis, grouped near the last tree, stretching up to watch me over the fronds. I stood for a moment, frozen with terror. If they attacked again, I didn't think the 'pus would be able to save me. I wasn't sure what it had done the last time—an explosion of some kind—but it had clearly used up its water doing it.

The minis didn't attack. They watched me for a minute and then turned and retreated back into the forest. The trees seemed to mark the edge of their territory.

So whose territory was this? I looked around with renewed fear, but couldn't see anything but waves of soft green, moving gently in the breeze.

I tucked the 'pus up under my sweater. Maybe the poor critter would stay a little moister under there. Then I struggled on, desperate for water.

*

I found the river fairly quickly, thank god. I was so thirsty and was starting to feel sick and dizzy, as well.

Knee-high ferns grew right up to the banks. Their dense roots formed a spongy mat that kept my feet from sinking into the mud.

When I reached the water's edge, it occurred to me that there might be aquatic predators to worry about. I took a few steps back and surveyed the river. It was wide, slow moving, and very clear. For some ways out, it was only a foot or two deep, but then the water darkened, as though with great depth.

I couldn't see anything moving out there, but that didn't really mean anything.

I sank to my knees and pulled the 'pus out from under my shirt. I lowered it into the water. It hung there limply for a minute, and I was afraid it had died. But then it unfurled its tentacles and relaxed into the water, its oblong pupil staring up at me.

"Drink it up, little guy," I said.

I leaned down and drank as well.

After a few minutes, the 'pus started crawling back up my arm, its cocoon of water reformed around it. I pulled it up onto the shore but was too weak to lift it—it must've weighed thirty pounds with its water coat. So I sat back and let it crawl into my lap.

Jesus, I owed my life to an octopus.

At least for the time being. I wasn't in good shape.

Why the hell had I left the rainforest? I'd been safe and well fed, there. Now I was injured—in a minute I'd have to try to figure out how badly—with no food, no shelter, and no possibility of retracing my steps. And so far as I could tell, I was no closer to finding help than I had been before.

I seemed incapable of making a good decision.

Moving slowly, I set the 'pus aside and stripped down to my underwear. My legs, hips, and rear were covered with bites and scratches, and I had some on my back and arms, too. None of the wounds were deep, but all were bleeding. From my woozy feeling, I thought the loss was adding up.

I sat there, stupefied. I had no idea what to do.

I should clean the bites, I thought.

The only thing I could clean them with was river water, and who knows what bacteria it held. Then again, I'd just drunk it. But what might I attract if I got into the water with open wounds?

I realized I was probably going to die pretty much where I was. I was too weak to keep going. It was late afternoon. The sun had already sunk behind the mountain. It wasn't as cold as it had been in the rainforest, but it would be chilly overnight. I had no food.

Really, what could I do?

I sat there a while, hurting and deeply angry at myself. Then I heard a strange, rasping noise behind me. I twisted around to look, too exhausted and low to be as afraid as I probably should've been.

The ferns were moving weirdly. I staggered to my feet, expecting a mini to come darting out, but after a second, I realized it was the plants themselves that were moving—not just near me, but as far out along the plain as I could see.

I stared in disbelief as they writhed.

Not long ago I'd wondered what kind of world a tree would invent for itself. The idea that a fern might work essence seemed even stranger. A tree had size, longevity. But a fern?

All the movement had purpose, I realized—the ferns were churning up the soil. The plants closest to me pulled something up with a small explosion of dirt. They grappled it upright and began to coil around it, like vines. They climbed to the top, then shot out feelers, questing for something else to grip.

I'd recognized the object before they covered it. It was a massive bone, half as tall as I was.

With another burst of soil, a matching bone emerged and was propped up and covered. Then two much bigger bones were passed up and woven into place atop the initial ones. Then two more. I backed away. More fern-vines boiled out atop the twin columns, which were by then two or three times my height. More and more vines grew, until a seething mass of green loomed over me, stretching forward as the columns swayed and bent.

As the ferns proliferated, more bones were brought up from the soil and passed into the mass of plant matter, which bucked and writhed itself into shape to accommodate each new arrival. As vertebrae were added, the mass stretched to create a torso and tail. Rib bones gave the torso depth and form.

I looked away from the spectacle, hoping to see an escape route, but similar constructions were underway all across the plain. I wasn't sure what to do. Were these things going to attack me?

I stumbled back as, almost at my feet, the plants churned up a massive skull. It was gigantic and had dozens of serrated teeth. As thousands of tiny vines passed it toward the growing creature, I scooped up my clothes. If this thing turned out to be friendly, I'd be surprised.

The 'pus grasped my calf and started climbing up. I limped downstream as fast as I could go, stealing looks over my shoulder at the growing monster I'd left behind. The skull was being hefted into place, vines wrapping around it at incredible speed. Even before it was fully covered, the creature shuddered and flexed, as though coming to life. It stepped forward and swung its head back and forth. Was it seeking me?

All over its body, vines shot into the air and rewrapped themselves in a frenzy, creating a churning corona of green.

Across the plain, other creatures were on the move toward me. The skeletons the plants had resurrected were all dinosaurs. Some were unbelievably large, dwarfing the huge carnivore that had been constructed closest to me. Others were small. Minis were well represented. They must've learned the hard way to stick to the woods. Many of the creatures looked like plant-eaters, but that didn't reassure me—some of them were enormous beyond belief.

Ahead of me, several reached the river bank and stopped, swinging their heads over the water. One of them was as tall as a five-storey building. Panicked, I stopped. Others closed in from the side and behind.

I waded out into the river. I'd have to swim across. It was a long way to the other side, and I didn't know what was in it, but that was my only hope.

About twenty feet out, there was a sandbank. The water there was less than a foot deep. On the other side of the sandbank was a drop-off. I stood looking into it. Things were swimming in the deeper water. Really big things.

Dozens of plant-dinos were massing where I'd stepped off the bank. They opened their mouths, as though roaring, but the only sound was the rasp and slap of fern vines. I was paralyzed, too terrified to jump into the deep water, with its huge, unknown creatures, but clearly unable to go back to dry land.

One of the dinos stepped into the water. Jolted into action, I turned and splashed my way down the sandbank, but I ran out of bank long before I'd passed the crowd of creatures waiting on the shore.

The splashing seemed to key them into my location, and

more began stepping into the river. Desperately, I turned back to the deep water. Something huge was swimming in there— something twenty feet long, at least. I just couldn't jump in. I stood there trying to make myself, and I just couldn't.

I felt the 'pus tighten around my waist. A wall of water rose out of the river and, faster than my eye could follow, smashed into the nearest dinos. An avalanche of bone and shredded vines blasted back through the assembled creatures. The river churned, almost knocking me down.

I couldn't sense whatever was happening, but it had to be the 'pus.

More dinos surged forward, and the 'pus flung another water wall at them. Then it did it again. And again.

Behind the carnage on shore, I could see the vines putting the destroyed dinos back together. The 'pus wasn't going to save me. It was just delaying the inevitable.

And the delay was brief. Its sixth strike was noticeably weakened, and its seventh did little more than knock a couple dinos down. It tried once more, and only succeeded in misting the creatures with water droplets.

Its grip on me tightened for a moment, and then it just fell off. It landed in the water, slid off the sandbar, and sank.

With a cry, I lunged for it, but it had disappeared into the deeps.

I knelt there in the water, stripped of every hope. I held my hands up at the oncoming creatures.

"Stop! Please!"

They didn't stop.

Things seemed to slow down. I saw the way individual plants unwrapped and rewrapped themselves over the bones as the creatures picked their legs up and stepped toward me through the shallows. I saw the gleam of their ancient teeth as they opened their mouths in soundless calls. I saw my own bones being passed through the ferns, being picked clean and buried in the peaty soil, locked in this place forever. I saw them resurrected into some horrifying parody of my body to destroy other intruders and add them to the sentinel horde.

The very core of me said, *No.*

Inside me, something tore. In front of me, something exploded. A roaring sound deafened me, and a wave of superheated air threw me back into the river's deeper channel. Disoriented, I struggled for the surface, panicked and flailing.

When my head broke the surface, I saw fire. Not just fire—a wall of flame. The air scorched my lungs. I ducked back beneath the surface and swam for the shallows. When I reached the sandbar, I crawled out onto it.

The far bank of the river was untouched, but the side where I'd walked was a work in devastation. The ferns near the river were gone—only blackened earth remained.

Unsteadily, I stood up.

A wall of flame hundreds of feet long was marching away from me across the valley, toward the mountain. The bank was littered with bones. The smaller ones were burned almost to ash. The larger ones were still burning.

The wind kicked up from behind me and, in the space of a minute, rose to a gale that almost knocked me down. It howled past me, plastering my wet hair across my face. The fire accelerated and grew. As I watched, it reached the tree line and began sweeping up through the canopy.

I'd done this. I didn't know how I'd done it, but I had.

Exultation coursed through me.

Those things had tried to kill me, and I'd killed them instead.

I started shaking. It took several long seconds to realize

why—I was laughing. I sat down in the water and let it take me, the weird, crazy laughter.

Finally, the laughing stopped, and I just sat there, too exhausted to move.

Eventually I realized I was quite cold, so I waded back to the bank and pulled myself out onto the warm, blackened ground. I had no idea where my clothes had gone, and there was no sign of the 'pus, so I just sat there, shivering, as late afternoon became night.

Chapter 23

IN THE WEE hours of the morning, Ghosteater padded across the burned plain, the fine ash and crunchy cinders shifting beneath his once-paws. He had almost reached the valley the evening before, but the firestorm had sent him racing back up the mountain. The tree-creatures' rainforest had sheltered him from the flames, but reaching it in time had been a near thing.

How close I had come to killing my rescuer.

He saw me from far off, huddled on the bank, shuddering with cold. He noted my lack of garments and thought it strange. Then, ever cautious—or usually cautious, at any rate—he sat down and considered me.

I was undoubtedly the source of the working. My trace was all over the marrow of the place. A fire-worker, then? He opened his mouth, tasting. No, not fire—heat. The marrow was thrumming with the echoes of the energy it had been worked to produce.

The isolate's cinder-filled wind played through his fur. It spoke to him, but he couldn't understand what it said. This world was not his; its language was foreign.

He looked back at me, curled up on the blackened earth.

Perhaps the wind said, *She-pup*.

Perhaps it said, *Run*.

Chapter 24

"Pup."

I just about jumped out of my skin, then scrambled around trying to get up.

"I will not hurt you," the voice said.

Finally I managed to get to my knees. It was hard going—my muscles were cramped from the cold.

I stared into the night, my breath coming in gasps. I couldn't see whoever'd spoken. There were about a million stars in the sky, but no moon. It was very dark.

I tried twice to speak before I managed to make any sound.

"Who's there?"

"Ghosteater."

My mind wrestled with the word, trying to understand. Madisyn's giant doggie? Here?

"Ghosteater ... from Dorf?"

He materialized out of the darkness, silvery coat luminous in the starlight, and walked toward me on his footless legs.

"Did you come here for me?"

Stupid question. Why else would he be here?

"The émigré Cordus sent people. I came too."

He looked up at the stars and took several deep breaths. Then his golden eyes came back to my face, and he studied me in silence for some time. Finally, he walked up to me, circled like a huge hound, and lay down.

"Lie here," he said. "I will warm you."

He'd get no argument from me—I was freezing. I lay down next to him and nestled my back up against his belly, which was soft and very warm. I was still cold, but it was a lot better than before. I fell asleep immediately.

❧

In the morning, Ghosteater used his keen nose to find my jeans and sweater, which had drifted some way downriver. While he was off retrieving them, I searched up and down the river for the 'pus but couldn't find it.

After Ghosteater returned with my clothes and I laid them out to dry, he gave all my bites a thorough cleaning with his tongue. I had trouble thinking of him as an animal, so it seemed weirdly intimate. I tried to squirm away, but he put a massive foreleg across me and held me down. Then he caught a large fish in the river and watched as I ate it. I felt like a toddler under the eye of a stern parent.

Once I'd pulled my still-damp clothes on, I started to search again for the 'pus.

"What do you seek?"

"I had a tree-octopus with me yesterday. It fell in the river right about here."

Ghosteater waded into the water, passing his nose delicately over the surface.

"It is dead."

"You can't possibly know that!"

The great beast stood in the water, looking up at me in silence. Then he came back to shore and shook himself.

"Scent tells the story. There are great fish in this river. They eat small creatures."

I stared at him, not wanting to believe it. He just looked back at me, matter of fact, emotionless.

I sat down. All the exultation I'd felt the night before turned to bitterness. I'd managed to save myself from my own idiotic decision to leave the rainforest, but I'd gotten my friend killed. It'd died trying to save me. With all the power it had, no fish could've gotten it if it hadn't depleted itself fighting the plant-dinos.

Ghosteater sat nearby. For a time he watched me in silent interest.

"Big things eat little things," he said at last. "Big things die. Then little things eat them."

"It wasn't just a 'little thing.' It was my friend. It sacrificed itself for me. It's my fault it died."

He pondered me, tipping his head to the side like a dog. He seemed to find my attachment to the 'pus mysterious and interesting.

"Can you tell if it was male or female?"

Ghosteater thought for a few seconds, seeming to roll the remembered scent over his tongue.

"Female."

I nodded, feeling empty. I wished I'd known before.

✿

My rescue may have been well in hand, but the next day and a half weren't pleasant.

I didn't really understand Ghosteater's explanation of how Graham's rock had brought me here. He could speak to me, yes, but communicating complex ideas seemed beyond him. I could only take his word for it that some of Cordus's people were coming.

I wanted to leave for the coast immediately, but the beast refused. It would take me several days to climb back up the mountain, and we had no way to carry water. Furthermore, my wounds had left me weak and in a lot of pain.

So there we stayed, waiting for the rest of the party to catch up. Ghosteater caught fish. I watched. He ate them. I ate them. He drank water. So did I. I tossed and squirmed, trying to find a way to sit or lie that wasn't painful. He sat and watched me, always silent unless I asked him something. At night, I curled up against him and tried to stay warm.

On my third day in the valley, I saw Zion, Kara, and Williams coming down the mountain. It was humbling. The walk that had taken me five days had taken them less than three.

I got up and walked across the blackened plain to meet them, Ghosteater by my side. When they saw me coming, they broke into a jog. But despite the hurry, when they reached me, there was an oddly awkward moment where we all just stood there, looking at each other. I was thinking it seemed weird to see people here. I don't know what they were thinking. Maybe they were amazed I was alive.

Kara broke the silence.

"Beth, are you all right?"

It seemed like a bizarre question. There were a dozen ways in which I was and wasn't all right. I thought about it. In the end, I just said, "Yeah."

She came forward and took my hand. Her eyes widened.

"Jesus, what did this to you?"

Williams studied me with an unreadable expression.

"What's wrong with her?"

"She's covered with cuts and puncture wounds. It's like something bit her all over."

"Mini-dinosaurs," I said.

That was greeted with silence.

"We didn't see anything like that," Zion finally said.

"The fire killed them," said Ghosteater.

Had I really killed them all? I felt sick.

"Okay, then. Let me just fix those cuts," Kara said, sounding disturbed.

It was a quick healing. When she was done, I felt a million times better. She even took care of my sunburn. Then we walked back to the river.

Ghosteater declared the huge fish in the river harmless to humans, so the rescue party members bathed. I sat there feeling beyond pathetic for not just swimming across when the plant-dinos were after me. Then again, there were ferns on the other side of the river, too.

Zion built a fire and Williams set up tarps and sleeping bags for the night. Ghosteater fished. We roasted what he caught over the fire.

Eating cooked food was good, but it felt wrong not to have the 'pus there to share it with.

While we ate, night fell. I finally got a comprehensible explanation about Graham's rock: it was one-half of a "carven strait," a rare and ancient device used for traveling. They didn't have to be opened with a working. Instead, they generated their own opening: if someone touched one stone, they'd be transported to wherever the companion happened to be. Apparently the art of making them was lost, and Cordus had been extremely surprised to find a set of them at large.

So although I hadn't noticed it, there had to be a stone ball in the sea where I arrived that matched the one I'd touched in

Justine's room. Touching the one here would take us back to Cordus's estate, where Graham's rock was now.

After these explanations, an uncomfortable silence fell. No doubt they wanted to know what had happened to me, but I didn't want to talk about it, especially not about the fire. Kara asked me a few questions, and I answered monosyllabically. When she persisted, I just got up and walked away, tossing them some lame excuse about stretching my legs.

I kept going a ways, well out of the circle of firelight. When I finally stopped, I looked up at the stars. There were so many of them. They were amazingly bright. I didn't recognize any constellations.

I could taste the pervasive flavor of soot at the back of my throat. The wind blew the stuff all over the place.

I had done this. I'd come to some little corner of the S-Em. I'd found Octoworld, Miniworld, and Fernworld, and I'd destroyed two of the three. I'd made a generous friend and gotten her killed.

At the same time, I'd survived. I'd survived what Graham did to me, and I'd survived my own bad choices.

The wind found the holes in my sweater, chilling me.

Eventually, Kara came looking for me, and I went back to the fire.

Everyone except Ghosteater crawled into a sleeping bag. No one said anything.

Climbing back up the mountain took almost two days because everyone had to stick to the slower pace I set. As we finally crested the summit, I was terribly afraid I would find the tree-'puses' rainforest burned as well, but it was intact.

The fire damage stopped abruptly as we walked into the rain: there was blackened earth and torched trees on one side of an invisible line, lush ferns and towering trees on the other.

"Is there a barrier, here?"

"Yes," Ghosteater said.

I wondered why we could go through it but the fire couldn't. I didn't ask, though. If I raised the subject, it'd invite questions.

We stopped for the night shortly afterwards. The forest was too dense and wet to build a fire, so we huddled under the tarps, eating dried meat and fruit. Once everyone was settled in their sleeping bags, I slipped away into the darkening forest and found a 'pus. I coaxed it into my lap and then explained what had happened to the one I'd carried with me—that she'd saved my life, and that I knew it was my fault she was dead, and that I was sorry.

The 'pus stared back at me, its strange oblong pupil reminding me of my friend's. Not surprisingly, it didn't respond. I had no idea if it understood me.

When I was done talking, I sat there for a long while, stroking the 'pus and feeling strange. Part of the feeling was sadness, and part of it was remorse. But there was also a striking sense of having been changed in ways I couldn't understand. I was at a loss.

Eventually I got up to head back to camp. Oddly, the 'pus wanted to come with me. When I got in my sleeping bag, it settled on a root near my face.

I woke up several times during the night, and each time it was still there. In the morning, it was gone.

A day and a half later, we reached the shore.

Williams led us out to the point where rocks and water met. We waded into the gentle waves until Ghosteater indicated the strait was beneath us. I looked down. The water was clear, but it was impossible to pick the stone ball out of the rocky seabed. As I watched, Ghosteater dove down, kicking vigorously to reach the bottom. We all watched as he touched a certain place with his nose, then disappeared. The water tossed violently as it filled the space he'd occupied, and I lost sight of the spot he'd touched.

"Ryder," Williams said. "Go."

Taking a deep breath, I bent down to the place I thought the strait was and began feeling around with my hands. On the third try, I must've touched it because I found myself sprawled on the tile floor of a windowless room beside a stone ball—the matching strait, the one Graham had been carrying.

"Move away," Ghosteater said from the corner.

I scrambled over to the wall and waited while the others appeared one by one.

Once everyone was there, I thanked them for coming to get me.

"Sure," Kara said, "no problem."

Zion shrugged. "Not like we had a choice, right?"

Ghosteater cocked his head and stared at me.

Williams said nothing—just grabbed a towel from the pile that had been left in the corner and walked out.

"Don't mind them," Kara said. "They're assholes. It's not your fault you ended up there."

"It is your fault we had to go so far to find you," Zion said, toweling her hair. "Next time, stay put."

Her words stung. I felt defensive, even though I'd been berating myself for that exact mistake.

"I didn't know if anyone would come for me. Or if Graham or Lord Limu might be the one who came, if anyone did."

"Exactly," Kara said staunchly. "I would've been on the move, too."

Zion rolled her eyes and left.

Kara and I dried off, then stood there awkwardly.

"Well," she said, "we'd better go find Lord Cordus. I mean, you'd better go find him. Hopefully he won't need to talk to me."

"Yeah. Okay."

She gave me a pained smile and left. Ghosteater slid out behind her, leaving me alone in the quiet room. The carven strait sat on the floor, shining dully. It was a profoundly anticlimactic ending to ten days of wonder, terror, and pain.

Chapter 25

CORDUS STRAIGHTENED UP, closing his hand.

We were sitting in his office in our usual training spot. He'd spoken briefly to me the day before, then sent me to my room to rest and recover. Today, I was resuming my old schedule. Our lesson had gone as usual: I still couldn't see workings.

He sat in silence for a time, then broached the subject I'd been dreading.

"As I understand it, you may have manifested a gift while in the isolate."

Knowing it was unavoidable, I described all that had happened to me and what I'd apparently done. He didn't seem shocked by my having incinerated a vast stretch of land and everything that lived there, but he did ask a number of very detailed questions.

At last, he sat back and started some serious foot-tapping.

When I couldn't stand the silence anymore, I spoke.

"So, am I a fire-worker, like Lord Limu?"

"I think not, Miss Ryder. Based on your description, I believe you are a worker of light."

You could've knocked me over with a feather.

"I did that with *light?*"

"Not the variety of light humans are capable of seeing," he said.

He got up, went a bookcase, and pulled out a volume.

"An explanation based on human science will be easiest for you, at this point."

He paged through the book and then brought it to me, opened to a colorful diagram.

"The electromagnetic spectrum," he said, sweeping his hand over the pages. "At the center are the wavelengths that human eyes can detect. Some Seconds can see more broadly, of course."

Right. Of course.

"I suspect you produced a powerful burst of electromagnetic energy in these wavelengths," he said, pointing to the infrared area of the spectrum. "Such a burst would ignite or incinerate flammable material, such as plants."

Plants, bones, minis.

"Or people?" I said, looking up at him.

He looked back at me, expressionless.

"People are indeed flammable, Miss Ryder."

I sat there for some time, reading the diagram's brief descriptions of infrared and other waves.

For once, Cordus was the one to break the silence.

"With time and practice, you may be able to produce energy across the entire spectrum."

I looked up at him, then back down at the book. Microwaves. X-rays. Gamma rays.

"I don't want this," I said.

I wasn't sure where the words had come from. Some deep, instinctual place. They surfaced and demanded expression. I spoke them without thinking.

"You have no choice as to the nature of your abilities, Miss Ryder," Cordus said softly. "When you have learned to control them, however, you will be able to choose how and when you employ them."

I was surprised at the obvious lie. There'd be no choice. I'd have to do exactly what he told me to do, and if that meant incinerating or irradiating people, then that's what I'd have to do. I doubted I could even choose my own death instead. He could get inside my head and control me like a puppet, so that disobedience would be literally impossible. That's what he'd done with the green man.

I suppose he took my silence for acquiescence, because he went on.

"As you know, the emergence of gifts is the second caste of Nolander development. Usually, one does not enter the second caste until one has spent several years in the first. You are now in the radically anomalous position of possessing a gift without being able to sense workings. You can make what you cannot perceive."

I nodded dully.

"Given the life-or-death situation you describe, I believe your capacity was once again forced into untimely growth. As a result, it seems to have become even more irregular in its shape."

"So, I'm lopsided?"

"I suppose that is as good a term as any other. In fact, the metaphor is useful. As you know from mundane experience, lopsided things tend to be unstable. Likewise, your capacity is unbalanced and is likely to function unpredictably for some time. Our lessons should be safe enough, but I must ask you to continue to refrain from attempting to sense workings outside my presence. In addition, you must not attempt to use your gift without my assistance. Any such attempt could be extremely dangerous."

"Don't worry—I wouldn't know how to use it if I wanted to," I said.

So far as I'm concerned, I thought, *I'm never using it again.*

❧

During the ensuing days and weeks, I slid back into my routine—workouts with Gwen, combat training with Tezzy, lessons with Cordus.

My "spa week" in the S-Em, as Gwen called it, had brought improvements to two out of the three areas of my education. I'd lost fat and gained muscle, which pleased Gwen. I'd also apparently gotten something Tezzy called "focus." She talked about my "deepened commitment to the art" and my "predator's eye." It sounded like mumbo-jumbo to me. I think she basically meant I wasn't quite as easy to knock over.

In my lessons with Cordus, however, I remained unable to sense the little heat-working he held out. My progress with Baasha was slow—even mastering the alphabet was a struggle. Fortunately, he remained patient.

I went back to visiting Justine, who'd survived being buried in the sinkhole. She continued to vacillate between fear and anger, and I continued to dread seeing her. I also reconnected with Tiffany, who'd been frightened when I stopped answering her calls for a week and a half. Ben still didn't want to talk to me, though Tiff said things seemed to be getting a little better.

As I returned to my routine, the estate around me appeared to assume its usual condition. Ghosteater disappeared. Williams and Kara went back to Minnesota. Cordus held court weekly.

I knew things weren't wholly normal, though. Cordus never looked ruffled or distracted, but his desk, once a model of neatness, was increasingly piled with old books and papers. Sometimes strange people visited the estate, and he spent hours talking to them privately. I was certain he was trying to find out more about the Eye of the Heavens and Limu's stolen weapon.

The few times I asked him about it, he shut me down immediately: "That conversation must wait, Miss Ryder," or, "This is neither the time nor the place, Miss Ryder." It was Cordus-speak for, *Jesus Christ, woman—shut up!* So I stopped asking.

It was hard not to feel tense about the situation. Limu scared me. Was he still in New York? Every time we drove into the city for court, I wondered if he was going to pop out of an alley and torch the car. And Justine just weirded me out. She both was and wasn't my sister-in-law. It was disturbing.

There wasn't much I could do about the big things, so I focused on small goals: running a faster forty-yard dash, mastering the ready stance, convincing the stable master to let me go riding.

No, that's not entirely true. I did tackle one big thing: trying to figure myself out.

I knew everything that had happened had changed me. Hell, that much was obvious: my life had been altered in nearly every way I could imagine. But my experience in the S-Em had done something on a different order of magnitude. It had reached way down deep inside me and shifted something. The closest I could come to pinning it down was this: death had come for me on that sand bank, and I'd said "no," and death had obeyed.

It wasn't a pure feeling. It was mixed with guilt and horror at what I'd done, with frustration at my mistakes, with anger at all that had been done to me, and with fear of what the future would bring. But it endured those things and held its own. What that meant for me I wasn't sure, but I knew it was important.

⚘

I looked up at Gwen, seeking reassurance.

"S'okay," she said. "He really is helpless. You'll see."

I nodded and knocked on the door she was guarding.

"Come in."

I opened the door slowly and peeked around it. Graham was sitting on a couch at the far end of the room. He looked surprised to see me.

"Hi," he said. "Come in."

I stepped in, closing the door behind me. I approached the sitting area and chose an armchair.

Long seconds of uncomfortable silence followed.

"How are you?" he said.

"Okay. You?"

"I'm okay."

He didn't look okay. He looked sick. Cordus was keeping him drained. I didn't know how he drained someone against their will. Maybe it felt like what Williams had done to me. At any rate, the effects were clear. Graham looked too weak to stand, much less cause trouble.

We sat there in silence.

"Beth," he finally said, "why are you here?"

I searched for an answer.

"I'm not sure."

I'd come planning to demand an explanation.

The more I'd thought about what Graham had done to me, the angrier it had made me. A lot of what had happened to me could be categorized as "my fault" or "just the way things are." Even the many cruelties I'd experienced and observed were the result of individuals acting according to their overt natures. Graham stood out from that. What he'd done—sending me to that place and leaving me there—seemed different. It felt like a betrayal.

But sitting across from him, that distinction seemed silly. He too had been acting according to his nature. I'd just been too naive to recognize his nature for what it was.

"Were you hoping I'd confess my sins?" he said, his voice taking on an edge. "Do you think you'll get 'closure,' or something?" He made sarcastic air quotes.

I stood and walked to the door.

"Wait," he said. "Wait."

I stopped.

"I'm sorry. I didn't mean that. I'm just tired."

He cleared his throat. "Hey, I haven't had any visitors. Why don't you stay a bit? You can tell me about where the strait took you."

"Would that be entertaining? Hearing the tale of how you almost killed me?"

He flushed and dropped his eyes.

I waited for a few seconds, then realized I was standing there hoping he'd produce a sincere apology. God, when was I going to learn? I turned to go.

"Beth, wait," he said, sounding upset.

Against my better judgment, I stopped again.

"I'm sorry I did that to you. It wasn't supposed to happen, and I just panicked. I should've come after you."

"Yeah, you should've. It would only have taken you a

couple seconds."

"But I didn't know where you'd gone. I mean, the companion could've been inside a volcano. It could've been in outer space."

"Nonsense," I snapped. "Limu wants Justine alive. You wouldn't have done something that stupid."

He stared at me, and I saw that expression on his face again, the one I'd seen at the mill—the trapped-animal look. At last he looked away, his expression bleak.

"There's a death sentence on my head. Limu figured that out and gave me a choice: be his man in Cordus's organization or face the music."

"Why were you sentenced to death?"

He shook his head and didn't answer.

I stood there a while and thought about what he'd said. Did it make me feel better about what he'd done? Maybe. A little. A death threat was a less-bad motive than greed or ambition, I guess. I remembered how I'd gone haring off to Nebraska after Williams had assaulted me. Profound fear could make you do things ranging from idiotic to evil.

Then again, why was I believing him? I opened my mouth to question his story. What came out was, "Did you really seduce Kara when she was fifteen?"

A second later, my brain came back on line. Why the hell had I said that?

"Yeah."

He shrugged, as though it was no big deal.

"Because you wanted to control her?"

He looked at me like I was nuts.

"No, because I wanted to fuck her. Isn't that why that kind of thing usually happens?"

Wow, classy, I thought.

"She was just a kid. It's statutory rape."

"Not where I'm from. Look," he said, sounding exasperated. "I probably shouldn't have done it. Whatever. It's all water under the bridge, now."

Unsteadily, he stood and walked over to the window, clearly annoyed with my moralizing. A silence stretched between us.

"What's Lord Cordus going to do with you?"

"Hang onto me, for the time being," Graham said. "He has a dispute with the elder beast over my ownership. Once he gets clear title, he'll execute me himself."

I frowned, confused.

"Elder beast?"

"Giant wolf, a million years old, no feet—I think you know him."

A million years old?

"You mean Ghosteater?"

"Yeah. He hunted me down in the city and claimed me. Cordus found some loophole. I think they're deadlocked, at this point. I'm being held until they find a neutral arbitrator."

I turned and walked to the door, then looked back. Graham was watching me. The soft June sunlight illuminated one side of his face. The other side was contoured with shadow. Even pale and sick, he was striking.

"Good luck, Graham."

"Beth," he said, as I reached for the doorknob.

I turned back one last time.

"That mouse you picked up on Rib Mountain? Don't tell anyone about that."

"Why?"

"Just don't."

An apprehensive shiver passed over me. I stared at him for

several long beats, but he'd looked away. Disturbed, I opened the door and left.

"Are you certain, Miss Ryder? Your visit was an anomaly in Mr. Ryzik's schedule—the only anomaly, in fact. Are you sure he said nothing of an impending escape?"

I was sitting on one of the straight-backed chairs in front of Cordus's desk. The man was doing something I'd never seen him do: he was pacing. He strolled from one side of the bay window behind his desk to the other, hands clasped behind his back, gaze distant. It looked leisurely and contemplative. I wasn't fooled for a moment.

"No, Lord Cordus, he didn't say anything. I'm quite certain."

Four days had passed since Graham's absence was noticed. His escape was a mystery. A tracker had followed his trail from outside his bedroom window to the edge of Cordus's property, but there was no sign he'd crossed the barrier. Zion, called back from an assignment in northern Virginia, had confirmed the trail but hadn't been able to get a fix on Graham's current location, which suggested he was far away. Cordus had people combing the city anyway and was checking with more distant contacts. No one had turned up anything.

Back and forth he walked. Back and forth.

This was the first time he'd questioned me. Only that morning had Gwen told him about my visit to Graham. Weirdly, she'd forgotten about it, and apparently no one else had known of it. I hadn't mentioned it myself. I hadn't thought it mattered.

"Why did you go see him?"

"I was hoping he'd explain what he'd done. It was bothering me."

"Were you lovers?"

I bristled. What business was that of his? Rather than snap at him, I just didn't answer.

He looked at me sharply, like some bird of prey seeing movement in the grass. Slowly, he came to a standstill.

"And what story did he spin for you, pray tell?"

"He said he'd been sentenced to death and Lord Limu used that to coerce him into being a double agent."

Cordus cocked his head, continuing to stare at me.

Did he really think Graham would've told me about his escape plans? That wouldn't make any sense.

"What else did he tell you?"

"He said he'd slept with Kara."

"And what else?"

I stared at Cordus, trying to decide how to answer. Graham had said not to mention the mouse, but it was just a mouse. Why should it be a secret?

I thought of his face, pale and lovely, touched with sunlight and shadow. And suddenly I knew: at the very last, he'd said one true thing. A tiny gift, one without cost. But perhaps priceless.

"He didn't say anything else."

"Nothing?"

"Nothing."

Cordus stalked toward me. He loomed over me for a moment, then reached down for my hand and pulled me up. He stepped closer, then closer still, leaning into me. I couldn't look away. I watched the tawny starbursts in his irises expand as his pupils dilated. My heart rate spiked. He traced a pattern on the back of my hand with his thumb. I jumped as his other hand slid around behind my neck and into my hair. He lowered his lips to my ear. On the way, they brushed against my cheek. A little sound came out of me before I could stop it.

"Miss Ryder," he whispered, nuzzling my hair, "why are you lying to me?"

His breath was warm. Awareness of him flooded my body. I saw only him, heard only him, felt only him. Desire pooled in my belly, hot and insistent.

"Tell me what he said."

His lips brushed over my cheekbone to my temple. He released my hand and drew his fingers lightly up my arm. His thumb brushed the side of my breast. I shuddered.

"Why would you lie for him?" he murmured, his lips moving slowly down to my jaw line. "He sent you to an isolate. He searched for Limu, intending to buy his freedom with your life."

He kissed my cheek, ever so lightly, then moved toward my mouth. My legs would barely hold me up.

"He sent you to a land of monsters. Did he try to save you? No, not once during all those days."

His breath was sweet. When he spoke, his lips moved against mine.

"And yet you lie for him?"

I stood there, eyes squeezed shut. If I spoke, if I moved, if I looked at him, it was all over. Second after second, we stood there, me shaking, my breath coming in gasps, him utterly composed.

"Very well, Miss Ryder."

He stepped back from me.

I reached out and grabbed the back of the chair I'd been sitting in, almost upsetting it. He moved away, unconcerned. Warily, I watched him retreat behind his desk and begin to sort some papers.

"It may interest you to hear that Mr. Ryzik went through the carven strait. Two different trackers confirmed his use of it this morning. I had thought the strait wholly out of reach. It seems that little is impossible, when it comes to that one."

He tapped a sheaf of paper on his desk, then slid it into a folder.

"Trapped as he is in an isolate, I shall very much enjoy hunting him down. You may go, Miss Ryder."

I made my way to the door, feeling like I was about to fall down. As I turned the knob, his voice stopped me.

"Miss Ryder."

Filled with dread, I turned.

He looked up, meeting my eyes.

"I hope you will remember what did not happen today."

Mouth too dry to speak, I nodded.

He looked down.

I opened the door—too fast—and left. I made it around the corner before my legs went all bendy, and I had to lean against the wall, sick with new self-understanding.

Oh shit, I thought. *I am so screwed.*

He hadn't used his mind-control thing on me. He hadn't needed to.

Epilogue

GHOSTEATER EMERGED FROM the silence into the springtime forest.

He had left the émigré's home some days before, angry at the man's refusal to hand over the golden-haired native. The émigré had spoken for hours. Laws had been invoked, wrongs had been weighed, a compromise had been sought. None of that meant a thing to the beast. Either blood would be shed over the matter, or it would not.

In the end, Ghosteater had chosen not to defend his claim. He'd staked it on a whim, and fighting the émigré might be fatal. It just wasn't worth it.

But anger, oh yes, there was anger. And disgust at these late-born creatures who knew no honesty. Their brains were too big for it. Revolting.

As the beast left the émigré's land, the wind had curled around his ears, whispering, suggesting a path. Ghosteater panted, taking in the air, tasting what it offered. Incompletion, fragment. He knew that scent. The strange woman, Justine. Tears and sunlight. He knew that scent as well: the pup, Beth. Heat and serpents: the émigré. Other scents, too. Intrigued, he turned aside and took one step on the wind's path, then another. Soon he was on his way.

The path led a few hundred miles north. After several days of travel, he had recognized his destination—a strait that had appeared recently in a small human structure some ways inland. He had noticed it during his last wanderings through the area, perhaps two hundred years ago. Made of heavy logs locked together, the structure had been built as a place of refuge during warfare. Perhaps the rage and hatred and blood of the place had drawn it closer to the other world. It was hard to say.

Ghosteater stepped into the roofless dwelling. Unlike the carven strait, which contained its own capacity, this one did not tug at him. It would have to be forced open. His ability to do such things is what made him, like the man Cordus, an émigré. Once, in the distant past, he had opened a strait without understanding what he did and had crossed through, finding himself in another world.

The other world. He had not been back there for some years. Unlike most émigrés, he did not consider the Second Emanation his home. This continent of this world was his place, however changed it might be.

Still, the scents on the wind were interesting, its words tantalizing.

Nosing at the air, he could barely feel the strait's presence. It was so young. He sensed the very edge of it and seized it, then adjusted his grip. When he had it firmly in his teeth, he touched his vast strength and worked the marrow of being, sending a shape spooling out through the darkness between worlds, connecting the young strait to something on the other side.

Where it went, he didn't know, but it smelled of trees and horses and dusty roads and fat, stupid deer. And of incompletion, tears. Sunlight, serpents. He cocked his head and listened again to the voice of the wind. Then he stepped through.

About the Author

BECCA MILLS TEACHES literature and writing at a small liberal arts college in the northeastern U.S. She has loved fantasy since, at age seven, she listened to her father read Tolkien aloud. *Nolander* is her first book. The next volume in the Emanations series, *Solatium*, is forthcoming in spring 2013. If you'd like to contact Becca, you can do so through her Facebook page (www.facebook.com/bccamlls) or her website (www.the-active-voice.com).